JOYRIDE TO THE MOON

MARK L. WILLIAMS

INK START MEDIA
265 Eastchester Dr Ste 133 #102
High Point NC 27262

JOYRIDE TO THE MOON

(WITH COMPLICATIONS)

MARK L. WILLIAMS

For
Christiana, Puppie, and DeeDee

THE CHALLENGE

The smoke wafted ceilingward in a curious, hypnotic helix. I smelled the sulpher. I exhaled. A billow of cigarette smoke shattered the lazy, ephimeral spiral of the match. In a matter of seconds, the smoke alarm would scream. Officious underlings would, doubtless, rush in – no few with fire extinguishers. There would be a great brew-haha. I'd be invited to an inquest and – I don't smoke. Well, I didn't until the previous evening. That was when I decided that I had had the proverbial *IT*.

When I was invited to join the International Space Administration (INSPAD), I was eager to be a part of the greatest scientific adventure since the sailing of the *Beagle*. I started out in Operations, where the action was. I was – or so I *thought* – an "ideas man." I had a ton of ideas on what to explore and how to plan missions. Unfortunately, I had no advanced degrees. My ideas were taken up by the big shots, and I was shunted from one subdivision to another until I hit rock-freaking-bottom: public relations.

Mel Harden walked in unannounced. He, too, joined INSPAD with high expectations. He was a hulking black man who, once he entered my "office", left little room for anything else. We arrived in Atlanta on the same plane and met at baggage claim. Before we collected our modest checked bags, we were friends. We graduated to best friends before we were assigned quarters.

Mel wanted to go into space. They'd just finished Moon Base (soon to be deignated Base One). He knew enough engineering to rate an assignment, but he was too tall and too heavy. Even if he lost twenty pounds (he'd be forced to amputate an arm or a leg because Mel Harden is all muscle and sinew), Mel would never be allowed to work on the moon – even if they could transport him thither, he'd spend all his time in a crouch.

Hail to thee, political coercion! Mel is black. If there is one thing that makes INSPAD quiver and quake, it is any allegation of political blasphemy. Should a drunken loon in a remote area of Antarctica "suggest" that INSPAD deep-sixed someone due to their epidermis, heads would roll. The "governing board" of INSPAD is a corrupt batch of immoral blood suckers. People will allow open thievery – will, in fact, applaud it *if* this international governing body supports the social cause *de jure*. The "hail to thee, black person" motif is required, entry-level bigotry. Mel's size and weight disqualified him from crew rotation. In the eyes of the pressure groups, however, his skin color trumped every other card in the deck. The people who "governed" INSPAD were smart enough to know that time and effort required to beat back determined protests would seriously reduce their bottom line. Graft and embezzelment are much more lucritive when you aren't forced into propaganda wars.

When Mel "flunked" his physical, INSPAD accepted him as an instructor. He went through the same training as any other space hopeful (graduating with full marks) and put on "alert status." It was all PR crapola, of course. INSPAD and Mel both knew that he would never fly. They assigned him to the training facility. After three years, he was the director and chief instructor of crew training. Nobody, not even those in the top tier of INSPAD, flew unless Mel authorized it. A couple pompus baboons tried. They remain chained to the earth.

The moment Mel squeezed the door closed behind him, he grabbed for my cig and crushed it out under his foot.

"These people will give you the boot for chewing gum," he reminded.

"The only thing I want from INSPAD is severance pay," I announced. "Smoking in a "STRICTLY no-smoking" area, added to my many, previous transgressions, will force their hand."

"You ain't happy? Quit."

"I want severence pay," I reminded. "If I quit, I get bupkis."

He leaned back against the door. I was tempted to pull out another cancer stick and light up. Mel, however, might bop me on the head.

Mel's "bop" would constitute a pile-driver from a mere mortal.

"Things might change," Mel suggested. "Rumor has it that INSPAD is about experience an office coup."

"I've heard that crap since I got here," I snorted.

Mel wouldn't hesitate around me. He trusted me in all things; I trusted Mel in all things. We shared unauthorized information precisely because we knew it would remain between us.

"Agamemnon," he announced, softly.

"I'll play," I replied. "How about *Endymion?*"

Mel ignored me.

"I've overheard a few things," he reported. "Something is up. It's organized, and it's code named *Agamemnon.*"

I thought it over for a few moments.

"Some underlings want a bigger share of the graft?"

Mel shrugged. The air in my "office" rearranged itself.

"Likely, but . . . well, there's a general feeling that we need an overhaul in operations."

That was encouraging.

"It could be nothing," I reminded. "There are always rumors."

"True. Still, what would be the harm in hanging on here for another three or four months?"

I didn't answer. Even had I desired to, the knock on my thin, plastic, airline lavatory door destroyed the opportunity. A moment after the bold knock, the door was violently thrust open. Mel and I occupied most of the available space. The door could not swing in more than a few inches.

"Duvall?" a voice inquired from beyond my portal.

"Guilty," I replied. "I'm in conference at the mo."

There was a brave but futile effort to force the opening wider. He gave up.

"So – damn – small," the voice complained.

"On Moon One, this room would be considered a luxury apartment," Mel informed.

"Well, this ain't the moon!"

"Who are you, and what do you want?"

This was my contribution to breaking the impass.

"Merkle," came the frustrated reply.

Jordan Merkle, is a carrot-topped moron of tender years whose powers of observation can best be described as "dorment." If he noticed any forbidden smoke, he was too obtuse to pay the slightest attention. He is the kind of person who felt every mission, no matter how mundane, constituted an emergency.

"From Ambercrobie," he announced, thrusting a two-inch thick stack of computer printouts. "Ya, gotta sign for it."

The papers were bound between two, cheap, plastic covers. The front cover had a document memo attached by sticky goo. I read it quickly. It was the normal, bureaucratic, yellow inter-office joke. I signed in the space specified, tore it off and returned it to the hand sticking through my door.

Mel didn't waste a moment. He leaned into the door and closed it none too gently. If the kid's hand was still inside – well, it wasn't.

"You are an important man," he announced.

"Don't be fooled by the thickness," I advised.

INSPAD, as with any bureucratic conglomoration, liked to impress itself with supercilious verbosity. Most of it was a reiteration of INSPAD rules and by-laws so the suits had cover if the low-level slaves (like me) screwed up. Fortunately, the PR branch made a real effort to give the slaves an even break. Someone, likely on our level, reviewed the edicts of the mighty potentates and translated them into English. The summation consisted of four green pages at the end of the mighty tome. I gave these studious attention for half a minute or so.

"I'm in charge of a special project," I informed Mel.

"What is it?"

Logical questions frequently confused Merkle.

"It's a publicity – *thing*."

INSPAD did not do "stunts;" it did "projects." In Merkle-speak, both *projects* and *research missions* were cleverly reduced to the one, catch-all word: "Thing." For Mel's benefit, I employed Merkle-speak. I knew Mel was as fed up with INSPAD red tape as I was.

This "thing" was really rich! I, Brice Duvall, was to spearhead the P.R. stunt to define all P.R. stunts. It was a lottery of sorts. My mission was to gather a team to find two common citizens, one male and one female, and bring them in for five-weeks of training (Mel's job). These "fortunate" two would be sent to the moon for a three month stint at a research station. They would be ferried up with regular relief crews. They would live and observe our trained professionals in action.

"I think a little mutiny is in the offing."

"Need any help?"

"You clued me in with this mysterious *Agamemnon* plot. I think, I'll call mine *Festina Lente*."

Mel moaned and planted his shoulder against the door.

"You are out of your tree!" he affirmed. "Of all the rediculous sayings in the history of the world, you have hit upon the most outragious."

I've known Mel long enough to know he was both knowledgeable and articulate. Still, he seldom ceased surprising me.

"You know Latin?" I asked, trying my best not to sound pompous.

"I've studied enough about Roman history to know that knuckle-headed old saw. Who needs to know Latin?"

I knew I could trust Mel. The thought of keeping confidence never crossed my mind. Still, I didn't want to make him a co-conspirator if (or when) the excrement meets the rotating blades. I compromised by avoiding the plans my brain conjured.

"I have to take my time," I mused. "Still, I have to get my ducks in a row before anyone knows I'm not – well, *exactly* following their directive."

I provided a synopsis of the summary pages.

"So," Mel concluded, "you have to present a male and a female by – what? – a year and a day from today."

I shook my head.

"I only have to find a female."

Mel caught my meaning instantly.

"You wouldn't dare, man."

"*Festina Lente* – man."

Asians, I thought. There was a prestigious university which declined to accept Assians in a by-gone decade. Picking a couple Asians would get up the noses of somebody! Unfortunately, five Americans of Asian descent were among the top field operatives in INSPAD. One was a team leader on the space station; one was in charge of both moon bases, ES (earth side); three were the key people in mission plans and operations. None of them, coincedentally, were graduates of a certain snooty university.

I began paging through the volumenous "appendix" in search of eligibility requirements. I discovered only three.

1. Applicants must be between the ages of 18 and 40.
2. One finalist must be male; the other must be female (biologically).
3. Neither must be associated with INSPAD in any capacity. Preferably, they should have little or no knowledge of INSPAD missions or proceedures.

After twenty minutes of flipping through the pages of beureocratic pablem, I found no further parameters. I tore a page out, turned it over, and began writing on the blank side of the printout.

    A. Weight requirements must be the same as for all active researchers.
    B. Must be literate
    C. Must speak fluently – no drug-culture slang or incoherent babbling
    D. Must be attractive – not beautiful or handsome, neccesaily. However, visible deformities will not do for a PR scam
    E. Must be eager but not foolhardy
    F. Must sign a waiver – no law suits or public recriminations over accidents or death
    G. No science degrees or space addicts – a common man or woman on the street

There was one more requirement, but it was so obvious I didn't bother to add it to the list. The lucky duo must be fluent, or reasonably so, in English. That was the language of INSPAD. Researchers could talk and joke and gossip in any language they fancied, but all official communications (oral and written) must be in English.

Toward the back of the p.o.s., there was a "suggested" budget. I was authorised fourteen underlings; two for each continent. (INSPAD recognized the sub-continent as an entity.)

I didn't need fourteen people. Joe Ambercrombie could do this alone – and for much less than the spendthrifts were willing to cough up. That would put their noses out of joint. INSPAD considered anything requiring less than three billion baloons per anum was was "petty cash." When I filled out an expense account of a couple hundred thousand, INSPAD would have to covine an international committee to discuss and review such a tiny project. After weeks of *per deim* and cash bar, they'd fire me.

I would get my severence pay, sure.

Meanwhile, I had an INSPAD expense card. There were fourteen additional cards awaiting my "team." The suits would assume that I'd blow through a month or two of expenses in selecting my team. There would be no team; there was me. Ergo, I had sixty days (maybe). After that, the "project manager" would start asking questions. On the other hand, the administrators of INSPAD (including many of the project managers) skimmed off the top. To find that I was making this a solo project would, possibly, pass muster if they knew (or suspected) that I was pocketing INSPAD money. There might be sharp words directd at me, but the suits would let it go for another month (or two).

Festina!

I booked a flight to Samos. There would be three connections and one very long flight. I could plan on the plane. There would be a couple additional days on Samos. I'd be able to fill in the details in the air and on the island.

ON YOUR MARK

Public relations people are the fungus of any meaningful endevor. Save for those at the top of the totem pole who must suck up to the politicians, PR people are the headlice of INSPAD. "Get rid of the bastards quickly so we can concentrate on the mission," is the mantra of any INSPAD employee worthy of his underpaid position. When properly handled, my PR position and rank became a valuable weapon.

I approached my supervisor with the first (and only important) page of the bulky memo I'd since consigned to the trash. I returned to my hovel and called every hour, on the hour, for word of approval. When five o'clock arrived, I fled the building for my modest apartment.

I lounged away the evening with a bottle of red wine and a good book.

Leaving for "work" the following morning, I took along two books. They were from the Hornblower series. Though I'd read them both, at least twice, it had been years. There was no reason for me to not enjoy meyself between hourly calls.

The secretary began getting snippy. By noon, she had a name for me. It was not flattering. I was delighted. The more I got on her nerves, the harder she would push her boss to get me off her nerves.

Another day, another pair of books to help the time pass.

It was just after three thirty when my computer dinged. My mission was formally approved.

I printed out six hard copies.

It was too late to start shaking trees, so I left work early.

What could they do? Fire me?

First thing the following morning, I made myself a nuisance at HR. It took a couple hours, but I left with an authorization for myself and fourteen team memebers. From there, I went to Section Five, the INSPAD designation for monitary dispersals. They wanted to issue fifteen cards and balked when I insisted upon one – mine.

"My team will report to me," I announced. "I will dole out cash as required. We're on a mission. No one is going to run up bar tabs or sign up for Country Club Family Memberships. This operation is business only."

They tried to talk me out of it. Everyone at INSPAD was feasting at the trough. Business-only missions were discouraged.

"Call the chief," I dared. "If I can't run this show my way, he can get another boy!"

Nobody called the chief. No one knew who it was. Neither did I; I'm gald they didn't ask.

As with any project, INSPAD issued me with a PoCo (portable communication device). I took it to my "office" and left it there. For certain, the device was fitted with a tracer. INSPAD, at any time – day or night – knew of my location to within fifteen meters. I desired to be on my own. I took my personal PoCo. It was three years old, but it *might* have a locator feature. The vendor insisted that it did not, but I retained serious doubts. Regardless, the company PoCo was equipped with one for absolute certain. At least, with my ancient PoCo, I had a chance.

THE JUNKET

INSPAD consists of the scientific (government) communities (governments) established by (government) treaties (government) brokered by the United (government) Nations (government). The resulting (government) bureauocracies patched together one huge "administration" that was answerable to the HQ (government) scientific (government) bodies of the several (governemt) national (government) scientific (government) bodies. The individual (government) bureauocracies created a single, ruling (governement) bureauocracy. As a result, there are (literally) millions of places to hide. A clever person could pull down a very healthy salary without ever having to report to anyone. "Scientific wealfare" is the term most often applied.

I am not a clever person. However, I knew the world was my oyster. The card issued to me was like having an inexhaustible bank balance. When my mission was completed, my expenses would be tallied and sent to someone who would pass it on to another person who would ship it off to another department, and – it could be decades before anyone examined it. Come the day when I am summoned to justify my expenses, I'd be in the ground.

It is estimated, by government agencies, that twenty-two percent of INSPAD's budget is spent on operations. Non-government offices insist the number is lower.

INSPAD members are The United States, Canada, Great Britain, France, Germany, South Africa, India, Japan, and Australia. Chile, Iceland, New Zealand, and Uzbeckistan provide INSPAD with key researchers, observatories, and facilities; they are "associate" members in fact if not in name. Naturally, they are obligated to put money into the INSPAD till.

As a boat rocker, I narrowed my search down to citizens of non-INSPAD nations. This might encourage someone to examine my expenses, but I could get away with it. Ignorance so completely insulates modern policy makers that I would pretend to be similarly insulated.

Duh and *Uhm* are the most popular responses to tough questions. I was determined to become fluent in the *Duh-uhm* language.

My first port of call was Athens. After a night at a modest hotel, I arranged a sea excursion to Samos. I could, likely, fly commercial, or charter a plane. However, Agamemnon didn't fly across those waters, and I had plenty of time on my search clock.

I got sea sick!

Those waters, even on temperate days, are not for the timid.

Why, you ask, must I divert to such a tourist trap?

Elementry, my dear Watson.

Samos is the home of Pythagoras, perhaps the greatest of all the early philosophers. I could never hope to make such a journey on my modest income, but, with the might of INSPAD behind me, nothing was beyond my reach.

By the time I got my "sea legs," we arrived. Though no longer green, the capacious void in my stomach was not yet ready for nurishment. Just as well. I was not here to suffer the plague of the tourist throng. I was on a mission. In the parlance of my employer, "The mission comes before any other consideration." (That, of course, was strictly for the worker bees. The "Admin Branch" of INSPAD insisted that boondoggles and cash bar came first, last, and always.)

Well, I considered myself a worker bee with administrator's priorities.

It took me less than an hour to find the workshop I sought. It was just beyond sight of the harbor and was ignored by most of the tourists. There, I expended another hour meticulously examining the wares.

Years before, I vowed to purchase a made-in-Samos Pythagorean cup. I could order one via computer, but that would be akin to ordering a gourmet meal from a five-star Parisian chef; it would lose its luster en route.

I sought one, but I couldn't limit myself to just one. I found four candidates. Each had hand-painted designs in the motif of ancient Greek pottery.

What the hell!

I bought them all but insisted they be packaged and sent individually. If one or more got broken or lost, I'd still have a chance. I paid out of my own pocket. In the unlikely event that INSPAD would audit my expenses and demand restitution, my Pythagorean cup would be beyond reach (I *hope*).

One bucket-list item down. (In truth, *two*; twisting bureaucratic tail remains an on-going project.) One major item to go.

This one was rather "iffy," and not devoid of danger.

From Samos, I contacted a friend of days gone by. We met during my early days with INSPAD. Ralph, however, bailed out early. He was a scholar and an adventurer. Boondoggles and cash bar held no allure. We kept in close contact over the years. When he told me his next port-of-call, however, it doubled – ney, quadrupled – my desire to get that INSPAD severance package.

Will arrive soon. Must secure transport. ETA unknown.
Will advise. Need a man on the inside. K?

From that moment, and for the next seven hours, I checked my PoCo.
I was enjoying a light meal at my INSPAD-financed hotel when Ralph's response arrived.

Come ahead! Will arrange ground trans and lodging pending
details.

"Damn! This will be fun!"
A passing waiter eyed me suspiciously. He kept his eyes on me until I left for my room.

IT ISN'T THE END
OF THE WORLD

(but you can see it from here)

When I was at university, I explored, vicariously, Timbuktu. I even wrote a paper on the subject. It has fascinated me ever since.

At a time when Europe was convinced that the sun revolved around the earth, and the Emperor Charlemagne struggled with letters (he could read, so his biographer tells us, but he couldn't write – hand-eye coordination problems, no doubt), Timbuktu was the repository of the most advanced scientific research findings. It was, in a very real sense, the inheritor of the Library of Alexandria. What was worth knowing was found in a desert oasis. European scholars risked their lives to trek hither. Many of those who attempted to return to Europe and propogate the fruits of their study died in the attempt. Even in the world of INSPAD, there was no guarentee of a round-trip visit.

For most people, Timbuktu is a synonym for *nowhere.* For me, it was a siren's song. As with my journey to Samos, Timbuktu was a budget buster – as far removed from my work station as the moons of Neptune. With my INSPAD expense card, however, it was only a matter of enduring hardship.

The "international" airport has a very short runway. Only smaller planes could access the remote, Sahara suburb safely. Getting to a feeder airport was no mean task. Further, flights were frequently delayed or cancled. Driving in was left only for the resourceful *and* foolhardy. If the vehicle broke down, or the petrol ran out, one might remain stranded for many days before hitching a ride on an overloaded truck or bus.

I opted for a trip up the Niger River. The *only* good thing, safety-wise, was that a disabled craft would float downstream and, eventually, a return to civilization.

The "ferry," as with the motor vehicles, was crowded, overloaded, and – in a serious wind gust – in danger of capsizing. There were no cabins, no AC, and no toilets worthy of that designation. Under the aluminum awning, one baked in oven heat. On "deck," one fried under the relentless sun. There was a kiosk – so named by some bureaucrat, no doubt – that served up warm, bottled water and food both unidentified and inedible. When the sun went down, I and the forty-some passengers, panted for the evening breeze. It was a warm wind, but welcome after hours of basting.

My PoCo was useless. I was in a "dead" area – one of the few remaining on earth. As I slowly passed from rare to medium, I recalled *Heart of Darkness*. True, there was no jungle and no hostile natives launching spears at us, but I identified with the narrator as I watched the shore creep, very slowly, past. It was possible to lean over and splash a handful of river on neck, face and shoulders. One, however, must exercise caution. The Niger was not the purest water in the world, and malevolent microbes abounded. Additionally, I feared that if my hand dallied too long in the river, I mightn't get it back. I was not informed of flesh eating critters, but this part of the world is not known for salubrious fawna.

As only one of five occidentals aboard, I was the subject of continual observation. A few people spoke to me or about me in dialects and languages unknown (to me, at least). It seemed that every passenger had his or her own language. Only a handful spoke French, the *official* language of Mali. My French, which had served me so well while studying in Dijon, was indecipherable to my fellow passengers. Their French was, as Mark Twain might suggest, "too clever" for me.

I listened and nodded my head a lot.

For thirteen blistering, unending hours, I half stood and half squated on a tiny space. If I moved, a dozen or more people must make way. There was traffic for water and whatever the kiosk designated as "food." I fasted and made a valient effort to make my bottled water last as long as possible. By journey's end, I had bullied my way to the kiosk six times. No one took offense – just as I took no offense when I was forced to make way for other passengers coming and going.

The smell of sweat and human waste bothered me at first. By nightfall, however, these odious oders ceased to overpower me. When I nodded off, I enjoyed visions of sitting in a tub filled with tepid water.

We "put in" several times during our "voyage." When passengers and cargo were discharged, there was a brief few moments during which one could stretch. Alas, the cargo and people brought aboard soon restored the crowdedness to "normal." Waiting for three or four days at an airport where one could, at least, stretch out on the floor and have a brief nap, became an overwhelming desire. I'd be sorely tempted to depart by air. Perhaps, the aircraft might be a cramped and crowded as the ferry, but I've never been unending hours on a plane.

I was told, by several people for whom the sight of white skin constituted an anomoly, that the temperature, normally, is more moderate. It was simply my bad luck that I'd hit in the midst of a scorcher. I suspected that they blamed me (or my white skin) for bringing such intemperate weather with me.

The recollection of *Heart of Darkness* returned. Every eye directed my way seemed resentful – or hostile.

Eventually, shortly after noon, the ferry arrived at Port Korioume. The unloading facilities were – ahm – *primative.*

I stood back and allowed the natives to experience freedom first. I didn't care to be "accidentally" pressed, face down, into the mud or risk being trampled to death by those who held me responsible for the miserably hot journey. Mali is an Islamic nation, but many, if not most, of the natives held to their tribal superstitions with tenacity.

When the crowd had disembarked and began tending to their own individual businesses, I tossed my back pack onto the mushy sand. I feared falling on my face and proposed that such an embarrassing eventuality would not be compounded by having to wrestle with my traps. After snapping up my gear, I slogged through the swamp and onto loose sand.

From river to desert in a matter of seconds and a few centimeters.

"Are you Brice Duvall?"

I looked up to find a tall figure in canvass work pants. The ensemble of *it* (the gender was not obvious) consisted of a worn, orange, long-sleeved shirt, a yellowish vest, yellowish baseball cap and gray, highly worn and abused athletic shoes.

"Is this Brice Duvall wanted by the authorities?" I asked, ever cautious.

"Monsieur Endicott sent me," the apparition informed. "He described Monsieur Duvall as an *occidental*. You strike me as the most likely candidate."

Its was the best French I'd heard since arriving in West Africa. The voice was high, but not too high. This could be a young man or an adult woman. One false move or careless remark could nominate me as guest of honor at some primative ceremony.

"Your powers of deduction do you justice," I advanced, ever cautious. "What is your mission."

The "meeter-greeter" eyed me suspiciously.

"Monsieur Endicott is, unavoidably, occupied. He hired me to take you to your hotel."

"My hotel?"

Well, that gave the game away. *Its* expression confirmed it.

"You expect to sleep in the desert? That's – pardon my boldness – for tourists. I was under the impression that you are here on business."

"And so I am."

It stepped aside and gestured to an ancient side-by-side. This vehicle had experienced a brutal life. I could hardly ignore what was, I'm positive, a bullet hole.

"I am Aissata Sissoko," *It* announced.

"Brice Duvall," I countered, extending my hand. "Of course, you knew that."

It eyed my hand with coumpound suspicion.

"You're an American," *It* concluded, announcing the verdict in English.

"I am."

Only when the conclusion was confirmed did *It* take my hand. The grip was sure and strong, but the fingers were decidedly feminine.

"I assumed – that is, your name – Duvall . . ."

"Mister Endicott never said."

"Does it make a difference? Your English is very good."

It smiled with pride.

"I learn English by listening to tourists, movies, and the radio. Come; we have some distance to go."

It wasn't that far, but *Siss* (as *It* adopted as a diminutive) drove at slightly above crawl speed. There was a stream of people headed for Timbuktu. Some led, rode or herded animals. There were camels, sheep, donkeys, goats, and a few oxen interspersed with a flock of people. Driving at speed, even to my untrained eye, was to invite a stampede and multiple injuries among the pedestrians.

The roar of the engine precluded further social exchanges. I held tight to the vehicle lest I be ejected. The road was rutted and bumpy. There might have been, at one time, a paved surface. The desert sand had taken over, however.

Siss helped by lugging in my pack. I was debating how much I owed her (I convinced myself that *It* was a female) for taxi fare. This proved moot. The last I saw of Siss was the back of her vest.

Registered
Guide

The letters were professionally embossed in two languages.

Check-in was a simple matter of filling out sparse information and signing my name. I hesitated to state that INSPAD was my employer, but I was ignorant of Mali law. Long prison terms were known for rather innocuous (by my standards) transgressions. If the desk clerk was as contemptuous of my organization as I, he hid it. For a brief moment, I had the euphoric sensation that the stoic, middle-aged man was blissfully unaware of the International Space Administration. If so, I was, truly, at the end of the world.

WHO WOULD A THUNK?

My room was very modest by INSPAD standards. I reminded myself that I was in Timbuktu and not Paris or, even, Sparta. By local standards, mine was, probably, considered "first class." Notwithstanding tiny holes in the pillow case and a face cloth that was several miles beyond warranty, I was dog tired. I readjusted the AC to a less frigid setting, plopped down on the bed and was transported to dreamland in record time.

The knock at the door was enough. I've always been a light sleeper. My miserable ferry ride hadn't squelched the habit of a lifetime.

I lept from bed and checked my watch. It was twenty after six. That confirmed that my "nap" had set a new, personal record.

Trusting fool that I am, I flung the door wide. Had a band of brigands been in the hall, I'd have bought it, sure. However, the form filling the doorway was that of a familiar friend from days gone by.

Ralph Endicott was browner and more leathery than I remembered. The climate, doubtless, contributed these alterations. However, he appeared to be the same rock-solid former wrestling champion of our younger days. He was a "seeker." Once he got a burr up his butt, he'd go to great lengths to satisfy his voracious curiosity. He'd come to Timbuktu, like me, on a whim. He stayed to examine the ancient scrolls at the university, but remained to gather all the information possible about ancient trade routes. He was, so he told me, working on a monograph.

"Ain't ya gonna invite me to dinner?" he croaked.

"INSPAD is footing the bill," I replied. "Want to catch a drink at the Stork Club first?"

He broke into a wide grin. We shook hands fervently.

"This place is about as good as you'll do in this part of the world," he informed. "Don't order suckling pig."

We marched down the hall, down the stairs, and past the main desk. The "supper club" was little more than a café, catering to the spoiled tourists with money to spend. I took an immediate dislike to the place. There was a well-stocked bar and a cigar counter. It pained me that the hotel staff was made up of local hires. Booze and smokes constituted a poke in the eye with a sharp stick. I hoped that the insurrection would be delayed until after I left.

As the two "early birds," we were the first customers. A well-togged gentlemen in a white, Panama suit was at our table before we were properly seated.

"Good evening, gentlemen," he greeted in precise French. "Would you care for a cocktail?"

I cringed.

"Nothing for me," I replied at once.

Ralph shook his head.

We were presented with two single sheets of paper featuring that evening's fare. There were three mutton dishes and three goat dishes. All six came with cuscus. There was, also, a sirloin steak with potatoes for a price only Andrew Mellon could meet and a fish platter, equally suited for the INSPAD expense acoount. I didn't bite. Such items must be frozen and air-freighted in. The portions were sure to be microscopic. I was hungry, so I opted for roast lamb. Ralph ordered goat.

"Sorry, I didn't meet you," he began. "I had some survey work to do, and I had no clue as to your arrival time."

"Forget it," I assured. "You're still studying water systems? Save for wells and the Niger, what's to study?"

He wagged a cautionary finger at me.

"You'd be surprised," he warned. "A large city like this in the middle of the Sahara – it's been here for centuries, remember. They began with just one well. I'd give a mighty amount to know how those nomads discovered water."

"Desperation, probably."

Ralph shrugged. It was clear that he considered me a hopeless case.

"What brings you to this place?" He asked.

"It's as far away from INSPAD as I can get without leaving the planet."

"They will ask questions?" He advised.

"Let them," I announced. "Speaking of questions, who was that person you sent out to meet me."

"Siss? Reliable, dependable, patient, and so on."

I cleared my throat.

"Is Siss male or female."

He leaned back as if amazed by my question. I caught the twinkle in his eye when he leaned way forward.

"Who is Siss. What is she?"

I ignored the Shakespearian allusion and leanded back in my turn.

"So," I announced. "I thought she was female. She didn't have a face cover, but I haven't seen many in this country."

"She's Catholic."

I had to think about that for a bit.

"Catholic, in an Islamic city? Is that healthy?"

He waved my comment aside.

"People come here from all over the world," he reminded. "This may be the middle of nowhere, but Timbuktu is pretty cosmipolitan. People, and their religions, come from every point on the compass. A few even make their homes here."

I was struggling to come to terms with a Christian resident in Timbuktu. Ralph's attitude was amazingly calm and reasoned. I have renounced calm and reason. INSPAD will do that to a person.

"She chopped off most of her hair."

That was the best I could do.

"Ask her," Ralph advised.

I crossed my arms and waited for the food to come.

"You can't stand a mystery, can you? Got your notebook? Try this."

He'd been teasing me. He expected me to grab him by the shirt and shake him until he confessed to murder. When I sulked, instead, he decided to spill.

Aissata's mother was born a slave. Siss was the third child of, presumably, three different fathers. At a young age, Siss was part of a payment for services rendered. She was accepted with the understanding that she would become a house servant. Her new owners decided she was still too young to trade, so they sent her off to "school," a euphemism for something I'll not record here. By the time she was old enough to bleed, Siss decided to make a "career change." She ran off with a caravan – yes, they still have them. She worked for food by carrying out whatever task was assigned.

Long story (with glaring omissions) cut short: she was taken in by a Catholic missionary where she got her primary religious and parochial education. It didn't take long to discover that Siss was both smart and precocious. She lived with two other women in the city and worked for food and university tuition. She was, by American standards, a sophomore.

Ralph did not know her chosen course of study.

The meal was filling. There was a fruit dish for dessert, mainly dates laced with a few "exotic" extras like shredded coconut and cherries. We passed the bulk of our evening talking of the bad old days at INSPAD. His monologue about desert water systems was far more interesting.

We ordered a glass of mineral water as our after diner cocktail. We agreed to meet up for another evening meal. Ralph promised to take me to a "place" he knew. I didn't fall off the turnip truck; there weren't any restaurants in the city – nothing that would fit the accepted paradigm. His invitation, therefore, reeked of intrigue.

I like intrigue.

I lay in my room and studied the ceiling.

INSPAD wanted to send a pair of "commoners" into space. A black, female, former slave who knew nothing of her father or mother (or, even, her birth place and country) couldn't be more common. As a public-relations scum sucker, I realized Siss was made to order. As a human being, I rejected arm twisting. If I could talk with her and introduce the proposition – well, she'd maintain veto power. However, if she was keen . . .

My INSPAD financed world tour might be cut short.

Oh, no! INSPAD would not get off so easily. I wanted my pound of flesh, and I was determined to have it!

LOOK AND YE SHALL FIND

(maybe)

Try to locate a particular person in a thriving desert city. Aissata Sissoko (a name she selected for herself after arriving in Timbuktu), was a registered guide, to be sure. However, her employeers (plural, since she was listed with four tour agents) were not keen on surrendering details about my former guide. Cosmopolitan or not, there were people in the city who didn't care for Catholic-mission alumnus. More importantly, local businessmen (they were, seemingly, *all* men) remained very wary of white people asking questions. This, no doubt, was a holdover from colonial times.

I tried the university. The registrar's office, if I can use that term, flatly refused to give out student and former student information. If, they reasoned, Siss wanted me the know her whereabouts, she'd have told me.

I quickly gave up the fatuous notion of treading the sand-laden streets until I spied her. In a city of more than sixty thousand, chance encounters are rare.

After four days, my appetite for goat, sheep and cuscus had been satisfied. It was time to move on. Ralph, however, suggested I stay for a big "rock concert" slated for the following evening. Curiosity pricked me. A "rock concert" in an Islamic city was certain to be beyond my imagining. The concept demanded investigation.

I stumbled upon one of the satellite souks not far from the hotel. There I purchased a brown, paper bag filled with dried dates. Fearing they might create an adverse impact on my digestive tract, I tried to ration myself. However, the taste of anything goatless or cuscusless was overwhelming. Bread might insulate my stomach. The moment I caught a whiff of baking bread, I altered course and homed in.

There are communial bake ovens in every neighborhood. I'd seen dozens. They were adobe-like, inverted bee-hive structures roughly six feet high. I didn't understand how they worked and wasn't curious enough to investigate. However, I fancied that a bit of penance and, perhaps, a couple of coins, I might persuade the bakeress to allow me a bit of crust.

The woman, as you may have guessed, was my prime candidate. She wore one of those sari-like things. She was dressed for work, not for fashion. It had been a shade of brown once upon a time. Age, relentless sun, and the ubiquitous dust made it a burlesque of itself. Under this pathetic atire were a pair of weather-worn, bluish athletic shoes. Apparently, she was measuring baking time by her nose; her eyes surveyed the sky as if predicting weather or, perhaps, searching for migratory fowl. Whatever her purpose, she noticed me not.

"Mlle. Sissoko," I hailed as I approached.

I was careful to moderate both volume and tone. I knew, from books, that, in the Arab world, one did not follow a woman in a veil. Though veiled women were scarce in Mali – or, at least, Timbuktu – it wouldn't do for an occidental to shout out a woman's name for all an sundry to hear. Siss, was neither offended nor peturbed. She turned all her attention to my approach.

"M. Duvall."

We established that we not only recognized each other, but that we remembered the correct monikers. She was holding a long handled impliment with which to introduce and retrieve loaves of bread from the bakeoven. There was not the shadow of doubt that she would use the device as a weapon if she suspected anything untoward. With this in mind, I made no mention of my four day search. If she knew I'd been asking around after her, she might decided to strike first and ask questions later.

"I have a dozen or so dates here," I gestured with my bag. "I'll trade them for just a little of your bread."

She smiled. It wasn't a particularly attractive smile, but, then, Siss was not a particularly attractive women.

"You are welcome to some bread, but you needn't trade," she assured.

Ah, a sample of West African hospitality. This was unfortunate. I'd gotten off on the wrong foot.

"I don't want to deprive you of your bread without some recompense."

Her brow wrinkled. Her English, apparently, did not reach that far. I repeated it in French. She smiled again. Either she found my rusty, Parisian French amusing, or I had mangled the sentiment beyond comprehension.

"You are enjoying your visit?"

An adroit means of skirting the issue.

"My friend, M. Endicott, and I are going to the concert tonight. Will you be there?"

"Barring unforseen circustances."

"I'm still a stranger here," I reminded. "Would it be rude to ask you to come to the hotel this evening? The three of us could go together. We may need a guide to get us there."

She felt that either I or my suggestion was harmless.

"I would be delighted."

"Would it be indelicate to ask if you require renumeration for services rendered? I ask as a visitor unfamiliar with local customs."

"Are we friends?"

That was a surprise.

"I hope we are friends," I said, cautiously.

"If we go as friends, it is not business. I shall be pleased to show you the way. I suspect M. Endicott knows the way. *Renumeration*, in that context, would be inappropriate."

Was she pulling my leg? No matter, I was curious to know which English movies, tourists, and radio she'd encountered to soak up her eclectic diction. I was expecting "Howdy, Partner." Being confronted by "Would sir prefer Samuel Johnson elocution with his afternoon tea?" was pleasing if unsettling.

Who, I wondered, was sounding out whom?

A TIMBUKTU CONCERT IS LIKE . . . AN ADJECTIVE SHORTAGE.

Headliners, for reasons that are too obvious to explore, eschew the Sahara Desert. When, therefore, there is a concert, it is done with local talent. Groups, within Mali, have a respectable fan base, and appear infrequently at the end of the earth. Ergo, Timbuktuians are the featured staple of local festivals. The remoteness of the venue, however, does not blunt either the verve or quality of local talent. Indeed, the city's isolation promotes quality; there are fewer distractions.

Three groups were on the bill. Electric guitars, African drums, and portable keyboards were the featured instruments of all three agrigations. There was, additionally, one bass fiddle player and an African descendant of a clarinette. The featured vocalists were all women. Men made up the bulk of the "backup" singers.

All the numbers were up-tempo. If I, as an outsider, expected an Islamic city to partake of dirge-like offerings, it is only natural. These people, however, love to "whoop-it-up." The stage was a blur of excitement, and the audience clapped and danced and became a part of the show. There were no seats; there was no need. The audience constituted part of the program. Passive people remained at home.

"Where do they generate all this electricity?" I shouted into Ralph's ear.

Where, indeed? There were several flood lights and a follow spot aimed at the stage while the "auditorium" (a large market square during daylight hours) was bathed in a Broadway-like blanket of illumination, both natural and artificial.

Ralph couldn't explain. Even if he knew, his response would be limited to signs and gestures. This was a "blow out." Dance, sing, clap, hoot, celebrate life, but expository discussions were, clearly, not on the agenda.

I was impressed enough to join in the frivolity. Siss, who was all business when driving, tour guiding, or bread baking, was as animated as any enthusiastic American music aficionado. Timbuktu proved itself a twenty-first century city with a twenty-first century population. True PoCos were few and service was unreliable, but that did not blunt or inhibit the citizens one iota. They are "with it!"

Brushing aside the concept of Timbuktu as a cultural center, the ceremony was far livelier than I imagined possible. My notion that I could be alone with Siss long enough to "proposition" her was doomed from the start. I could hardly introduce INSPAD business with Ralph, a chronic INSPADophobe, as a member of our party. Further, Siss's two hutmates arrived and made a congregation the proverbial crowd.

I don't regret the five of us attending a truly remarkable concert. Indeed, watching the three woman gyrating and displaying amazing dexterity in their footwork made the musical event an even greater delight. Ralph and I attempted to keep up with the trio which delighted them no end. Their lilting, uninhibited laughter added to the acoustical largess.

When the event disolved and the disappointed audience began to disperse, it would have been rude to the nth degree to *not* see the ladies home. Their mud hut was, essentually, a storage unit. It resembled the early moon "blisters" INSPAD errected. In Timbuktu, the circular dome was handmade, probably in the previous century. It was a place to store the women's modest pelf. There was, of course, a dirt floor. The "beds" were simple, rush mats with folded jackets for pillows. The blankets were thin and locally weaved.

The women slept there, but they lived outside. When not occupied, they would sit or stand outside and entertain guests.

For a brief moment, I considered inviting Siss to the hotel for a coffee. This idea was discarded instantly. Even if I could get rid of Ralph, the hotel staff would hardly allow a man (particularly a foreigner) to be left alone with a woman citizen – even if we remained in public areas. Further, it would not be acceptable for me to "see her home" after our conference. I could hardly send for a taxi.

"I have a tour group arriving in the morning," she volunteered.

"At the port?"

She shook her head.

"By bus," she informed. "I will meet them at the mosque."

"When?"

"Whenever they arrive."

In the desert, time is measured by *morning, afternoon, evening* and *closed-for-business*. Long water and land journeys to Timbuktu were subject to a myriad of delays.

"The university mosque or the main mosque?"

She looked at me as if I had no sense.

"I want to talk with you," I said, boldly. "I'll meet you. Hopefully, we can talk before your group arrives."

"Okay."

Okay by the way, is the local word that covers everything from assent to disaster.

IT AIN'T EASY

It seems so simple.

"Wanna go to the moon?"

If I asked that question in a crowded auditorium, I'd risk being crushed. That's assuming those assembled realized that mine was a legitimate question.

"Wanna go to the moon?"

If I asked that question in a crowded auditorium, people would get up and walk out. That's assuming that those assembled knew (and felt about) INSPAD as I did.

Well, I was in Timbuktu. For these isolated people, INSPAD was both as remote and inconsequential as a rain shower in the Solomon Islands. True, Siss was a cut above the average. She was inherently bright and determined to further her education even if she had to do so in bite-sized increments. She was pushing thirty hard, if she wasn't pulling it. Due to her early history, no one could know, for certain, either her birth date or birth place. She'd carved out a comfortable niche for herself as a reliable and respected citizen. Throwing that away for a pig in the poke (poor choice of words, forgive me) was not an easy choice.

There was another, equally formidable, problem.

How do I present the offer.

"Wanna go to the moon?"

That question wasn't worth a blank by way of reply.

I daren't explain INSPAD in any detail. My natural distatste was certain to bubble up.

I daren't explain the publicity angle – which was the entire reason for the project. Siss did not strike me as a person who craved attention. She was a respected woman who enjoyed a close circle of friends. Her cup runnith over. The idea of becoming a world-wide celebrity would, likely, frighten her. It might actually horrify her.

I daren't try the science angle. She knew more math and science than ninty percent of her fellow citizens, but atrophysics, geology, and biomedicine were far beyond her rudimentary knowledge. She'd be petrified by her ignorance.

If only I were a real PR pro. I wasn't. I was put in public relations because it was INSPAD's answer to sweeping me under the rug. They suspected that I wanted to be fired and decided to deny me that because – well, because, they are a bastardly gang.

So, here I was, at the end of the world and on my own. I had only my wits. I am, by nature and nurture, witless. Despite my insane vendetta, I liked Siss, and I wanted her to have this one-in-fifty million chance. More to the point, I wanted her on the moon. Of course, she'd be remorsely exploited by every scum-sucking scribe with an imagination. Being at the mercy of publicity, Siss might be driven to an early grave. However, I thought she could survive. She had resources I could not fatham.

What to do?

I was at the mosque at the proverbial crack of dawn. The call to prayer was blasted from the ancient walls by modern-day sound equipment; it was probably heard in Malta. There were the devout who responded as expected. Many Timbuktuians, however, were – how shall I say? – fair-weather Muslims. Indeed, Timbuktu was an amalgamation of religious beliefs. There were even a few Shinto followers, or, more accurately, believers *influenced* by Shinto traditions. Somehow, the locals were tolerant and respectful of the many faiths that settled in this arid land. No one cast hostile or accusatory glances in my direction when I sat, placidly, in the dust under the shadow of the mosque.

Eventually, Siss appeared in the same guide uniform she wore on my arrival. She saw me and approached. I was still in a quandary and very nervous. The perceptive woman detected my unease. She offered no greeting, but settled down next to me as if to meditate. We remained mute for several moments.

"Do you ever think about the moon?" I asked.

That was near enough "Wanna go," but slightly more urbane.

"I ponder some nights," she confessed. "I think about the people who work there."

I couldn't muster a cogent rejoinder.

"What, exactly, do you think about the people who work there?"

Several seconds had elapsed before I spoke. Several more seconds ticked past while her thought procees suspiciously examined my query.

"I think," she began slowly and thoughtfully. "I think how focused they must be. They have work to do. No distractions. No appointments. No obligations. No outside commitments. For company, they have only those few people with whom they work. They can remain silent for hours and not fear being thought a snob. And, the view . . . I've never seen the Mediterranean – nor the Atlantic, come to that."

"You can see them from the moon," I reminded.

"Well, yes, but . . ."

I let that hang in the air for several seconds.

"What if I told you, I could send you to the moon for a three month stint? Maybe, four."

She didn't answer. Her eyes locked onto mine as if to dare me to produce a punch line.

"What could I do on the moon?" she demanded. "I have no scientific training worthy of the name. I could contribute nothing."

"The people I work for are looking for volunteers."

I'd choke if I said INSPAD, so I substituted an acceptable collective noun.

"They want two *ordinary* earth citizens to experience, observe, and report the experience. There would be minor tasks, to be sure. However, you wouldn't be expected to be a geologist, a physicist, or an astro-physicist. Still, you couldn't help but learn. I bet your university would allow you a few credits for your adventure."

She either refused to speak or couldn't.

"By the way, I do not consider you *ordinary*. You are a remarkable woman."

"There must be millions of people better suited than I," she objected.

"Perhaps, but I cannot meet and get to know millions of people."

"But, my skin color and my – uhm – *history*."

"I was not sent out to pick physical characteristics or personal histories. I was sent out to find a citizen of the earth as a represenative of the non-scientific people of this planet. Of course, you'd be in for a lot of publicity, but you'd have a great story to tell."

She looked for the approach of her tour group. There was not so much as a dust cloud in the distance.

"It is something to think about," she concluded.

"You think about it, then. Before I leave, I'll provide contact information."

"Please," she began with the air of urgency. "I don't do well with strangers. If – if I decide to – do this – thing, I'll deal only with you."

"I'd be honored."

She nodded.

After a silent, and respectful, few minutes, I got up and sauntered away.

Quiet Colloquy

Ralph was exploring the desert with a gaggle of fellow scientists and their ground- penetrating radar, electronic gear, and a plethora of additional ultra-sophisticated equipment. He might be gone for three days or three months. The duration of their expoditions was predicated entirely upon their line of supply. Their work, in short, was limited by the same conditions as our three moon bases.

I wasn't prepared for another meal of goat or sheep and the insipid side dishes served up at the hotel. It was as near Western-cuisine as one was apt to find at the end of the world, but I'd had my fill. Ergo, I haunted the market and gathered up items that didn't require preparation. Dates, it seemed, would constitute the bulk of my evening repast. It wouldn't do to smuggle my evening meal into the hotel, but I could sit, cross-legged, in the dust of several dozen streets and partake without attracting much attention. Any occidental, of course, would gather a much more substantial quota of curious glances, but Timbuktu – at least in my limited experience – was a leave-the-bastard-alone metropolis.

With nothing to do, and the balance of the day to not do it, I retired to my room. It was air-conditioned, but not up to the needs of outsiders. Sweating moderately while reclining on the bed and watching forty-year old American programs (dubbed into French with subtitles in two local tribal dialects) was as good as it was likely to get.

During my thrid nap, the phone rang.

It could be Ralph. It was possible (but highly unlikely) that his PoCo signal could get into the local phone system. Even so, what was the purpose? A social call in the heat of the afternoon was, decidedly, ill-timed. If he called to ask if I could bring him a candy bar to some bizarre set of desert co-ordinates – well, that would not promote civility on my part.

"M. Duvall?"

I recognized the voice.

"Mlle. Sissoko?"

"Oui."

Sparkling converstation.

"I have only a few minutes," she continued. "May I meet you at your hotel in a couple of hours. I have some questions."

I looked at my watch.

"At six o'clock," I replied. "I'll be waiting in the lobby."

She said something unintelligible. Perhaps, she was speaking to another person nearby. The line went dead.

I wondered if her tour group would lodge at my hotel. That would make things so much simpler. However, these want-to-be nomads tended to "rough it" at one of several outdoor camps. Locals would find the accomodations luxurious. Rich tourists, however, would be thrilled by the primitive if rustic "atmosphere." They would, likely, dine on beef and reasonably fresh vegitables.

Damn!

I was seated in the lobby sipping the one five-star item the hotel offered – thick, sweet, sit-up-and-take-notice coffee. When the syrapy, bold liquid was gone, there remained a delightful residual of fine grounds. With the dainty spoon provided, I scooped out a little at a time and chewed it. I figured that feasting on coffee was infinitely preferable than masticating on goat, sheep, or lamb.

Siss walked boldly through the open portal like some Hollywood, western ruffian. Her kaki trousers, and shirt were as clean and neat as anyone had a right to expect in land of dusty streets and shifting sand. Her hiking boots were, however, scuffed and displayed evidence of many miles. The vest, identifying her as a certified guide in two languages, appeared older than the woman wearing it. Doubtless, the trappings of office were handed down from generation to generation; either that or public brawls were frequent.

I stood.

Proper ediquette demanded I do no less. Such practices were discouraged by modern society which is exactly why I continued to exercise them whenever possible. Nevertheless, my gallant gesture was mocked by circumstances. I knew Siss was a woman. Any casual bystander, however, would be confused. Siss looked quite manly in stature and form. Her feminine attire of the previous evening flattered her only marginally.

"I could have found you," I reported for want of better. "I know the way. It's unfair to bring you out of your way."

She remained stoic and shrugged her shoulders.

"Father Bornik remins me that slothfulness is a sin."

I had a reply to that, but I stiffled it. One does not make friends by gainsaying religious teachings. I'd learned that lesson early in life.

She was troubled. It was not my place to compound them with trite chitchat. I placed my cup back on its saucer and moved to the door. She, the woman, waited until I passed through before falling into step behind me. I wanted to scold her for being so staid. I much preferred walking with someone rather than leading them. However, her town; her rules.

Siss's hutmates were darker than she. They had short, dark, tangled low-maintenance hair. They came from different tribes and kept their respective religions, accpting Islam and tolerating Siss's Catholicism. Despite their three different cultures, languages, and belief systems, the trio got on as best friends. Perhaps, the rest of the world should learn from them.

Our meal bubbled in a pot as Siss and I arrived. The aroma made my nose prickle. I detected spices in the thick soup. When Doris (not her real name) stirred it with a industrial-strength wooden spoon, chunks of something made a brief appearance before vanishing back into the swirl. Siss ducked into the hut and reappeared with four, hand-carved bowls and wooden spoons.

There were (prayer?) rugs arranged equidistant around the pot, but not too near. I folded my legs as best I could and settled onto the mat assigned me. As the guest, I was the first served. I waited until the others all had a bowl full, and I waited still. I didn't know the proceedure and didn't want to behave like an uncultured lout. I waited for the others to show me how it was done.

Siss ate with chopsticks. There was an interesting story there, but I promised myself to postpone any interrogation for another time.

She was as adroit and neat as Chaucer's Nun. The food, both chunks and the thick liquid she slurped quietly, went into her mouth and nowhere else. Fearing that I'd wear part of my dinner, I used the spoon with precision.

The – whatever it was – did contain more spices than I cared for, but I put it away with ease. The "chunks" were very tender. I hoped it was chicken meat or, failing that, chicken parts. I daren't ask. Aside from being inexcusably rude, I risked being informed that it was dog intestine or something equally repellent.

Often times, ignorance *is* bliss. It was tasty and satisfying.

The younger woman, the one who knew a peculiar brand of French but very little Arabic, fished out all the chunks with her spoon and ejoyed it along with the juice. When the chunks were gone, she drank from the bowl. The older woman carefully ladled out the juice (gravy, soup, whatever). When only the chunks remained, she picked them up individually with finger and thumb and ate them like peanuts. Siss ate exactly as a Japanese woman would eat. Her slurping, however, was less pronounced than one finds in the Orient.

We paused after the first bowl. I wanted seconds, but sat quietly waiting for one of my hostesses to show me the way.

"I have three jobs here," Siss reminded at last.

I was eyeing the residuals in the pot. There was a chance I'd be offered seconds, and I didn't want negligence to rob me of that chance.

"Once you are accepted, you'll get recruit pay," I promised. "That won't amount to much, but you'll be living in restricted barraks. Aside from hygenic needs, there is no opportunity to buy anything."

"My sisters rely on my paying my share," Siss announced.

These women were not "sisters." However, I allowed the word as a sign of the bond which existed among them rather than an exceptionally transparent lie. I did not consider Siss a dumbass. I was confident she didn't think me one.

"We can make arrangements to send most or all of your pay here – well, not here where we are sitting, but the bank, telegraph office, or to Father – your priest."

I couldn't recall the man's name, and, *yes*, Timbuktu has a telegraph office. It doesn't do dah-dit-dah, but the Mali varient of a portable communication device does send and receive messages just as in the old days – to include a word limit. Cash transfers are among the services available.

Six eyes engaged in tacit, hurried conversation.

"What if I am not accepted?"

"Then, you come back and take up where you left off. No, Mlle. Sissoko, you do not return your training pay."

I charged ahead. I really wanted more of that soup, stew, or whatever it was. My stomach churned in anticipation – for a change.

"Once you complete your training, you are paid basic officer pay. It isn't princely, but it is three or four times above your training stipend. The moment you leave earth, you draw half your officer pay, plus your base officer pay. You continue getting pay and a half until the moment you return."

One of the "sisters" made a hand gesture. Siss saw it. She knew I noticed it. Rather than be offended or suspicious, I admired how people can communicate without words.

"Do I have to stay in the service?"

"Only long enough to be debriefed. INSPAD will want to get, in writing, everything you did or saw during your tenure."

"I can write well in French," she interrupted. "My English writing is not so good."

"I doubt you will have to write anything," I replied. "They will record your report, in any language you like. Someone else will enter it in a computer file. In any case, unless you partake in something scientific, your debriefing will be confinded to your thoughts and feelings. It shouldn't take more than a couple hours. Once debriefing is over, you can quit on the spot."

Siss was thinking hard. Her sisters helped her, though not a word was exchanged.

"I can't afford a trip to America."

Of course, I invited that! Sometimes, I don't cover the most obvious details.

"INSPAD pays for your transportation to training and your return. You must return to Mali," I warned. "If you decide you want to relocate to Ulan Bator, it will have to be on your own. You must return here – INSPAD will insist."

I added this last to reassure the sisters that Siss must come back "home." If she decided to stay in the States, INSPAD would be more than happy to deny her return fare. I doubted Siss would abandon her sisters and Father Whoseits, but one can never be certain.

"I will think on these things," she promised.

The bad news was that I'd be stuck here for however long it took. The good news was we could resume our meal.

I WAS NEVER AWARDED A PARTICIPATION TROPHY

(So I Stole One)

INSPAD is a quazi-political organization which uses science as a front for laundering money and awarding cash prizes to people for keeping out of prison while actively fleecing the general public. Because it is so huge, governments yield to its power and promply comply with its every demand. Every member state, and (within limits) every "associate" member state contributes thousands of pages of rules, regulations, policies and proceedures. Many of these are in direct violation of each other. As a result, any clever employee can play INSPAD like a toy piano.

As a clever person, I am on par with an entry-level grifter. Were I bold enough and smart enough, I could take INSPAD for several billions. I could buy Mali (and everyone in it) and set myself up as His Imperial Majesty for as long as it pleased me.

Fortunately, for Mali, I am not overly greedy and nowhere corrupt enough to promote myself to such a level of depravity. My criminal activity was confined to ticking off rather innocuous wishes: buying Pythagorean cups, for example, and traveling to interesting and remote parts of the world. Best of all, my wish list was paid for by a corrupt organization. True, the money I spent was extorted from a billion or so people who were, essentially, slaves to corrupt governments.

One of those slaves was Brice Duvall. Another was Aissata Sissoko. With a modicum of luck, we could game the system for our own selfish ends.

I vowed to leave Siss alone to ponder her future and her current options. I refused to bully her – that was INSPAD's preferred method – nor would I pressure her. I was on a mission to obtain a pound of flesh from my employeer. Siss could be an important asset, but I was not Little Ceasar. If Siss joined me in my adventure, she was welcome, but I would not hold a knife to her throat and force her to do something she didn't want to do.

It should be easy, in a city as large as Timbuktu, to avoid a particular person. However, it seemed that Siss and her "sisters" were ubiquitous. I had to sneak in and out of the markets. Most of the citizens walked to and through these daily. I saw many familiar faces. Many people greeted me pleasantly without knowing my name. It was rather like being Pepe Lamoco. I was as conspicuous as a lighthouse – a *white* lighthouse. My method was to know *exactly* what I would purchase; I'd dart in, buy the desired goods, and leave the area as quickly as possible. All the while, I kept my head moving. My eyes were constantly searching for those I most wanted to avoid.

After my first, nerve-racking forey, I hired an employee of the hotel to do my purchasing by proxy. In exchange for a bit of folding money, young boys would vie to do my bidding. This made it impossible for me to remain in the hotel. I'd be surrounded by a gaggle of employees, plus their cousins, sons, daughters, friends, and sundry others. Once my evening meal fixings were securely stashed, I'd leave the hotel with all due haste.

My preferred venue was a level patch of ground near a school. Decades of tiny feet had so compacted the dirt and sand that the "park" had the texture of asphalt. Any time during daylight hours, young boys (and no few girls) would play "football." Now, I am to international football what a kazoo player is to a symphony orchestra. However, the children were delightful. They laughed at my lack of coordination and enjoyed "showing me up," but we all had fun. After three-day's practice, I could dribble the ball for five or six seconds at a time. Inevitably, however, some young kid would steal the ball away. I tried hard to steal the ball from the kids, but they were too adroit. I never had a chance.

The kids had great fun. They enjoyed making a fool out of me. I enjoyed watching them make a fool out of me. When I needed a drink (of water) or a bit of rest, I'd just sit on the ground and watch them go at it. They liked showing off for me. I applauded when appropriate, and they were appreciative.

Some of the kids spoke French. Most, however, spoke one (or more) tribal languages. They awarded me a name. I cannot record it here – the vowel sounds, particularly, cannot be reproduced with our alphabet. I never knew what this moniker meant in either French or English. Likely, it amounted to "Clumsy White Guy," or something equally unflattering. It made no difference to me. I was so enthralled by their youthful effervescence that language and meanings were superfluous. Regardless, I learned a few of my friends by their names, though I never succeeded in pronouncing them correctly (they often laughed when I tried).

This, I concluded, was the discovery of my fatal weakness: I enjoyed watching children having a good time. If I could do anything to advance this cause, I'd do my damnedest.

Playing with eager, young children and watching them at play was good for my soul. Remember, though, I was not acclimated to the local environment. It wasn't as oppressively hot as I expected, but the air was arid and the relentless sun was not merciful to my, hitherto, sedentary lifestyle.

Upon leaving the hotel one morning, I felt a bit shaky. Eager though I was to be with my newest frineds, I realized I wasn't up to the task. Should I beg off, they might consider it a hostile act. They didn't mind me sitting and watching, but they turned curiously petulant if I didn't chase them around a bit. As I could not risk upsetting them, I opted to take the morning off. They were not slaves to schedules or time clocks. There was never a ceremonial "changing of the guard," but idividuals did come and go throughout the daylight hours. Should I return in the later stages of the afternoon, I was certain to find a few of the "regulars" who could explain my innocuous nature to any child who might consider my presence sinister.

This desperate notion might contain more fancy than was wise, but I clung to it.

I decided to seek admission to Sankore University – not as a potential student, but as a "clumsy white guy" curious about course offerings and facilities. It would get me out of the relentless sun and, possibly, into an airconditioned environment. Further, I might mention Siss. I was certain she had made an impression on university staff as she had with me. Several insightful anecdotes might await me there.

Surprisingly, my entrance went virtually unnoticed. A dozen or so students (I assumed they were students) passed me by in both directions. If they were either bothered or surprised by my skin color or my foreign attire, they disguised it masterfully. They were either off to study or headed home to the ever-demanding chores of desert life. There may have been security people about, but they remained inconspicuous. In short, no one challenged me or bothered to ask why I was there.

I wandered around for a few minutes.

Eventually, I found myself in a common area. Several students and, I presume, faculty members were seated around a number of tables. The furniture represented an amazing, and eclectic, collection. I doubt there was one table that matched any of its mates. There were wooden tables, plastic tables, aluminum tables, particalboard tables, and one olive-drab field table I'd seen during my brief stint in the Army. Likewise, the chairs presented a tribute to variety, though there were a few (a very few) that matched.

The students and staff assembled were engaged in various activities. Some read texts, some deftly utilized the keyboards of their laptops, a few discussed over a flury of lecture notes, and a group of three were collaborating over mastery of some device I didn't recognize. A chill went up my spine. There was no chit-chat, no slurping of coffee or bottled drinks, no sign of frivoulous activity of any kind. Were there sanctions over occupying space in the common? As the only person not involved in some form of study or production, I might be uncerimoniously escorted out of the building.

At the far side of the common was a bookcase crammed with tattered volumes. There were no few paperbacks among this collection. I'd been around enough to know a book swap even in this most unlikely of cities. I quickly busied myself with examining these cast offs.

My hotel, by Mali standards, was "comfort class," but – outdoor concert aside – there were few entertainments available. There was no live music in the dining room – no piped-in music either, now that I think on it. The three TV channels were occupied by Islamic devotions, news shows, and sports. One channel featured ninety to two hours of imported programs in the evening. These were (almost) exclusively American with subtitles. Alternatively, a single person dubbed the audio of *all* the characters into French. Watching forty-year old American TV shows turned stale very quickly. Still, "when in Timbuktu …"

The sight of those hardbound books was positively intoxicating! Additionally, it provided me with an occupation. If loiterers were discouraged or, worse, expelled, I needed an excuse to avoid admonishment.

I found an abridgement of Dr. Johnson's Dictionary. Knowing that he enjoyed injecting saterical comments along with his definitions, I felt this volume was worthy of my attention. The text was in English and the binding remained immaculate despite the early twentieth-century copyright.

A moment after tucking the volume under my arm, I spied a mystery by Dorothy L. Sayers. It was in French and had been subjected to a hard life. A few of the pages had been torn but none were missing. Someone did some serious underlining, in ink, and made snarky little comments in the margins of several pages. Both the text and the annotations piqued my interest.

The idea of reading a French translation of an English mystery quickly promoted itself from a casual interest into an obsession. Despite my best efforts, my French lacked proficiency. Perhaps, if I could learn from an author highly regarded as a scholar . . .

Shedding my coyness, I approached a man sitting errect in his chair and reading an Arabic text. My menu-Arabic and a carefully drawn and highly detailed illistration on the facing page suggested it was an Indian veda – Gilgamesh, parhaps?

"*Pardon,*" I said, tentatively.

The man wore thick, black-rimmed glasses. He took a deep breath.

You're for it, now I thougt to myself.

Letting out his breath, he turned to look at me. His annoyance was quickly replaced by curiosity. Apparently, he was – until that moment – unaware of the *clumsy white guy.*

"I took these books from the shelf behind you. Are they for sale? Whom do I pay and how much?"

He glanced at my books. His attitude and expression communicated both knowledge and wisdom. He knew English and French and, I suspect, had a very good idea about the contents of my selections.

"You needn't pay anything," he said in perfectly enunciated English. "If you can make use of them, take them."

How did he know I was an English speaker? Was my French really that bad?

"I'm not depriving anyone?"

I was clutching at straws. The *clumsy white guy* didn't belong here. He certainly had no liscence to remove books from the university.

"Hardly. If you insist on a *quid-pro-quo,* perhaps you could bring them back when you're finished," he suggested. "Alternatively, you could bring in a couple other volumes you judge to be analogous."

"Thank you, sir," I replied while trying to maintain a non-groveling attitude. "I graduated from an American university, but I like to examine items I have not, formally, studied."

"A healthy attitude," he pontificated. "I wish you success."

"And you, sir."

He rose and inch or two from his chair and nodded as if imitating a bow. I replied with a polite, if abbreviated, bow of my own.

It wasn't only the children that delighted me! The gentleman, either a professor or a well-advanced graduate student – was a person I'd like to know.

I left the university with much more than two didactic volumes.

Did you ever page through a dictionary edited by a man whose heart just wasn't in it? As I understand, Johnson was part of an eighteenth century version of I-can-do-anything-better-than-you. The French collected and defined a mountain of words under Voltaire who had dozens of assistants. Johnson's patron commissioned him to do a better job with fewer helpers.

Lexicographer : A writer of dictionaries; a harmless drudge
Compliment: An act . . . of civility, usually understood to include
        . . . hypocrisy
Excise : A hateful tax
Ingaunation : A word neither used nor necessary
Pension : . . . generally understood to mean pay given to a state
        hireling for treason to his country

Oh, how I'd love for Sam's return. I'd love to see his definitions of those words most often brandished by INSPAD officials! If only someone offered me a reasonable emolument, I'd begin work at once. Of course, I'd probably spend the remainder of my days in a bomb-proof bunker or cave.

Would it be worth it?

Hummm. I'd have to think hard about that.

Meanwhile, do not take my historical snippit too seriously. Voltaire sprang to mind only because no other candidate did. Since I made no effort to check the veracity of my statement, it isn't impotant to me. If the reader is fastidious about truth, let him research it. I've worked for INSPAD long enough to know that dogma and coercion are sacred; facts are nasty little things summarily discarded in favor of expediency.

Have I made my attitude clear?

INSPAD, because of its international protocols (many of them secret), its vastness, its undecipherable layers of bureaucracy, its huge (secret) budget, its ability to overfund or syphon off huge chunks of cash has made it the most evil and corrupt institution in the history of our home planet. One might think I was motivated by greed. Perhaps, that influenced my action no little; however, I was after a pound of flesh (as mentioned previously). Alas, a pound – or even several tons – of flesh is likely to go unnoticed. If any particular "lord" noticed a shortfall in the season's graft, he (or she or the "gang") could restore monitary balance by dipping into petty cash. No one would ask questions. In fact, only a fool or a masochist would dare suggest that theft and extortion existed anywhere, to any degree, in the vast INSPAD leviathan. Such people were known to "disappear."

Mr. Big Mouth, formerly a low-level INSPAD employee in the geology department, was transfered to East Anglia recruitment division. However, after eight months, Mr. Mouth has yet to report in. Inquiries are being made.

This, and a myriad of similar notices, are so common that the London *Times* dedicats two pages a month to list them all. The public is encouraged to report any sightings or contacts with these "missing" persons. However, all but the dullest of readers knows that a "notice of transfer" is tantimount to an epitaph.

Well, I knew when I applied that INSPAD might, literally, be the death of me. I had no one the blame but myself. Regardless, I wanted that pound of flesh – not just for myself, but for those who dared to question methods, procedures, or corruption. I was well aware that my neck was sticking way out, but I knew where most of the lines were drawn. In a conspiracy of millions, the odds were *slightly* in my favor. It was the nameless and faceless who disappeared. I would, if I suceeded, be known to the world, as would Siss. Our "disappearance" would create a bumper crop of questions and bad publicity. Mob bosses hate that!

My plan, however, was audacious.

I once heard of a British MP who illistrated *audacious* on a BBC chat show.

"*Audacious*," he pontificated, "is best exemplified by a fly, climbing up a hind leg of an elephant, intent on rape."

Okay. In the world of INSPAD, I was more insignificant than the common house fly. However, I knew the system. Additionally, I knew where many bodies were (metaphorically) buried. I wasn't interested in the money. My mission was to twist the tale of the beast. Siss would be a part of that – a citizen of a non-INSPAD country, a former slave, not at all photogenic, moderately educated, highly respected in her community, and from a remote corner of the globe. These qualities would have several of the most corrupt INSPAD officials crapping coconuts! They wanted "ordinary" people to be a publicity front for them – the glitering object distracting public attention. Siss, if she agreed to join my conspiracy, would constitute a poke in the eye of the dictators. Their publicity people would have to work overtime to placate a restless public who, just possibly, would rally around Siss, a symbol of the downtrodden.

I'd love to see these officious bastards forcing toothpaste back into the tube.

WE ARE GO FOR LAUNCH

Now that I had people to help me pass the time in relative comfort, Siss informed me that she (with the eager encouragement of her "sisters") agreed to volunteer for the Into Space program. She was in a hurry to get to work. She didn't specify what her work was. In addition to being a certified guide, she worked, by the hour, for at least three other employers.

Ours was the briefest of conversations because she daren't be late. That particular work-ethic was all Siss. In Timbuktu, working hours (starting time, specifically) was, essentially, a concept.

If, for example, your workday began at eight in the morning, anything between seven and ten was close enough.

"Two months," I told her.

First, I had to get out of Mali. If I departed at eight (or ten, or noon, or dusk) the next day, I *might* be out of Mali within the week. Regardless, Siss would have sixty days to inform her commercial contacts that she would be leaving.

"How long will I be gone?"

In the civilized world, this is a legitimate question. In the Sahara, Junetember was as specific as the actual date of return.

"Eighteen months," I replied. "Maybe, two years."

Siss was acclimated to both the Western and Timbukian calendar. She was, also, intelligent enough to convert the one to the other.

Previously, I explained that INSPAD time is exact once the clock is started. Let's allow two weeks for orientation and paperwork; six to eight weeks of training; two or three months to fix the "departure" date; a four or five month "tour;" and three weeks of "debriefing." There would, inevitably, be personal appearances, chat show interviews, book deals, and other publicity junk.

Siss might not want to play the game. She might run off in the dead of night and be lost in Timbuktu. Any eager "journalist" who thought to corner her in her own city would find it rough going. Those who knew Siss would protect both her and her privacy.

It could get ugly.
Good!

I hurridly made arrangements for my egrees. Despite the discomfort of river travel, the boat/ferry system promised to be the most expeditious. Road travel, judging by the vehicles I'd seen arriving and departing, promised a myriad of potential disasters. On the river, even if the engine went tango uniform, the current would carry us downstream. Once I got to Kinshasa, reliable air travel was available.

TESTING THE WATERS

The "ferry" was within thirty miles of Kinshasa before I enjoyed PoCo service. INSPAD offered a satellite PoCo system, *but* each nation had to pay the subscription rates. Many poverty-stricken countries didn't pay – couldn't pay, that is. The big shots in the Mali government had a "limited" subscription. People in or near government offices could buy and use PoCos. However, most governments monitor these freeloaders. The possibility of a coup is ever the concern of authoritarian regimes, and doubly so among the poorest counties. For once, an INSPAD PoCo would be safer. No government on earth will mess with INSPAD. Regardless, I felt brave.

I spent several minutes catching up on world events and discovered that the International Court had agreed to hear a case brought against INSPAD. There were charges of "misappropriation of funds," but formal arguments were fifteen months away. Perhaps, I'd be called to the stand. Actually, I hoped I would be, despite my own misappropriation of funds. However, a joyride to Samos to purchase Pythagorean cups (purchased with MY money) hardly rated a pimple on a flea's butt. Still, I suppose, every little bit helps.

Next, I checked my INSPAD feed. There was nothing directed *to* me, but there were two brief comments about my "disappearance." Since I was not a VIP, these were hardly worth anyone's attention – to include my own. However, an INSPAD big cabluna was off to South Africa on a "fact-finding mission." This is INSPAD-speak for some high official with a summer resort home (the South African summer is the Northern hemisphere's winter). Somebody wanted to sip mint julips in the sun on the backs of the low-level slaves who contributed (involuntarily) to his or her financial status.

I had a sneaking suspicion as to this person's identity.

Under ordinary circumstances, I'd drag my feet and take in the sights. I planned to catch a cargo ship and go to its final destination. Unfortunately, I couldn't rely on Mr. Big to stay at his vaction home for an extended period (So many banks to defraud; so little time). As a result, I booked, through INSPAD, a flight to Durban. I had to change planes four times.

I rented a car, through INSPAD, and hustled down the coast to, almost, East London. Dieter Rolf commisioned a royal residence not far inland from a marina built with the rich and famous in mind. It was not, perhaps, as stately as the "digs" built by Kubla Kahn, but it was grand enough for an average king. It was built high enough to afford a magnificant ocean view, but it would be vulnerable to cold winds in the winter.

There was security, of course. The first layer consisted of two uniformed sentries stationed at the grand gate. In the civilized world, it would be placed at the end of a stately drive. For Rolf, however, the stately drive was designated a "private highway" by the grand signage at the road junction and along the single-lane highway. There were two additional signs announcing, among other things, *private* and *no trespassing* and *subject to arrest.*

Hey, I was INSPAD! I had my ID and I had my a copy of my mission orders (reduced to a laminated file card), and my INSPAD payment card. For me, or any other INSPAD swag, the word *private* and the phrase *no trespassing* did not exist. I was INSPAD; the law does not apply to me.

The tallest of the two sentries came forward, his right hand near his pistol. The second guard remained at his post. He was black and built for no nonsense. Additionally, he had a rifle at port arms. It was as nasty looking as the man who expertly held it.

"My name is Adam Kane," I announced, boldly, while flashing my INSPAD ID card.

It is my experience, powerful and influencial people anoited themselves "sophisticated" and reeking of class and knowledge. In point of fact, however, such pretentious dolts considered anything prior to the twenty-first century as prehistoric and, thus, of no value. I, however, was well versed in the culture of days gone by. Not so, the sentries. They, obviously, knew nothing of the Springbock Radio series *My Name is Adam Kane.* I'd listened to several episodes and was facinated by the authoritative, slangy baritone of the lead actor.

I doubt the sentries knew of the existance of radio.

The lead flunky was far more interested in searching for guns and explosives than he was in examining my ID card. I stuffed it into my shirt pocket as if to say "you had your chance."

"I'm here to see Herr Rolf on INSPAD business."

The guard's brow knitted. He didn't like me.

"Have you an appointment?" he damanded.

"If I had, you'd have waved me through," I reminded. "I was scheduled to meet him in London, but my bosses insisted that I see him as soon as possible, so, here I am. Tell him I'm here with revised specifications for the moon station."

There was one on the drawing board, but the brass was highly dubious. The establishment of an luner orbital station would threaten the existance of our dark-side moon base. The fight over initiating construction or scrapping the project would go on for a year or longer. There, certainly, was no hurry. However, the report of a London-based official traveling half the world to see a man whose suck-power in the project was minimal – if, indeed, it existed at all – was bound to pique curiosity. Herr Rolf might think he'd been handed a special project – one rife with corruption just begging to be exploited.

Greed is a mighty force.

Twelve minutes after announcing myself, the palace gates swung open.

I'd seen movies made during the Great Depression. They generally featured wealthy people dealing with such horrific problems as which car to take to a snooty gala or cooks who are so judicious that they tested the cooking sherry four or five times an hour. There was no place in films for the reality of a nation in want.

Suddenly, I found myself in just such a film. A black, meticulously togged gentleman met me at the front doors (plural – they were broad, arched and so white one had to squint when approaching). He held the door open and made a sweeping gesture with the other.

"Herr Rolf will see you in the library, sir," he announced in a business-only baritone.

I walked across the impressive entry hall in the direction indicated. I stood stock still as Jeeves opened the door for me. I entered a large room with plush furnishings, a plush carpet, plush hanging lights, and an unmistakable aroma of "plush." There was one large, black walnut bookcase containing three and a half dozen books. The rest of the space was dedicated to trophies – a mounted pistol of early frontier vintage, a crystal decanter with matching goblets, a jeweled and gilded egg (which, I assumed was Faberge), and several additional bobs and jigerdos unidentifiable by me save for the fact that they would fetch stratospheric bids at auction. The books were ancient and with bindings predating anything I'd seen previously.

Library, my butt!

These books were for show, not for reading.

The door clicked quietly behind me.

I'm not the brightest lamp in the world, but even I knew one does not leave a stranger in a room full treasures unless there were cameras – lots of cameras! I fought down the temptation to have a flip through of one of those volumes. I was here to push my luck as it had never been pushed before. To ruin this opportunity by risking the ire of a man whose bodyguards, udoubtedly, had orders to kill –

A door opened in the back of the room. I did a double take because there was no door in the back of the room. Well, of course there was or it wouldn't have opened, but it was so cleverly camoflaged that your average person (i.e. *me*) would never notice. Doubtless, Rolf's inner sanctum was on the other side of that portal. Doubtless, also, as in the White House, there would be other entrances to that "operations center" just as inconspicuous as the one in the "library."

"Who the hell are you?"

He had a puffy face as one would expect. His physique suggested he was, once, a man one would either greet with a bow or step aside to allow him space. Years and high living had made him soft and his voice gutteral. He was used to issuing orders and having them obeyed. In his declining years, he cultivated a voice that sounded as if his throat had been scoured by a cheese grater. It was intimidating only if one realized he had hired thugs to "take care of business."

"My name is Adam Kane."

In for a penny; in for a pound.

It was clear that, ancient books aside, Herr Rolf knew as little about Springbock Radio productions as the flunkies at his front gate.

"Is that supposed to mean something?" he demanded.

"Just being polite. We work for the same people."

"Not the ones I work with," he reminded.

"Not yet," I dared.

He stared at me as if he expected me to burst into song.

"This is a nice place," I began. "I wouldn't mind living in a place like this, but my place in INSPAD is too humble to presume. You are a clever man with clever associates and good connections. I'm just a card stacker. However, I think INSPAD is big enough for us both."

"Who sent you?"

"Why, the big pooh-bahs in the States," I replied without batting an eyelash. "I'm supposed to have team of – well, enough to get a nice, fat expense account. However, there's just me. So, while I'm performing my mission alone, I am enjoyng travel, accomidations, and top-of-the-line chefs. The wine cellars ain't bad, either. That's just the crumbs. I'm after bigger game."

Max das Messe (as near to Mack the Knife as my playground German would travel) glared at me with all the contempt I deserved. He was a high roller. He had neither time nor patience for small-timers.

"You didn't come here to boast about petty larceny," he growled. "This would be a good time for you to crawl back into your hole."

"I didn't come for a chat, sir. I came here because I need help – the kind of help that comes from the top down."

"Not interested."

With each passing second, my life expectancy was rapidly fading. If I pushed too hard, this character could have me thrown out with the rest of the garbage.

"I've completed my mission," I announced with more confidence than I felt. "I have two ordinary Joes to send into space and get in the way of that handful of people who are actually doing cutting-edge science. I don't like red tape. I'd like for you to – well, exercise your considerable influence to get my selections approved without INSPAD bureaucratic jiggery-pokery messing things up."

Mr. Big was pissed, but curious.

"What the hell do you get out of it?" He demanded.

I grinned. Getting his attention was half the battle.

"I've had a nice, little joyride on the INSPAD dime, but I can make more – a pile and a half. Not so much as to afford a place like this, but I can settle for less. The beauty of it is that I can make that pile legitimately."

He was still pissed, but he was interested. Maybe, I, the stupid peasant, had hit upon something he and others of his class had missed. True to his creed, "There's no such thing as too much," he was willing to hear me out.

"How?"

I nearly put my head in the noose. It was on the tip of my tongue to say something like *we smoke pipe of peace, hunt many buffalo.* I caught myself in time – thankfully.

"Publicity, Herr Rolf. Publicity."

One of his eyebrows arched, but his steely glare reminded me that I remained on very thin ice.

"The press does its damnedest to make hay by doing interviews with those who come back off the station and from the moon. But they're all scientists. Their lives are predicated on observation, experiment, evaluation and hypothosis. The public doesn't want that. It wants simple stuff. How do you pee? How can you survive without your PoCo? How do you have sex in space? Do you want to be in movies? You know: simple things for simple people with simple tastes. To hicks fresh off the street corner – *tabula rasa*. Toss the press a bone or two and they make up their stories as they always do. It's all fluff, fiction, and nonsense. However, before they can print or broadcast, they must get permission in writing."

Rolf nodded his head.

"Exclusive contracts," he mused. "It has some merit."

"Thank you," I nodded. "However, I can't be certain my handpicked candidates will go through. You know INSPAD; give them the chance, and they'll make a soup sandwich."

He took a deep breath.

"I don't like to rock the boat," he announced. "I'm doing okay. Why should I stick my neck out for a publicity hound?"

I had one card to play. It might be an ace. It might be a joker.

Several days before, Mel used a word so fatuous that it refused to leave my head. The fact that the word was whispered added to my suspicion.

"Are any of those books first editions?" I asked casually. "Anything by Aeschylus? Maybe, in ancinet Greek? *The Suppliants*, perhaps, or even – *Agamemnon*?"

I kept my eyes on the bookcase, but I had to force myself. When there was no sound for several seconds, I looked at Herr Rolf.

Max das Messe was gone. In his place was a wide-eyed man with dilated pupils. The skin of his full face seemed to sag. When he gathered his wits, he closed the distance between us, very rapidly.

"What do you know about Agamemnon?" he demanded in a voice resembling a frog's croak.

Bullseye!

I was elated and scared out of my wits. No matter what I told him, he'd not believe it. Moreover, if this was some super-secret scam, my silence must be secured. I know how thugs secure silence. One word from Herr Rolf, and his hired guns would make short work of me.

"I know absolutely, positively nothing!" I announced, trying hard to keep the panic out of my voice.

Rolf was on the very edge. I hadn't counted on this, but I knew it was "think-fast" time.

"A friend mentioned it to me," I reported. "The way she talked, um, *he* talked, he seemed to think I knew all about it. I went along with the gag. He told me nothing because he assumed I knew what he did. However, he expects to hear from me by the end of the week. If he doesn't hear – does the word *panic* mean anything to you?"

I threw in the mixed pronouns on purpose.

"What does this "friend" know?"

"Your guess is as good as mine. I didn't ask and . . . *she* didn't explain."

He didn't believe me. Still, he couldn't take the chance. If I disappeared, and if I really had a friend . . .

"You breathe a word to anyone and you're dead."

He meant it, but he was crapping his drawers – figuratively, at least.

"I can't tell anyone anything I don't know," I assured.

It was guts for garters time.

"Do we have a deal, Herr Rolf? Will you help clear the way for me?"

He tried to stare me down. I stared back. If I screwed up now, I mightn't get back out that front gate.

"You know what will happen if you squeak?"

People who are sure of themselves don't make threats. They don't have to. Herr Rolf was shaken, but the color was returning to his face.

"I might – you know – *forget* to call my friend. Oh, and FYI, you won't find – *him* listed on my PoCo, if that's what you're thinking. *He* is in an area so remote, there's no PoCo coverage, so my only means of contact is by primitive means."

"You're lying!"

"You have the dice. You know the point."

That was sheer bravado. If I'd been Herr Rolf, I'd have shot me on the spot. Whatever Agamemnon was, it must have a huge payoff. My guess is that several higher-ups were in on this. If so, one mistake by Rolf might not bode well for his future. Corruption and corrupt people can be so very useful at times. I prayed this was one of those times.

I was shaking when I climbed back into my rental. I spent much of my drive back to Durban looking over my shoulder. If I kicked over a hornet's nest, the best place for me was on the moon.

THE EARTH MAY NOT BE SAFE

As mentioned earlier, I didn't carry an INSPAD PoCo. The "organization" assured us that the issued PoCos did not have a locator chip. Only one out of every ten thousand employees believed that. However, each employee was issued a PoCo. Many of those who had no dishonerable intentions used the INSPAD PoCos. Others, such as I, placed their company PoCos under a rock somewhere and bought their own from a commercial vender.

Dieter Rolf, the German embezzler with two first names (likely, neither belonged to him), would "protect his interests." He'd want to know if I was INSPAD or just some street hustler. When my PoCo buzzed, I checked the readout.

Okay, Rolf had checked on me from his inner sanctum. He knew I worked for INSPAD. Doubtless, his first step would be to call my PoCo. Getting no response, he used his "contacts" to find my active PoCo. He wanted to talk. The moment I picked up, he'd have access to my exact location. Ergo, I didn't pick up.

I was smart. Was I smart enough?

If he called, it was unlikely I was being followed. Of course, he might *want* me to think that. Regardless, he must realize that Durban was the nearest major airport. He could have a dozen or more goons waiting for me there. From the office cams, he could ditribute my picture to make certain the goons got the right guy.

I took an exit to a just-happened-to-be-near-the-highway village. I turned off on a dirt track before getting to the edge of town. I left the car and made myself comfortable in a handy hedge several meters away. There I remained, quiet and camouflaged, for nearly two hours. No other car exited the highway; no one walked over to inspect my abandoned car.

Either I wasn't followed, or I was survailled by a drone or, even, a satellite. If so, someone would be on the ground snooping. Rolf's goons would be ready at short notice. If Agamemnon was of vital importance, so was I. If I dropped out of sight, someone would get edgy. Perhaps, I hadn't dropped out of sight. It was possible that an INSPAD drone had my infrared signature displayed on Rolf's monitor at that very moment.

After another hour, the shadows drew in and darkness descended. If Rolf knew my location, he'd call the police to report an abandoned car. That's assuming, of course, that he wouldn't dispatch a couple of his thugs to "chat" with me.

I concluded that I'd stuck my foot in it – both feet. If Rolf had decided to call my bluff, he had all the assets on his side. That left me with bupkis. My only hope was to keep Rolf's "employees" behind me, rather than in front. He was certain to have a team at the Durban airport. Due to the lengthy delay, he may have people in Kimberly and Cape Town as well.

Cautiously, I headed back to the car. I had sense enough to keep it in view, so anyone who planted a bomb inside must be very good, indeed. Of course, a high-powered rifle with a night scope could be anywhere.

If Rolf was determined to get me, I was –

Aposiopesis will do here. Even a dolt can complete that sentence.

I drove as fast as local laws allowed. Several vehicles were not similarly inclined. I cringed whenever one passed me. If the shooting started, I judged my chances would be slightly better if I turned into the gunfire. Going off the road would likely kill or seriously injure me. If I managed to avoid those eventualities, I'd be left afoot and defenseless.

East London Airport had flights to only two destinations: Cape Town and Durban. They did, however, have a charter service.

The six days following were nightmarish. My INSPAD expense card was leaving behind a paper trail that any fool with half a brain could follow. However, it kept any persuers behind me – no "cutting him off at the pass."

The moment I landed in Cape Verde, I accumulated provisions and chartered a boat to take me to one of the lesser populated islands. My luck held. I was deposited on a sandy beach. The local inhabitants, all fourteen of them, greeted me as if I were a messanger from another planet. They survived by fishing and spearing wild game (they'd run out of amunition years before and decided that they could spare expensive cargo space on supply craft by using indigenous materials).

It was made to order. No one could get to or onto the island without being observed. Rolf may have had suck power enough to order an airstrike, but there was no way of assessing the damage by remote control. Sooner or later, someone would have to set foot on the island.

Fortunately, I was within PoCo range, so I could check propaganda reports. I daren't call up specifics; that would give away my location. Well, I'd stay put until I got a boost in confidence or until I was satisfied Rolf was not hounding me. The overwhelming odds were if he wanted me at room temperature, he'd have caught up with me before I got out of South Africa. Of course, he might assume that "my friend" was, also, holed up in Cape Verde.

That opened a fresh can of worms.

Just as I considered throwing caution to the wind, a PoCo headline caught my eye. Three of INSPAD's leading grafters went down within hours of each other. They didn't fall into the hands of the law, of course. In typical beaurocratic fashion, one stepped aside to "spend more time with his family." A second major figure would undergo "lengthy medical proceedures" that would keep him from (get this) "judiciously performing his duties." The third victim suffred from "overwork" and required an "extended, recouperative vacation."

These press releases were aimed specifically at the ignorant and the gullible. Anyone with a nodding aquaintance would know, instantly, that there had been a silent coup. Three of INSPAD leading white-collar felons had been ousted to make way for the latest crop of embezzlers.

Undoubtedly, this was "Agamemnon." It had been in the works for months, if not years, and the fruit was harvested at precicely the moment when the trio was ripest. Predictably. Herr Rolf was tapped to fill one of the vacancies. I saw another palacial mansion in his immediate future.

Okay, Rolf, you are now first at the trough. Let's see how long you can keep it!

The three former officials were very lucky. Before, those in the way met with serious "accidents." Topping three big shots at once would be a tough sell, even for the masters of propoganda. However, I was no longer a security risk for Rolf and his co-conspirators which meant that I could move around freely.

Caution demanded that I keep my PoCo silent. I'd have to wait for the weekly supply boat to arrive. I'd slip a message and a bit of "coffee sweetener" into the sweaty hands of the pilot. A day or two later, a sport cruiser would be out to fetch me. I'd catch the next flight to Dakar and be back in the States a week or two later.

I continued to look over my shoulder, but I wasn't as paniced as I'd been after leaving Rolf's South African palace. Assured, or reasonably assured, that I wasn't being stalked, I considered flying to Europe to catch a commercial flight home. My PoCo informed me that most of the (as yet) unfilled seats were going to New York.

I wouldn't go to New York for twenty million credits!

It took a few days, but I reached Lisbon where I enjoyed a quiet two days before boarding a flight to the Azors. With my INSPAD credentials, I entered our military facility there and bullied my way onto a MATS flight to Charleston.

My pride in myself and my 007 imposture took a severe and unexpected beating.

After leaving the aircraft and entering the arrival facility, I was greeted by a bull-neck civilian holding a sign. It was made from the side of a cardboard box which was not trimmed. The large, black letters were stenciled the military way.

ADAM
KANE

This was not a good sign!

The hulk holding this masterpiece looked bored, but he was big enough and appeared strong enough to snap my spine to relieve the tedium. I was wary, but what could I do? If Rolf had traced me to Charleston, he, and his resources, could locate me no matter what I did or where I went.

"My name is Adam Kane," I announced, a twit feigning bravado.

I'd adopted the line as often quoted in the radio show. There was little need to discard it. If this giant was an assassin, it would serve as a great exit line.

The giant reached inside his jacket. On a military base, in front of God and everybody, this man was going to take out an equalizer and equalize me! It was too fantastic to credit, but my blood – and the rest of my body – froze.

Good-bye world.

His hand emerged with an envolope – *not* a handgun.

"You were to get this the moment you arrived," a gravely, baritone voice informed.

I took the message and gulped hard.

The giant, his mission completed, turned his back to me and set a methodical yet unhurried course for the egress. I watched him while my blood pressure eased its way back toward normal. As he passed a trash bin, the giant deposited the Adam Kane sign. He exited both the building and my sight. I waited several seconds, fearing he'd return with a high-powered rifle or a samarai sword.

He didn't.

I moved into the proximity of a uniformed SP before finding a seat and settling in. Only when my breathing regained normalcy did I dare to examine the envelope.

Brice Duvall

Message received. Rolf knew my true identity. Obviously, he'd been tracking me despite all my precautions. I imagine he got a good laugh over my Cape Verde hideaway.

Calculating that the situation could not get any worse, I tore open the seal. Inside, I discovered a short missive. It was in a script font, but was computer generated.

Adam:

You kept your cards close to the vest. Well played.
Submit your selections for Project Blue Moon,
They will be approved. Get any static, contact me
through the chain.

R

Did the project have a name? I didn't find it in the prospectous, but, of course, I hadn't paid the pile of paper much attention. I was encouraged by his promise, but I know the chain of command for junior nobodies like me is, normally, a tediously long process. Still, it was better than sleeping with the fishes.

More than ever before, I was certain: the best way to remain safe lay in vacating the planet.

I was relieved to be alive and whole, but I was, also, angry. In my youth, I considered INSPAD to be the source of all adventure. The human race can speak of conquoring space, but the notion, itself, is fatuous; it is clear evidence that the earth is inabited by flea-brained humanoids so bold as to assume we *know* anything. Whatever we discover, scientifically or otherwise, underscores our monumental ignorance. Nevertheless, for an eager young boy who burrowed in science texts and science-fiction novels, INSPAD was the entry into knowledge and exploration. Only after I gained employment did I discover that the orginazation was corrupt and dangerous. No matter what dedicated scientists learned by studying the earth from space or the moon from research stations, it was filtered through several layers of money-grubbing, chair-bound morons. The people at the top were there only to siphon off as much money, and corrupt as many elected patsies as possible.

Miffed and incensed as I was, I used my INSPAD card to buy a car. I'd drive back to Atlanta. When I submitted my expense voucher, I'd be honest. My pleasure cruise to Samos and my using INSPAD money to buy a car for myself would be set down undisguised. Chances were, I'd never be audited. Chances were, no one would review my account. I'd come home far, very far, below the allocation set forth in the prospectous. My anemic spending wasn't worth anyone's attention.

I alerted Aissata Sissoko. Rather, I initiated an alert. It would not reach her for three or four days, and she'd require time to settle affairs before leaving home. On acceptance, she'd be on INSPAD pay, to include a generous expense account. I thought I knew Siss well enough have confidence that her expenses would be modest. However, who could know? Give Cinderella the keys to the Caddie, and she might spend like an INSPAD administrator.

PASSING THE TIME

Once upon a time, I lived in the INSPAD facility – a euphemisim for the company dormitory. It made the morning commute to my cubicle very easy. When my infatuation with INSPAD began to wane, I took a small apartment in a highrise filled with small apartments catering specifically to INSPAD underlings. That apartment was vacated when I began my mission and, assuredly, housed a young, eager sucker. Since my credentials would soon be invalidated, the INSPAD guest house was, also, off limits.

I drove to the home of Ellen Lindstrom. Her husband was one of the first scientists sent to the space station. He and three colleagues were exposed to a huge dose of radiation as a result of a design flaw. When he returned home, he and his family knew he had only a short time to live. The Widow Lindstrom worked like a galley slave to keep her family fed and sheltered.

The time has come, the Walrus said . . .

Space voyagers (INSPADspeak) are paid the same as newly commissioned military officers but ONLY during training. Once they were sent to one of the "bases," they were paid by the academic institution or research foundation from whence they came. They were required to sign a waiver. Any injury sustained while "on duty" was not the fault of INSPAD. Since insurance companies are not eager to sell policies for anyone leaving earth's atmosphere, it is understood that the scientist and his or her family were participating in a crap shoot. Harold Lindstrom didn't make his point. The only thing INSPAD paid for was the headstone.

What a nice touch.

I never met Dr. Lindstrom, but my heart bleeds peanut butter for his family. I visited their modest hovel several times and slipped them cash or credits from time to time. If INSPAD got wind of my "transfer payments," I'd be "dealt with."

After checking into the hobo motel, I drove to the Lindstrom address and signed the title of the car over to the widow. Wheels would make her life easier. Failing that, the resale value would keep the family in chinks for a few months.

My cubicle was just as I had left it – cigarette ashes and cracker crumbs included. I fired up my cumputer, wrote out a terse two-week notice and sent it to the "proper authority." It would languish there for a few weeks, but my copy of the document was on file and ready for inspection when the crap came rolling down the hill.

I phoned the proper office and left a message.

Three days later, I got an "invitation" to come to the "office" and present my "report." Well, I knew how that stuff worked. I'd be treated like dirt by every person in the office (to include the cleaning crew). After I'd been sufficiently chastized by all and sundry, I would present my report in writing.

"Tell me what's in it," some officious boob would demand.

Heads and subheads of departments at INSPAD do not read reports. They require a verbal synopsis – preferably with words of one syllable. Printed material was left to the officious underlings. Doubtless, they would check for spelling errors before stamping it, reducing it to a micro-record, and filing it away in the memory bank of the gargantuine HR computer where it would remain, unnoticed and forgotten.

Stuff them! I had less than two weeks before I'd present my single digit salute. If this PR gag was important enough, some smug office slave would be dispatched soon enough.

I passed the time by paging through Dr. Johnson's dictionary. How fun it would be to insult and cuss those who lorded over me without leaving them a reference point.

Eventually, someone came by to ask if I had returned my INSPAD expense card. I replied that I had. It is doubtful that anyone would follow up. My expenses were so meger, by INSPAD standards, they'd never rate an audit.

Two days later, a smug peon walked into my booth without knocking.

"Where's your report?" he demanded.

I felt sorry for the man. His brown hair was sprinkled with strands of gray and his eyes squinted through a pair of rimless glasses. He may have been employed in the PR department for decades – or he may not. Regardless, he was a go-fer – as low as a slave can be in this outfit. Either he was a dunce or he really pissed somebody off.

"Pull up the trash can; I'll give it to you here and now."

I was not too surprised when he did exactly that. As a sign of contempt for a person who worked in a booth rather than an office, he turned the trash can over before sitting. What little I had tossed was scattered about the cheap carpet.

He listened. He ignored my flippant remarks. He did, however, ask three salient questions. My respect for him grew substantially. He was a galley slave, and he knew it, but he wasn't some empty-headed fool like most of the others on our level.

When my recitation ended, he stood up and offered his hand. I accepted it. He thanked me for my time and returned to the plantation. It's a pity I didn't ask his name. I imagined that he and I could grow to be friends. Likely, I'd never see him again.

My computer was up and running, but I had nothing to do. Since I was the man without an INSPAD, I was tempted to log into a site not approved by the monitors. What could they do? Fire me? That would be nice, but I had pushed my luck beyond tolerable limits. If I pushed too hard, "security" might "accidently" stop my breathing. I got what I wanted; it was foolish to taunt the sharks by sticking my hand in the water.

I picked up a book and attempted to read. My mind wouldn't focus, however. If I didn't find something to do, I'd lose my sanity and, with it, my ticket to the moon.

My reverie was shattered when my door violently flew open. I pushed my chair away from the explosion in self-defense. Alas, it wasn't an explosion. It was something equally as terrifying – well, it would have been had not Mel Harden been the door smasher-inner.

This sable skinned "man mountain" possessed ripples that had ripples. He'd dominated in both football and amateur boxing. He was a man to stand aside of if one dared anger him.

"Hey, Mel," I squeaked, hoping that I had done nothing to arouse his ire.

"Hey, yourself, Brice. What the hell are you doing?"

I cleared my throat.

"I resigned," I announced. "I'm just twiddling my thumbs until my two weeks are up."

"Well, pack up, bud. We need this – phone booth."

I was relaxed by this time. If Mel had anything to say to me with his fists, he wouldn't be flapping his gums.

"I can't leave," I reminded. "The suits would mark me absent and send me to the slammer."

"Get out, Brice. You is fired."

My eyes must have grown to the size of beachballs.

"Fired?"

Mel shrugged his massive shoulders.

"I suggested it," he responded. "I suggested that you are a loose cannon, and might just do something more agrivating than you done did already."

Mel could speak better English than many PhDs. However, he would use his getto slang when he wished to promote his volitile nature. When he sounded threatening, people could see his point of view more readily. So far as I knew, he'd never used his iron fists in anger, but nobody – myself included – wanted the honor of being the first recipient.

"This is on the level?"

"Check your mail," he suggested. "They should have sent out the pink slip by now."

I did as ordered. Sure enough, I was a *former* INSPAD employee. I'd get the severance package!

"Mel, I think I owe you a drink."

"Just one? You'd better dig a little deeper in those pockets, pal."

"Let's go."

He held up a large, restraining hand.

"You're a free man, but I'm still on the clock. Where's your digs?"

I told him.

"I'll come by around six," he announced. "I'll buy the eats; you can keep my glass full."

"Look forward to it."

He wanted to pump me. I had no problem with that. In fact, I was eager to tell him my whole, sordid plan.

Mel and I joined INSPAD back in the day when we thought that space exploration was a great, scientific adventure. We would give of ourselves to expand the frontiers of knowledge. Oh, we were so idealistic, we didn't stop to consider that we brought no useful skills. We both came to INSPAD with a college education, but we were not aeronautical engineers, nor did we have any scientific background. Mel would make a terrific astronaut; he could get scientists to and from where they would do the most good, but – he was too big and too heavy. Meanwhile, I could – contribute – nothing.

We thought we were *so lucky* to get a job with INSPAD. That didn't last long.

When it comes budget time, INSPAD deals with the number one. How many zeros are appended to *one* is predicated upon the number of hands in the cookie jar. For example, if INSPAD requires one million credits for – say, moon geology analysis. Dieter Rolf gets the first crack at that money. Naturally, the Head of Lunar Research must get a piece of the action, as well as the Chief of the Lunar Geology Department, and Office of Lunar Personnel, Lunar Reasearch Coordinator, and so and so and so. By the time the one million trickles down to the knuckle scrapers, there *might* be a hundred and fifty thousand left for the purchase and up-keep of equipment. The geologists, themselves, would be paid through their research organizations or the university where they were tenured.

It was bad when Mel and I joined. Now, that INSPAD was financed by a myriad of countries, the number *one* is followed by two or three additional zeros. A modern government is administered by the greedy and the corrupt. INSPAD is made up of an international gang of grafters and embezzlers. My joy ride to Samos and Timbuktu as well as my "vacation" in South Africa and Cape Verde (to include the purchase of a car) hardly constituted a pimple on a flea's butt. Nevertheless, it was a great screen. Rolf, and his fellow hoodlums thought I was just another "grabber." In truth, I was simply biding my time. One day, somehow, I'd get my pound of flesh.

Mel's feelings were similar. It was his job to train those who went to the space station and the moon bases. These were experts in their chosen fields. They were not astronauts. It was Mel's job to make them "space savy," so they wouldn't do something stupid – like removing their helmet to scratch a nose. Because INSPAD had sense enough to know that big brains often lack workaday intelligence, the pressure suits, clothing, and food supplies had to be, virtually, idiot proof. Still, these researchers had to be trained so they could get to the assigned station, carry out the assigned research, and return to earth alive and kicking.

The next round of basic training was to begin three days after my return. Mel wanted me in that class of candidates and lobbied for my firing. I'd join five other trainees. Siss would undergo the same training, but in a later class, predicated upon her arrival.

The training cycle was six weeks followed by a two week break before the next class was ushered in. Not every graduate went into space. Those trained would go into a pool. When a particular skill was required, the best qualified would be selected from the pool.

Ironically, Siss and I would go to the head of the line. That's cheating. However, that's INSPAD; one more reason to want to poke the beast.

Security be damned. Mel was my friend. I gave him a play-by-play of my boondoggle. He'd not "leak." Even if he did, what could happen? Well – now that I think on it, Dieter or one of his lackies, could make me stop breathing. Still, my trust in Mel was absolute.

We settled down in a nice booth in an upscale eatery. We enjoyed a cocktail while waiting for our steaks.

"Tell me about Aissata," he whispered, emphatically.

"She's as tall as I am," I reported.

His eyes lit up.

"Go on," he encouraged.

"She's not much to look at."

He sighed.

"She's no crone," I continued, "but her face and body are hardly – well, she's on the subtle side."

His attention departed forthwith.

"You're looking for the furture Mrs. Harden? You're in the right place."

Mel made a face and took a sip of his beer.

"Most of the females are married," he responded. "Those that aren't are, mostly, PhDs. I'm out of the game before we snap the ball. Those that are fairly good looking are pressed into service by their bosses who are too old or ailing to go themselves. Most of these are married – and their husbands are real exited about their wives going away, unescorted, for three months at a whack."

"How about the ones who are not married?"

"They're in love with going on a space adventure. They won't take any chances that their dream might get derailed."

Mel drove me to his home. We stopped at my former mail box and picked up my Samos cups. I had to clear out all my things (including my – "ha-ha" – pay checks) so that my replacement would have an INSPAD address. I showed him how the cups worked, but over the sink. It would be great fun to see Mel's face when he got a lap full of wine. However, he was in charge of my training; I wasn't anxious to have him think he owed me "special treatment."

We used water rather than waste wine. He was eager to know how the cups worked. Hell, I didn't know.

"It's been around for centuries," I reminded. "Ask one of the brainiacs to explain it for us both."

After several attempts to understand it, I announced that this was not a parlor trick; it was science and math. A parlor trick we could figure out – eventually. Science and math – well, if our high school and college instructors couldn't get basic science and math into our heads, we lacked the tools to figure it out.

INSPAD SPACE ASSETS

The space station, cleverly code named *S-1*, maintains orbital parameters of low earth orbit and very high earth orbit. There are three available slots are for meterology; currently, all these slots are filled. Radiation and gravitational studies had up to five slots, but there were seldom more than three positions filled during any once cycle. Astoroid studies and mapping were vital to the next "phase" of exploration. There were five slots devoted to this activity which were closely linked to ground instilations the world over. However, any cycle with more than two of these allocated positions filled was rare. There were three slots set aside for communications and, you bet your sweet bippy, all these are filled.

Communication is vital. It isn't as taxing, perhaps, as air-traffic control, but the eight-hour shifts leave those manning the comm equipment constantly screaming for more people. INSPAD "can't afford" any additional people.

Four people are assigned as maintenance personel. There were four slots which *must* be filled during every cycle. These are hand-picked experts in all the systems. They are known as Space Monkeys and it is their job to keep themselves alive in a very hostile environment. If they stay alive, so do the others. When a Space Monkey issues an order, it supersedes *everything* else.

More about the Space Monkeys anon, but these people handle everything from DTRs (duct tape repairs) to hull breaches. Nobody messes with a Space Monkey!

In addition to the billeted crew, there were three or four cargo and rations personnel. They were responsible for all provisions and equipment transport. Some of the cargo is stored in the station en route to the moon bases. These people seldom eat or sleep in the station, but there are areas set aside for unforeseen circumstances.

Moon Base One is the first of the lunar bases and the crown jewel of scientific exploration of an extraterrestrial body. It started as a primative igloo, but a dozen years of planning and application of newer "space-age" materials have made it very special. There are six, science slots. There is always a geologist, at least one and often two. These "rock punders" are often referred to as the "wedding cake" squad. Each level of geological exploration is predicated on the study and evaluation of the team preceeding. The big university dollars go toward looking for specific kinds of rock to amend and expand our theoretical models. Nobody has made any "moon-shaking" discoveries as yet. Instead, our geological exploration is predicated upon a step-by-step method. Of course, if someone stumbles across a fossil of a living organism – well, the egg heads will have to revise their "model."

There is a medical doctor assigned to study the long-term impact of prolonged tours in an artificial atmosphere and low-gravity. Twice weekly exams of each team member and observations of mental health and stability keeps the medical profession on earth in voluminous data for study and evaluation. Once, a crew member came down with a case of the common cold *after* a thorough medical exam before leaving earth. This created a lot of excitement, but the contagion was sucessfully contained. That one, unfortunate scientist kept the earth-bound medcial community in valuable data for months.

There are astronomers on the moon base. With the sun beating down on the facility, there are precious little visual or radio observations, so the bulk of the work is on the sun and earth. When the blanket of dark decends, the astronomy shifts average fourteen hours. INSPAD tries to keep, at least, two astronomers at the base, but this is contingent on those available in the pool *and* the ability of the university or research organization to pay them.

The other scientists based at Moon One were selected on the basis of the research program submitted from a reputable organization ("reputable" is a concept not found at INSPAD, so I suspect – there's no way I can be certain – that some of these "scientists" are joy riders). Solar flares, meteorological study, radio and radar tests, biological experiments – some with lunar soil – and other research far beyond my ability to comprehend are all done at Moon One. Then, there are equipment tests. If INSPAD comes up with a "better" construction material, EVA suit, water system, environmental device, insulation material, or similar inovations, they must be lunar tested by those who design or manufacture such items.

Communicaton is, as ever, a major concern. Much of the preliminary data gathered is shot back to earth three times a day. These are "insurance" drops. In the evnt of a "catastrophic event," and the Moon One personnel are "terminated" (dead), the scientists on earth can salvage something.

One of the engineering triumphs was a "land line" for communications with Moon Two. That was a major project which ate up four cycles. If, for whatever reason, radio communication links went down, Moon One could remain in phone contact with the crew at Moon Two. The real reason, however, is the crews could converse freely without fear of being heard by some officious, INSPAD pooh-bah. Otherwise, free speech was discouraged. Any punk kid with the know-how could make a receiver and tune-in to moon chatter. If punk kids can do it, propaganda organizations can do it. It won't do to have the world know about every space peccadillo. There were frequent arguments, disagreements, and lapses in civilized decorum that are better kept secure.

Moon One is the Lunar Hilton. There is a "plush" (by moon standards) crew lounge, and the sleeping quarters were the best in the history of space travel.

Moon Two is much closer to the lunar equator and on the rim of a major crater. It is more protected (from small meteor downstrikes) and has better earth-monitoring equipment. There is more "moonwalking" done from here than from the other bases – and further afield. Much is made of the "camping trips" of three or four days duration. These, and the vehicles which make these treks possible, are all Moon Two projects. There is one base "commander" and up to four "pedestrian" scientists. It is rare to have more than two "camp outs" during any given mission, but trios are not unknown. Regardless, one of the team (at least one) must remain at base and monitor (or supervise) every second of every "field trip."

Conversations between base and the "campers" often became heated. The radio links between were electronically scrambled, but the most tumultuous exchanges were made in short bursts. One was ever aware that whatever can be scrambled can be unscrambled.

"Always remember, somewhere out there, is a sixteen year-old kid who can make a radio out of a potato peeler. He will know when you scratch your balls. He will be eager for an audience."

This, or any, similar warning was issued before any "moonwalk." Scientists, by virtue of their profession, have very high boiling points. However, when they boil over, they don't speak scientifically. They can be quite creative.

Moon Three, a.k.a. "Dark Side," a.k.a. "Sparta," is the most remote human habitation in the solar system. Because of the SETI project, this base is completely cut off from direct communication with earth. In truth, the SETI "observatory" consists of a single radio telescope which is, periodically, aimed at "likely" planetary systems (i.e.: the ones of which we know). Since any two-way communication is measured in centuries, no one expects anything to come of it. However, picking up a "being-sourced" signal from a distant galaxy would excite half the world and panic the remaining half. INSPAD would determine *if* and *when* such a discovery would be made public.

The "Dark Side" Station can host four researchers. To date, there have never been more than three. There has been considerable talk of laying a land line (Lunar line) from Base One to Dark, but it would require too much material and manpower. There was serious discussion about constructing two relay towers for radio communication, but that entails nearly as much supply and people as the antiquated telephone line. Moreover, the scientific community would go bonkers; the entire reason for the Dark Side station was to avoid all the electronic *pollution* earth facilities produce.

It is very quiet at Delta Sierra. The only human sounds come from those stationed there. Additionally, if there is an emergency requiring evacuation . . . well, chances are, no one would know to send help or lay plans for evacuation.

That brings us to the Space Monkeys.

These men (and they are mostly male) are heavy equipment opporators and repair experts. There are twenty-eight highly trained, highly skilled, and highly tough creatures who serve a six-month tour. They are the highest paid of the INSPAD employees. The big shots, like Dieter Rolf, rake in much greater amounts, but the bulk of their "earnings" are embezzled. The Space Monkeys earn theirs under circumstances that would drive most people insane.

There are two "transports" on the moon. It took two years to ship the parts and assemble them (each) on the lunar surface. Supplies, from water (much easier, and *lighter* to ship as oxygen and hydrogen and "manufacture" on the moon), to scientific equipment are moved from the supply "zones" to Base One and Base Two.

The Space Monkeys must live on the Transports. They are each assigned a small space "called a telephone booth" in the bowels of the "Crawler." This is their home for six months. If there is room at a Moon Base, one person may spend a night in the "plush" environment of the "guest room." Alcohol is prohibited beyond the earth's atmosphere, but Space Monkeys are not searched during pre-flight as carefully as the moon-base crews. They always seem to have a stash hidden away on the crawlers. Since resupply is impossible, there are no (reported) incidents of drunken crew (thus far). However, four ounces of "juice" can buy a hell of a lot on the moon.

There is room for only one driver. The lunar speed limit is twelve (earth) miles an hour. Driving, therefore, is the most tedious, tooth-achingly dreary activity in the solar system. A two-hour shift in the driver's seat is considered punishment. Often, however, "vistors" were encouraged to "volunteer" to drive the beast. Navigation is simple: one simply follows the ruts created during previous missions.

Much time and effort was spent in providing all the tools required to keep both the crawlers and the moon bases up and running. These tools were pure gold. If one has a "flat" or a broken hose, one does *not* want to discover a required tool was left somewhere else. There were strict rules in place. There were tools at the each base for all the installed equipment. There were tools on each crawler for every item on or in it. Should any tool be dicovered where it did not belong, an investigation is launched. If blame can be assigned, that unfortunate person (scientist, Space Monkey, or tourist) was guarenteed a minimum of five years in an earth slammer.

This is one of the few things about which INSPAD is judicious!

COMPLICATIONS

Festina Lente was falling into place well. Should Herr Rolf get careless and be ousted from his perch – well, it was almost certain to happen. Even with the help of the big kabloona, there remained the problem of my employment. The criteria for the PR scam would be made public soon. INSPAD needed a shiny object to distract the public. News outlets, those not owned and operated by INSPAD or corrupt governments, were muddying the waters. There was no immediate threat, but there were plenty of whispers that the INSPAD "reorganization" was, in fact, a coup. The more corrupt an organization was, the more damaging "unauthorized" information became. The (so-called) news media was constantly beating back "leaked" information which confirmed the major news organizations were the puppets of the rich and powerful. Crooks and assassins that control or form a mighty conglomerate are careful to project the image of sticklers for honesty and integrity.

Soon enough, the "comman man and woman" would be announced, officially. There would be much noise about the criteria established for the selection "committee." No INSPAD employee was allowed.

I had to become a former employee before the announcement was offical. If I quit too soon, INSPAD would sweep me under the rug – or make a valiant try. If I "resigned" too late, I'd be bounced in favor of someone INSPAD selected – a close relative of Dieter Rolf, for an example. There were a myriad of "examples." There could be a major blow up. INSPAD might collapse under the weight of its own corruption.

Well, if I could be the catalyst to bring down INSPAD, I'd make the sacrifice with a smile on my face. However, there could never be a guarantee. INSPAD had dodged damning scandals before. I couldn't risk it. I must continue to advance my own interests. That's the INSPAD way!

Mel Harden is the one person I trust above all others. I would be his subordinate for the duration of my training. In any new endeavor, there exists a certain amount of hit-and-miss. There was one death on the station which led to Mel's appointment as Chief of Training. It is an impressive title, but as in all INSPAD projects, there are layers of desk jockeys over him. Anytime a "superior" scratches his or her butt, a new directive lands on Mel.

The good news is, the "idea goons" wouldn't be caught dead around us slaves. Therefore, Mel disregards the garbage they throw at him. He keeps meticulous files, however, against the day when a goon comes around (they always notify people of their arrival date to make certain the red carpet is rolled out). Mel will page through the goon's directives to make certain he pays proper lip service during visits.

Mel's personal (and primary) mission is to teach every trainee how to survive when a catastrophic event happens. Two of his trainees nearly died on the moon. Many people would be haunted by these "accidents" Such a person will reflect that he (or she) "might have taught them better." Mel would have no such sentiments. He insists that each trainee do *exactly* as he teaches them. If a trainee cannot master a skill (any skill), or if a trainee insists on taking "short cuts," that trainee does not get Mel's certification.

Without Mel's certification, nobody – that means *nobody* – leaves the earth's atmosphere.

Should Dieter Rolf desire an "on-site inspection," he'd have to go through Mel. This was one of the few iron-clad regulations at INSPAD. It would take considerable muscle and facing-down a mountain of bad publicity to bypass Mel.

"I'm going to ride you," he warned me. "If you mess up, you will think a ton of bricks fell on you!"

He was not jesting. We were friends. We were good friends. He would be rougher on me than anyone else because he wanted to make damn certain I was coming back. If something happened, Mel would *never* wallow in that I-could-have-trained-him-better syndrome.

I had gamed the system to hitch a ride to the moon. With Mel the games would stop. He would be on my case every minute of every day. If that was the price I must pay to cheat the cheaters, I would pay it.

It was four days prior to the next training cycle. There were only five other qualifying candidates in my "class."

"All the easier to keep my eyes on you, trainee," he reminded.

To get me started, we adjourned to his digs and spent an evening going over manuals, devices, and procedures. This one-on-one instruction would give me both a head start and a leg up when the training commenced. I might be able to assist my fellow trainees and take some of the load off Mel's broad shoulders.

That first night, I invited myself to Mel's digs. Like most of the INSPAD peasants, it was "cozy." Single occupant residences are looked down upon. My hotel room (*hotel* not *motel*) had room for my ass and a pot to pee in. Mel enjoyed a "living room" and a "kitchen." These two chambers were not segregated. If Mel sat at the kitchen counter, I could lounge in the only chair situated, strategically, next to a wall-mounted reading lamp. The most spacious chamber in Mel's residence was a capacious closet. As a result, Mel's wardrobe was the envy of all. Most of us had two or, if we were lucky, three changes of clothes. Mel could step out ten or eleven days in a row in different togs.

What a waste!

Mel wore only his INSPAD officer's uniform at work (six days a week). However, he had three uniforms.

I brought along a bottle of Riesling and two of my Pythagorean cups. As we sipped our wine, we made a cursory tour of three technical manuals. The material therein would be studied thoroughly during our training cycle, but a "sneak peek" of coming attractions was not going to kill anyone.

After we dispatched our first measure of wine, we contemplated a refill. However, the Pythagorean cups were designed, specifically, to discourage an excess of sprits. Instead, we went to the sink and attempted to discover the secret behind the "disappearing water." Better, we agreed, for water to go down the drain. The wine deserved a much better fate.

Our second evening began with a vow to enjoy the wine residuals. I left my cups at home, so there was no danger of the bottle surviving.

We paged through two more booklets, but I lost interest quickly. My friend, who knew the material front-back-and-sideways was, decidedly, most *un*interested. He was between training cycles. He wanted a break from the "space poop."

Absolutely devoid of prodding, we walked a half mile down the street to a fast-food emporium. It was too early for the teen revelers and too late for the afternoon or early-evening clientele who sought a break from office drudgery. There were two pairs chowing down with purpose, and an older man studying a newspaper over a cup (half-empty) of coffee. We had a clear field to the order window.

The woman behind the counter ceased whatever she was doing and sauntered over to the register. Mel looked over the woman's shoulder at the menu. I studied the woman.

Why?

Allow me to elaborate.

Why?

Now, I must divulge something that makes me a bit uncomfortable. You see, I like women. I am particularly attracted to *attractive* women. I have been known to ogle any pretty woman who crosses my path at INSPAD HQ. I enjoy examining oil paintings of attractive women (sorry, Leo, the Moaning Lisa leaves me cold). I study the "architecture" of any appealing visage. Oh, a pleasing figure never comes amiss, but the body – particularly when it is tucked inside any sort of clothing – isn't as mesmerizing as a well-sculpted face.

Siss, let me remind you, had very few physical attributes, either in body or in facial features.

The "order-taker" was as hypnotic as a cold, left-over sausage patty. She had an oval face, high forehead, big (well "larger" ears) and a trio of minor blemishes on her left cheek. If there were another female in sight, I'd hardly have paid this woman any attention. She was as plain as yesterday's socks.

Once again, *why?*

Mel, in his authoritative, drill-sergeant voice, submitted *our* order without bothering to consult me.

"Two gut-bombs with the works, two coffees, black, and a girl on the side."

The woman didn't bat an eye. She didn't smile – not even a little – nor did she scowl – not even a little.

"You don't want anything on the girl," she surmised.

In all my time with and around Mel Harden, I never saw him at a loss. This record was broken that early evening. Similarly, I was stunned – only momentarily.

"Let's sit down before she calls the cops," I suggested while attempting to stifle a laugh.

A defeated drill sergeant backed away in silent defeat.

I stepped into the breach.

"Looks like I have to buy," I informed her.

She didn't feel the urge to comment.

I produced my INSPAD card and ran it over the screen. The register beeped. The slug heads at INSPAD hadn't voided my mission expenses yet.

"Congratulations," I smiled. "I've never seen my friend chopped down with such elegance."

"I had him pegged as harmless," she reported. "If I thought him a pig, I'd have let it be."

Thus far, we've had three *whys* – by my count, anyway. Well, let's have a few more.

"You're not wearing a ring."

If there is anyone (not affiliated with INSPAD) who can explain *why* I made such a vacuous remark, I wish he, she, it, or they can explain it to me. I'm at a loss. I needed a Pythagorean cup of the brain!

Well, if I hadn't made an absolute fool of myself, the woman opted to compound my embarrassment. Was she a sadist, or was she merely vindictive?

"Master has twenty-eight wives," she announced. "One runs out of rings, eventually."

Okay, Mr. Big INSPAD shot; it's your turn at bat.

"Must be tough," I sighed.

This woman had yet to change her expression. She was willing and able to take our orders, but she had to cease some other occupation to tend to our flippancy. Clearly, she felt her interrupted and menial task was of greater importance than either Mel or I.

"Tough on Master, perhaps," she informed. "He has to explain to twenty-seven of us who he was with the night before."

Not once did this person show the slightest emotion. Nevertheless, it was a TKO. I drifted over to Mel without daring to spar with her further. I was embarrassed and ashamed. This – *female* had been hardened to the point where she could cross swords with any know-it-all. I wondered if she could dispatch drunks or acidheads as adroitly.

Why (that word again) did I need to know? Why would I want to?

Mel sat mute. He was nursing his wounds. He enjoyed teasing people when – I add hastily – he wasn't on duty. It, apparently, never occurred to him that people might tease back.

"She's good," I informed, unnecessarily.

"She'd be even better if she showed a little emotion," he replied.

That, indeed, was true. However, her humor was made sharper by her deadpan delivery. I hoped that was part of her routine. If not, then there was a story behind it; a story that mightn't be felicitous. Mel may or may not reflect my feelings, but our "boy's night out" had assumed a much less jaunty mood. In the world of INSPAD, there was little joy and precious little pride.

We conversed softly. Our concern turned once again to the Pythagorean cups. They were amazing, but we weren't certain if we wanted to know how they worked.

"I don't want to know," Mel concluded.

"Why not?"

This was the first cogent *why* I conjured since our arrival.

"There is a basic, scientific answer," he began. "The ancient Greeks figured it out, and their science was still fairly rudimentary . . ."

"Not," I cautioned, "In the theoretical aspects."

Mel nodded. He conceded that point.

"In applied science – the screw, for instance. The Egyptians used it to transfer water from the river up to the fields. So simple, but so profound. If I understood what makes those cups work – well, I just don't want to know. It's better this way."

I nodded without knowing – you know.

"Some mysteries are more interesting than facts," he pontificated.

Try telling that to the scientists on the moon.

I thought that sentiment but didn't vocalize it.

We allowed ourselves to be distracted by our philosophic colloquy. The stoic order-taker set one burger in front of Mel before providing the same service for me. This was not done. When our order was up, it was announced. We were expected to fetch it ourselves. We sent questioning glances at our waitress.

"There's an eight-year-old in the kitchen and she's shivering," she informed my companion. "Is it okay for me to tell her to put her clothes back on?"

I sensed that Melvin was just about to launch an invective. It might be intended as humor, or it might not. This was my opportunity to keep things light.

"Ma'am, we're perfectly capable of waiting on ourselves," I reminded.

"My name is Happy, as you can see."

She thrust her bosom in my direction. There was no name tag appended to her uniform, but the company logo was conspicuous.

"I'll be back with the coffee," she said without further ado.

The dynamic had morphed completely. The rather plain woman had transformed into an enigma. When I entered, she was just another woman working a crap job to earn enough to keep body and soul together; she was just one among thousands. Within minutes, she was a mysterious stranger and very alluring.

When she returned with our paper cups of brutal coffee, I could not let her off. As she so assiduously observed, this branch of the Happy Burger franchise was not crowded.

"What do you do when you get off work?"

It was trite, but I am not famous for my snappy repartee. I think I stole that crippled line from a film made in the very long ago.

"I'll hurry home to make sure the sitter has the kids in bed."

"May I call on you some time?"

"I don't know. *May* you?"

"Look," I said, struggling to keep my oar in. "We have so much in common. I'm Happy Brice. You're Happy Burger. I think we should talk over all our *happy*."

She looked me in the eyes.

"You his friend?"

Her glare shifted to Mel.

"I have the honor," he replied without a moment of hesitation.

"Talk to me," she dared.

Mel cleared his throat.

"I've known Happy here for several years. He's as punch drunk as they get, but I've never known him to lie or bite dogs."

She remained stone-faced and silent.

Mel glanced at me for only a second.

"He's got something nobody else in this city has."

Happy's forehead blossomed into inquisitory ripples.

"This man – sitting right there and looking like a hound dog passing peach seeds – this very gentleman – well, maybe not a true gentleman, but a nice guy for sure – is the proud owner of four – four, mark you, four Pythagorean cups. He'd be thrilled to show them to you."

"No etchings?"

"No etchings," we assured in unison.

"Alright, then," she nodded. "I'll give you my PoCo before you leave."

"I won't abuse the honor," I said, trying very hard not to grin.

She looked once more into my eyes. Her expression was very hard, indeed.

"If these Pythagorean cups are cheap imitations, I'll smash them over your head."

"Fair enough," I agreed.

She didn't know a Pythagorean cup from an ichthyosaurus, but she was game. Well, so was I.

"Where did you get that Oxbridge locution?" I asked my friend once Happy was out of earshot.

"Where did you get the notion of chatting her up?" he challenged. "She says she has kids."

I nodded.

"And no ring," I reminded.

"That could mean any one of several things."

He replied by taking a healthy bite of his burger.

WHY?

Mel is the guy who chats up women. He's very good at it. I doubt that he ever tried to chat up a Happy Burger employee; he preferred women with a bit of culture and education. He promised me that he had never hit on a trainee. I believe that. His mission was to prepare those people for survival in a hostile environment. Rigging a test or a simulation in exchange for a little whoopie was stepping over the line. He'd never do such a thing.

In fact, Mel Harder didn't have to bribe (or blackmail) women. He was Mr. Smooth. I, on the other hand, am Mr. Hopeless. I am to women what a Pythagorean cup is to a drinking orgy.

What a stupid I am!

Why would I chat up Happy Burger? She wasn't very attractive – in fact, my initial impression of her was hardly an impression at all. She never varied her expression; she didn't bother with make up or jewelry; she was rather small; her figure was – well, obscure; she looked sexless in that gaudy Happy Burger uniform. However, she had a razor-sharp wit. What she lacked aesthetically, she compensated for with her border-line humor.

She scribbled her PoCo code on a paper napkin. I nearly tossed it out with the residuals of our burgers. Instead, I stuffed it in my pocket and resisted the urge to call.

Two days later, I figured that I couldn't be any greater fool than I'd been to date. No matter what, I'd never see the woman again, so what could she do me?

"Hello?"

What do I say?

"Happy? This is a former customer. You gave me your PoCo."

"You're Pythagoras!"

This was not the monotone she'd used during our visit. There was warmth and excitement in her voice. Obviously, she'd researched my bait – well, the bait Mel used on my behalf.

"I am that he."

I tried to keep things light – as if I'd been turned down by better women than she. Little could she know, I'd been turned down by, practically, every woman I'd approached. It was my bravado. I wanted her to think that I had plenty more fish to fry.

"I have a son and a daughter, Pythagoras. Do you really have those cups?"

"Indeed, I do."

"At the risk of being forward, could you come to my apartment and show us how they work? I'm very interested. I know the children would really be excited about them."

What the hell?

"It would be a pleasure," I assured. "Just to ease my mind, you are the cashier at Happy Burger – well, the other night."

"Yes, yes, of course I am."

"Just checking, I didn't recognize your voice."

"I'm not working," she reminded. "I'm not using my work voice."

"Well, uh – yes. When should I come? And where?"

"Tomorrow. I don't work weekends."

She gave me her address and apartment number. I was excited but wary. What if she was playing with me? What if she had given me the address of Margret Hamilton? Even if she hadn't, was I expected to entertain her kids?

This relationship might meet with a sudden end.

Still, what did I have to lose?

I arrived at the apartment early – too early. I figured if I caught her on the hop and she told me to pound sand, I could take my time running the errands I had ignored far too long. If I caught her with her guard down and she didn't hold it against me, well . . . that circumstance opened the door for interesting possibilities.

Alas, tunnel vision is my most dangerous trait. My first date with "Happy," (I still did not know her name) involved complications.

The woman who opened the door was of mature years. Her visage resembled that of "Happy," but it had weathered many a year. She eyed me suspiciously – why would she not?

"Do I have the right apartment?"

I am as suave and adroit as a Mexican stevedore.

"Whom do you seek?"

Whom? Who uses that brand of locution? The anomaly was compounded by a thick, unidentifiable, foreign accent.

I nearly swallowed my tongue. I didn't know the woman's name. That was damned awkward. If I asked for "Happy," I'd likely get an abrupt response.

"She wanted me to show my Pythagorean cups to the children."

The woman smiled and opened wide the door. In the background, very feint, wafted the strains of Debussy's fawn. The woman, slightly stoop-shouldered but, otherwise, carrying her years well, encouraged me by gesturing with her arm. I entered. She closed the door behind me.

"These are the cups?"

As a gesture of good will, I offered my package. She took it but did not investigate.

"Please, sit."

She placed the package on the coffee table. Behind it was a small couch. I moved toward it but did not bend my knees. There was a woman, standing. My ancient upbringing would not allow me to sit until the woman took her place.

"I am Ksenia, Elena's mother. She's walking with the children. Please, sit."

"After you," I insisted.

She smiled before occupying a small armchair very comfortable in appearance. I was on my way down but popped back up when the woman jumped excitedly.

"Sit, please. Sit. I am only to get something. I am a moment."

Against my better judgement, I sat.

The room was small – lunar-like. There was a plush, woven carpet with an intricate Slavic design. On the wall opposite me, there was a modest icon in the Byzantine style. The floor lamp was late-American ugly, but the couch and reading chair were enlivened by – I assumed – homemade shawls bordered by delicate little – balls (I guess).

To my left was a lunar-like kitchen which was spotless – I mean, operating theater spotless. There was a short hallway down which my aging hostess disappeared. There was a door on either side and another at the end. A bathroom and two bedrooms, likely. The bedroom at the end of the hall must have been the largest.

Did the people eat standing up or did they snuggle up around the coffee table?

I worry about things like that.

Not many moments passed. Whatever my hostess fetched, it must have been instantly accessible.

"My Elena!" The woman announced with obvious pride.

She held a manuscript-sized album. She sat down beside me and opened the volume. There were papers and certificates and documents all neatly arranged in book-page order. Then, there were a myriad of photos. Many were of a young girl.

The woman chuntered on excitedly. She spoke in Russian (?) – very rapidly. She wanted me to experience the history. Doubtless, she feared interruption.

There were photos of a baby, a young girl, a teenager whom I recognized, eventually. Happy had one, ice-cold expression during my sojourn at Happy Burger, but the teen had a smile that could knock over a moose. She also had an overbite that was at once slightly freakish but highly seductive. The only other common characteristic I found in these photos were two bright, rosy cheeks. The very plain woman who'd sounded so cynical and boorish at Happy Burger had been, and likely still was, a looker.

How the woman gushed over "her Elena."

There were academic awards and photos of a schoolgirl beaming over plaques and certificates. Then, the sports photos; there were a ton. Elena (always *my* Elena) was an athlete. She played basketball, ran hurdles, played volleyball, and was a speedskater! She had a collection of ribbons and trophies to confirm her prowess. Then, there was a photo of *my* Elena holding a pair of skis in one arm and, from the opposite shoulder, a target rifle was slung at the ready. There was an accompanying document in French – a language with which I had a nodding acquaintance.

Fifth place in the Olympic biathlon.

The Olympics!

!!!!!!!!!!!!!!!!!!

Oh, but the "*my* Elena saga" continued. There were photos of this remarkable woman in attractive fashions – slacks, pantsuits, dresses, skirts and vests – holding a microphone. The deluge of unfamiliar words and phrases were superfluous; *my* Elena had been a sports reporter for some visual network.

Ah, then the wedding photos. It was one fancy event. *My* Elena's dress resembled a coronation gown. The duds worn by the groom were similarly grandiose.

There followed the family photos.

I felt like a snake in the weeds.

What was such an august person doing in Happy Burger? What circumstances forced her to work there? What right did I have to address her – never mind chatting her up and making a date with her?

I was so lost and confused, I hardly noticed the commotion in the stairwell. Suddenly, a key rattled in the lock. Three figures spilled into the room, two little ones and one not so little.

"MAMA!"

Happy was mortified. She's caught her mother and me with "the book."

She was not happy. Her face flushed, she scurried over to grab the book and slam it shut. Her rapid Russian was fire and brimstone. She was embarrassed, humiliated, enraged and ashamed all at one go. She issued commands to her children who did not tarry while carrying them out. With the speed of light, she got the book out of sight and out of the room. When she returned, very soon after, she continued her furious lecture. The older woman said nothing. She appeared to accept the admonishment without complaint. When the tirade began to subside, the woman stood and spoke softly and briefly.

My Elena's cheeks were still puffed out with rage, and her lips were tightly drawn. Her eyes were wide and angry. After holding her furious pose for a few more seconds, she relented. She took her antagonist in her arms and hugged her warmly.

The woman took her cue. She retired to one of the other rooms with the children.

Happy looked down at me. I had no ambition to be the next target. I got to my feet quickly. My amazement at witnessing the drama had swept away my manners. The face I studied was embarrassed and – dare I say – repentant.

"My mother," she announced. "My babysitter. Also, my best friend. She treats me like a goddess, and she is so proud of me, but – sometimes, I just want to crawl into a hole."

"Why shouldn't she be proud of you?" I demanded, perhaps too indelicately. "I'm proud of you, and I don't even know you."

"I'm Elena Ilyaovna Sidorov Yelagin," she announced abruptly while extending her hand.

Was she being a smart ass? I could play. She bested me (and Mel) at Happy Burger. This was an opportunity to show that I can ride a horse as well.

HOWEVER . . .

What if this was straight up? I'd look a fool if I made fun of her name – should it prove to be her correct moniker. If not – if she was just pushing my leg again . . . Well, I'd survive.

"Brice Duvall," I replied, seizing her hand.

She smiled. It was pleasing and – that overbite! If I snapped a picture of her at that moment, I'd carry the image with me during the day and sleep next to it at night. Elena's smile did not stop with healthy teeth and delicious lips. She was on her way to cultivating a proper double chin. Quite unexpectedly, this added to her allure.

"French?"

"You're the second person to ask that," I informed. "No matter where the name comes from, I'm an American for several generations."

"I'm Russian from Novgorod. *The* Novgorod, the city of Rurik, not that cheap imitation on the Volga. It's called Veliky Novgorod, but it's *the* Novgorod."

"We must meet again later so you can tell me how you really feel."

She smiled again. She didn't resemble the plain stone face of Happy Burger. When she smiled, she was disarmingly attractive.

"Are these the cups?"

An abrupt change of topic like that put out the No Trespassing sign. There was no way she could erase my memory of the *My* Elena documents and photos. She made it quite clear, however, she did not wish to discuss her history. I would respect her wishes, but I was composing an extensive list of questions. Heading the inquisition was the issue of her personalities (plural!) The woman standing near an icon was *not* the woman I chatted up at Happy Burger. These were two distinct people.

First, she admired the cups and their hand-painted images.

Next, she called her children and her mother.

Finally, she ushered the crew into the kitchen and demanded a demonstration.

The children were mesmerized. They insisted it was magic. Elena explained, but not too scientifically. I got the feeling she knew how the cups worked, but the young people wouldn't understand the physics involved. I made a mental note to inform her of the treaty struck by Mel and me. I didn't want her to destroy the mystery.

Both the boy, Eduard, and his younger sister, Arina, were over the moon. Each had to try. They must know if the magic worked for them as it did for me. I was reticent. I didn't want them to break one of my treasures. We had to hold the cups over the sink or risk getting water everywhere. There were just too many hard objects near our "laboratory."

I needn't have worried.

Elena didn't indulge. She reveled in the children's delighted exclamations and joyful cheers.

I wanted to get to know Elena better. I invited her to dinner the following night. She made a face.

"I have to work until seven," she announced. "You'd be surprised how a shift at Happy Burger can kill an appetite."

"Breakfast, then."

She wasn't keen. She cast a glance in the direction of her children. Then, she looked at me. I don't know what she sought, but she found it.

"How about Bean and Cake?"

It was a bit high-hat for my taste. I suspect Elena felt the same. Perhaps, that was why she wanted an "escort." A place like Bean and Cake is decidedly *not* for the businessman or businesswoman on the go. People went there together to be together. Of course, it is a specialty establishment. The coffee beans are roasted daily and on the premises; the biscuits were made daily and on the premises. No few people are satisfied to have only two biscuits with butter and jam for breakfast. Stubborn people might ask for biscuits and gravy, but only once; the management might be tempted to serve it in your lap.

"I'll call for you around eight."

"No."

It was as if she were on the verge of panic, but she recovered quickly.

"I'll meet you out front *at* eight."

She was prompt and prim.

She wore trendy blue slacks and matching pumps with a sleeveless white blouse. The sleeves of her pale blue sweater were tied around her neck. Save for her watch, she wore no jewelry.

We were shown to a quaint table for two. I fancied biscuits and gravy, but that's like ordering a peanut butter sandwich at the Savoy. I had, instead, a vegetable omelet. Elena opted for a fruit cup.

I didn't have to pump her. She was so distressed by her mother's "showing off" that she was bubbling to set the record straight.

Elena's father, Ilya, was Jewish and passed away when she was thirteen. Elena and her mother were Orthodox. Well. "modern-day Orthodox." The icon in their living room was ornamental. Thoughtlessly, she disclosed something indelicate about her mother; something so innocuous that I hardly noticed and don't remember. After committing her trespass, however, Elena quickly crossed herself.

This gesture was simple and inconspicuous, but I found it endearing.

Elena was a scholar and an athlete. She won awards both academic and sports related. She was the champion biathlete in her city, district, and, ultimately, the Russian national champion three years in a row. Her husband-to-be was infatuated by her press and publicity photos. He decided he wanted to meet her. As the heir to a multi-million ruble heavy-equipment manufacturing firm, his desire was made manifest.

It was love at – well, second or third sight. They had a blow-out wedding – no expense spared. Fedor seldom had the opportunity to see her compete, being up to his ears with his father's business. Elena hated being apart, but she was driven. She made a name for herself in speed skating and short-distance hurdling, but she could shoot the pimple off a flea's butt, so she was "encouraged" to dedicate herself to that.

She "retired" when she got pregnant with Eduard. She was awarded a spot on a news network. What Elena didn't know about a sport – any sport – was inconsequential. She traveled all over the world covering Russian athletes.

More time apart from Fedor.

Elena was an only child. There was something about the status that haunted her. She wanted another baby. Fedor was not keen. Elena won him over, but two children with both parents hip deep in separate careers produced strain. Ksenia became the live-in maid and babysitter. Mother-in-law and Fedor got on well enough, but husband and wife became despondent when two or three days might pass without their seeing each other.

After seventeen years, they divorced.

They still loved each other, but they were frustrated by never being together – or being together so seldom that it became insufferable. Fedor inherited the business, which required constant supervision, glad handing, and paper pushing. Elena was a national broadcast celebrity who was frequently out of the home and out of the country. Ksenia was the best mother a child could have, but she was not the mother of Elena's children. That added to the stress.

Ultimately, she renounced her career in order to be a mother.

I did the math in my head. Elena was older than I was. She was pushing forty pretty damned hard. However, I knew why Fedor wanted to meet this woman. She was smart, articulate, a champion athlete, and skilled in three languages.

"I'm serving my penance," she announced. "I've had my whole life handed to me."

"I disagree," I objected. "You worked your butt off."

"For what?" she challenged.

I let that lay on the table for a few moments. I was about to say something when she charged ahead.

"I wake my children in the morning," she said. "I put them in bed at night. I get to take them for walks, read to them, play with them. That's worth more to me than anything."

"You came to America to work at Happy Burger?"

"I don't need the money," she replied. "Fedor supports us, but I want to set an example. I can't do this at home. I'm a celebrity. Only two people in a thousand in America know who I am, and those two would dismiss the notion that Elena Sidorov would be caught dead at Happy Burger."

"Doesn't your husband miss the kids?"

"Of course, he does. Still, if we lived in Novgorod, he'd only see them for a few minutes during weekends. He's just – it can't happen. I live for his PoCos, but ours ceased to be a marriage when he took over from his father."

I was ill.

Here I was, Brice Duvall, super con. I'd faced down Dieter Rolf. I was poking the INSPAD giant. I was breaking a score of regulations and, perhaps, a few laws. I was pleased to do whatever I had to do just to obtain a small sliver of satisfaction from the corrupt organization employing me – until recently, that is.

Suddenly, I was frightened.

If I bluffed my way onto the moon, it would be months before I'd have a chance to see Elena again. If the INSPAD Gestapo came after me, I mightn't see her for months or years or . . .

I called Elena. I had no excuse.

"I wanted to hear you smile," I confessed.

"In Novgorod, we have a word for people like you."

Did I care? I was infatuated with the dual personalities. At Happy Burger, Elena was stoic, and her soft monotone was a brilliant backdrop for her sarcasm. Away from work, she sparkled. She was effervescent, chatty and enthralling. She loved her mother despite obvious frustration over the woman's machinations and lack of judgement. She loved her children and indulged their mischief. Alas, she still loved her ex-husband. Their divorce was amicable; it recognized that their lives were banished to separate orbits.

Elena didn't have to work. Her ex-husband provided her with a more than generous "allowance," but the woman was too proud to become an idle socialite. Her athletic career was behind her. To rest on her laurels or, worse, to selfishly flaunt them ran counter to – dare I say? – her philosophy of life.

Elena Ilyaovna Sidorov Yelagin was no "cover girl." When she turned on the charm, however; when she smiled, her eyes danced. Those eyes . . . Once, I read of an artist who insisted that there were women who could "paint you" with her eyes. Only after experiencing Elena in her home did I understand: she painted her mother, her children, and *me* with her merry, dancing, all-seeing eyes. Her smile – well, it radiated a warmth that I felt right down to the soles of my feet – *and* that overbite!

One did not *know* Elena. One *experienced* Elena!

What I knew of this woman was biographical and *superficial*. Her personality, however, possessed depth. How I wanted to plumb those depths, but . . . If I were a poet, I might – just maybe – express my feelings. What, however, would be the point?

I was not in love with Elena; I was in *infatuation* with her. I was like some pre-pubescent kid who was head over tea kettle with a model or movie star or singer; a person who spoke in sighs and feasted on adoration.

Well, I'm not a poet, so futile, confused, inadequate prose must serve – and it served so very, very badly.

There was nothing wrong with Dieter Rolf's prose, however. It was as blunt as a nuclear accident.

Your affiliation with INSPAD is dissolved upon receipt of
this message. Any personal items will be packaged and
returned to you. If you attempt to enter any INSPAD facility
you will be escorted out, by force if needs be.
Your INSPAD credits are, henceforth, void. Orders for your
assignment to the training facility will follow. An expense card
will be issued at that time.
Caution, Adam Kane. Don't be Russian into anything. Do well
in training and follow INSPAD and mission rules.

My skin crawled. Rolf knew about Elena. Even for a dictatorial organization, that was crossing a line. Of course, I could do something to embarrass or piss him off. What could he do?

I figured the very worst punishment he could administer would be to send me to the moon and not allow my return. However, he could punish me by doing something to Elena.

Prior to this message, I wanted only a pound of corrupt flesh. Now, the war had escalated. Perhaps Rolf didn't intend to threaten Elena, but that's how I interpreted it. Well, if he wanted to make this thing personal, this scam entered a new phase.

DISTRACTION

We'd made our "date" the evening before. I made certain to leave my PoCo at home. If Rolf had some goon tracking me, that was the surest way. Of course, PoCos sold for private use are guaranteed to be free of tracing "pills," but these same manufacturers guaranteed your "personal" PoCo conversations were "eavesdropping proof." Well, I knew that one of these "guarantees" was false. Chances were excellent the other one was equally void.

Mel had his INSPAD PoCo. He was required to always have it with him. Ten will get you forty, INSPAD could listen to any conversation at any time – even if the PoCo was turned off.

I brought a copy of Rolf's message and a notebook. The first thirty odd minutes of our conversation that evening consisted of scribbling incomplete sentences in the notebook and sliding it back and forth across the table. Mel thought I was being an alarmist. There was nothing to be gained by threatening Elena, and certainly no gain in carrying it out. He noted that Rolf had not stated any conditions beyond doing well in training. He, further, assured me that I would do exactly that, or Mel, personally, will flunk me and my moon mission would be denied.

I still felt threatened. I didn't like INSPAD spying on Elena, her mother, and the kids.

Did you trigger Rolf by mentioning Agamemnon?

I nodded.

He mentions "Russians" – no names. It's his gotchya

How I wanted to believe that. Still, I was a bundle of nerves. I wanted to see Elena again. I wanted that very much. However, I did not want to make her a target. I did *not* want that.

I wanted to drop by Happy Burger to warn Elena. Mel thought that was a very, very, very bad idea. If Rolf was just teasing, my "warning" might cause her to worry needlessly and, perhaps, introduce paranoid behavior. If Rolf intended to harm Elena or her relatives, warning her would do no good. Rolf and his Gestapo had too many resources. They'd do whatever they had in mind, and no one could stop them – particularly if the "no one" was on the moon.

The bottom line was that Elena could not be in any more danger (if she was in any danger). I could see her as often as I pleased. It would alter nothing.

We could have, or would have, conversed for some while about my wanting to see Elena at all. True, she was sharp as a tack, but Mel was nonplussed. He considered her as plain as an INSPAD door frame. He did not have the opportunity to bask in her personality or respond to her smile (and that magic overbite).

I "just happened" by Happy Burger that afternoon. I "just happened" to slip her a note while she was tending to a customer. I retreated to a neutral corner and waited.

Elena was "stone face" once more. She took and rang up the orders. She was terse and employed her monotone. I saw her reading my note which she disposed of immediately. After taking another order, she looked at me for only a second. So immediately did she return to her work that she couldn't have seen my nod. To remain would make me look even more silly and suspicious.

I left.

When I returned, I leaned up against a skinny tree near a transit stop. It was a quarter after eight when Elena came from the side of the building. She must have exited from the back. She wore jeans and a sleeveless pullover. In her left hand was a small canvass bag. I assume it was her Happy Burger uniform which she'd launder preparatory to her next shift.

"Nice of you to see me home," she said without enthusiasm.

"I have ulterior motives," I replied.

"I suspected as much."

"Do you have your PoCo?"

"At work? You must be daft."

"I asked because, we may be under observation."

She didn't laugh, but she didn't cringe. To her credit, she didn't accuse me of being *daft*.

"My husband and I still love each other," she informed softly. "We ended our marriage because we couldn't be together for more than a few minutes a week. He isn't the jealous type, and he would never consider spying on me."

"It isn't your husband."

Full marks for composure. Elena did not demand an explanation.

"Oh?"

"I'm the one being watched. Because of me, some loathsome people know of you and might start watching you."

"Good luck to them. Unless they are captivated by the sight of me selling gut bombs and playing with my children, they are likely to die of boredom."

I cleared my throat. That put her on full alert.

"They might come after you, or the kids, if they want to warn me – or frighten me."

Full marks again. She didn't demand an explanation. She didn't go into seizures. She didn't scream, and she didn't demand.

"I know you're a good shot," I continued. "Do you have a gun?"

"No. I know where to get one."

I didn't elaborate.

"The thing is, you see," I began cautiously, "I want to see you again. I want to see you often. I might, eventually, ask to be your second husband."

She didn't break stride, but she turned her head and examined me critically.

"You don't know me," she dared. "That stuff my mother fed you was only window dressing. That sports ____ (she used a word here, perhaps Russian, I do not know – but it was obviously contemptable) and the broadcasting – *thing*; that isn't me. Fedor fell in love with that – other person. Not that it made much difference, but it made for a bad start."

"I saw the real you when we were playing with the cups," I responded. "You were winding up those kids and making it into something special –"

"Well, it was!" she interrupted.

"But you made it into a production," I insisted. "When those children are as old as you are now, I guarantee they'll remember that very special time."

She digested that for several meters.

"Do you really believe that?"

It was a dare; not much of one, however.

"Yes."

We were nearing the entrance to her building.

"If one or both of us is being tracked or followed, there's no need to be coy. I will call you. I want to see you again."

"You're a strange one, Brice Duvall. Could we go out to eat some evening or, maybe, see a play or pitch horseshoes? Those are things Fedor and I seldom had an opportunity to do."

I didn't bite on horseshoes. I'd convinced myself that Elena was extremely cosmopolitan.

Instead, Adam Kane stepped to the fore.

"I would be proud to, *but* –"

She stopped.

I stopped.

She looked up at me.

I looked down at her.

"*But* what?"

"May I kiss you goodnight?"

"I have to bribe you?"

"You don't *have to*."

She studied me momentarily.

It is difficult to determine who kissed whom. It was not one of those, over the top, kiss- me-as-if-it-were-the-last-time things. In fact, it was quite innocuous – puritanical, almost. It was enough.

It was more than enough.

"You're asking for trouble, you know," she smirked.

"Some troubles are worth having," I replied.

You will find that line in Henry James, on the exact page I did. It was a very Adam-Kane thing to do, and I was (am) proud of it.

She studied me carefully. I imagine she was trying to decide if I was insane or sincere. I leaned over and kissed her cheek – the left cheek. I kissed her right on top of those three, gnat's-egg-like, blemishes.

I was ready for the worst INSPAD and Mel Harden could throw at me.

BACK TO SCHOOL
THE
MEL HARDEN WAY

I hadn't nerve to ask Elena for her picture, so I "casually" mentioned the idea to "Mama."

She gave me my choice of an impressive collection. She was quick to tell me which were her favorites and which Elena wanted burnt.

I selected one from the "burn this" file. It was not nearly as glamorous as half the others, but it depicted Elena as I most wanted to remember her.

I suspected it was snapped during her sportscasting days. The person to whom she was speaking was out of shot. This person, apparently, made a comment that struck Elena as witty – or, perhaps, ironic. She turned her head to the right and smiled a genuine smile, not that pasty, hideous thing she conjured when posing. Her gnat's eggs were well masked by makeup, but not well enough to make them invisible to someone searching for them. Her overbite was well displayed squinting eyes as if she enjoyed whatever comment launched her reaction. Cute, light brown bangs cascaded over her brow and nearly touched her eyebrows.

Elena had dark hair. However, light brown tresses looked very good on her.

This and my selections of Johnson's Dictionary were the only personal items I brought. Each "candidate" was allowed six items, but I wasn't certain I owned six items. No PoCos were allowed which sent three of my fellow trainees into a fit of depression.

We were issued space (fire resistant) clothing: underwear, work suit, space socks, and space shoes. We were assigned our "sleep quarters," a small, closet-like chamber with two bunks mounted one above the other. Our class was small enough that we were allowed "private" quarters. We were each issued a light-weight space "blanket." These were for psychological purposes since the "space environment" was judiciously set at sixty-eight degrees.

The materials in our "mockup" were the same as we would find on the station and the lunar bases. The layout was as near a duplicate of Base One. Since there were more trainees in any given cycle than one would ever find on the moon, certain accommodations were put in place. There were more "sleep chambers," obviously, and the common area was considerably larger.

For the first six days of our cycle, we would work and study in the space quarters. However, lectures and equipment workshops were conducted in a hangar-like facility which can be accessed only through the "living quarters."

INSPAD, in its infinite wisdom, subjected trainees to cramped quarters for the duration of the training. That monolithic collection of grafters and conmen thought this would discourage people of the low order who had anemic bank accounts. What INSPAD hadn't counted on was that most academics would suffer any hardship to advance their academic standing or to expand the book of knowledge. To date, only one trainee opted out. Several others had been dismissed for "failure to qualify," an INSPAD euphemism for "troublemaker."

Our first full day was dedicated to studying and reviewing human systems and procedures. In short, we must follow the rules. When we broke for lunch, three of my fellow students ate in the common area and quizzed each other. I enjoyed a Spartan meal in my chamber studying my notes.

Before breaking for our evening rations, we each took a test on INSPAD organization and procedures. I got ninety-seven out of one hundred. One of the women passed with an eighty-two, but Mel flagged me. I had to pass a retest in the morning and get a higher score or I'd be escorted out on the street for "failure to qualify."

I shot Mel a malevolent glance which he ignored.

A joke is a joke, but certain things are not funny. I let him know as much when he filled the entrance to my sleep chamber. I was propped up on my bunk nibbling at my rations. Mel might have come in, but there wasn't enough room.

"I warned you, Brice," he reminded.

"I guess I didn't catch the part about flighty, scatter-brained females skate with an eighty-two, but I am held to a different standard."

"The difference is, Brice, I don't give a damn about her. She'll manage well enough. You're the best friend I have in this part of the world. I'm taking no chances with you."

He had me there.

"May I retest tonight before lights out?"

Mel would have shrugged, but there was precious little space for his massive shoulders to shrug.

"Suits me."

"Give me an hour."

He nodded, but he did not retire. I glared at him. Couldn't he see I was eating?

"Happy Burger has really got under your skin, hasn't she?"

For Mel, Elena was one more female in a city full of females. He thought her bright and witty – wit with a dangerous edge to it, but she was hardly aesthetic. That's because he had not experienced her beyond the workplace. Elena possessed a myriad of hues and emotions; her face could run the gamut from homely to charming to knock-down gorgeous – and complete the course in a matter of seconds.

Mama showed me a formal portrait of *My* Elena. She wore a dark suit; her hair was jet-black and in curls and bobs; her lips were coated with blood-red lipstick.

She was so ugly!

Who was it said, "she made you want to burn every bed in the world?" That photo of Elena would put the Mongol Hoard to flight.

Makeup is supposed to make you look *better*!

Elena didn't need lipstick – or only a very pale layer, if she was a slave to supercilious customs.

As these thoughts raced through my brain, I could not gainsay my friend and tormentor.

"Yes, she has," I admitted.

"You must put her out of your head, buddy."

That's all I needed: trite!

"You can say that because it's not your skin she's under."

He sighed.

"Ya know, partner," he mused. "Iffin I keep hangin' round you, people gonna think I a white man."

In a different venue and in different circumstances, I would have chuckled. Suddenly, I wasn't in the mood. Mel, thinking I was still irked about his arbitrary ruling *vis* my test score, moved off and let me languish.

Mel is a clever guy. The test questions were reworded and appeared in a different order than I found them on the first test. This was, I suppose, standard practice. It forced me to consider each question anew rather than scroll through them until I found the ones I'd muffed.

It made no difference. I got a hundred.

The following morning, we practiced the hokey-pokey – that is egress and transfer.

First, we practiced leaving the transport and entering the station. Everyone must go through the station to get to the moon. Barring an emergency or an abort, the moon voyagers would never see the interior, but we must be prepared. A select few, normally established staff, remain there. The aces, that is, those who have been to and through the station more than four times, are very adroit at these transfers. Further, the airlocks are so voluminous that two, or even three, aces can enter and exit at the same time. Regulations and procedures (remember the test) are very specific: only one customer in the airlock at any one time.

Once aboard the station, a mockup, we toured the facilities. Devoid of the scientific equipment, there was considerable room, save for the sleep cells (which come in only one size).

There are hundreds of stories of "sex in space." However, a couple had to be very determined or very devil-may-care. It's a job for just one person to sleep in a cell, never mind two people "docking." The alternative is to "make the sign of the tree-sloth" in front of all and sundry. To date, no one has been observed using either technique, but the stories continue to thrive. In fact, now that space travel has become something of a yawn in the minds of the general public, the only space entertainment consists of "pitching woo in close quarters."

Romance in a landfill would be nearer reality, but when has the entertainment industry been scrupulous about facts and reality?

After our abbreviated tour, we transferred to a transport. Mel, the only one not in a pressure suit, shouted and swore all through the procedure. Of course, even the highest scorer on the test (me) required remediation when it came to applying the theories we'd memorized.

Mel was so annoyed with us that he had us return to the station and transfer again. Since the only way to get back aboard the pretend station was to transfer, we each got two more practice sessions – with Mel supplying the background music.

Once aboard the mockup transport (at least the interior; the exterior was plywood and cardboard), we broke for lunch.

The rations were filled with protein and the drinks were filled with electrolytes. Both were insipid. Again, dedication to science allowed for our voluntary sacrifice. Even I, whose only purpose was to show my middle finger to INSPAD, was properly motivated to masticate our assigned rations.

After lunch and a round of critiques by Mel, we transferred to the landing craft. Then, we transferred to a crawler.

(If there is any moon snogging, the crawler is the place.)

The only part of the crawler mockup available was the service and cargo transfer area. We'd not train in a full-sized mockup until later in our regimen.

By this time, we were fairly adroit at transfers. One wouldn't think so from the way Mel carried on. He slapped my butt when I did not meet his exacting standards. I couldn't feel it inside the pressure suit, but the smack (silent on the moon) was audible in earth atmosphere.

One more transfer to our assigned moon base. When we emerged, we found ourselves back in our living quarters area. There, dripping with sweat and gasping for breath, we were allowed to remove and store our assigned pressure suits. We were all in damp flight suits.

"On the station or at a moon base," Mel announced, "The showers are tiny little things. You remove your flight suits and throw them into the chute to your right where they will be processed and returned to you. The average time is three hours. That's why you each have two flight suits. You lather up *before* you enter the chamber. You get a shade less than a gallon to rinse with. Not all the gold on earth will buy you a drop more. Your filthy rinse water will be processed and, likely, you'll be drinking it later."

We all knew that, but our imagination went into high gear over this prospect.

I've known men who like to pee in the shower. I've done it myself. In the station or on the moon base, this was a capital offense. Urine is collected and processed very carefully. There are things in human pee that are required in station and base equipment. The water, of course, is treated and becomes a part of the hydro-system, a complex reclamation that keeps things (such as the air cycle and hydraulics) functioning. Of course, part of our pee goes to our oxygenator. We get to breathe it.

The greatest quandary facing the scientists (since INSPAD doesn't give a fig) is what to do with human "johnny-dos." It just won't serve to toss poop all over a virgin environment. Digging a shaft and covering it over wasn't an acceptable option. If lunar scientists and their sponsoring organization have a "prime directive," it is Recycle *Everything*. A laudable goal, but once the human machine discharges waste, there is precious little useful employments for it. Fertilizer, of course, but horticulture and the lunar surface are mutually exclusive.

The scientists experimented with agriculture "bubbles." These are hastily constructed devices intended to produce greens for consumption. For a year and a half, agronomists toiled and sweated and shook their rattles, but Project Grow was written off as a failure.

Firstly, the INSPAD "nutrient packages" are exactly that. There is precious little waste to excrete. When scientists and Space Monkeys return to earth, their most frequent comment were focused upon the "blessing" of "going" once a day. On the moon, people have been known to go several days before acquiring enough "mass" to "eject."

Until biologists and the medicos solve the problem of poop, it is "processed" and compressed to a fare-thee-well and stored in biodegradable tubes. Since there are no bacteria to biodegrade, these tubes are stored out of sight until a solution is found. Solutions, so far, are either bizarre, cost prohibitive, or both:

1. Load the tubes into a container and drop them into the earth's atmosphere. They will burn up and – problem solved. The meteorologists had a field day with that idea: Warning, today's forecast, scattered patches of shit through the morning.

2. Load the tubes into a container and shoot it off until the sun's gravitational field draws them near enough for total incineration. Warning: Aside from the cost of such a program, Poop Pods might wander around the inner solar system for decades or centuries, thereby creating hazards to navigation during future space missions.

Fortunately, after the first thirty hours or so, humans become so acclimated to the station and moon base atmosphere that the olfactory sense is deadened. Those people who return to earth after a prolonged period in space don't recover their sense of smell, completely, for three or four months.

There are two "cleaning stations" in the "Space Academy." One is for the little boys; the other is for the little girls. There's a modesty curtain between them, but it is little more than an idea. Nature has provided the women in our cycle with natural defenses; no male of my acquaintance would be tempted to peek even if they were desperate. Similarly, the males (me included) are pretty much flirt proof.

Mel was with us for end-of-day *stuff*. There was room enough because of our modest numbers. He ate the same rations we did. This was a gesture much appreciated by those of us who found space food filling but repulsive. Had Mel my scruples, he'd smuggle in a few Happy Burgers. We'd worship him as a god and submit to any punishment he saw fit to mete out. Well, Mel is strictly a by-the-book kind of guy. He'd probably consumed more space rations than any person in history. Incredibly, he was still alive.

He provided an oral critique of our day's training. He insisted that personal hygiene was extremely important in close quarters. Showering daily was such a bother in space and most unsatisfactory. People, particularly exhausted people, were tempted to skip the fuss and bother of a shower. If any crewmates to date let them get away with it, I am not privy to the exceptions. Even the Space Monkeys, who would kick moon dust in Mel's face just to show their contempt, even these rule-breaking, bare-knuckle, booze hounds wouldn't put up with body odor. They have been known to strip and scrub the recalcitrant, regardless of age or gender.

"Nobody is an expert at egress and transfer," he assured us. "The key is to take your time and know exactly where your limbs are. Duvall, you get the award for Most Likely to Puncture a Pressure Suit. You better get your head on and take this seriously, or you gonna die. It is, exactly, that simple."

Was he digging at me again, or was this an honest evaluation? Until our training was completed, I'd not know.

The *oxygenator* (a name pirated by INSPAD) is *the* key equipment in establishing permanent lunar bases. It is a huge piece of equipment and a pain to transport, assemble and maintain. It "produces" oxygen. How it does so is the only closely guarded secret of INSPAD. Why? Who can guess? Maybe, INSPAD thinks that people might invent a better oxygenator in their basement and make millions of dollars by gaining a patent on the improved technology.

The oxygenator is a huge, bulbus container with an instrument interface. Anyone on the station or at a lunar base will see two digital displays; one displays pressure (92 psi is the "normal" reading) and the oxygen content. It isn't pure. It "manufactures" a gaseous mixture roughly (very roughly) akin to what we breathe on earth. Periodically, one must insert a fresh cannister, cylindrical in shape and highly pressurized, to "refresh" the process. The "air" is circulated and run through "scrubbers" to extract the carbon dioxide.

The carbon, as is everything in the lunar cycles, is processed and distributed to other systems for – whatever . . . Someone, not Mel, explained it all to me in precise detail, and I still haven't a clue. Suffice it to say that the lunar environment cycle is enclosed, and everything is reused.

The oxygenator "manufactures" miniscule amounts of oxygen while making highly productive use of what humans require. That will have to do.

Clumsy humans can do little with the oxygenator other than perform periodic maintenance. Under Mel's tyranny, we learned to perform checks and ensure the valves, pipping, vents, filters, and so on are serviceable and functioning. If the oxygenator fails (how? There are no moving parts), the crew is left with only the atmosphere trapped in the habitation unit. Ultimately, carbon dioxide will build up until the environment can no longer be sustained. At that point, it's into the pressure suits. That will allow a person to live for another twelve to eighteen hours. If the crawler doesn't reach you in that time – well, that's tough. Very tough! If the monkeys cannot fix the equipment, the options are so simple that not even an INSPAD administrator could mess this one up: evacuate or die.

Mel was determined to remain a tyrant.

There were other candidates in our cycle, but Mel dedicated most of his venom to me. He even applied a dope slap. It hurt. I resented it.

All candidates are quarantined during training. Mel didn't leave the facility during the cycle. If trainees couldn't leave for fear of contracting some contagious malady, then Mel felt living at home defeated the purpose of the quarantine. One will not find this in any INSPAD directive, but Mel paid no attention to them, relying, instead, on his own (excellent) judgement.

"I got a knot on my head where you clipped me," I complained.

"Sorry," he muttered. "I can't hit any of them. They might sue INSPAD which would make me a candidate for the cemetery."

"It put the fear of Mel into them," I agreed.

"When this is over, you are entitled to one poke in the snout," he promised.

He knew damn well I'd never collect. Still, I appreciated the offer.

We were drinking coffee. It was INSPAD coffee so it was, practically, tasteless. To supply real coffee would cut into Dieter's graft, so corners are cut – particularly when the people who are subjected to privation hadn't either the power or the position to raise objections.

"We've lost people up there …"

I was about to introduce an objection, but he made a warning gesture.

"Every hour of every day, I wonder if there was something I could have – *should* have taught them that would have made a difference. I refuse to lose you, Brice. If a slap to the head will help you remember something you must know or do, you'll get a slap in the head. I'm not being mean; I'm being selfish."

I kept my mouth shut. I wasn't going to thank him for beating me senseless.

"I hope you'll exercise restraint when Aissata gets here."

"'Ain't struck a woman yet," he replied. "She ain't getting' no favors, Brice. I know you picked her, but if she don't cut it, she ain't goin'. The big shots can override me, of course."

I pondered that for a few moments.

"I don't think they will," I concluded. "It's a publicity stunt. If it blows up on them, the publicity will be all bad. If there's one thing a gangster hates, it's a tarnished reputation. For what it's worth, I think she will do fine."

"For you, Brice, I'll keep an extra special eye on her."

There was no need to thank him. I trusted Mel in all things. I was certain that I would be well qualified to go to the moon. Siss would be equally well prepared. Mel would make double certain of that.

Beginning with our second week, the morning hours were devoted to physical fitness. We ran three miles every morning (no mean task in a closed environment). There was no time limit. The object was to increase lung capacity and efficiency in breathing. There was strength training as well. We would lose muscle power in a low gravity environment. Unless we were eager to collapse upon our return to earth and struggle with ordinary tasks, we required the exercise equipment installed in all extra-terrestrial venues. Because INSPAD devoted so much of its funding for the care and feeding of Dieter Rolf and his fellow thugs, the PT equipment on the station and on the moon were built on the cheap. They required frequent repair which, of course, required blood, sweat, and exertion. It was a win-win for the grafters, but field personnel frequently applied generous amounts of *to-hell-with-it* with any equipment not essential to their research. Even INSPAD realized this; ergo, there were stiff regulations about keeping PT equipment in full working order. The penalties for failure to comply were equally rigorous.

Part of every afternoon training session was devoted to equipment maintenance – specifically, the physical conditioning equipment. We learned to hate those devices as much as the field personnel did. Nevertheless, it wouldn't do for a "space hero" to die from a preventable malady soon after returning to earth. It was bad publicity. Bad publicity might impact Dieter's bottom line – and those of his hangers-on as well.

The "training" quickly evolved (or *de*volved) into part one and part two.

At six every morning, we ran three miles. This, according to the propaganda, was to get maximum efficiency from our breathing. Air (with much higher oxygen content than on earth) was the most valuable commodity in space and shouldn't be wasted.

After the run, we "showered" dressed and reported to the lecture room.

Most lectures were dedicated to INSPAD policies and procedures. There were regulations about farting, nose picking, fingernail cleaning, shaving, drinking, eating – if a human is capable of performing it, strict INSPAD regulations covered it.

The afternoon was much more interesting. We learned how to repair equipment and perform basic tasks in a less than one G environment. The scientists were tasked with the equipment they would find on the station or the moon bases. These devices were far from the ultra-sophisticated laboratory equipment with which they were familiar. Much of the data collected must be radioed to proper facilities. Samples and other data not conducive to transmissions would accompany the scientist himself or herself.

Low-G training was fun, but preparations were tedious. I, and the other moon-bound personnel, worked in harness. The machines were adjusted to our exact weight so the harnesses would duplicate our "moon mass." Caution is the key feature in a low-gravity environment. The quarters and facilities have very limited space. If we are seated and attempt to stand up as we've learned to do since birth, we run the risk of fracturing our skull on the ceiling of our moon base.

You'll not find this written down in any of the manuals, but one learns not to be in a hurry. Take your time and always remember that once your body mass is in motion, you must either brake efficiently or bounce off things like the steel sphere in a pin-ball machine.

MEETING UP

Part one of our cycle lasted three weeks and two days. We were then allowed to rejoin the world of the living for six days. At the end of our vacation, we had to submit to physical exams anew and go through "disease control." Before we were allowed back into quarantine, we must be free of viruses. Prior to this indignity, however, we were free to enjoy proper showers, proper food, proper bathroom visits, and (most glorious of all) the enjoyment of a proper living space.

Mel would put us through the ringer for three more weeks. The "final exams," both written and performance would take up the remaining week. The six-day vacation was inserted mid-cycle to encourage trainees to brush up on their learning and to devote themselves to the study of those procedures and requirements in which they were deficient.

"In truth," Mel confessed. "I need a break."

The trainees might manage for the length of the course, but Mel was cooped up in a simulated environment for half to three-quarters of the year. Half or more of the people he trained would go into space or to the moon. Mel was earthbound. He needed a break far more than any of the peons.

At the end of the training, trainees (unless they "washed out) we promoted to flight status. Once qualified, the graduate and members of his or her sponsoring institution would meet with INSPAD personnel. A research plan must be submitted for approval. Once approved, the principals would determine what equipment was required. Obviously, INSPAD could not afford to transfer tons of equipment. Therefore, existing equipment would be modified, if possible.

Few of the scientists worked with materials to exacting specifications. All stood for unanimity in one basic tenant: a half-assed research project is far superior to no project. The procedure to produce a half-assed project was extended. If a mission was approved in a calendar year, it constitutes a major triumph. By then, of course, the scientist tasked with carrying out the mission objectives must undergo two weeks of "refresher" courses before being transported to the research station.

Mel didn't do refreshed training, but he monitored it as much as time allowed.

I got word that Aissata was in town. I'd told Mel about her and provided a thumbnail biography. He was intrigued. I warned her that she wasn't much to look at.

"Neither is your Russian girlfriend," he taunted.

I said nothing.

Mel knew Elena only from our Happy Burger foray. I got to see her out of uniform and devoid of her *miss-on-you, -pister, -you're-not-so-muckin-futch* demeanor. In truth, I was afraid. If he knew Elena as did I, the bastard might try to steal her away. For the sake of our friendship, I was determined to keep him out of temptation's way.

It isn't encouraged for Mel to fraternize with trainees. However, he voided this unwritten rule with me. Using his INSPAD contacts, he obtained the address of Aissata's digs. Anxious to see her again myself, we "just happened" to "drop by" one morning.

"She ain' in," the crusty landlady announced.

Hers was a hostel for "ladies." The crusty old woman made clear her feelings about two un-women daring to sneak past her to bother (or molest) one of her "ladies."

"Do you know where she am't?" Mel inquired.

He was always the smart ass. Apparently, Elena's resourceful put-down did not break him of the habit.

"Don' know. She leave 'bout eight er nine ev' morn' and comes in roun' eight er later ev' even'."

We knew, instinctively, that returning in the evening might result in a police call-out. Mel was disappointed.

"I have an idea," I prompted.

"You haven't had an idea in all the time I've known you," he scoffed.

"You have someplace to be?"

"No."

I assumed as much.

"Follow me," I suggested.

Forty minutes later, we entered the public library.

There was considerable debate over public funding of a building built to house antiques. Nobody, or so we are told, reads books anymore. Hellfire, you can read anything you want on your PoCo – if your eyesight is a hundred percent and you're *really* determined. Nevertheless, there are people like me (millions of us) who still feel that turning a page is one of life's few genuine pleasures.

"You start at the top and work down to the third floor. I'll meet you there."

"I don't know what I'm looking for," Mel complained.

"A black woman, fairly thin and tall," I reminded. "If you find one, you know where I'll be."

He shrugged.

Mel eschewed the elevator. He worked hard to keep in shape while existing inside a sardine tin for weeks at a time. He mounted the stairs and climbed.

We did, indeed, meet on the third floor.

"That her?" he whispered.

There was a youngish woman seated at a table. She was studying one book which lay open on the tabletop. Near her right elbow were two stacked books. Next to her left elbow was a veritable tower constructed of books, magazines and pamphlets.

"Indeed, it is."

Mel was impressed. I, however, owe it all to basic reasoning. If Siss was an off-and-on university student, she would consider the public library a cornucopia – or an oasis.

"Aissata."

She was startled. Who, in an alien world, would know her? Her grin testified to her relief.

She stood at once.

"I'm pleased to see you again," she announced.

We shook hands.

"Allow me to present my friend, Mel Harden. Mel, this is Aissata, of whom I've spoken often."

Siss had hand out in a flash. Mel took it. Were he able, he'd have blushed.

"I'm happy to meet you," he said with a trace of awe.

"Enjoy your time together," I cautioned. "Mel will be your primary training instructor. He will not be nice to you, but he will prepare you well."

"You don't look like an ogre," she said, calmly.

"Brice knows what he's talking about," he replied, honestly. "It's my job to see that those who go to the moon return alive. A few students don't take it seriously. That makes me angry."

"I assure you, sir, I take this very seriously. I'm honored to be considered. I will work hard to keep you from becoming angry."

"In any case, don't take it personally," I injected.

Mel nudged me gently, reminding me to keep my oar out.

Mel and I have exchanged many personal details about ourselves. We were good enough friends that we could swap personal information without the assistance of alcohol – though there were a few times when we suffered a hangover the following morning. Regardless, I knew that Siss was not Mel's "type," and vice versa.

Mel Harden started his professional life as a chemistry teacher. It didn't take him long to figure out that the kids ran the school, and the government sided with the kids. He threw it all up. He was determined to find work in a job where either his clientele or his colleagues wanted to learn and wanted to do things right. He was at sixes-and-sevens when he discovered INSPAD. What he wouldn't give to study reactions in low or zero gravity! He put in his name and went through the training. Only after he'd completed his cycle was he told he was too big to leave earth.

Mel was not disappointed; he was angry. Typical INSPAD: they trained him and made him ready then flatly rejected him. Our bond was forged in our mutual distaste for a certain international organization.

Several times during Mel's training cycle, he questioned much of the instruction. He didn't think it was complete; he didn't think it was rigorous enough. There were some tasks and requirements he felt were stupid if not dangerous. He began raising hell until someone, doubtless a subscriber of the kids-run-the-school syndrome, had the proverbial *it*.

Mel was assigned as a trainer. It took only eighteen months until those over him were either promoted or dismissed. Mel Harden was now *the* person who decided which people were qualified and which weren't. It was raw meat to a ravenous dog. The people who wanted to do research in space were motivated and keen to learn. The prima donnas and screw ups were not selected by academic and scientific institutions to do research in space.

Because I know Mel as well as I do, I know there was no "spark" between he and Siss. He admired her humble birth and was enthralled by her insatiable appetite for knowledge. Siss was the kind of student he'd always wanted in his basic chemistry classes. She wasn't paging through back issues of fashion magazines or reading racy prose, she was seeking to add to what she'd learned at university.

I tarried for a few minutes until they began discussing the properties of water in a low gravity environment. Ten minutes into their discussion, I, casually, stole away.

Forty minutes later, I was at Happy Burger. Elena was not behind the counter. Note to self: write down Elena's workdays rather than rely on a poor memory. I used my PoCo.

"Brice," a familiar voice greeted me. "I was wondering if you'd left the country."

"No luck. Are you home?"

"No, Mama and I are spoiling the kids at a playground park."

"I'd like to see you. Could I take you to sit-down meal?"

"Someplace where they serve Vegemite?"

I made a face. Happy I was that she couldn't see me. I knew the stuff was popular with Space Monkeys. There was, in fact, a big blow-up. Even INSPAD drones will realize something is amiss when the crawler toilets require frequent repair.

"If you like."

I was feeling brave.

"Yuk! Find someplace else."

My spirits rebounded.

"Happy Burger?"

"Getting close, but I think you can do better."

The sparing resumed later at a bistro that, apparently, existed on pretention alone. The food was good, but hardly epicurean. The wine – well, when the waitress mispronounced *Riesling*, there is little more need be said.

"My father wanted me to play football," she announced, after she finished the weather report and the antics of her children that day.

"That's the one sport you never went near," I concluded.

"Do you read people's minds?" she asked, sharply.

"Your best friend is *Mama*," I observed. "Her husband is *my* father's clone. You aren't very subtle."

She blushed momentarily and played with the napkin in her lap. When she replied, she made certain to look over my shoulder.

"I didn't like my father until after he was – gone. He was always rather aloof and – frightening. I thought he hated me, or . . . well . . . He said and wrote many loving things about me, but he could never talk to me. He never said *I love you*. Mama knew him well enough that his words and his tone were inconsequential. Only when I read through his letters and papers did I realize how much he cared for me. So, I carry that guilt around. I never knew him or understood him, so I didn't love him until too late."

She thoughtfully sampled her salad.

"You did love Fedor," I pushed. "You told me that you still do."

She took another sample as an excuse to formulate her response.

"The problem is, Fedor married his father's work before he even knew of my existence. He thought he could handle both his work and his marriage. Brice, he was out of the country six months out of every twelve – and not to those places where his family could go, not safely at any rate . . ."

"You say he came onto you," I prompted.

She glared at me.

"I don't like your tone."

Here was a conundrum. Her voice and her flinty eyes made it clear that she objected to my crude diction. The rest of her body, however, remained as natural and relaxed as ever.

"Sorry," I proposed at once. "Maybe, if I could speak Russian, I could made it sound less objectionable."

She gave me a momentary pout and resumed chewing her greens.

"He saw pictures of me in the papers and magazines. He fancied me, but we didn't congregate with the same people. He used his father's influence to bring us together at some Moscow fete. He confessed later that it was all staged, but we hit it off from the start. He's charming and erudite and attentive in a way I found very attractive. He would call me. I would call him. We had amazing conversations about – well, about everything.

"We spent a weekend together. Then, we spent two or three weekends together. We got married. Our honeymoon – is that what you Americans say? We spent three days in Perm. What's in Perm? The Eiffel Tower, Big Ben, the Grand Canyon? What difference? We never left the hotel. Then, he went back to work, and I went back to training."

I'd not put my foot in it again. I spooned up my soup, being extra careful not to give my yellow shirt a case of measles. It was a good soup. I did not slurp. This occupied my mind.

"Right after I retired, we made a baby. Mama had to tend to it because Fedor was occupied with business, and I was flitting about Europe covering sports events. I quit that when Fedor agreed to make another baby. Then, Mama and I teamed up to see that they were properly nurtured."

"He wasn't keen," I noted.

I wanted her to know that I had paid attention during our previous conversations.

"No," she confirmed. "He didn't like the idea of raising our children by proxy. So, I quit because Fedor couldn't. In our seventeen years as man and wife, we were together for only a fraction of that. He apologized for being so selfish and insisted I divorce him. On what grounds? The Church is very – what you say? – *pursnippity* about the reasons for divorce."

"Close enough," I acknowledged.

There were times to offer tips concerning the English language. Our dinner date that evening was, decidedly, not the time.

"So, Fedor has his business for a wife, and I have his children – and Mama. We're all jolly good friends, but we don't see each other any more than we did when we were married."

It sounded too phony to be phony. Elena had an aura about her. She was a straight shooter, in my estimation. As her initial confrontation with Mel indicated, she was ready and able to play games, but she didn't strike me as the kind of person to conjure convenient inventions.

"And America?"

"I'm too well known in Europe," she responded immediately. "Very few Americans know my name and none, or nearly none, would recognize me."

Speaking for myself, I'd neither know of her nor recognize her had not "Mama" and her pride made me cognizant.

"But . . .," I began, cautiously. "Happy Burger?"

She sighed audibly.

"I told you, Brice – by the way, may I call you Brice?"

"If I may call you Elena," I replied automatically.

She smiled. She didn't show any teeth (none of that to-die-for overbite), but the gesture made manifest her pleasure.

"I told you, Brice," she repeated. "This is my penance. Fedor sends us more than we need. I'm an independent woman, or very near. During my sports career, I was financed by people who believed in me. It paid for my training, equipment and ammo. When I became a *star* sports reporter, I had dozens of people whose job it was to make me look and sound good."

The emphasis she placed on that word *star* might be offensive to social-justice slaves. She packed considerable meaning into that single word.

"For the first time in my life, I'm on my own. I take pride in being proud of myself. I've been promoted twice, you know. I'm a shift supervisor. I have between two and five people who must report to me. I didn't get those promotions because I'm famous – or was famous – or because my big, high, mucky-muck husband was leading interference for me. That was me! Elena worked her way up. I'm being considered for another promotion. It feeds my ego and sets a good example for my children."

"Why Happy Burger?"

She shrugged.

"Why not? I doubt I'd earn two promotions in twenty months if I worked for Boeing."

"I'm not so certain," I responded. "Your English, and your mode of expression, are head-and-shoulders above most Americans I know."

She glared at me once more. This time, she directed no hint of hostility my way.

"*Head-and-shoulders*," she repeated. "That's a new one. Did you just make that up?"

"No, and I'm surprised you haven't heard it."

She shrugged before shaking her head delicately.

"Perhaps, I have. Mind if I use it?"

"I'm certain it's in the public domain."

When she finished her salad, she folded her cloth napkin just so and placed it near her wine glass.

"That's Elena Sidorov," she announced. "She's been properly examined. Now, Mr. Brice Duvall, you owe me. Let's hear your history."

I deserved that. Unlike Elena, I am not proud of my accomplishments. I certainly never earned anything. Since falling in with the INSPAD mafia, I was demoted several times.

"I come from a small town in Kansas, I was never married – or divorced, so I have no former spouse to support me. I support myself the INSPAD way, I lie and cheat. Given the proper circumstances, I'd steal – from INSPAD at any rate."

Her expression dared me to continue. I did not continue.

"There is much more," she insisted.

"Elena, I like you very much – very, very much. I would give nearly anything to impress you, but I've got nothing; I've done nothing."

She shook her head once more. It was slow and limited, but it spread dubiety across the table. It was more subtle than a slap in the face, but just as emphatic.

"Not, true," she murmured. "You knew about Pythagorean cups. You went to Samos to fetch them. You enchanted my children, and their mother, and their grandmother."

"Pythagoras I know about," I insisted. "That does not make me a learned man."

She sighed again.

"This is really sad," she half-whispered. "You know so little about yourself. You are learned and, more important, you are kind and caring."

I felt myself blushing.

"More important*ly*," I corrected.

She laughed. It was reserved and befitting our environment, but her teeth showed and that overbite caused a burst of electricity to travel down my spine.

"Gotchya!" she said, pointing a finger at me and allowing her double-chin-to-be to enhance her visage even more.

"I laid a trap and, snap, you fell right into it. I knew you'd correct me. You want me to speak better English. You'd have done the same for anyone – I'd bet on it. You do not give yourself credit. Well, Mr. Brice Duvall, I do."

How could I sink any lower?

"Would you say that last part in front of a Justice of the Peace?"

She wrinkled her nose.

She did not agree to my terms. More importantly, she did not refuse.

FOCUS

Elena, meaning "shining light" in some ancient tongue, not only got under my skin, she crawled up my spine and burrowed at the base of my neck. Hers was the most magical visage I'd ever beheld. Depending upon light, shadow, and a variety of other variables, Elena could appear homely, sprite-like, morose, exuberant, brilliant, attractive, and radiant. Frequently, she ran the gamut through them all in a few short seconds. I doubt anyone would ever describe her as beautiful, but no one would ever avoid the temptation of a second, more interested survey.

I made an absolute fool of myself because of her. I had, in the clumsiest means possible, proposed marriage twice. She shrugged them off effortlessly. I hardly knew the woman, despite her autobiographical narrations. More to the point, she hardly knew me. She foolishly analyzed me on exceptionally superficial evidence. I was flattered by her conclusions but doubted their veracity. However, she had yet to dismiss me.

Hope is the refuge of the weak and powerless.

Mel escorted me back to the facility two hours ahead of the deadline. Before we entered the training unit, he gripped me firmly by the arm and pulled me aside. His vice-like fist hurt me no little.

"You're making a damned fool of yourself over that Russian burger flipper," he announced. "You've got to focus, buddy. If you screw this up and don't qualify, what happens to Siss? You are – *were* the program. INSPAD wanted *two* common people. What will they do if they're left with one? They might cancel the whole show."

"I've done well enough so far," I reminded, hoping he would release my me and restore circulation to my lower arm.

"Well, I'm going to camp in your back pocket every minute of training. If you screw this up for her, I won't leave you with a single tooth in your mouth. Do you understand?"

"Yes, drill sergeant."

He gripped tighter (if that were possible) and shook me.

"I don't want your shit," he bellowed. "I want an answer. Do you understand?"

"I understand."

He released the vice. My arm tingled at the reintroduction of blood and oxygen. I shook it to make certain it was still attached.

"Permission to speak, Mel."

I wanted this off the record, but I didn't want my best friend to take offense. He glared at me with flinty, malevolent eyes. When he was satisfied that this was friend-to-friend rather than victim-to-assailant, he relaxed.

"What is it?"

His voice was calm.

"How much has Siss got under your skin?"

I expected him to flare. He didn't. We were friends once more. We could talk freely.

"It ain't exactly the same," he said, calmly. "I'm not milk bottle over tea kettle like you, but I want her to have this, and every other opportunity possible. She has insatiable curiosity. If I say something she doesn't understand, she wants me to explain it. If I bought her a Happy Burger, she'd take it apart, bit by bit, in an attempt to understand how it works."

"That's a bit of a reach, isn't it?"

He shook his head emphatically.

"Maybe, but I won't tempt fate. I attempted to show her some of the sights. I gave up after a couple hours. She wants to know how apartment buildings can avoid collapsing. She wants to know how water is fed into the fountains and ponds. She wants to know how the streets are paved and what with. Even if I knew the technical explanations, I'd get worn out – and fast. When I admit that I don't know or understand the engineering, high-level chemistry, and the math required, she looks disappointed. Because she wants to know everything, she's disappointed that I don't. I swear, Brice, that woman should have a degree in hand right now: a degree in Astrophysics at least."

"I told you she was keen," I reminded.

"*Keen* ain't the word. You told me that her mother was a slave. She told me that her mother was a slave – and so was she, early on, but – damn! It's one thing to know so much, but she insists on *understanding* everything. You can't have a normal conversation with her. She will stop you and ask this, that, and another thing. It's maddening. At the same time, it's inspiring."

I thought for a moment.

"Let me share my experience," I advanced. "Ask her about her home – her daily life, the women she lives with, her university experience. It will give you a break. Moreover, it will fascinate you. You might start asking *her* questions. She's got a lot to say, Mel."

He looked as if my suggestion had merit.

"Thanks for the tip," he said at last.

"*Da Nada,*" I responded.

"It won't save you, understand? Once we go through this door, I'm going to kick your ass every chance I get."

"I understand how you feel, Mel. I will work hard to keep the need for ass kicking to a minimum."

He nodded.

"Focus, Brice," he reminded. "Just keep your focus and we will all be happy."

GRADUATION

In order of frequency, the second half of our training consisted of 1) physical training, 2) transfers between where we were to where we needed to go, and 3) the other stuff. By the close of the third day, I thought I'd scream if we executed one more air-lock exercise. I didn't scream, but it was a near thing.

Mel was right. He told us a dozen times a day that transfers were a pain in the ass. However, should anyone get careless, one person could kill themselves and all those on both sides of the airlock. No matter how efficient we became, no matter how many times we practiced, we must be perfect.

The physical training was salt and pepper. None of us had appreciably "decayed" in our brief time off. Still, an efficient circulatory system was vital. After graduation, each person was encouraged to keep in tip-top shape. If, or when, a graduate was called up, he or she would undergo serious, remedial physical conditioning. Those who showed up in poor condition would be scrubbed from the program; guaranteed! Those who reported in "fair" condition often wished they had been scrubbed.

Scientists are dedicated. They know if they didn't serve a cycle when called, they would let down the university or research facility that nominated them. For a dedicated researcher to let down dozens of colleagues and the project they sweated blood to produce and submit would negate their reason to exist. Three such people, who realized their scientific career was over, committed suicide.

It should be no surprise that insurance companies would not insure any of the INSPAD extraterrestrial facilities or the people who manned them. Husbands, wives, children, relatives were left at the mercy of others should a space scientist not return.

INSPAD refused to transport bodies. If a person died on the moon, he or she was sent out in a crawler. The Space Monkeys would leave them by the wayside and, theoretically, pile rocks and moondust atop them. They might or might not leave or improvise some kind of marker.

If anyone ever dies in the space station – well, as with moon deaths, there was no established procedure. The only certainty is that the body will not remain on the station.

These morbid topics were briefly addressed during a morning briefing.

Mel, as promised, was on my case every minute of every day. My minor transgressions (that an academic might commit without serious admonishment) brought down both brimstone and wrath. He dissected my every move, particularly during airlock transfers. The others might drop or mishandle a tool without a major eruption. When my screwdriver slipped and made a scratch on a control panel, however, Mel applied extreme unction. In short, minor mishaps by the eggheads earned corrective punishment. For me, anything not up to Mel's exacting standards met with memorable punishment.

I gritted my teeth. I knew Mel considered me to be the nearest he'd come to space travel. He wanted me to be as perfect as he would expect himself to be in my place. Above the worst of his temper, however, I knew he was my friend, and he did not want me to screw up. If I died, he would console himself with the certainty that he did all he could to prevent it. Unfortunately, and despite all his bluster, Mel would blame himself – forever.

The graduation "ceremony" was brief and sparsely attended. It was held in the training auditorium situated inside the ring of space station, moon base, and crawler mockups. For once, we did not have to suit up and transition via airlock. The auditorium could be accessed by a subterranean feature which (owing to fire regulations) had a twin on the opposite side. This discovery finally put an end to hours of speculation. We trainees were subjected to lectures by experts who did not use either pressure suits or airlocks to reach the podium.

It was simple as is befitting its status. Our training merely put our names on a lengthening role of those qualified for space travel. This was a brief and pedestrian "chapter one." The scientists would be subjected to months of battle with INSPAD over their proposed research projects. Special equipment would doom any proposal. INSPAD insisted that existing equipment must be used or modified. Frequently, the cost of such "improvements" were twice or thrice the price of devices designed specifically to fill the mission objectives. Nevertheless, INSPAD refused to be a cargo handler. Make do with what we have or pound sand.

Three of our "graduating class," two men and one woman, were Space Monkeys. They required an additional four months of extensive training. Roughly half of that time required them to work in pressure suits. If they passed a series of rigorous hands-on tests, they would be welcomed to the Monkey Pool.

It was the most thankless cycle in all of space travel. They were paid enough to buy eight or ten scientists, but they were six months on and nine months off. When not working, they didn't get paid. When on duty, they couldn't spend any of their emoluments. They had to live in the crawlers. It was as cramped and filthy as the inside of a World War I submarine. Further, they had to handle all repairs, conduct required maintenance, and respond to every "emergency." Most emergencies resided in the heads of panic-prone scientists, but they had to be addressed. However, when a genuine emergency existed, a Space Monkey was the difference between life and death.

There was no lack of Space Monkey candidates, but only the best and most experienced were considered. Of these, only a third could undergo the rigors of basic training. Of those remaining, only one in five would make the grade in advanced and specialized training. For every hundred candidates, only five to eight would be put into the rotation. The desire to shorten the Space Monkey cycle to three months on and nine months off would remain a dream until there were a hell of a lot more monkeys than existed.

The ceremony was sparsely attended. The graduates and their families attended. It was enough to fill most of the assembly area. Some INSPAD poo-bah (one of the many I never knew and never knew of) gave a vapid twenty-minute speech after which Mel and the Director of Training (an official of whom I knew nothing and who, likely, didn't direct anything) called up each graduate to present the certification card. We few, many of whom might never leave earth's atmosphere, were now, "officially" on flight status.

We shook hands with Mel and the officials. We shook hands with each other. We helped ourselves to refreshments (finger sandwiches, coffee, tea, juice and an assortment of cookies). After ninety minutes, we were ushered out of the facility so it could be locked up.

The facility would undergo repairs, renovations, and major scrubbing before the next training cycle.

Because I was one of two "commoners" selected for an INSPAD publicity rip off, I expected to be confronted with a bevy of "journalists." Dieter and those far down the food chain realized that I was a loose cannon. They would "brief" me to a fare-thee-well prior to meeting with the cretons of the press. Further, Siss was bound to be the publicity darling. To roll me out prematurely would seriously impact the desired result. There would be no press conference until Siss and I appeared together.

Before I left the training facility, I was called in for a conference.

The Godfather, or his stand-in, sat behind a huge, imitation mahogany desk. He was flanked by two burly goons with another "guarding" the door. He introduced himself. His was a name alien to me and instantly forgotten.

The bespeckled INSPAD official invited me to sit down in one of two plush chairs facing his desk.

I sat down.

It took him roughly five minutes to praise INSPAD and scientific research to the sky. I didn't bother to listen. He was, I'm certain, on the take. Whatever his official position, he filled it because he had a lot of suck power with someone (or several) up the chain. I doubt he could boil water. I very much doubt he could even explain the process.

"We decide when we can exploit the maximum publicity from the project," he said, at last.

"Understood."

I shouldn't have spoken at all. It was understood that I was a slave and would remain mute unless *ol' masa* gave me permission to speak. I suppose, that's exactly the reason that I piped up.

I expected him to shoot me a warning glance or exhibit a bit of temper. He did neither. I was a nobody – a nothing. He simply ignored me and continued to adore his own voice.

He took, roughly, an additional five minutes to tell me to keep my mouth buttoned. Until the official press conference, I wasn't to allude to the project or disclose my participation in it.

"Do you understand?"

Permission to speak. Well, I didn't care to. Perhaps, I was expected to fall to my knees and kiss his ring.

I stood.

I nodded my head.

I turned to leave.

The goon at the door opened it and closed it behind him. He escorted me out of the building.

He said nothing.

I said nothing.

TRAPPED

Because of the Pythagorean cups, little Eduard, aged seven, thought the sun, moon, and stars rose and set over me. It was a relief for Elena and Mama. Eduard has eclectic interests, and it is difficult for him to get much attention. Arina, however, remains focused. At the age of four, she became enamored with figure skating. Unlike her brother, she nurtured her desire for an entire year.

Elena's forte is speed skating. Arina's "training," therefore, is very restricted. She was promised lessons from a professional if she remained serious.

Mama seldom left the apartment save for family walks through a nearby park. I eased the burden of babysitting the elder child while the two "girls" were busy on the ice. Eduard and I would wander off for fun and adventure. After ninety minutes of swinging, teeter-tottering, monkey bars, gathering flowers or apple windfalls, we would return to fetch Mommie and Sis.

Eduard is exceptionally gregarious for his tender years. He appreciated the attention of an older male. There could be no doubt that he loved his mother and grandmother, but his feelings for his precocious sister were conflicting and transitory. He envied her for having established an interest in one thing: figure skating. He explored every rainbow but had yet to fall in love with any one activity.

Never once did I forget Dieter Rolf's threat. Maybe, he wanted to yank my chain. A gang boss, however, is a dangerous thing. An overheard lament resulted in murder in the cathedral; a desperate desire to please a czar led to decades of tumult. Who knew what Dieter said when his underlings were nearby? Who knew what independent action they might initiate if they thought it would curry favor with "the boss?"

I was willing to take my chances. However, I feared for Elena and her family.

I kept my head on a swivel.

After my earlier enigmatic warning, Elena was true to her word: she knew how to get a gun. It was the .38 police special, and she carried it in her purse. It remained a secret from Mama, the children, and me. Only after I procured a weapon of my own did she show me hers. I honored her by not asking if she knew how to use it. Granted, there are light-years of difference between a biathlon target rifle and a pistol, but Elena is no fool. If she said she knew how to use it, she *knew* how to use it.

Mel obtained a nine-millimeter automatic from "somewhere." While I trusted Mel implicitly, I was nonplussed to discover the serial number was filed off. That did not mean the gun couldn't be traced, but it implied that the weapon had been in the hands of people who did not want their names and faces known to all and sundry.

I was careful to buy ammo through a third party. I hoped, but did not ask, Elena if she had taken similar precautions. I stuck the pistol in my belt and left my shirttails out. At the end of every day, I cleaned it behind locked doors. It wouldn't do to suffer a misfire because some stray bit of lint found its way into a vital area.

It was all false bravado, of course. If Dieter's goons were stalking us, they'd use high-powered rifles from considerable distance. Our little pop guns would never be effective, even if we knew the exact location of the shooter. We'd have a better chance of defending ourselves by throwing our pistols at the assailants.

Nevertheless, the INSPAD mafia was in the business of maximizing profits. To take care of two, inconsequential punks might require finding assassins on the cheap. Against them, we had a chance. However, if we were targeted and escaped, there wasn't a hole deep enough to protect us from the next round of thugs – they would be professionals.

I kept telling myself that Rolf was teasing me. My Agamemnon comment clearly startled him. Well, his "Russian into things" comment was terrifying and revenge enough. Still, with the likes of Rolf and his gang, it is impossible to ignore or dismiss a threat.

My only refuge was the conceit that some Matt Dillon type would ride into Dodge and clean up the town. This was as likely as creating a pine forest on the moon. Still, there was a chance – a very slim chance – only a whisper of a chance, but hope springs eternal.

Meanwhile, I took delight in entertaining Elena's children. I was the man with the "magic cups." I could do no wrong. If Eduard felt I was paying too much attention to his sister, he would go to great lengths to be a pest. Strangely, Arina was never jealous. She'd retire to a neutral corner and play with some toy or spruce up her dolly. Eventually, Eduard would be satiated and drift off somewhere and attend to something else. At that point, the patient girl would come over to me as if to ask "now, what will we do?"

One evening, as I was leaving, Elena saw me to the door.

"Are you trying to seduce me by winning over my children?"

My smartass gene kicked in automatically.

"Is it working?"

She was taken by surprise. This unexpected response caught her off guard.

"Yes," she concluded.

It was my turn to confront the unexpected.

"Good," I replied after an awkward pause.

I was beginning to sweat. If I continued this farrago much longer, I'd end up as a damp puddle on the floor just outside her apartment door. My experience with females, to date, had never progressed to "intimacy" – a word used by the coy or prudish to infer exactly what I *did not* intend.

Elena was a bit older than I. She was a celebrity in her country and much of Europe. She married and divorced a man she couldn't quite give up. She needn't work, but she did to boost her self-esteem. She was, I was certain, flirting with me, but she did so with such subtlety and reservedness that I was perpetually off balance.

She was a spider. She had led me into her web. I allowed it.

However, I could not tolerate another lengthy pause. Inevitably, it would be the precursor of another. My nerves could stand the strain no longer.

It was time to absquatulate.

DOUBTS AND RESOLUTION

Mel, as always, billeted with his trainees. Siss was among a group of twelve. This was larger than the norm and extra precautions must be taken. So many people crammed together in such limited space is asking for trouble. Mel had the experience and could recognize the early symptoms of "space happy" personnel; he would defuse explosive problems before they got out of control. He felt the heat, however. Siss had him sweating mightily. She was INSPAD's million-dollar baby, and if anything happened to her or – worse – if she failed to qualify . . .

I knew. Mel knew. Dieter knew. If Siss did not qualify, Mel could expect immediate termination. If he were very lucky, he'd only lose his job. Mel was on the razor's edge. However, the man would not allow his professionalism to be compromised. If Siss didn't measure up to his exacting standards, he'd flunk her. Doubtless, some grand poo-bah would overrule Mel. If Siss was sent to the moon and she was killed, the INSPAD publicity stunt would become their worst nightmare. Of course, they couldn't chance Mel remaining silent. INSPAD might be forced to "take steps."

Mel was in an untenable position.

Perhaps, being under the blow torch prompted Mel to violate his own rules. His situation couldn't get much worse. He liked Siss. He admired her perspicacity and her desire to know all that was knowable or quantifiable. This made matters worse. He would never send an unprepared or improperly trained person to the moon, but there was no way to stop it.

He wasn't so crass as to smuggle in a PoCo. He could, however, lay in a text line. Every second night, he would employ Morse to tap out a brief message to fed into his personal computer. I had access to both his digs and his computer. If I inserted a lemon into the message port, I could be on my way in less than twenty seconds. Once at home, I'd transfer the message from the lemon to my computer. Once there, it was the simple matter of converting dots and dashes to letters.

Siss was doing fine, according to reports. Despite her eagerness, she knew the risks and worked hard to do exactly as Mel demanded. I knew he'd ride her, as he had me, but for different reasons. Once she was known to the public, Siss would be under the microscope. Should anything go amiss, all that attention would be deflected on one person.

Meanwhile, I thought it was right and proper to maintain an aesthetic distance from Elena. I didn't know if she was coming on to me. I thought I handled her so expertly and delicately, but there was always a lifeboat. Suddenly, she was uncomfortably bold.

It's possible that she was simply yanking my chain. Perhaps, she was. On the other hand – well, there wasn't another hand. If she was teasing, she'd forgive my "disappearance" for a few days.

I'd allowed myself to be spooked by Rolf. My nerves told me that my next breath might be my last; my brain told me that I was being taunted for that Agamemnon thing. Regardless, once on the moon I was beyond sniper range. However, Rolf could "arrange" a one-way journey.

I lay on my bed. The window was closed, and the curtain drawn. There was minimal illumination. It was time to confront my sins of commission and omission. Perhaps, a wallow in remorse might clear the air. There was nothing lost if it failed.

My PoCo beeped.

Let it beep, I thought. It might be an eager assassin trying to lure me to the front door of the dormitory. I'd be a fat, juicy target. Hell, even I could make that shot!

Five minutes later, Po beeped again.

It couldn't be Mel.

Heaving a mighty sigh, I grabbed the device and glanced at the ID. None registered. It was a spammer. Normally, I wouldn't give these leeches the slime of day. In my high-octane mood, I spoiled for a fight.

"You've got five seconds! Make it good!"

"Don't take that tone with me!"

It was Elena. She was either at work or preparing for her shift. Because there was no ID, she wasn't using her PoCo. I assumed it was the Happy Burger device. It would allow only limited service options.

"Sorry. I thought you were a spammer."

The tone of my voice was much changed.

"You promised Arina to take her to the park," she scolded. "Just the two of you. She's been looking forward to it all day. You, Brice Duvall, should be ashamed."

Damn! Our caustic farewell at her apartment door had erased my memory.

"I'm sorry – I – uhm –"

"*You forgot*, I know. How proud you must be to break a little girl's heart."

"I'm on my way," I promised.

I canceled the connection before she had another chance to bury a knife in my ribs.

It is amazing how a broken promise can banish the fear of death. My exit, however, was very swift and sudden. A well-trained assassin would not be deterred by my amateur theatricals, but it made me feel slightly better.

I collected Arina. She was in the act of drying her tears, but my arrival perked her up quickly. Mama, however, sent a withering look my way. Doubtless, she was the angry one. I imagined Elena hurrying out the door.

"Don't worry, Mama," she'd say. "I'll take care of this!"

Had Elena reneged on that promise, the atmosphere at home would turn very chilly for a day or three.

"My stagecoach was held up by Black Bart and his gang," I explained.

Mama didn't understand much English, but she was in no mood to accept even a legitimate excuse. The child was hopeful, but her tender years did not make her stupid. I'm certain her mother had dispelled most of the wild and woolly American stereotypical episodes that pass for children's entertainment.

We left the building hand in hand. She maintained a bit of a sulk, but she was recovering. It took us only five minutes to get to the neighborhood's communal kiddie park. There was a large sign at the gate.

Adults Must Be
Accompanied
By A Child

This notice might have lacked authority, but the myriad of security cameras would give even the most dedicated pervert pause.

We did the castle bit, with the swinging bridge and the slide. Before long, she graduated to the see-saw. She sat on her end; I stood near the fulcrum and pushed down with my arms and applied resistance on the downward phase so she wouldn't crash into the ground. Then, she struggled with the monkey bars before turning green on the spin-and-puke.

It was a nice "date," but I was anxious to return to close quarters where I'd get a break from being spied upon. I knew I was under observation. There was no point in trying to locate the spy. I hadn't any training in such matters. The best I could do is make the goon think I was as stupid as I was expected to be. That might work to my advantage further down the line.

"Just a minute," Arina promised – seven times.

She was having a great time. I was not. However, I owed her for being remiss in keeping our "date."

There was a discovery that I found interesting: Arina was blond! There could be no doubt. I'd inspected thoroughly if surreptitiously. This was an authentic Russian blond. I didn't think such things existed, except in cheap detective fiction.

Here was a mystery to take my mind off other things. I knew Elena changed hair color regularly. Since meeting her, I'd seen light brown tresses and reddish brown. Her pictures as an athlete were notable for her dark hair. Eduard, also, had dark hair; I took that as the baseline. Where, I wondered, did this blond color come from? Mightn't that have become a divorce issue?

I liked Elena enough to hope that her lies were of the little white variety. If – well, there was the disturbing possibility that she might be using me. She'd get away with it because I can resist everything except temptation. Still, I'd be disappointed. Further, I liked Arina very much. It would hurt me considerably if I discovered that her mother was – well, not the *My Elena* as advertised by Mama.

Finally, the blond sprite relented. I assumed it was due to the lengthening shadows. When we got to the apartment, however, she sprinted for the bathroom. Had she not been "stricken," we might have been considerably longer in the park.

Mama's ire had, apparently, been soothed. She no longer gave me the evil eye. Eduard seized the opportunity to accost me. He had stored up an entire day's adventures, and I was to get a detailed account of each one. I listened patiently. I really wasn't interested, but I had nowhere to be and had nothing to do.

We were interrupted briefly when the blond sprite flew into my arms, thanked me for our "date," and kissed me on the cheek. She was gone in the proverbial trice leaving her brother free to resume his narration. Mama watched the tableau with a satisfied smile.

I felt, however briefly, like one of the family.

I'm not a trained professional. I'm just a pushy little punk who held a grudge against his former employer. If I was being followed or monitored, those doing the job were pros. I tried every trick I knew, i.e.: suddenly changing direction, looking for reflections in store windows, and suddenly stopping to tie my shoe or pick up some pretend object I'd spotted. Not once did I spot anyone suspicious.

Of course, I might be tracked by satellite. That would be cost prohibitive. Additionally, it would be akin to using an elephant gun to combat a bothersome gnat. They might use drone, but they are so easily spotted, unless they are the high-altitude jobs which would be nearly as expensive as spy sats.

They got a make on Elena. True, she was a well-known celebrity, but someone would have to photo ID her, get her fingerprints or shoe size, or something. Top-flight assassins are also a spendy proposition. Those sorts of assets cost money. People in Rolf's class don't spend their ill-gotten pile so freely. Hiring a detective at a low daily rate is more his speed.

If Elena and I were being monitored, the hirelings were very good. They might tire of us. They might get careless. They just might turn up the heat by going after Arina in the kiddie playground – a symbolic "shot across the bow" thing. That would push the envelope and take us beyond recall. I hoped that if someone was ready to stoop so low, they'd be too dense to realize I had John Roscoe with me. Elena had one as well. She mightn't be as familiar with pistols as she was with target rifles, but she'd not hesitate to aerate anyone who threatened her kids.

Well, the best we could do was hope. If Rolf had us tagged, he'd opt for low-budget muscle. If they were too stupid or too eager, we could defend ourselves. It was a slim hope, but it provided just enough succor to allow us to drop off to sleep at night – eventually.

A beep woke me. I glanced at my watch. It was early.

If this was a call from Dieter, I promised myself to be very rude.

"This better be good," I snarled.

It was Elena. She was too chipper and chatty for so early in the day.

"On behalf of Goldie Locks, I want to thank you. She was gushing last night. It took Mama and me an hour to get her into bed, but she wouldn't shut up. She thinks you're the kindest, most fun person in the world."

"This couldn't have waited another hour?" I mumbled.

"What have you to do this day that's so urgent?"

"Getting my nap-nap in."

"I'll treat you to breakfast at Argo," she chirped.

"Eight thirty?"

"If you don't show, I'll hunt you down."

"Deal."

I showered and shaved. I put on my cleanest dirty clothes. Laundry night was the afternoon prior, but I had a date with Goldie Locks. I vowed to stifle my curiosity, but Elena begged my intrusion by using that moniker.

I hustled over to Mel's and captured his latest message. It took no time to decode. It was three short words only.

Goodxverygoodx

Satisfied that Siss was up to the mark, I left the apartment building with dispatch.

Argo is a Greek place. Originally, it was Argos, but the terminal letter was lost during a tornado. Rather than redo the sign, the owners changed the name.

I wondered what a Greek breakfast was like. Dates and olives with bread and retsina. I wasn't certain I could handle that. A cup, or two, of Greek coffee would open my eyes, but, unless there was something to spread on the bread, the coffee would have to hold me until I found a quick-snack place – Happy Burger, for instance. They sold very nice breakfast sandwiches.

It was a relief to discover my morning worry was wasted. Argo had a page and a half on non-Greek fast breakers.

She paid very little attention to her appearance; her hair was slightly disordered, and she was devoid of makeup, so her gnat's eggs were clearly visible. She tried to hit her mouth with a bit of lipstick but missed. She dabbed away her mistakes leaving her with asymmetrical lips.

She was bubbly. The thrill of seeing her rather taciturn daughter so vociferous the previous evening was like a strong dose of adrenalin. She was so wired that I was initially overpowered.

I ordered a Denver omelet with wheat toast.

"The same," Elena chirped while bouncing in her seat.

"You don't know what I ordered," I accused. "You weren't paying the slightest attention."

She smiled as only Elena Ilyanova Sidorov Yelagin can smile.

"Only once before have I seen my little girl so excited," she beamed. "When I finally fell asleep – I was so excited, I only slept for three hours or so – I dreamed delicious, marvelous, beautiful, fantastic dreams! I'm a happy, excited woman, and you are the cause."

This was exactly the moment to ask her for the launch codes.

"How did your daughter inherit blond hair."

If we lived in a normal world, this would be Elena's cue to stand up and slap me across the face. My words and tone were inexcusably accusatory.

She laughed. Then, she smiled – even better than before. A thousand watts of energy flowed across that table. It wasn't as abrupt as a slap, but it was as emphatic. She leaned over. Fearing she wanted me to lean toward her so she could bean me with the sugar dispenser, I remained coy and in place.

"Novgorod!" she reminded. "The house of Rurik. He came from Scandinavia early on. We are of that stock. My maternal family runs right back to those first foreigners. We have blonds every second or third generation since the ninth century."

This was too much.

"No one can trace a family back that far," I asserted.

I don't care how much I cared for her, nobody can lie to me without being called out. Still, she didn't moderate either her mood or behavior one iota.

"DNA, you silly cow," she gushed while wrinkling her nose. "Mama and I have Scandinavian DNA. So do the children. Eduard's genes are recessive. I know what you're thinking – all that traveling, all those Olympic athletes, all that attention, a husband who was seldom at home. Well, my children are legit, and I'm proud of them – and of my heritage. Now, Mr. Dubious, tell me about your DNA. Do you have any philistines up the branches of your tree."

I sighed.

Elena could read me like a book. She knew I could check her story. One does not have DNA testing without careful documentation. Was this a result of her husband? Did he share the same suspicions as I had? Well, that was a query best reserved for another time.

TENSION

I tried to recall how much I'd told Elena about going to the moon. I wasn't supposed to talk. That was the order given by the local thug-in-chief. Well, I was careful to heed the "advice," but these guys and reason are mutually exclusive. If Mr. Big was upset, it would do me no good to tell him that the objectional information was released before he gave me his "mouth-shut" order. I'd been rather – um – injudicious in my bearing and curtness. These bullies resent that sort of thing. When they realize they have power over you, they treat you like a slave.

Elena had gotten under my skin and was burrowing in my every thought. I didn't know where our relationship was headed, but I wanted it to last long enough for me to figure out what our relationship was.

One afternoon, Elena pleaded with me.

Yes, *pleaded*.

First she beeped me and asked to meet her on her way to work. I had no problems being her slave, I agreed at once.

I met her at the door to her apartment building. I figured we could talk as we walked. If we never talked, just having her within arm's length would satiate me for a day or two.

"Mama and I want to visit the Civil War Museum. We're both very keen, but the children would be – well, adventurous. I realize this is a cheek, but could you stay with the children for a few hours tomorrow?"

"I don't know," I replied. "I'd have to check my social calendar."

"You don't have a social calendar," she reminded. "In fact, if it wasn't for us, you'd have no social at all."

I wasn't all that keen. Being with the children when there was adult supervision was one thing. Being left alone with them – well . . .

"You took Goldie Locks to the park that day," she reported, reading my thoughts. "You both survived. We will leave you some snacks to give them. They like you, Brice. They'd, probably, want to entertain you."

I remained non-plussed.

"I don't speak Russian."

I was grasping at straws.

"They grew up with English. Mama and I are teaming up to teach them Russian. We take care of the languages. We'd like you to take care of the children."

I knew she would twist my arm until I relented, but I continued to hope for a reprieve.

"Please, Brice. For me."

Damn!

I'd crawl on my belly over broken glass if she asked. She was asking.

"For you," I emphasized, "I'll do it."

Waiting for Siss was torture. We'd be trotted out for the press. It would be INSPAD's answer to a freak show. I didn't mind because I was ready to embarrass the whole corrupt outfit any way I could and at every opportunity they allowed me. However, Siss didn't deserve this. She would be used by unscrupulous publicity hounds. They would squeeze her dry. When they could use her no longer, they'd throw her out with the rest of the trash.

You did that, Bric! I told myself. *You will burn in hell for this.*

I had so much to answer for. Further, there was no way I could ever make it up to the woman. I'd never draw a clean breath again.

Funny, isn't it? Because I knew that I was destined for one of the circles in Dante's inferno, I had an odd but genuine sense of freedom. I could enjoy myself because there was no chance of escape. If I was very skillful, I could do things and make gestures to placate Siss. If she had the sense to match her innate intelligence, she'd survive purgatory and emerge stronger and tougher than ever. One day, she could return to her desert hovel and live the life of her own choosing.

There was only one balm applicable to me: *salve*. Wasn't that the greeting Goethe used? He certainly splayed that word on a myriad of his personal possessions (including, I think, his house). Well, there was only one way I could "be well," and that was to help those in need. I fumbled the ball with Siss, but that did not prohibit me from being of service to her.

Meanwhile, Elena and Mama needed some mother-daughter time. I was flattered that they would trust me with the children. It was a trust I'd not take lightly.

The little hellions were fed before my arrival. I had strict instructions concerning snacks. They were allowed, but between-meal chow was strictly rationed. I was warned that they would pull the old "but Mommie always lets us have extra _______ (insert item)" scam. I promised, in front of the prisoners, that I would adhere to the house rules.

Eduard was disappointed that I hadn't brought a Pythagorean cup. I considered that. It would have kept him entertained for, perhaps, the duration of my watch. The risk of breakage was too great, however.

Arina had a tea party planned. She had a large toy samovar and a quaint set of toy tea items. Of course, I was obligated to join her first thing through the door. Eduard was above such "kid's stuff" and settled down to assemble a model airplane with snap-together plastic parts.

The tea was tepid, but it was the real stuff – sweet and spiced. I sipped daintily with my pinkie in the air. My hostess regaled me with neighborhood gossip (the antics of her dollies and stuffed toys) and complemented me on my manners. I wish I could have talked her into signing a statement about my good behavior. For some obscure reason, her opinion of me was very important.

Eduard finished his plane. I expected him to rush to me and show it off. Doubtless, he'd expect plaudits. I was not disappointed when, instead, he asked me to play a game of chess. Arina had pretty much exhausted her party-hostess play and was eager to initiate something else. While she hustled away, I joined her brother.

I sat on the couch. Eduard sat Indian style on the floor across from me. Arina returned with two of her dolls and a stuffed, toy puppy. She offered them all tea and began to inform her "guests" about what that "nice Mr. Duvall" said and did at the party just concluded.

Now, I admit that I've never been a chess player. I remembered the pieces and moves from my youth, but that was about it. Nevertheless, if this seven-year-old kid thought I'd let him win – well, he was going to be disappointed.

That seven-year-old kid won three straight games. He did not play like a seven-year-old kid. He considered his moves carefully. He, obviously, knew chess strategy. I'm ashamed to admit that he irked me no little. Twice, I thought I had him on the ropes, but he was just too good.

During our fourth game, Arina and her puppy came over. She, silently, climbed up onto my lap. She made no demands and, in fact, said nothing. She watched the game as she gently petted her puppy.

That was the picture Mama and Elena were treated to when they let themselves in. I was a bit ill-tempered. I was determined to trounce that precocious little imp and was busy planning a combination that would aid me in that effort. I was too tempestuous to realize that my doom was sealed.

I do not refer to the chess contest.

Elena told me, much later, when she saw me sitting intimately and placidly with her two "darlings," that our friendship increased by several degrees. She'd always found me "nice" and "charming" in – as she put it – a rather "brutal" way. I'd been good company in her estimation. When I practically accused her of being a woman of easy virtue, she wasn't insulted. Indeed, she thought it rather funny.

On that hazy afternoon, she decided it was her turn to "chase" me.

Mel is a professional. He liked Siss and admired her insatiable appetite for knowledge. He would have loved to hang around with her during the break in training, but it wouldn't look right. More to the point, even his innocuous relationship with her would be seized upon by the Propaganda Ministry. It would *insist* that Siss would get a spot on an early cycle because Mel was more than just her mentor. It was equally as likely that INSPAD was using them both to funnel more "illicit" wealth into the INSPAD coffers. If Siss died "up there," the propagandists would come down on Mel and the INSPAD Training Center like a ton of radioactive plutonium. There was a very real possibility that they would come after me, the person who searched the world – well, the Mali portion of the world – to find a sacrificial goat.

The Propaganda Ministry had long ago shed any credibility it once enjoyed. Even the most gullible creatures realized that the concept of "truth" and the more tangible examples of "news reports" were mutually incompatible. However, the propagandists had considerable suck power with government agents and offices. The greatest fear of Dieter Rolf and his henchmen was that the propagandist would single them out for their special brand of slander. Too many people could be swayed by "investigative" reports. Indeed, it was a propaganda caper that made Project Agamemnon possible.

The best way to protect himself from a potential pogrom was for Mel to be seen, frequently, in the company of potential witnesses – even a few of the water-carrying propagandists. If a story emerged of Mel cutting training corners favoring Siss, he would have witnesses who could affirm that he was *not* having an affair with Siss. Of course, the propagandists could lie or, at least, propose a fanciful "report," but only if they had a reason to target Mel specifically.

My defense against the propagandists was simple: I didn't give a damn. Of course, these scum suckers could "destroy" me, but how? I was a nobody. I had no job, no influence, no position, no celebrity status (or, potentially, very minor status), and no fortune to seize. I could go back to Cape Verde and join the fishing fleet.

Well, my relationship with Elena changed everything. She, and her family, had a lot to lose.

If my mission to poke the INSPAD tiger left me unscathed, or nearly so, I'd turn my attention on the "eyes and ears of the world." These capricious bullies and character assassins needed a comeuppance. Maybe, just maybe, I could poke out a few eyes here and there.

Well, that was in the future. I was trapped in the now. I would flaunt the yellow press and take my chances. That did not, however, mean I'd not take precautions.

I "just happened" to be in the library at the same time as Siss. I wasn't being followed (openly, that is), and I doubt Siss was – she was, at the time, a non-entity.

She was hunkering over a thin, cloth-bound book. Her brow was wrinkled with concentration. She looked up when I drew out a chair opposite her and planted myself. She smiled. It was a smile worth observing.

"I was studying INTRANS," she informed.

Good luck with that!

INTRANS was not structurally affiliated with INSPAD, but INSPAD was its only regular customer. It was formed in the early days of planning for the space station. Transporting the equipment and personnel required to build the station was financially impossible by the traditional rocket method. The greatest aeronautical and propulsion engineers formed International Transit. The headquarters were, and still are, in Trinidad. "Happy engineers are productive engineers," was the company mantra. It didn't adversely impact the paper pushers either.

The company, through hard work, trial and error, and a huge influx of cash, designed and built the Space Master (they could afford the best engineers and administrators on the planet, but "Space Master" was the best name they could conjure. It's rumored that an employee's pre-teen son had invented the moniker).

The Space Master was, likely, the ultimate in secret technology. Compared with the INTRANS team, the Manhattan Project was a public development. It just would not do for some math and science whiz to build a functioning model in his garage.

The Space Master is the largest, fixed-wing aircraft ever built. It was powered by six, huge electric-fan engines. These monsters were powered by – wait for it – nuclear "power plants" (*not* reactors). These "plants" produced incredible electrical power. They lifted the giant aircraft off the ground and kept it going for the thirty-six-hour flight to the space station.

Once the monster was beyond the atmosphere, smaller, liquid propellant engines took over. The massive nuclear plants and the liquid-fuel tanks accounted for nearly half the craft's size. It could transport tons of equipment and people to the station and, ultimately, the moon.

There were two Space Masters in use with a third under construction. Space Master Alpha would service one cycle. Space Master Bravo would service the following cycle. Three-months of maintenance was cutting safety margins "too close," so INTRANS insisted on introducing a third monster.

The maximum speed of the Space Master was four hundred eighty miles an hour, but it seldom violated the manufacturer's cruising speed of three hundred ninety miles an hour. That wasn't just "slow" by modern standards, it was glacial. Nevertheless, the Space Master was not designed for speed; it was designed for lifting heavy payloads to super-high altitudes.

Siss was looking at the schematics and illustrations of the interior. The Space Master could transport up to thirty scientists and Space Monkeys. Additionally, there were two flight teams of three to pilot the craft or, at least, to monitor the systems during every minute of every flight. There was a galley, sleeping quarters, he and she potties, and a "lounge." As with accommodations on the moon and in the space station, the living areas were "very cozy."

There was nothing I could tell Siss about the Space Master. I was a rookie too. However, even the "frequent flyers" knew very little about the craft. Even the flight crew was kept in the dark as to how, exactly, the power plants and engines worked. If a power plant or an engine failed, the return to earth promised to be very exciting. Such failures had yet to occur, but all the flight crews were rigorously trained in emergency procedures.

For all its mass, the Space Master, according to the manufacturer, was one hell of a glider. That, too, had yet to be tested.

"How's your training going?" I asked, to avoid a technical discussion of the Space Master.

"The transfers are really getting on my nerves," she confessed.

"That's why they do them," I said, quoting Mel. "You mess up a transfer only once. You'll be too dead to try again."

"I understand," she nodded. "I'm very aware of why we must do so many, but they take a lot out of me. I've lost ten pounds."

Siss, despite her size, did not have ten pounds to lose.

"You will make up most of that just by drinking more water until you go back."

She nodded.

"Are you having second thoughts?"

"Oh, no!" She was emphatic. "I really want to do this. I've learned so much. Once on the moon, I hope I will learn even more."

"How are your sisters."

A pained expression crossed her face.

"They miss me," she reported. "I don't understand how they can miss me as much as I miss them, but we cope. This is the first time any of us has been out of Africa. It is so different here – and the food! Every day, I try something different."

"Happy Burger?" I asked.

"Not yet," she replied. "I'm sure to try soon. I hear the others talking about it. Our meal conversations are exclusively about *real* food."

I didn't laugh. It wasn't funny.

It was early. Elena wouldn't check in until much later.

Siss was anxious but not visibly nervous. She didn't like the idea of ordering anything from an overhead menu, even when accompanied by photos of each item. She trusted me to order for her since this was only a "test flight." Recalling the meal she and her "sisters" prepared in Timbuktu, I considered ordering something spicy for her. In the end, I played it safe and ordered the "standard:" hamburger deluxe. Additionally, I got us each a vanilla shake. We could have coffee or ipecac later, if required.

Siss, obviously, is an adventurer. She wanted to experience new things. I had a feeling that she would praise this newest taste experience, even if she had to lie. She'd do it to be polite since I knew her well enough to know she is not in the habit of INSPAD-speak (a.k.a. lying one's ass off about everything!)

As we waited, Siss asked me to explain orbital mechanics in a way she could understand. Yes, she was that desperate. I knew so little – the math far beyond my understanding – but I made crude diagrams on a paper napkin.

"We take the Space Master to the station, meeting it at perigee, that is when the station's orbit brings it closest to earth. We ride the station for three or four days – however long it takes it to near apogee, the farthest orbital point from earth. We transfer –"

She groaned at the word *transfer*. I backed up a bit.

"We get onto the lunar lander, and it launches us on a course to the moon. We are close enough to the moon's gravitation, that we don't require much thrust. Soon, we are captured by the moon's gravity."

"I know the rest," she interrupted. "Thank you for showing me. It's much easier when I can see and hear at the same time."

When our number was called, I collected our tray and returned to the soon-to-be African Astro "scientist." There is nothing in the INSPAD lexicon to designate a *visitor* or a *joy rider*. She wasn't the first "black" person (the more I see and hear that phrase, the more I despise it) to visit the moon, but her credentials are unarguably the most unique to date.

Siss bit into her burger cautiously. She chewed slowly before making an appreciative sound.

"This is good," she announced. "Lettuce and tomato with meat. A veritable burst of flavor."

I chuckled at her diction. Lettuce and tomatoes are scarce in her part of the world. Meat – well, that term when used in fast-food joints, is relative. There was probably some beef in the burgers, but the party was rounded out with whatever else was handy, pork, chicken, mutton, and who knows? The important thing is that it – whatever it is – is inspected prior to being made public.

Siss didn't mention the bread. We call it the bun, which I thought was the best part of the Happy Burger. A woman brought up on the African version of bread would never think that a bun qualified for such a lofty title. I should have mentioned this, but I kept my thoughts to myself.

With nothing to do and with the rest of the day in which to do it, I opted to drop in on Elena. With luck, I'd catch her on the hop. If so, I could bid the family a friendly greeting without being tied down. There was a part of me that wanted to sit across a chess board from a precocious little irritant. Now that I knew what I was up against, I'd like another crack at him.

I did, indeed, come at exactly the wrong moment.

The children were helping with clearing up after an early meal. Arina was carefully wrapping and putting away residuals while Eduard helped Mama dry and stack the dishes. Elena made a brief, harried appearance. She had her Happy Burger uniform draped over one arm, her anti-slip work shoes on her feet and very little else. She said something emphatic to Mama in Russian and paid me no attention whatever.

I knew I was pushing hospitality beyond reason, but I hardly expected to see an ecdysiast.

In truth, I was not overly impressed. She was getting on a bit in years and her merciless athletic training produced an abundance of muscle and sinew. On her left shoulder was an ugly cicatrice, a souvenir of a major operation, I suppose.

Well, in her bra and undershorts, she was a far cry from the voluptuous cuties one finds in clubs about town, but she had my undivided attention. *As ye show, so shall we peep.* I'd heard or read that somewhere; I accept it as a truism.

Mama said one or two words. Elena made a face and disappeared.

Not wishing to be mistaken for a voyeur, I remained. The children, Mama, and I exchanged meaningless homilies for two or three minutes. Elena returned, in full uniform, and made a grab for her handbag.

"May I walk you to work?"

She was harried by something. It was difficult for her to acknowledge me. Perhaps, I had done or said something that irked her. If so, I was anxious to make amends.

"I can't find my ID," she sighed.

"Was it lifted?"

"I'm sure not. It's here somewhere, but I don't have time to search."

"All the more reason for me to escort you," I chirped, thankful that I was not responsible for her mood.

She nodded her thanks, but her umbrage remained overt.

We were out of the building and well on her way before I broke the silence.

"I took a colleague to Happy Burger for lunch."

Elena was not whelmed. The place was a popular lunch venue.

I told her about Siss and how we met. She was visibly interested in hearing about this mystery woman and our initial meeting. Immediately, she peppered me with questions. I answered insofar as I was able.

"I'd like to meet this woman," Elena reported.

"I will make that happen."

She remained upset about her missing ID, but when she reported for work, I took my leave. She wished me a good afternoon upon our parting. It was platitudinous, but it eased the tension considerably.

SHOW DOWN

After introducing Elena and Aissata, I became the third wheel – or the fourth or fifth. Elena was thrilled to meet someone from a truly exotic place. Predictably, they hit it off like sorority sisters on the eve of the Spring Ball. Twice, I helped Mama tend the children while "My Elena" went off with "My Siss." Only the resumption of training separated the two new best friends.

"I love the way she speaks French," Elena gushed.

"You know French?"

I was slightly miffed to be denied this item previously.

"Not enough to hurt me," Elena shrugged. "I know enough to have fallen in love with her French."

Aissata's French, heavily seasoned by her Mali environment and tribal influences, was – in Elena's estimation – "charming." Parisians mightn't care for it, but there didn't happen to be any among either of their close acquaintances.

After Siss disappeared for her second phase of flight training, Elena gave me a play-by-play of their time together and a synopsis of their voluminous conversations. She, then, excused herself to reintroduce herself to her children. She made it clear that my presence was persona-non-needed. She wasn't so rude as to throw me out of the apartment, but she suggested I not darken her door for a couple days.

Banishment was but one of my problems. Despite Mel's glowing reports of Aissata's progress, I was as nervous as a kitten surrounded by a pack of wild dogs. When a day passed without a report from Mel, I convinced myself that the wheels were coming off the wagon. If Siss tanked, Rolf and his Pretorian Guard would be out for blood – mine! The program was financially closed. Someone from way upstairs would have to find a replacement – two replacements since my head would belong to Mme. La Guillotine.

I lay down on the floor of Mel's cell and slept with my arm for a pillow and my jacket for a blanket. I remained there, fasting, for twenty hours.

Finally, Mel's computer dinged.

Onxcoursex

Good news, but this was just the beginning of round two. I had confidence in Mel and confidence in Siss, but too many things could go too wrong. At least, I could breathe again. How long that would last would depend upon things beyond my control.

I hustled back to my digs for a shower, shave, and a bout of proper sleep. I didn't wake up until nearly noon. My breakfast was a slice of stale bread and a small block of sharp cheddar cheese. I put on clean clothes and went to see Elena.

The woman looked like I felt. With her gnat's eggs uglier than ever and her hair in a flurry of disorder, she was as appealing as a hand grenade.

"Coffee?" I croaked.

She bid me enter. Mama was tutoring the children, in Russian, and in another room. Elena quietly and efficiently got the coffee gurgling. While we waited, she gestured toward the couch while she knelt on the other side of the chess table.

"You're going to the moon."

It wasn't a question.

"That's classified information," I warned. "Don't noise that around."

I was scared. If she told me that she'd been informing every Happy Burger customer that a "guy" she knew was scheduled for a lunar holiday, I would be in deep poop.

"Is that why you didn't tell me?"

"Would it have made any difference?"

She pressed her lips together as if to contain rage.

"I came out of the bedroom and found you here – that day. It was too late to be coy, and I'm too old to be embarrassed, so I felt the situation couldn't get any worse."

"Yes," I nodded. "I saw rather a lot of you that afternoon."

It wasn't funny. She didn't think so either.

"Well, the fact is, it happened – add to that, the way you are with the children. Brice, you're a part of the family."

I cleared my throat.

"Even if you suspect me of thinking you're a good-time girl?"

She snorted.

"I'll not defend myself, but I'd be interested to examine any evidence. If you think I am what you say, I can't stop you. It hurts, you know. I'd like to think you'd examine any evidence very carefully. I was married for many years to a man I seldom saw. Now, I start feeling toward you – well, the way I feel toward you. Next, I learn you're leaving the planet for however long. I'm in a rut. It's ending, just like the first time. This time, however, we never really got started."

I was confident enough to issue a dare.

"If you tell me to never come here again, I shall obey."

She looked directly through my eyes and into my thoughts. I don't know what she found in there, but she trolled for an uncomfortably long while.

"I never would have agreed to divorce Fedor if he hadn't insisted," she announced as she settled in for a bit of introspection. "He thought I deserved better and could do better. Until a few weeks ago, I doubted that. You make me very confused."

"Confused or torn?"

As with all things important, she pondered my question for some while.

"I cannot answer that. It isn't that I *won't*, it's just – I'm no longer certain who I am. I've had two careers. I outgrew them both. Now, I'm focused on maintaining my self-esteem and preparing my children for the future. Beyond that . . ."

Beyond that *what?*

"Elena, if I may be so forward, I would appreciate being a part of that future."

She smiled, but only for a moment. She was not a beauty, to be sure. Her smile, however, was a balm to my existence.

"You're going to the moon," she reminded.

"I went to Mali to find Siss," I reminded. "I came back."

"You didn't come back to *me*."

As previously noted, Elena Ilyaovna is a tough read. Her sense of humor is tuned to a frequency beyond my range. Similarly, her sarcasm is razor sharp but cleverly cloaked. She could rip me to shreds and leave no trace of blood. I didn't know if she was mocking me, joking with me, criticizing me, or toying with me. Because of my feelings for her, I decided to be cautious.

"I never knew you existed," I began, hoping my tone of voice would not provoke her. "I never followed biathlon, and I don't watch or listen to sports features in English, never mind Russian. I didn't know you until I turned up at Happy Burger one evening. I am committed to the moon mission. I was on that very night I first met you. The idea that I am running away from you is misplaced."

"You think I'm fishing?"

"I know damned well you are," I responded, feeling much more secure.

She took a breath and pursed her lips again.

"I suppose I am."

It was my turn. I knew this better be good.

"Elena, I love you."

She perked up. Skepticism radiated from her expression.

"Now, the question is: am I *in love* with you? I cannot honestly say. I think about you every day. I feel so good when I think I've pleased you, but you are –"

I could not complete that sentence.

"I *are* what, Brice?"

I needed a script writer. My feelings refused to be translated verbally.

"You are the most fascinating and insightful person I've yet to meet, but there are times when you scare me."

"How? What do I do?"

"It isn't anything you do or say. It's just – you."

She was clearly nonplussed. Was she getting angry? Who could tell?

"That's clear enough, I guess."

I took a deep, deep breath and hoped for something either inspired or cogent.

"You threw Mel for a loop when you presupposed he wanted nothing on the girl he ordered. It was so funny that I was too stunned to laugh. Later, you told him there was a naked child in the back and would Mel let her put her clothes back on. That crossed the line – for me, anyway. That was outright obscene. I wasn't certain that I ever wanted to see you again. I certainly didn't want to know you."

She examined me closely. She didn't urge me to continue; her eyes and visage made her desires very, very clear.

"There is an aura about you," I began.

I was starting to tremble. It was my goal to explain myself, but I was limited by words, and words betray and miscarry. Beads of sweat were forming on my brow.

"Just when I think you've pushed too far, I find you – suddenly – so attractive and – well, *safe*. I like to be with you. I *want* to be with you."

Elena cast a furtive glance at the short hallway. Mama and the children could not remain occupied forever. There remained a bit of air to clear. I'd said things that amazed me. I wasn't, however, satisfied they conveyed my feelings adequately.

She stood and went to the machine. I heard her take two mugs from the cupboard; I heard the coffee being poured. Moments later, she was at my side. She offered a mug which I accepted. Then, she used her hip against my shoulder. Understanding her intent, I slid to my right. Elena didn't wait. She settled down onto the area just vacated. There wasn't enough room, but, without either of us spilling coffee, we were sitting side by side. There wasn't enough room to sit side by side. I had room enough to make space, but the warmth of her body made me greedy. I would yield not an inch more. If Elena objected to my un-gentlemanly behavior, she failed to express it by word or action.

"Against my better judgement, I trust you," she announced. "You opinion of me matters very much. Let me confide in you."

"Do you think it wise?" I asked with no little concern.

"Who am I to judge?"

Deuce. It was my serve, but I couldn't.

"I've been with two men where we – ah – actually got something straight – uhm, mutually."

That was amusing but bordering. I didn't think it prudent to speak.

"The first was when I was fifteen. He was a classmate and I thought he was the – how is it in English? – the cat's meow."

This was no time for trading English language euphemisms. My mouth remained clamped shut.

"It was horrible, Brice. I mean, it was so – bad, so unspeakable, so – just so worse than bad! This is supposed to be an expression of love? I – I wanted a lobotomy. Never would I be able to erase the horrible, terrible, despicable experience from my memory. I shudder just thinking of it after all this time."

She held the mug to her lips, but I don't think she imbibed any coffee.

"When Fedor – well, when it was getting very serious, I knew that – well, I knew I'd have to relent. I was really scared, Brice. I wanted Fedor, but I didn't want that – other stuff. Well, I gritted my teeth and did what was expected of a loving, dutiful wife. Brice, it was the most exciting, wonderful, magnificent night of my life. In fact, it changed my life. I thought I was in love before, but – my love increased a hundred times because of that one night."

"You are under no obligation to tell me any of this," I reminded.

"Shut up, Brice."

I shut up.

"Then, we had Eduard. He was a tangible expression of our love. We were thrilled. Then – then I recalled my life as an only child. I didn't care for that, Brice. I don't want to talk to Mama about it. I suspect there was a reason, and I don't feel it's my place to demand an explanation. I wanted Eduard to have a sibling. Fedor was cool about it. He – he wasn't home often, but when he was – I mean when the temperature and time were right – I was the boldest, most unabashed vamp that ever was! Well, even when we missed, we still had fun. But – the important thing is I got Arina. Whatever Lola wants, Lola gets!"

This time, she sipped some coffee with an unmistakable sense of satisfaction. The air had cleared. A state of equilibrium returned.

"Does Lola want me?"

That was bold. However, I wasn't quaking anymore.

She turned her head and eyed me very thoroughly and very carefully.

"Yes, Brice. I think Lola does."

"*Think?*"

"Let's say I have a supreme interest in you."

It was time to chop wood.

"May I kiss you?"

Her face exploded in mirth. Her nose wrinkled, her lips spread wide around gleaming teeth and that magnificent, hypnotic overbite.

"This isn't Italian opera buffa," she snickered. "You don't need permission!"

"*Permesso.*"

Instantly, she was as sober as a hanging judge. She looked at and right through me.

"*Prego.*"

I leaned over and kissed her. It wasn't very passionate. It certainly wasn't very seductive. However, it was soothing, and exceptionally warm.

"*Grazie,*" I whispered.

Mama, apparently, knew her cue. She'd hit her mark in time to witness the comic event. Elena and I realized our faux pas together and too late. Elena said something in Russian. Mama snorted as only a Russian mother can snort. Nevertheless, it did not escape our attention that Mama's gesture lacked any sign of disapproval.

WORLD, HERE WE ARE

Aissata came through with flying colors. Mel assured me that he cut her no slack. She experienced several minor mishaps, but so did we all. None of these "demerits" were classified as life-threatening. One demerit rated punishment and remedial training. With two demerits, the candidate is escorted to the parking lot and warned never to approach an INSPAD facility again.

Three days after Siss graduated, she and I were seated on the dais inside the training ring. It was the same area where we trainees endured our training lectures, slide shows, and systems orientation. Due to the limited area, the number of reporters was kept down to a dozen and a half. The press corps had to draw straws, take a number, or murder someone else to join the elite few who were allowed to put some fun back into the news cycle.

Space, by this time, had become old hat. Of course, if there was a lunar crash or a system failure in any of the extraterrestrial facilities, there would be round-the-clock "make-it-up-as-you-go-along" reporting. It made for great, world-wide entertainment since the "news" media eschewed verified facts. It was all "human interest," a.k.a. *gossip*.

We were briefed over what to expect in the way of questioning. We were not coached in our answers, but there were strict parameters imposed. We must not, ever, in any way, embarrass or impugn INSPAD or any INSPAD official.

Dr. Davis Mannion introduced us and provided a biographical sketch of us. No mention was made of my former affiliation with INSPAD.

Siss and I were allowed to make an "opening statement."

Siss stole the entire show. Her skin color, accented English, and "native costume" (INSPAD made certain she wore something "native") made her the focus of the world.

Mannion, a person I never knew before and never saw since, explained how INSPAD wanted the public to have access to the lunar experience of "ordinary" people. I bristled at that. Scientists, even those thrilled to go into and return from space, are considered uppity and dull. *Ordinary*, somehow, was touted as the new chic.

My presentation did not take more than half the time allotted. I spoke briefly of my origins, family, education, and work experience with a "major corporation." I was not allowed to name the "corporation," least INSPAD be accused of providing an unpaid commercial for a *private* business. If anyone discovered INSPAD had been my employer, the digested matter would hit the revolving blades.

Siss took more than her allotted time, but no one complained. She is both personable and interesting. She was, also, literate and articulate.

Then, it was question time.

"Miss Sissoko," some smart-assed punk began. "Are you aware that the United Nations declared involuntary servitude eradicated two decades ago."

Typical. Being born a slave was a publicity gold mine. Here was a gold miner cursing his own, chosen profession. I couldn't help myself.

"You're saying the United Nations lies?" I asked. "Please, don't let me think you are calling Miss Sissoko a liar."

The slimy little butt was suddenly stumbling over his own tongue. He'd put his foot in it, and he was trying to pretend it never happened. Siss saved the day with her staid demeanor and her soothing voice.

"Like Mr. Duvall, I have no living relatives," she began with perfect enunciation. "What I know of my first years comes from a Benedictine monk who knew my mother and her history. I, personally, have no knowledge or recollection."

That was too diplomatic. Perhaps the slave markets were gone ("perhaps") but I'd been to Africa, and I harbored strong suspicions about some of people I met along the Niger. I wanted to punch that officious punk. Failing that, I wanted him to look like the officious fool he was in front of the entire world. Instead, I reminded myself that I was only a syllable away from meeting one of Dieter's goons.

The bulk of the questions were directed at Siss. She was the star. I fielded a paltry few, which suited me right down to the ground. My answers were terse and, I hope, polite.

After what seemed years, the party broke up. Siss and I would be hustled off to our respective hovels in INSPAD vehicles. First, however, the prevaricators were herded out before they could create news rather than lie about what had taken place. I was reminded, with amazing subtilty, that my whole purpose in life was to be a publicity plaything. It wouldn't serve to insult a reporter or aggravate one.

I was contrite. I knew he was correct. My personal animosity toward reporters and my hostility toward INSPAD would be used against me.

Siss and I were "invited" to INSPAD Operations Central. I was not surprised to see a crystal chandelier, but I hardly expected the modest lobby underneath it. I wondered if the ostentatious decoration was a tax write-off for the resident graft artist. As two moon voyagers did not rate a reception in the inner sanctum, we were told to make ourselves comfortable. I deferred to my fellow traveler.

Aissata had acclimated well. It was clear that she had accumulated some cosmopolitan experience before finding the Atlanta Public Library. She motioned me to a beige colored sofa. It was designed for three, so we could be comfortable without violating propriety. Now that we were in the public domain, the vultures would be lurking everywhere. The camera does lie; it all depends upon who is pointing it and who is writing the caption. The penny-press would lust for a scandal and were ready and able to manufacture one.

The Sex Life
of the
Moon Couple

That would sell subscriptions all over the world. Siss was aware of the evils of the press. Photos of us may be snapped surreptitiously. If so, Siss and I were obligated to appear as innocuous as possible.

Soon, a portly man with a receding hairline and gray streaks around his ears appeared and headed for us like a homing pigeon. He introduced himself. I stood, as expected. He shook hands with Siss first, as expected, and she remained seated, as expected. After shaking my hand, he helped himself to the space between us. In his free hand, he had a file folder. It bulged slightly.

I don't recall the man's name. For all I knew, he was the low-level spook who moved into my cubical when I was evicted.

He leafed through the papers contained in the folder. They were offers from various media outlets. We had the option of "selling" ourselves for the exclusive rights to our "stories."

We would be built up prior to our departure and "interviewed" upon our return. During our cycle on the moon, we would be reported upon. There would be constant communication with Luna One, and our thoughts and experiences would be broadcast to the peasants daily.

Mr. Port gave us a brief synopsis of each proposal to include the monetary incentives. There was, as always, a catch. Certain media concerns had to be financed which, traditionally, was deducted from the "package price." Mr. Port and I reviewed the proposals with Siss for the better part of an hour. I encouraged her to accept one from a European-based group. It had as good a reputation as any media outfit. In English, that means the media consortium issued lies that were, at least, plausible.

"It's a nice price," I suggested. "It will pay for your college no matter where you decide to study."

Siss trusted me (the fool) and opted to sign with the Europeans. Mr. Port promised to have the INSPAD lawyers draw up the necessary papers for her signature. I knew, from experience, that INSPAD had a surplus of lawyers and many of them specialized in contract law. Siss would be protected from the garden-variety sharks by the INSPAD sharks. Of course, they'd have to be paid from their clients proceeds. Regardless, Siss would retain an impressive pile of chips.

"I don't want a contract, and I won't sign one."

Mr. Port examined me as if I'd lost my marbles.

"It's for your protection," he reminded (as expected).

"I don't want to be gaged," I replied. "If someone asks me a question, I reserve the right to answer without having to go through a mountain of legal mumbo-jumbo."

In short, I wanted to be able to shoot off my mouth on the off chance there is one "journalist" on the planet who is more interested in facts than what makes for "good copy." If I'm asked for my opinion, he or she will get my opinion, with the caveat that it is my opinion only. I had things to say about INSPAD that would not pass muster with the propogandists, many of whom were, also, on the take.

I was not forgetting Rolf's threat. If I became a liability, Elena and her family might suffer. Still, Dieter Rolf would remain the tip of the pyramid only until the next gang boss ousted him. The new guy (or un-guy, as the case may be) mightn't hold a grudge.

After our dismissal, I tied up with Mel for a romp through our favorite bars. I wanted to retain my faculties, however. I would be with Siss when she met with her legal team. There was no assistance I could provide in matters of law, but my presence just might discourage the suits from dealing from the bottom of the deck. I didn't give a damn about INSPAD or the lawyers or the monetary dispensations. I did, however, care about Siss. I got her into this mess, and I would protect her if I could. Regardless, I'd be there for her.

Prior to our introductory news conference, I warned Elena that I would be *incommunicado* indefinitely. The propagandists would squeeze me dry before plaguing anyone I'd been in contact with during the past decade. Exercising revenge for my daring to have a very placid existence, hitherto, they'd grab Elena by the ankles and shake out of her any facts that could be the foundation for the myriad of lies they'd throw up. In no time the reporters, a.k.a. creative fiction scribblers, would have Elena draped with an Olympic gold medal (provided, of course, they only allowed her one gold medal). Happy Burger would be so crammed with frauds and hacks that the franchise employing her would be forced to either fire her or close its doors. Every closet she'd been in since childhood would be inspected for skeletons. If the bastards found none, they'd fabricate a dozen or two. Before they were finished, they'd "prove" that Eduard was the rightful Czar of Russia.

My PoCo would be monitored (never mind that doing so was illegal). If Elena coded me, the press would be on her before she closed the transmission. Doubtless, our conversation would be recorded and edited beyond the bounds of reason or propriety. Similarly, if I attempted to code her – well, she'd pay for it.

Though it was ancient history, the Lindberg kidnapping was much on my mind. The mere thought of authorities digging up the remains of young Arina would feed an entire stable of nightmares for years to come.

Goldfinger! Beware his web; it's the kiss of death!

Mediafinger! Beware their lies; they'll make you pray for death!

Mel would risk my company because he was protected. First, he was a black man; the media hesitated to play hardball with a black man because it would cost them a lot of suck power with militant organizations. Second, he was employed by INSPAD; no one risks the ire of an organization that powerful. Bothersome people have been known to disappear.

I toyed with the notion of using Mel to slip written notes to Elena and forward any responses. It was too dangerous. The slugs would suspect. Sooner or later, the messages would be intercepted, checked for "spelling errors," and made public. Would they cast us as lured sex maniacs, or would we be spies for an army of international conspirators? Curious to know how our relationship would be spun, I realized it would put Elena and her family – to include her ex-husband – in considerable danger.

How I missed the Postal Service. At least the government would protect our exchange of missives, but no one wrote letters or sent postcards anymore. I'd have to figure something out on my own. It was better than two to one that my conversations with Mel, even in a noisy bar, would be monitored. There were directional audio receptors, both cheap and easily disguised. Then, of course, there were the good, old lip readers.

Siss and Elena had become good friends. No problem there. Sable protected them from the malevolence of fiction writers. There was a real possibility that I could use Siss as a go-between. I hesitated to do so. Siss was a friend; I respected her. One does not use friends.

Elena and I had become very close – if you know what I mean. I remained nonplussed. I wanted her. Indeed, I'm convinced I was in love with her. However, Mama and the kids constituted obstacles. If Elena were forced to choose between me and her family – well, I preferred not to think of that. Further, what did I have to offer? I told Dieter I was a card stacker. Well, I was. Elena and her family deserved much better. Perhaps, under her influence, I'd make something of myself. I couldn't see myself as a Happy Burger employee, but, if Elena insisted, I'd shed my natural inhibitions in a heartbeat.

Elena had enjoyed fame. She worked hard to obtain it, but that part of her life was over. She wanted to be a small somebody. Her husband's continuing financial support made it possible. She could – and *did* – start at rock bottom. Somehow, I cannot imagine Fedor Yelagin's support extending far enough to provide a shady, younger hanger-on a safety net.

Conclusion: I was not worthy of Elena. I had no prospect of becoming worthy of her.

Conclusion: I must let her go.

It made me sick. No amount of card stacking was ever going to make me un-sick.

THE COUNTDOWN

In INSPAD terms, Siss and I were three days from departure.

We, and our chaperones, were ushered into a proper auditorium for a final, pre-launch press conference. There would be another shortly after our return, but that would come, if all went well, a little over four months hence.

There were thirty credentialed wire-service people who were allowed access. I was prepared for them to sharpen their fangs on us before plaguing more worthy celebrities. To my surprise, however, they were as gentle as little lambs. Well, I know about wolves in lamb's clothing. Nevertheless, I kept my natural distrust and coarseness under wraps.

"What personal items are you taking with you?"

Siss said she was taking a photo of her "sisters," her notes on astrophysics, a book of prayer, and a St. Christopher medallion.

I fully expected one of the pedantic know-it-alls to remind Siss that Saint Christopher had been demoted long, long ago. Imagine my surprise when no one made any mention.

"I'm taking a volume containing selections from Sam Johnson's Dictionary and a mystery by Dorothy L. Sayers, in paperback."

We would be quartered on Luna One, correct?

Siss, always the first to respond to questions addressed to us both, replied that INSPAD was reluctant to have two supernumeraries at the same facility. Luna One would be cramped enough hosting Siss.

Where would I be quartered.

"I asked for Dark Side. There seems to be a discussion about that. I might not know prior to our landing on the lunar surface."

Why the Dark Side.

Because, Dumbass, it's as far away from INSPAD as I can get.

"I'm addicted to adventure," I said, aloud. "I cannot expect anything more adventurous than being on the dark side of the moon where we will have no direct contact with anyone."

True!

For a few seconds, we could be in contact with the other moon bases and earth when the crawler was at exactly the right place. It would remain in motion, however, and line-of-sight communications relay would be very short indeed. The only communications directed to us would have to be hand delivered by the crawler crew. Our responses would, likewise, be hand carried.

As the current cycle ended, there were three scientists at Dark Side. Two of these, a Swiss geologist and a Canadian astronomer, were "cycling out." A French radio astronomer would remain for another three months. Imagine being isolated from the rest of humankind for half a year!

Bliss!

If I were granted permission to cycle at Dark Side, I'd be accompanied by a German astrophysicist who specialized in spectrometry. There was some concern about a Frenchman and a German sharing the same cramped quarters beyond range of any possible counseling or therapeutical services. These two "roommates" knew of each other's work, and it was decided that their professionalism would negate any natural animosity. The one good thing about INSPAD was how carefully they psych-profiled it's scientists. Anyone with a tendency for violence or heated argumentation is prohibited from moon and space station assignments. Further, nationalistic emotionalism is taken into consideration and carefully examined prior to assignments.

Still, I was slightly concerned. A Frenchman and a German, cooped up for three months in a hole in the ground – it was an explosive recipe.

What a fine mess I got myself into – and I did it all on my own.

Damn!

All I wanted was severance pay.

JULES VERNE REVISED

There were seventeen passengers and tons of food, supplies, spare parts, and mail. There were, also, pressure suits, belts, boots, gloves, sunglasses, unguents, deodorants, and a long list of items that wouldn't draw a yawn on earth. Aboard the space station and on the moon, the most innocuous item can push a person into a space-happy state if denied.

I knew that my many mental images of Elena, her mother, and her children would not carry me through three and a half months alone. Were I an intelligent being, I'd have asked Elena for some photo images. In a belated effort to preserve my sanity, I relied of Mel who "knew a guy." I do not know the identity of this "guy," nor did I care to. If he muffed his mission and Elena was tied to me, lives would be destroyed. In a belated effort to preserve my sanity, I tried to call off the cloak-and-dagger mission. The risks of a media snoop catching the scent were too great. Alas, Mel informed me, I was too late.

For three days, I crapped boulders in worry and, truthfully, panic. If my actions created hell for the people I loved, I vowed to remain on the moon. I wouldn't live there, but I would make certain I wouldn't be leaving.

We were in quarantine.

There was little danger that we'd carry a fatal virus to the moon. We'd been thoroughly tested and retested. The real danger, in the minds of INSPAD, was that someone would smuggle booze, drugs, explosives, or similar contraband and, potentially, destroy the entire project.

The quarantine facility was spacious – the last chance we'd have to spread out and enjoy freedom of movement. There was an exercise unit complete with an eighth of a mile track. The common area had tables and chairs for as many as fifty people. We could congregate together or spread out as we pleased. We were each assigned a sleep chamber large enough to contain a bed (a real bed, *not* a bunk), a chair, and a reading lamp. To ensure privacy, we had a key to our own assigned chamber. If we lost that key, we would sleep in the common.

Before we were brought to the facility, the cleaning and maintenance crews entered, one at a time. Each person stripped naked and was scanned. Once inside the facility, these people put on their respective uniforms (which had been cleaned, ironed, folded, and scanned previously.) When the work was finished and the facility was ready, the crew individually stripped and were scanned again. Once they were in their own clothes, they were free to do as they pleased and go wherever they wanted.

When we arrived, we stripped and were scanned at ten-minute intervals. Our street clothes were neither searched nor scanned, but they were placed in a reserved space inside a vault. That vault would remain secure until our arrival when we stripped and scanned out.

It took nearly three hours for our mission to enter. Once inside, the door was closed and locked. In case of fire, there were two emergency exits. One must press two panic bars to open those doors. Alarms would sound for miles. People and fire equipment would converge. If there was no fire, someone would go to the slammer because surveillance cameras were as numerous as dandelions at and near the emergency exits.

There were three cooks and a gofer who were sealed in with us and subject to the same strip-and-scan as we. They were well paid as befitted the prison atmosphere.

The food was top drawer. It was, in a very real sense, the last meals of the condemned. Once we left earth, it was "plastic food" until we returned. Even then, we would be held captive for ten days while we readjusted, in a series of small snacks, to real food. People who returned from months in space and chowed down on steak and potatoes were violently ill for days. After lengthy deprivation, the entire digestive system must be gently reintroduced to real food.

There were seventeen in our cycle. There were two flight crews (pilot, assistant pilot, and engineer), Siss and I, four legitimate scientists and five Space Monkeys. If an emergency developed, the flight would be aborted, and the Space Master would return to earth. It was mostly wing. For its size and weight, it was a great glider – or so we were told. No one had nerve enough to test this feature. There were only two in service and losing one during a test flight would, potentially, prove catastrophic.

At the very last minute (figuratively), Mel's covert agent managed to smuggle a photo of Elena into one of my books. I'd remain unaware until I discovered it in my "secured gear" on the moon. It wasn't the best photo of her, but it was taken during her sports-reporter days. Thus, she was all "glammed up." If only her facial expression was a bit brighter. Nevertheless, it was her photo. I recognized the expression she wore; I'd seen it many times. It was a true representation of the woman I'd fallen for. I loved to gaze upon it. Alas, I mightn't ever see her in the flesh again.

We didn't care to be cooped up. There were three communal PoCos available so that "the lepers" (as we called ourselves) could chat with friends, family, and sweeties. I called Mel twice, but I dare not ask about Elena. INSPAD-issued PoCos, likely, were monitored by people who mightn't have our best interest at heart.

Siss called Mel twice. Mel called and asked for her twice. She and I, Mel and she, got along very well. However, we were getting anxious. If we were going to catch up with the station at perigee, we had to begin our flight in three days.

We'd be served a light breakfast in the morning. Sandwiches and salads, both of high quality, were served as our midday snack. The evening meals, however, had copious bursts of flavor. The grumblings we shared during the day disappeared during the evening repasts. When we retired for the night, we were universal in our desire for a postponement of our scheduled take-off. It would mean many more of those delightful evening banquets.

Alas and alack, the facility director's voice was piped into the commons via the PA system. Mr. Director was not allowed access to the holy of holies, so his voice was brought to us from afar. We (all of us) had been given a clean bill of health by the rattle-shakers. We would not be taking communicable maladies into space. Therefore, we would leave the facility on schedule and in pressure suits to make certain we'd pick up nothing on our way to the Space Master.

No one was allowed to back out at this point. The offer was never made. I suppose some nervous Nellie may have gone into convulsions of cowardice and had to be left behind, but INSPAD and the research institution that sent them would be stuck with considerable financial outlay and nothing to show for it. Court proceedings were the least of that person's worries.

There was a large, digital clock in the commons. The moment the director's announcement ended, the clock began ticking backwards. When the device reached zero, we would be escorted to the Space Master. We were provided with one hour to get into the craft, stow any gear, and remove our pressure suits. The Space Master had its own environment. It was germ and virus free. The bulk of our boarding time was taken up with carefully recycling the pressure suits. There was one chance in ten thousand that a suit would pick up a contagion between the facility and the Space Master, but that was once chance too many. The suits would remain on earth. The Space Master had the pressure suits we'd use in space.

Everything was figured to the exact second. If we dropped behind by a few minutes, power settings would be upped slightly to make up the lost time. Similarly, if we found ourselves bucking a serious headwind, adjustments were made. We had to reach the station and remain in very exact tolerances, or the cycle must be scrubbed. This constituted hardship for those due for replacement and a greater hardship for those scheduled to remain – resupply was vital for both the station and the moon bases. There were contingency plans, of course, but these had yet to be tested. Mel once told me that these plans were extremely poor since they depended upon a very heavy dose of luck.

The Space Master was the largest transport I'd ever seen with a wingspan that defied belief. The passenger cabin was, however, very small. Space Master is, essentially, a cargo ship. The people were treated as cargo. There was seating with bunks in rows above the seats and others crammed between the rows of seats and the interior of the fuselage. There was a tiny "kitchen" where packaged rations could be heated. There was, also, an urn for heating coffee and another for water. Tea bags were available for those who shunned coffee.

A portion of our flight would be in a weightless environment. During that time, the kitchen was secured, and all liquids confined to interior reservoirs. We'd eat and drink through tubes inserted in heavy plastic bags. During this phase, we were "encouraged" to remain strapped down in our seats or our bunks and keep movement through the cabin to a minimum. There were two latrines for use for the bulk of our journey and two more for use in "low gravity."

We loitered in the cabin waiting for engine start. Unlike a rocket launch, the Space Master, thanks to its mini reactors, did not rely on an external power source. The cabin was well lit, and the air was cool and circulated reassuringly. There were no assigned seats. Only a few opted to settle down and, thereby, mark their territory.

Siss and I knew each other better than anyone else in our expedition. We tended to keep in proximity. I studied her as she scanned her newest surroundings. She appeared unsettled.

"Having second thoughts?"

She focused on me instantly.

"I wish I could have had another couple weeks in the library," she replied. "There are hundreds of book on hundreds of fascinating subjects; I'd have loved to explore further. This – thing is very exciting, and I'm looking forward to it, but there aren't many books where we're going."

"Sorry I got you into this."

Her expression transformed noticeably.

"Don't think that," she admonished. "If it hadn't been for you, it might have taken me decades to get lost in a huge library. Nobody reads books anymore."

"You do," I reminded.

"Yes. The library was, for me, a treasure trove. No matter what happens, I will thank God for the few days I had amongst all those great thinkers and scientists. I learned so much. Most important, Brice, I learned that I know next to nothing."

"That's an important thing to know, Siss."

"I'm happy to know I'm not the only one who feels that way."

Jens Schulte was the German astrophysicist who was assigned to Dark Side. He had more letters after his name than I had regrets. Though he had to be pushing forty, he looked like a college undergraduate. Jens was marginally attractive with light brown, almost reddish, locks. As did all Germans, he spoke textbook English. His CV suggested he was a brain with legs, but, unlike most Germans – particularly of the bookish sort – he was convivial and engaging.

Jens and I enjoyed a brief and amiable exchange. Siss helped herself to a paper cup of black coffee and joined us in a round of delightful conversation. I introduced them. After a brief exchange of friendly banter, Siss broached the subject that was foremost in her mind.

Previously, she asked me to explain the how and why of our space station and lunar rendezvous. I explained it all patiently. Unfortunately, mine was a layman's understanding. Siss, ever curious, sought a more scientific explanation. Jens was only too happy to explain – one scientific mind to another.

Siss was fascinated. The language of science was beyond my ken. What was riveting to the African was incomprehensible babble for me. I preferred to mingle with the less erudite.

We heard the engines whirr. The monsters were not as tumultuous as the liquid fuel variety, but they certainly made their presence known. A few minutes later, someone looked through one of the tiny view ports.

"We're moving," she announced.

No one noticed when the mighty Space Master began to roll, but there was no denying that we were approaching parking-lot speed.

"Ladies and gentlemen," a voice boomed over the PA. "We have started our takeoff roll. This would be a good time to find a seat and strap yourself in. When we leave the ground, we will climb at roughly thirty-five degrees. Once in the air, you will be free to move about the passenger cabin but be very careful. We will maintain a steep climb for a considerable while. Handball playing is prohibited. If you have any questions, the relief flight crew will field them. Be advised, they're a surly lot, so good luck."

We were all togged up in dark blue flight suits. Only the flight crew wore grey. If they were on flight duty, they wore a yellow vest.

We passengers prudently selected a seat and buckled in. After two more minutes, we were traveling at speed along the longest runway in the Western Hemisphere. There was a longer Space Master runway in Mongolia which was seldom employed but was at Space Master disposal should it be required.

Sooner than expected, we were pressed back in our seats. It was no longer possible to see through any of the tiny view ports since they were mounted too high. The electric powered fan "jet" made quite a racket. The vibrations made me very uncomfortable. Not once, during our training, were we told about noise and vibrations. It made me wonder: what else had they neglected to tell us?

Suddenly, the vibration stopped. Moments later, gravity planted us firmly in our seats as the aircraft's attitude was alarmingly nose up. Thank you, Mr. Pilot for telling us about that!

Over ninety minutes passed before one bold adventurer (or a desperate one), unhitched and struggled to get to his feet. There were seats and overhead rails. When one is confronted with an urgent need to visit the little boys' room, one learns to adjust to a steeply angled floor in a matter of seconds. Upon inspection, I discovered that the "men's rooms" were modified to accommodate steep-angle discharge. I'm certain the women's rooms were similarly adjusted, but I neither inspected nor inquired.

Five hours into our flight, the angle of our climb eased noticeably. We were able to navigate around the cabin with relative ease. We were informed that we were "cruising" at one hundred thousand feet. We were on course and on schedule.

With this reassuring news, we ambled to the "kitchen" and selected a meal. The persnickety lined up to use the "zapper." Most of us, including Siss, managed to gulp our rations at cabin temperature.

The noise of the fans receded. There wasn't enough air to maintain the cacophony, but the vibrations continued.

"I've had about all the fun I can stand for one day," I told Siss. "I think I'll look for my bunk and take a nap."

"We're over there," she pointed to the starboard sleeping balcony.

"*We?*"

She nodded, not the least concerned.

I expected the cots to be segregated. Well, they were. Siss and I constituted a "team." Jens, the team of one, was assigned a cot at the tail end of the Base One trio. Siss was next to me. My head would be separated from her feet by a quarter inch of INSPAD synthetic ply.

I suppose there was no need to be prudish. To make the sign of the nocturnal tree sloth, two people had to be both malleable and acrobatic. There's no doubt that people have tried. The Space Master would constitute the pinnacle of any Mile High Club. However, I wondered how many casualties resulted from such ambitious activities.

I wondered if anyone injured themselves while boinking. How could they do the jobs they were tasked? There are no chiropractors in space – few doctors at all, in fact. An amateur might be talked through setting bones or making a sling, but . . .

I was too tired to even think about it.

TRANSFERS ONE AND TWO

I never got a good look at the Space Station. I was told it was modeled upon the station dreamed up by the von Braun team when they were still puttering around with the von Braun designed V-2s for his new employer, the United States Government. It was a circular wheel with most of the consumables stored in the hub together with the oxygenator, mini-reactor, emergency batteries, water system, and supply storage. It was canted 38 degrees from earth's equator and set in motion by six small rockets attached to the hull. It "spun" (a word I don't associate with a slow-motion rotation) enough to produce centrifugal force enough to keep the people and equipment from floating around. In earth values, the station simulated roughly (very roughly) a "gravity" of point 37 of one g.

Rotating as it does, the station was basically a gyro. It would take a determined effort to knock it out of whack, but the scientists didn't want to take any chances. They lobbied INSPAD to keep transients off the vehicle. Those assigned to the station worked mainly on the study of earth's meteorology – not so much weather forecasting (the weather satellites handled that) but studying weather systems and cycles. Other scientists performed biological experiments and there was a concerted effort to map and determine the orbits of bodies in the asteroid belt.

Originally, the radio and optical equipment was computer controlled so that the equipment would be aimed at a particular point and remain fixed despite the rotation of the station. The computers, however, were foiled by certain variables that no human could detect or correct. The aiming point would slip, ever so slightly, from time to time. That was maddening enough in itself, but it, also, skewed a lot of data. Relief was found when INSPAD assembled a stable platform.

The RePlat (so designated) was in a slightly lower orbit. Its orbit mirrored the station's orbit so precisely that, in three years, it's distance from the station had increased by a mere eight inches.

Researchers on the station could point three "telescopes," three radio transceivers, and two radar devices and keep them "locked on target" for the time desired. All information was beamed to the station, picked up by any of the several arrays, and transferred to the proper equipment.

I was reliably told that observers on the station could spot RePlat with the naked eye if the sun hit it just right. It was eighteen earth miles from the station, but when people spotted a star where no star could be, it could only be RePlat.

Six tons of supplies and equipment were transferred from the Space Master to the station by a team of Space Monkeys. The specially designed crates were easily moved because they were, essentially, weightless. The crates, however, had mass. In space, when mass meets with mass, it's a mess. For that reason, Space Monkeys *only* were allowed to execute space transfers. On the moon everyone was expected to pitch in.

It would take us three earth days to reach the station's apogee. This was the launch point for those lunar bound. Because the transfer of supplies to the station was a delicate procedure, the Space Monkeys worked in three-hour shifts for most of our wait time.

Finally, the task was completed. We took aboard two Monkeys from the station, two scientists, and the station commander, a grizzled man in his fifties whose nine-month tour was done. He wasn't so much a scientist as an INSPAD "spy." I do not imply that his reports about the care, maintenance, and functions of the station are not important. They are. However, if anyone has a negative attitude about INSPAD or is convinced they are being treated unfairly, the station commander becomes that tattle-tale-in-chief.

With the veterans secure on board, the Space Master transferred two scientists, two monkeys, and a new station commander. When that procedure was completed, the Space Monkeys readied the Luner Schooner. They stowed the supplies and equipment destined for the moon bases; topped off the liquid fuel required and made the vehicle ready for flight.

Next, the two-person flight crew was hustled aboard. Three hours later, we Moon People were suited up and transferred. If our sleeping accommodations were Spartan on the Space Master, they were luxurious when compared with what awaited us on the Luner Schooner. If Siss were on one end of the cabin, and I was on the other, I'd need to have at least three others change places with me before I could get to her. We "Dark Siders" kept near each other to avoid creating ill will.

INSPAD assured me that my actual destination would be debated.

"If you don't hear anything while you're at the station, assume that your Dark Side billet is approved."

Nothing was addressed to me the entire time we kept station with the station.

Very likely, the geniuses at INSPAD just forgot.

There were two pilots. In truth, we didn't need one at all. Anyone who could operate a basic SynMax could fly the Lunar Schooner. Still, the rocket scientists insisted on doing things right. The computer was set, and the countdown was automatic. The pilot would do nothing more than monitor the system readouts. The second pilot was an apprentice – a trainee. He would take command should the pilot be killed or turn up missing.

I envied that pilot. He had half as much room as we peons and the most comfortable seat this side of Atlanta. The great thing about a weightless environment is that a person could lounge in a seat for days and never suffer cramps or saddle sores.

There was no announcement.

When the computer clock reached zero, there was a loud pop followed by twelve seconds of hissing. Nobody warned us. We thought there was a hull leak, and we made certain our pressure suits were nearby.

It takes so little to escape the space station at apogee. A quick burn of seconds moved us out of the last few miles of the earth's gravitational pull. We "puttered" along at slightly over a hundred miles an hour. By the time we reached the break, we were doing little more than twenty miles an hour.

"Capture," the pilot announced.

We were now in the Moon's gravitational pull. Our speed would increase gradually until it was time for insertion. We'd make two orbits of the moon to check all the systems in our craft and on the moon. Once everything was functioning as designed, we'd burn enough to bleed off speed.

It was a tediously long process, but the Lunar Schooner carried very little fuel. The lion's share was reserved for launching from the moon. There was a modest amount of fuel near Base One, in case of emergency, but it had yet to be tapped.

We waited and waited and waited as our orbit decayed and the moon grew larger and larger in our view ports. As with all the flight plans to date, everything was timed down to the microsecond. The final breaking burn occurred at exactly the right moment and lasted for exactly the right length. That left us vertical. We were sinking. We were in free fall. Granted, the lunar gravity is much less than earth's, but when you realize you are falling thousands of feet – and picking up steam every moment – it is pucker time.

There were two radars aboard. If the readings of one did not coincide exactly with the other, we would abort. The pilot had only two tasks: watch the radar data and keep his finger on the abort trigger. One of the pilots confessed, later, landing the Lunar Schooner is the most frightening task in the whole history of civilization. If the landing rockets failed to fire, if the thrust was not exact, if the pilot was a fraction of a second late in pulling the abort trigger, the Lunar Schooner and everything aboard would be reduced to a smudge on the lunar surface.

No sooner had I made peace with my maker than I got the most violent (and painful) kick in the ass. My body was traveling at, seemingly, thousands of miles an hour in one direction, and there was, in an instant, a violent lurch in the opposite direction. My stomach and liver continued downward while my kidneys and heart were eager to ascend. I must have weighed a thousand pounds at that moment – and a thousand pounds on the moon is chicken feed compared with earth measure.

For ten horrifying, painful, endless seconds the retro rockets pushed and strained. The moment our pads touched the lunar landing area, the retro rockets shut down and we settled onto the surface soft as an angle's kiss.

It took everyone, to include the pilot and the spare, a minute or two to get air back into our lungs and life back in our trembling bodies. No one spoke or moved for several seconds.

"Cheated death again," someone murmured.

I think it was the pilot.

Gradually, we unlatched our safety harnesses and began to move about.

We were ordered into our pressure suits prior to descent. I thought, at the time, it was a foolish procedure. Since we were forbidden to put on our helmets, the suits afforded no protection should there be a mishap. Suddenly, I realized why we suited up. In our confined space and after the ride from hell, we were trembling so much and left so weak by the assault on our bodies (and interior parts) it would take us weeks to get into those damned pressure suits. As it was, we had only to dawn our helmets and latch them. Even trembling fingers and unresponsive muscles could do that much.

We had to get out so those due for evacuation could get aboard. The Dark Side refugee and two Space Monkeys entered the Schooner soon after it emptied. Siss went directly into Base One with a "replacement." Jens and I waited outside the crawler as those monkeys due for rotation left it together with the departing scientists from Dark Side. I couldn't understand the delay. I remained a bit shaken up by the abrupt landing. I wanted to get into the crawler and take off my "hat." With luck, I might be able to rest horizontally or a reasonable *fac simile*.

Say what you will about the Space Monkeys (and many people do), they are sticklers for cleanliness. They scrubbed and polished prior to rotating back to earth, and those remaining scrubbed and polished before allowing the "newbies" access.

When we were finally allowed to board, I let Jens go first. I wasn't being polite. My nerves, muscles and bones remained unreliable. If I was going to fall face down into the dusty, rocky lunar surface, I preferred to have as few witnesses as possible. One of the monkeys, a veteran, diagnosed my condition and came to my aid. He took me by the arm and guided me to the airlock.

Only One Customer at a Time

The handwritten sign was affixed over the airlock. If it had been there long, the fastidious monkeys would have to redo the sign every few days. Any written message exposed to undiluted sunlight would vanish quickly.

Finally, it was my turn. How I wanted to be on the other side of that airlock! Regardless, Mel's relentless cursing and coaching (and, in my case, a dope slap) kicked in. This was one of those potentially dangerous transfers I would face. I did as I was trained. I was cautious and not afraid to take my time. I pulled the hatch behind me and dogged it down. I made certain the hatch was closed and sealed before turning my attention to the valves. I monitored the needle (no digital readouts on the crawlers) and made certain the pressure was within the required tolerances. Next, I turned the wheel reeling in the interior bolts. I expected the hatch to pop open. Alas, the airlock pressure was well matched with the interior atmosphere. Cautiously, I stepped into the crawler. Regulations required that I keep my hat on until the vehicle commander notified us that the airlock was empty and secure. I was very close to violating that rule. Had I, they'd have stuffed me right back into the Schooner and sent home with the rest of the "retirees." At that point, severance pay wouldn't look so good. A portion of the next several months would be spent in the sneezer.

Finally, it was all aboard.

Personal gear was stowed in a small cargo bay designed for that purpose. I'd have no access until it was off loaded at Dark Side. However, Space Monkeys had a network of sorts. Jens, the replacement Space Monkey, and I were each handed a small vile of Russian vodka. We couldn't drink until we got the all-clear, but we all had experienced the bone-rattle of a lunar landing. A good jolt of joy-juice would provide us with amazing recuperative powers.

A pressure suited figure from a hatchway above our heads gave us a thumbs up followed by a two-handed gesture resembling the removal of a helmet. To verify his message, he quickly unlatched and removed his hat.

I did not have to be told twice. My helmet was off, and two shots of vodka were down my throat within seconds. I gasped for air. What I got was the foulest breath I'd ever experienced. It may have resembled earth air, but it was unpleasant. My lungs felt as if they were being dipped in bronze.

"You Duvall?" our airlock assistant asked.

"You Tarzan," I replied.

My voice came in a higher pitch that I didn't recognize.

"They tell me you're the INSPAD spy."

Crying in a bucket! Rolf was after his pound of flesh. Doubtless, every person on Luna had me pegged as an agent for a corrupt and despised agency.

"I ain't no spy!"

I wish I hadn't said that. Some wise ass would assume that my double negative constituted a positive.

"If you say so," the burly mechanic responded.

He did not sound genuine.

"Dr. Schulte," he said as if I didn't exist. "How'd you like to drive for a while?"

This prompted a classic double take.

As he shook the cobwebs out of his head, I shook them out of mine. I was accused of being a spy, and the accuser asked Jens Schulte to violate INSPAD directives. That could mean that he didn't believe that malarkey, or he didn't expect me to report back.

Everyone knew that driving the crawlers at eight to twelve miles an hour was tooth-achingly boring. The Monkeys routinely passed this task off on whatever sucker happened to be handy. Still, it was strictly *verboten*.

At that moment, my eye caught a large metal protrusion that contained steerage linkage or a pneumatic shock assembly of some kind. I could not read the Cyrillic portion of the manufacturer's plate, but I had no problem reading the Roman letters.

RURIK

If I wasn't a spy before, I signed up in that instant.

In one of our rare, reflective moments, Elena revealed something which was of little consequence at the time. She related that Fedor's father, when he still headed up his company, was asked by INSPAD to submit plans for a moon crawler. If his plans were selected from among the other applicants, he'd be awarded the contract to build two crawlers. The major engineering feature was that the crawlers must be disassembled for transport to the moon where they would be reassembled by a crew in pressure suits. The challenge intrigued the old man, but he recognized, early on, that INSPAD consisted of unprincipled and corrupt businessmen – the kind of people who would cut costs at every corner, who would build a bridge on the cheap and pocket the money they'd make from phony purchase orders – and if the bridge collapsed and people were killed . . . oh, well.

This was back in the early days of INSPAD. It would take the world a decade and a half to figure out what Fedor's father knew from the get-go. He refused to have anything to do with INSPAD. He'd authorize no drafting of crawler plans, and no sales of parts of equipment to INSPAD.

Nothing.

Fedor, upon inheriting the business, continued the boycott of INSPAD.

One the moon, I discovered a unit made by Rurik Industries, a world leader in heavy equipment. This was not something INSPAD made from stolen plans or a copycat made by industrial spies. Such equipment would not have the factory name and a serial number. Someone, somewhere, was being very dishonest. Of course, Fedor or his father *might* have lied. That was a possibility. However, I knew from firsthand experience that INSPAD lies – and steals. I, myself, stole from the stealers.

Before I took another breath, I made a rule: keep your mouth shut. The thugs at INSPAD obviously did not think it worth the bother to remove identification plates from stolen parts. If they were so careless about these *little* details, there were probably a lot more *little* things. Perhaps, if I compiled a large enough list of *little* things, a few *big* things (and people) my topple over from the accumulated weight.

OVER THE POLE

The crawler began with a lurch. After four hours of loading, we began our trek from Base One to Dark Side. Much of the cargo we carried was slung under the behemoth. A few of the items, slated to be slung, found their way into the "living side" of the air lock. For starters the vets (a euphemism for anyone who had served one cycle and was starting another) were chomping down salted peanuts. The monkey who boarded with us did not get any. Jens and I did not get any. It was clear that those new to the grind were not yet entitled to those smuggled goods monkeys always managed to procure.

I adjusted to the arid air and its peculiar odor quickly. One of the vets told me that after two or three days, I'd no longer notice it.

Jens was driving. I opted to "spy." No one discouraged me from moving about. During my tour, I kept my eyes peeled for stolen mechanical parts. I noticed three, but no more clearly marked items from Rurik. Two of the monkeys who handled much of the cargo were stretched out on their tiny bunks. One was reading the *Feed-Box* newspaper. It was only a few days old. I wondered if they placed any bets. There was no chance of phoning their bookies on earth, but they could bet with each other. Of course, the "players" must wait three or four months to learn the results.

The crawlers "commander" was a balding vet who had fourteen cycles under his belt. This man was on the moon when the forerunner of the modern crawler was little more than a modified backhoe with a pressurized driver's canopy. Daniel Boone and Kit Carson surged through every artery in his body. Either he had several ex-wives to support, or he had run afoul of some Chinese tong. In a very real sense, this crusty old coot created Base One and Dark Side.

As an aside, Base Two was constructed by a private firm. By all reports, they did a cracker-jack job, but INSPAD didn't care for any freelancers. Apparently, there were fewer opportunities for graft and skimming off the top if you hired a reputable firm and allowed them to do things their own way.

Captain Ryan Jenkins leaned against the bulkhead and chewed his peanuts with much relish. He was "supervising" Jens. In truth, he was only three feet away if Jens had a question or needed help. He'd seen it all, and he'd been instrumental in the greatest scientific endeavor since the IGY of a century before.

"You won't get us lost?" I asked of Jens, still not used to the sound of my moon voice.

"Just stay in the tracks," he replied.

There could be no mistaking the path carved out of moondust by the crawler on many previous journeys. We were not going over the moon's north pole. Instead, the journey to Dark Side took us over the "eastern" shoulder of the moon. It was not a straight line. Hills, craters, and "suspicious soft spots" must be avoided. There were several serious detours. Some might have been unnecessary, but no crawler has been lost or damaged to date. A navigable path in hand was worth all the short-cuts through iffy geography.

As another aside, there remains considerable debate amongst the scientific community about directions on the moon. There are three major proposals under review. The discussions concerning these options are heated and verbose. The system used by the crawler crews is simple. It was established by Jenkins himself.

From the moon, he could see the area where earth's North Pole is located. He pronounced Moon "North" to be analogous to earth's. Facing moon north, to his right was moon east; to his left was moon west; behind him was moon south. It was so simple and practical that the scientific community couldn't comprehend it. Thus, while moon directions and coordinates are hotly contested, those who live and work on the moon use the Jinkins method. It gets the job done.

"You wanna have a go in a couple hours," the grizzled old bird asked of me.

"I was hardly through the airlock when I was accused of being an INSPAD spy," I announced.

My attitude was unmistakable, even in my unfamiliar high-pitched moon voice. Kit Carson Jinkins didn't interrupt his goober intake. He'd seen people come and go. I was just the latest in a long line of neophytes.

"So?" he dared. "If you're here, you do as you're told. At the end of the day, you need us to get off this rock. We don't need you at all."

Message received. There was considerable doubt that I would be allowed off "this rock." That doubt would shrink if I decided to be contentious.

"I'm not a spy," I responded. "I asked to go Dark Side because it is as far away as I can get from INSPAD. I'll help you and your crew anyway I can. The same with the scientists."

He nodded. I doubt he cared a pinch of owl dung one way or the other. Ultimately, my life was in his hands.

"Driving at a fast walk is boring as hell," he announced. "Anyone who volunteers to stand a watch is our friend."

"Consider me your friend."

He nodded again and continued munching.

After five hours, it was my turn.

Captain (Commander, Skipper, Big Cheese – whatever) Jenkins had retired to a game of four-handed spades down "below." The person who replaced him was that same punk who fingered me as a spy. The less intercourse I had with him, the better. I suppose the crew kept watch over the unauthorized drivers to prevent some rouge elephant from tearing off into the uncharted regions of the moon. It took two scientists, Jenkins, and three hardy souls, and three months to lay out the Dark Side Route. Moon quakes, sink holes, dangerous outcrops, and a myriad of additional considerations required a step-by-step, yard-by-yard approach to the problem. The original survey team took weight as their primary concern.

Any item weighing one hundred pounds on earth would tip the scales at approximately sixteen and a half pounds on the moon. The packing cases used by INSPAD were red lined at ninety pounds. Therefore, the Space Monkeys (always working in pairs) can (and do) handle the fifteen pounds with ease. The problem on the moon was hardly ever weight; the problem was bulk – thus two monkeys per crate.

The weight of the crawler was such that, on earth, it would be nearly impossible to move. Less weight (on the moon) meant a smaller electric motor. If, however, a crawler got stuck or wedged between moon obstacles, the chances of escape were problematical at best. Electric power plants just don't provide the punch that earth-moving equipment requires.

The outer hull of the crawler consists of solar panels. There is, also, a row of panels running vertical down the long axis of the vehicle. From a distance, it looks very much like those fascinating drawings of the stegosaurus in my elementary school science book. There were storage batteries which could keep the crawler moving at five (earth) miles an hour for twelve hours. That was the "predicted" and the "design" limit life of the batteries. No one was anxious to find out.

Though we traveled to the Dark Side, cycles were predicated on sun power. When the moon's orbit takes it between the earth and the sun, it is "high noon" on the dark side. When people on earth look at the sky and find no moon, or only a sliver of the moon, rest assured, it is extremely bright on the so-called dark side.

Jens was correct. It is impossible to get lost on Highway Dark Side. The accumulated treks to and fro made an unmistakable path.

I settled down into the "driver's seat" and strapped in – just in case a moon deer ran right out in front of the crawler, forcing me to hit the brake. I'd be safe. The monkeys below would still be traveling at five to twelve miles an hour. There would be injuries. Jens was warned about sudden stops. When my turn came, I was reminded again.

Emphatically!

The accelerator was as in the cars of old, and steering was facilitated by two "laterals."

Pulling back on the left lateral retards the treads on that side of the vehicle. The treads on the right continue to move at normal speed; thus, the crawler turns (skids, actually) left. By pulling all the way back on one lateral and accelerating, the crawler makes a very fast, very sharp turn (not recommended).

Within a few minutes, I understood why the monkeys hated to drive. Watching paint dry is more exciting.

Three hours into my turn, Jenkins called a halt. I stopped the crawler and moved the transmission lever to neutral. Within minutes, there were three monkeys and Jenkins unloading crates. They carried them to a pile of material only a few meters off the "road." It took them twelve minutes to move two crates and position them to Jenkins's satisfaction.

Twenty minutes after I was ordered to stop, I was ordered to "proceed."

Jenkins came up to relieve the monkey keeping an eye on the driver.

"If they go ahead with their plans to lay a land line to Dark Side," he explained to me, "They will place a way station here."

"Why?" I asked.

It was a reasonable question. It would be cheaper and quicker to just lay the line from huge spools attached to the back of the crawler.

"INSPAD." Jenkins replied.

That may have been the answer, but his explanation did not explain the reason. Of course, INSPAD directives and logic were, as expected, strangers.

The final portion of our transit was driven by two of the monkeys. We were out of contact with Earth Side and had been for some while. There was an "evening" transmission from Base One checking with Base Two and the mobile units. After everyone checked in, and Base One knew everyone was still alive and listening, there followed news and alerts. Meteor showers were predictable, and all the moon personnel were advised. If there were special orders or requests, they were handled during the evening broadcast.

The morning transmissions were the time to place requests for supplies or the report of any medical "problems" during the night. The most important information, however, were readouts of air and water reserves and remaining consumables (food).

Since I would be on the dark side, and out of reach of both the moon stations and the earth stations, I'd not be privy to any of these daily reports.

The procedure for exchanging personnel on the moon is much like a prisoner exchange during the Napoleonic Wars. The crawler growled to a stop and shut down all but interior lighting and life support systems. This occupied, roughly, three minutes. As if on cue, a pressure-suited form emerged from the Dark Side airlock. He stood forlorn and still. Jens egressed the crawler first since he was the lone man's legitimate replacement. I saw them shake hands just prior to being "urged" into the airlock.

I don't recall being informed of the identity of the departing scientist, but I shook hands with whoever he was. This ritual concluded, he stepped into the crawler airlock simultaneously with Jens closing the Dark Side airlock after him. For nearly five, extremely eerie minutes, I was alone on the lunar surface.

As I stepped toward the Dark Side airlock, a Space Monkey stepped out of the crawler. It is strictly forbidden for anyone to perform any task on the lunar surface when alone. Therefore, the monkey stood stock still as I entered the base "guest room."

It was stuffier in the moon base than it had been in the crawler.

A middle-aged man with sharp features and a splash of gray in his dark brown hair helped me out of my pressure suit. Once reduced to only my flight suit, the gentleman extended his hand.

"I'm Henri dela Cour," he informed as he shook my hand with genuine enthusiasm.

"I'm Brice Duvall."

The man smiled and began an oration in his native tongue.

"I'm not French," I interrupted.

"Oh," he said as if caught with his hand in the cookie jar. "*Pardon.*"

"I'm not a scientist," I explained quickly. "I won the INSPAD contest: free moon trip."

"Rigged, of course," he nodded, knowingly.

"Indeed, it was," I assured.

"No matter. Join us in the common while the monkeys place some contraband in the airlock. It's Christmas when the crawler comes. They leave us nice little gifts."

I was on the dark side of the moon. There were two men with whom I would spend three months. Nearby, there were five Space Monkeys, men who were paid exceedingly well by the mob because the moon bases could not survive without them. The Space Monkeys gave themselves liberties and privileges that the mob dared not deny. This, however, was the first time moonnicks (a pejorative employed by INSPAD) were openly praised.

Dark Side Station was in the early stages of "sunrise." The shadows were long, but the objects casting them were clearly visible. I could see the superstructure of the station from some distance. The huge SETI dish was a monument too obvious to miss in the lunar landscape. There was a smaller dish opposite. Gradually, I could make out the "observation deck," a low-profile protrusion which nestled between the huge globe of the oxygenator and the smaller, but equally protuberant water "reservoir." Further out was the reactor, supplying power for the facility and its batteries.

The worst-case scenario was a large meteor would strike a facility. It, and everyone stationed there, would be vaporized. The chances of this were slim – very, very slim. However, smaller meteors rained down constantly. These small objects could visit devastation on any of the facilities. Therefore, with every crawler visit, an extra layer of moon dust and debris was piled atop the exposed portions excepting the crawlers and the oxygenators. It was all carefully planned, of course. If the weight of the moon dirt became too much, it would crush the facility and everyone inside. I suppose, in battlefield terminology, the moon bases were fortified and camouflaged bunkers.

The Dark Side airlock emptied onto a small platform. From the platform, one must descend several steps to get to the living area. The crawlers, and their primitive predecessors, dredged out a series of trenches, covered them with heavy metal sheets, and buried them. These oversized ant hills were designed to keep the vital gasses contained inside, and the death-is-certain vacuum out.

The Dark Side Station is very primitive when compared with the older, more extensive bases. There are four coffin-like niches, each designated as a sleeping area. They look like something one would find in a Japanese capsule hotel. There was room for your ass, a blanket or two, and a reading light. One must read in the prone position – there was no room to read sitting up.

There was a "hallway" along which were the bedrooms. If two people met, one of them would be obliged to back up. The "bedrooms" and the "hallway" emptied into the "common."

There was a small square table around which were arrayed four "moon chairs." I suspect they were originally movie props used in westerns or action pictures when an actor is expected to slam someone over the head or across the shoulders. Those chairs, as would ours, would shatter and fly to pieces. On the moon, they were functional. That low moon gravity sure comes in handy.

It is best to stoop over when entering the common – unless one was below average height. Meals and meetings took place here – when mealtimes coincided. Many games of cards had been played on the flimsy, plastic table. The only currency that changed hands consisted of space junk – broken tools, pencils, erasers, paper clips, buttons and the like. It was a house rule, at least during my tenure, that all the tokens were returned to the game box to be divided equally among the players when a new round was in the offing.

Dr. dela Cour did not pause at the common. He led me along to the workstations. Possibly by design, the scientific portion of the station was spacious. I suppose this encouraged the scientists to spend most of their time doing what they had come here to study. Eight computers, each programmed for a specific research area, were aligned on proper tables with proper writing surfaces and stacks of printer paper in evidence. The chairs were of the metal folding variety, but they were earth chairs and did not have to be pampered like the moon chairs.

Considerable instrumentation was visible above the computer array.

There was a hatch leading to the "observation" area. We did not ascend. The hatch was opened only to allow people to enter and leave. In the event of a hull puncture, the underground portion of the station would remain functional. The person, or persons, in the observation area would be dead before they had time to blink.

"You would do us a big service if you would handle the SETI program," Dr. dela Cour announced.

"I'm not a scientist," I reminded him.

"What science? The program is all mapped out. Every two weeks, you change to the coordinates which are printed in the mission book. You check data once or twice a day. If you detect anything that may have an intelligent origin, note it and the people on the ground will analyze it. We're in daylight now, so the sun forces us to suspend for the duration. When it gets dark again, you just point the dish and let the computer do the work."

That sounded easy enough. It would take very little time (as if I had so much to do), and it would free Drs. Dela Cour and Schulte from a menial task which, likely, would not result in anything meaningful.

Back in the common, we found Jens sitting in one of the chairs. He would get a working tour later. Presently, he was patiently waiting for his equipment and personal items to join him.

I wasn't certain a Frenchman and a German would play well together, but they got off to an auspicious start. Jens spoke to his French colleague in his native tongue. Henri responded by speaking to the German in *his* own tongue. Both ends of this bi-lingual exchange were beyond my schoolboy knowledge. They both spoke English, fluently. English, after all, was the international language of science. Were my station mates sparing with each other or were they simply harvesting the fruit of months of labor in learning the other's language?

Tune in next week.

There was a closed-circuit camera pointed directly at the crawler's designated unloading zone. It had a fisheye lens so we could see a vast area though the images were distorted. The monitor was mounted above, between the common and the workstation. We knew the airlock was clear when we watched the monkeys re-mount the crawler. We waited a few moments. Finally, a signal light flashed from the driver's station.

"All clear," Henri concluded.

He led the way to the air lock.

I was eager to have my meager possessions, my books with which I would pass the time free from INSPAD's beck and call. Maybe, the crime family could do me serious harm – might even ruin me financially. However, for ninety plus days, I was beyond their reach and, blessings be upon me, beyond their voice.

Jens wasn't nearly as concerned about his personal items. He, like Henri, acted like a child on Christmas morning. It was an open secret that the Space Monkeys shared in the wealth of their smuggling. Happy monkeys and unhappy scientists made a volatile mix in an artificial environment. By tacit agreement, the two "labor unions" preferred to live in peace.

"That is damned nice of them," Henri said, in English. "The guys outdid themselves."

With only four exceptions, all the Space Monkeys were male. Female monkeys were highly prized, but not for the most obvious reason. Nearly all the monkeys were muscle, sinew, and bulk. Inevitably, there was a space on the crawler or at a facility where access was physically impossible. Slim, lithe, smallish women, however, could perform maintenance and address emergencies the burly men couldn't reach. In fact, the smaller the woman, the more prized her expertise. Being small was a decided advantage, but women must be as adroit in mechanics as their male counterparts. They must, also, be physically strong and mentally tough. The derisive comments about women drivers were standard fare with the crawler crews.

Nevertheless, I liked "the guys." It was a term of endearment. The "official" Space Monkeys was so impersonal. True, *the guys* is too gender specific for the fastidious, earth-bound social pontificators, but they don't have to rub elbows with those dedicated (and VERY well-paid) individuals who kept the moon's scientists in business. Further, I was assured that the certified female Space Monkeys are delighted with the moniker. When a woman won the approval of her co-workers, she was proud to be considered one of *the guys*.

Henri's appreciation was predicated on three large cylinders.

Oxygen!

Jens and I lugged one of the metal tubes into a bunk (easy to do in reduced gravity). Henri and I filled a second bunk. Henri and I wrestled the third one into a resting place. Before we considered anything else, we removed the protective hood on the first tube. Henri, the senior in rank because of his time on station, opened the valve. We enjoyed the welcome hiss as the life-giving gas escaped into our smelly, stale, restricted living area.

We could hear the noise of the machinery. The oxygenator now had a fighting chance to recycle properly. Our environment must remain at a fixed pressure, or the airlocks mightn't function properly. Further, too much pressure might create a breech and we'd die. The equipment kept the pressure within acceptable parameters, but the noise indicated that the inanimate motors, gears, and vents were pleased to deal with pure, unadulterated, oxygen. Other gasses would have to be added or we would soon be on an oxygen high or, as a former moon scientist once said, "moon inebriation." Before emptying the other cylinders, we stowed the other items left by "the guys." There were provisions, of course, and most of them were stowed under the long table in the work area. It made things very crowded, but space accrued with disturbing rapidity. There was, also, the extra bunk which could be filled without disturbing anyone.

It took us two hours to move and stow.

"Let's open the last cylinder after breakfast," Henri suggested.

Jens and I were feeling rather giddy. We were in no mood to challenge authority.

Henri pointed to an analog clock affixed to the wall of the common. It was recessed so its minimal thickness would not encroach upon the minimal living space allotted to us. The first station commander set the clock arbitrarily since sunrise and sunset are nowhere near the earthly phenomenon. Quickly, I guesstimate Dark Side "breakfast time" (0600) to the time in Atlanta. Our breakfast would be mid-afternoon at Happy Burger; Elena would be in the early stages of getting ready for work.

I JOIN THE WORK FORCE

Knowing, or strongly suspecting, that my presence in Dark Side would meet with saturnine reactions from the scientists, I opted to promote some goodwill. Mel knew a guy who knew a guy who was thick with several monkeys. I placed an order and a modest renumeration. I did not, however, expect much if anything. However, among the items placed in the airlock was an innocuous package labeled DUVALL.

I carried my treasure to my bunk and rested it atop the oxygen cylinder. With trembling fingers, I undid the package and was excited to find a small coffee maker, a packaged brick of German coffee and a large thermos filled with genuine earth water.

"Gentlemen," I announced loudly (in a voice much nearer my earth voice), "I brought you a nice housewarming gift."

Jens had been in the "bathroom" and was first to appear. Henri was busy organizing our "consumables." He lingered long enough to establish some sort of order. When he did arrive, his eyes were as large as the headlights on the crawler.

"Dr. dela Cour," Jens stammered with some difficulty.

The rest of his speech was in French, but I hardly required a translator.

As the senior member of the station and *de facto* commander, Henri must be informed of any startling developments. He appeared slightly annoyed, but sunlight curtailed much of his scripted program. There was no reason to hurry with his current task, but it would be a relief to have it out of the way.

"Ach, Du lieber Gott!"

If this continued for the duration of my cycle, I'd forget which one was French, and which wasn't. Despite my discomfiture, there was no doubt about either Henri's surprise or the glee in his expression.

"Just a little something," I muttered, suddenly embarrassed.

Jens and Henri, exercising their bi-lingual mode of conversation, were concerned that the coffee maker might not match with the battery ports. I had a strong suspicion that two accomplished scientists could overcome minor problems matching direct current with such a weakling of an appliance. It took them less than a quarter hour to fashion a coupling.

"The best way to test this is to make a pot," Jens whispered.

He was not afraid that his English would be overheard. Jens was still in a state of shock and anticipation.

Carefully – oh, so very carefully – the earth water was poured into the vessel. It would be both a shame and a waste to spill so much as a drop. Next, the coffee filter was inserted. It took two scientists working together three minutes to seed the annoying filter "just so." This experiment was very important to them. Everything must be done in accordance with a tolerance of exactitude. The carafe was inserted and adjusted so the handle was "just so." Finally, with a trembling finger, Henri pressed the "engage" button.

Eight or nine interminable seconds ticked past. No one breathed. Then – a gurgle! Then, another. Then, another.

We were breathing again. The smell of coffee, mixed with the oxygen-boosted air, made our noses prickle.

"Gentlemen," Henri announced in Oxford English, "I order everyone to stand down. This is an official work break. Coffee first, then we will return to work."

The sun was out. There was precious little to do. Both scientists were engaged in programs that required a night sky. When the sun was out, we were expected to engage in rock pounding and collecting. Geologists love such opportunities, but we had none on station. Therefore, the basic rule is "if you see something pretty or unusual, note the location and collect it." These "samples" were stored outside the station. There was no container, so we would just toss our finds into the existing pile of samples. One can "toss" a rock quite a distance on the moon. Naturally, rock tossing was the official sport of Dark Side. There were rules, of course, as there are in any sport.

Do Not Throw in the Direction of the Facility.

That was the primary restriction. After that, the rules were pretty much up for grabs.

We sat at the table and watched the coffee maker as if we expected it to burst into song. In a way, it did. The noises we were hearing were familiar on earth, but they were lacking on the moon.

When the appliance ceased gurgling and began spitting steam, Jens collected three cups and brought them to the table.

"Brice," Henri decreed. "You do the honors."

"No, sir," I protested. "I don't want the responsibility. I can't handle the pressure."

Henri eyed Jens closely.

If we messed this up, our next attempt would be with recycled and heavily filtered water. It was a poor substitute for the real thing.

"Okay," Henri sighed, employing the one English word found in every (known) earth language. "If I mess this up, remember, you forced me to do this."

Carefully, and slowly, he pulled the carafe out from under its hiding place. His hand shook as he poured the steaming nectar into my mug. It continued to shake as he served Jens. He paused for a moment and took a deep breath before filling his own mug. Without prompting, we held our mugs up and clicked them ever so delicately.

"Cheers," I said.

"*Zum Voll,*" Jens added, and I have no idea what he intended or what it meant.

For the next ten minutes, time ceased. No one spoke. Our taste buds frolicked.

I slept fitfully. Mine was the niche directly behind the common. The "navigation light" over the table was kept on. In case of an emergency, no one wanted to waste time looking for a light switch. True, there was a curtain, and I could have closed in much of the darkness. That lonely light, however, was my security blanket – my Teddy bear, as it were.

Jens was in the next niche on the airlock side. Henri was in the next den opposite me. There were no luxury suites in this hotel. If a member of the Saudi Royal Family visited Dark Side, he'd sleep in the same accommodations as we peasants.

The air in my confined space was moderated only moderately by our earlier release of pure oxygen. Upon our return, I'd ask Siss to propose ventilation fans be installed. They needn't be either large or of much voltage – just enough to establish an air current.

INSPAD would, at least, listen to Siss. I suspect that, upon my return, I'd be clapped in irons and locked away.

We woke and took "showers" prior to breakfast. Jens oversaw the coffee preparation. It would be made with recycled water, so we weren't expecting much. Nevertheless, adulterated coffee was better than none.

We released the last of the oxygen as planned. Refreshed and eager to work, we worried the empty cylinders into the air lock together with broken and discarded items. This accomplished, Henri signaled the crawler. He was flashed in return.

"What's wrong with a short-range radio?" I asked in my innocence.

"Transmissions on the Dark Side are strictly forbidden," Henri reminded. "If we allow transmissions to and from the crawler, we will be playing video games and relaying messages to people back home. We keep the lid on. No transmitting."

I learned enough Morse to have a jolly chat with the monkeys, but they were busy. Today was trash day. The monkeys would inspect the reactor, the oxygenator, the water system, and the exterior of our base. They would collect and remove everything in the air lock. The few discarded items Henri and the former cycle "stored" outside would be collected and removed.

Policy insists that one person always remain inside the habitation unit. Therefore, Henri escorted me outside to collect rock samples. He knew the terrain and those areas sampled previously. A rover would serve better. Geologists were ever ready to inspect virgin ground. The area within walking distance of Dark Side had been well covered. However, the fate of a rover rested with higher authority.

Don't hold your breath. The people in Project Control were nervous Nellies who hyperventilated whenever the crawler was out of communications range. A rover running around loose, without commo and systems telemetry, might result in mass heart attacks. It was bad enough that Henri and I had to communicate by hand signals only.

Well, that isn't quite right.

"When you transfer out," Henri began, "Stay close."

Was he afraid I'd run for the hills. Well, they did look inviting, not so far distant, gentle slopes, and no visible crags or crevices.

Henri was waiting when I stepped out onto the moon's surface. He motioned to me to come near. I was turned slightly, and I felt Henri's pressure suit against mine. His helmet touched mine; I could hear it.

"Can you hear me?"

The voice was muffled, but quite understandable.

"I hear fine," I replied.

"If we have something urgent to communicate, we touch helmets. Understand."

"Perfectly."

"If it isn't urgent, it's hand signs only."

"Understood."

"We can get far apart from each other, but we don't turn our backs – ever. No matter where we are, if one of us gets in trouble, the other will see and know instantly."

"Keep within sight of each other at all times," I summarized.

"Okay. Let's work our way southeast."

"I forgot my compass."

I heard the initiation of a chuckle before our helmets disengaged.

For the first part of our journey, I followed by staying on Henri's right so he could see me. Had he not given instructions, I'd have followed in his tracks. Had I, he wouldn't have me in sight. This way we could walk together rather than one of us walking backward.

Henri had a map. He consulted it twice. Finally, he signaled by pointing at his feet before opening his arms to the moonscape around us.

I tried to remember to look for pretty or unusual rocks. Too late to ask what an unusual moon rock looked like. To me, they were all unusual. Further, my concept of pretty did not serve well on the moon.

We remained for roughly half an hour. I picked up three candidates and placed them in my carry bag. Henri collected eight. I know because I kept him in sight. I could tell that he was watching me as well.

We'd gotten out of sight of Dark Side, so we navigated by walking toward the crawler. When we got close, we began waving at the monkeys who waved back. Henri stopped two monkeys on our way to the airlock. He touched helmets with each one. Later, he informed me that he thanked them mightily for the oxygen cylinders. Had I thought of it, I'd have done the same.

We deposited our finds in the "rock spot" before entering our home away from home.

Henri showed me where the geological logbook was kept. We entered the search area by a coordinate system the brainiacs "back home" devised. It was easier for any interested party to simply follow our tracks. There was no weather system to erase them.

We described our finds in non-scientific terms. If ever a qualified geologist came for a cycle in Dark Side, and he (or she) found a discovery-of-the-century in our rock collection, he (or she) would demand to know *exactly* where that specimen was found.

"If they find something that exciting," Henri theorized, "they won't stop until they find where it came from. They won't hesitate to search every spot recorded in the log."

I agreed with him. At the same time, I let him know my own opinion.

"That's a very unscientific approach."

Henri was not petulant.

"If you want something to do," he suggested. "*Scientificize* it."

He handed me the logbook.

I was not petulant. He was not baiting me. Even if he was, it made sense.

"I'll have to go out and examine that rock pile."

"Take Jens with you tomorrow," he suggested. "Meantime, why don't you draft a plan of action."

"I don't think it's that complicated," I protested.

"If you want it scientific, put it down on paper first. If you must revise it later, after you get your hands dirty, you can amend it as you go. Someday, a real geologist will check your work for spelling errors. If this helps them in any way, they will be grateful."

"Kind of like leaving them an oxygen cylinder," I suggested.

Henri's eyes twinkled. He smiled. It wasn't a huge smile; it was the smile a scientist would provide a student who understood some previously troublesome concept.

Okay! I came here specifically to get away from INSPAD while, at the same time, being a blister on their asses. Nevertheless, three months of picking my nose and longing to breathe normal air again was not my idea of a good time. If nothing else, creating a more exact and useful logbook would keep me occupied.

First, I must start with the basics. There are igneous rocks, then there were – the other kinds. What did I know about geology? Well, igneous came from magma. I must assume that, ultimately, all rock came from magma. Let's assume that the moon is composed of igneous rock.

If I find a crystal, or crystals in existing rock, I must assume that something with either significant force or heat would put them there. Meteor strikes would produce crystals. It's a good bet I would not find any eroded rock. If I did, I'd have every geologist on earth out for my hair.

Second, if I *did* find eroded rock, I would put it somewhere a *real* geologist would find it. Let him (or her) take the heat.

Third, segregate the rock pile into two parts: Igneous and crystal content.

So far, I had a project an eight-year-old child could handle. However, I had to start somewhere. I could, as Dr. dela Cour suggested, amend things as my work progressed.

Thankful that the modern moon base had ample notebooks and writing implements, I sketched out my Teach-Yourself-Geology program. It took only a few minutes.

While Henri and Jens went over the records and equipment in the "data room," I sat in the common with Dr. Johnson and the naughty Dorothy L. Sayers.

THE IGNORANT SCIENTIST

Henri and Jens had a mountain of planning and organizing to do. The moment the sun went away, they would be busier than a one-legged man in a butt-kicking contest. They would have to share some of the same equipment. They needed to plan, in advance, who got what and when. Of course, it's all paperwork, but there are times when plenary sessions are justified. The moon is a small sphere. Dark Side is a small environment. For the sake of peaceful coexistence, certain matters needed to be ironed out before they become issues – or a war.

The last thing in the world (ah, excuse, please: *the last thing on the moon*) I wanted to do was disrupt the work of legitimate scientists. Still, the freeloader had a job. It was a job I wanted to do. Brushing aside the fact that I had no expertise in geology, I wanted to give it my best shot. Eratosthenes began his brilliant career by recognizing he didn't know a damn thing. I don't claim to have the brain power of Eratosthenes, but I could begin by sorting and classifying. During the process, other concerns were certain to become manifest. I'd wrestle with perplexity on a one-thing-at-a-time basis.

I waited until we were having "evening" rations and coffee. I interrupted the bilingual colloquy when it began to wind down.

"I need to segregate the rock pile into original and modified exhibits."

The two learned men looked at me as if waiting for the punchline. Because I didn't know diddly divided by squat about geology, I shied away from scientific terms.

"You'd have to have one of us go out with you," Henri advised. "That won't work."

"So," I advanced, "Let's bring the pile in here."

Henri and Jens exchanged annoyed glances.

"We don't have any room," Jens reminded, as if he suspected me of being mentally handicapped.

"We have the empty bed and my bed," I explained. "I can sleep out here and get out of the way when you two go to work."

"The pile isn't that large," I continued. "I just need to separate the two main kinds of rock. When I'm done playing, we can put them back."

"What good would you do?" Henri challenged.

"I can write up my observations. I can take photos of anomalous rocks and send them – the photos – back with the crawler. Surely, there are geologists on the ground who will examine them and tell me what to do and what to look for. I don't want to get in your way, but I'd like to feel like I'm doing something constructive."

They remained silent for a long while.

"Dr. dela Cour," I said, looking directly at him. "You're the one who suggested this. If I call you away from your work, tell me and I'll shut down. I can't help notice that there isn't much you can do when the sun is up."

Another silence descended.

"If I catch you out there with a beach umbrella," Henri growled, "I'll lock you out."

It is amazing what you can get away with if you treat a guy to real coffee and the real water with which to make it.

The next day, when Dr. dela Cour took Dr. Schultz for a rock-collecting walk, I secured permission to access the observation deck. Permission was granted, but the commander would remain inside until he double checked the hatch to make certain it was secure. Only then did he join Jens who loitered about near the airlock.

I manufactured a crude gun sight, and, with the aid of a school-kid's protractor, I established a range finder. Once in a museum, I'd seen a model of an early twentieth-century Forest Service lookout station. In the center was a device for measuring where and how far a fire was from that location. I lacked a three-sixty view. Should the rock collectors search on the opposite side of the observation deck – well, there were only left-behind footprints to locate the search area.

Arbitrarily, I established due south, one hundred eighty degrees on my device. If the rockhounds strayed beyond one hundred twenty degrees and two hundred fifty degrees, my device would be useless. If they remained within that arc, I could record the azimuth and determine the range within two or three meters. The team would return with five of six samples. These I could examine. After making notes, I could place the samples in a sample bag together with an ID card noting date and location of collection. The bags could be stored outside the station so long as they were sheltered from the sun. Direct sunlight was brutal. A canvass bag would disintegrate after a few days and plastic, vacuum-sealed bags would melt.

Whenever I went out, I would bury the bags and pile up stones to mark their location. The chances were nearly zero that anyone would retrieve them, but science demands order and recording. Perhaps, someday, a real scientist would check my work and decide that Brice Duvall was much more than just a pretty face.

By the time the sun was beginning to set, I had examined all the rocks and recorded the anomalies I discovered on each. Every rock was assigned an ID number. Those collected after I took over the "rock garden" were also identified by date and location of discovery. However, my expertise remained simple: a rock sample was either igneous or bore some degree of crystal.

Dark Side was dark when the crawler reappeared. The monkeys left us with two cylinders. We feared that their source of supply may have been compromised and we mightn't get any more. We didn't dare ask. If we ever had to testify under oath . . .

It wasn't pure oxygen after all. Dr. dela Cour ran a sample through our equipment. It was, in his scientific parlance "hopped up earth air." It contained the same gases found in earth air with an extra, generous portion of oxygen. Call it what you like, the self-appointed scientist of this expedition (me) referred to the cylinders' content as "sweet ambrosia." (Look that up in the science lexicon!)

In addition to the glorious air, the monkeys delivered – wait for it – six oranges! The ceremony performed over these unexpected delights defies description. Never in my life did I ever expect to enjoy the unconfined joy of sticky, orange-juice fingers. I avoided washing my hands for several hours because my orange-smelling fingers provided a pleasing aroma wherever I went in the station. Further, the smell of oranges inside a pressure suit is a pleasure beyond measure!

So much for our brief sojourn in heaven. Returning to the mundane, I received a brief missive from Siss. Like me, she was sore afraid that she would interfere with or despoil serious scientific research. However, in a few brief days, she'd learned so much about weather and weather systems that she was seriously considering meteorology as a career. She got along well with both the monkeys and the scientists at Base One. She, also, thrilled at the sight of the earth and felt sorry for me because I couldn't see such a beautiful sight.

I sweated for more than an hour to compose a cheerful note in return. She had the earth for stimulation; I had oranges and the smell of oranges. I explained how I had become a part of an actual science project.

Dr. dela Cour was required to submit a report on each bi-monthly crawler visit. In it, he explained my participation in ordering and classifying geology samples. He requested that I be supplied with any geology-for-idiots material that may be on hand. The man didn't advise me of my request until after the crawler's departure. I was flattered to be included in his report, but I warned him that lower-level geology texts were tens of thousands of miles away.

"And how much did it cost me to ask?" he asked.

He had me there.

There is one thing I must mention.

Quiet.

When one is on the dark side of the moon, and one's only companions leave the station, it gets very quiet. I dropped a clipboard in the common one afternoon and it took twenty minutes for my heart and breathing to return to normal. To be swathed in quiet, then to have the quiet shattered by some clumsy mishap – one experiences undiluted terror. Indeed, the quiet itself is spooky.

Have you ever seen one of those war or horror movies? There is one B-picture cliché that never ceases to fetch a howl from the more sophisticated viewers.

"It's quiet out there."

"Yeah. Too quiet."

Well, being alone inside a lunar base – it is too damned quiet. When I didn't hear someone shuffling about or snoring or making some noise – any noise, no matter how soft and inconsequential, it was reassuring. There was someone else nearby. When you don't hear any human produced sounds – that's when you know you are ALONE!

Being alone is very frightening.

I can handle being alone if there's a radio. Even if everything is prerecorded, it is human produced sound. Had I a radio in Dark Side, I would hear nothing – absolutely, positively nothing. I doubt the AM band would even pop or squeak. Even if it did, it lacked one important quality: the pop or squeak was not produced by a human source.

I wanted to be Dark Side because I wanted to pretend that INSPAD didn't exist. When left alone in the station, nothing existed other than me. Even if I could see Henri and Jens in their pressure suits, I heard nothing.

Nothing.

Nothing.

Nothing.

Spooky!

Jens was taking a proprietary interest in my too-late interest in geology. He reviewed my collections and compared each specimen with the short write up I penciled out. He lauded my expositions but regretted my inability to employ scientific diction.

"Help me out," I chided.

"If I ever knew any geological nomenclature, it vanished long ago," he responded.

He chuckled when I showed him my "map" of the area around Dark Side.

"Let me show you something."

He guided me to one of the workstations and produced a topo map. It was a crude survey of the area around Dark Side. He used the computer to provide a larger scale map.

"Notice," he began, "the station was constructed to take the best advantage of the sun. We don't want sun, so we are pointed to keep it is behind us as much as possible. That's why the layout is skewed like – this. Your lunar *south* is very much – southeast."

He plotted lunar south over the topo map with a grease pencil.

I was a fool. What made me think I could contribute anything? I hadn't the knowledge or the scientific mindset. If I were a scientist, I would know never to take anything for granted.

Suddenly, I was Mister Attitude. I knew my *best* was *poor* because I had no training. However, I was the first person to attempt to bring order to what was, essentially, a pile of randomly selected rock samples.

"Columbus," I hissed.

"What?"

Jens was incredulous. Why should he not be?

"Columbus made a mistake. He didn't know he'd bumped into something he wasn't looking for. I didn't know the orientation of this station. Well, this is my Columbus moment and in *my* program, this is south."

I took the grease pencil and a straight edge and drew a line away from the station at a perpendicular. To make certain there was no mistaking my intent, I planted a large S at the end of my line.

"The science guys will make it right," I concluded. "Until then, this is south."

Jens smiled. It didn't matter to him in the least. He was after bigger game. He patted me reassuringly on the shoulder and left me in charge of *my* project.

"Hey!" I hailed.

He stopped and turned toward me.

"This does not mean I'm shutting you out," I reported hurriedly. "I can still call on you when I need advice."

Again, he smiled.

"I admire your determination," he said. "Insofar as I am able, I will gladly help. Any time."

That was as welcome as a good whiff of fresh air.

THE FLURRY BEGINS

When the sun went away, the stars came out.

I mean, they came out! The eerie blackness was splattered with stars – hundreds of thousands – millions! As a non-scientist, I was awestruck. I couldn't stop looking. They didn't twinkle; they simply shown like nothing I'd ever seen.

Henri and Jens were stuck to their workstations like flies on flypaper. I hardly saw them, but I heard them operating equipment as if their lives depended upon it. They seldom spoke. When they did say something, it was nearly always a cry of joy or frustration. They worked on separate projects, so they had very little to say. They were lost in their work.

I tried to beg permission to go upstairs to the observation area. No one gave me permission. However, no one denied me. They were so focused, I could have launched a Fourth of July rocket; they wouldn't have noticed. They wouldn't have cared.

I checked the instrument panel. These devices told me that the upper deck was habitable and pressurized.

I climbed the ladder, opened the hatch, climbed through, and (as per our s.o.p.) closed and sealed it behind me.

How long I remained there is beyond my knowing or caring. It was the greatest display I ever saw. I couldn't stop looking. Eventually, I fell asleep. When I woke, the same awesome vista remained as I had left it. Hunger did not register. However, there came a time when my body insisted I be somewhere else.

Reluctantly, and with the speed of a sedative-addicted tree sloth, I reentered the station. Jens and Henri were busy. They still didn't notice me, or much of anything apart from their work.

I emptied my bowels and blader. That was when hunger struck – with a vengeance.

I helped myself to a ration packet and some liquid – whatever. My mission was to return to the upper deck post haste, but my training and consideration for others plagued me. Quickly, I cleaned up my mess and stowed the trash as I always had.

Finally, I was back to witness –I was about to say, "the greatest show on earth." I suppose, it could be amended to "the greatest show on the moon." That isn't right either. Three totally unnecessary words remained.

Forty-five of forty-eight consecutive hours were spent in that greatest of all view ports. Geology didn't mean a thing – nor did INSPAD, or Henri, or Jens, or the moon, or the crawler, or everything I'd ever known or experienced. I couldn't look away. I couldn't force myself to look away. I had done a lot of dirty work to get that view. After experiencing it, I'd have assassinated half the world's population to earn that spectacular vista.

That's the most regrettable feature of my life in Dark Side. I couldn't tear myself away from the *ultimate* view. When I did break free, however, morals and mores renewed their grip, and I was human once more.

There are no words that can describe that sight. *Awe* is too short and too inadequate to come within a millionth of an inch of describing that hypnotic panorama. The view from Dark Side makes insignificant every superlative ever created.

Henri and Jens did not want to "waste" a single moment of darkness. They observed, plotted, sampled, recorded, evaluated, dissected, and confirmed every shred of information they gathered. Personal hygiene and dietary requirements went out the window. Whenever I snapped out of my coma, I would exit the observation level and check on my comrades.

"I made us some lunch," I announced.

"I'll just be a minute," Henri muttered.

That minute, according to the station clock, lasted three hours and eighteen minutes.

"Don't want to waste this dark," Jens announced as he took a moment to rehydrate.

I didn't either. My inclinations and desires were overridden by my non-scientific desire to live. The stars, I told myself, will still be there when I return.

I caught Henri in a drunken stupor. There were no "stimulants" other than medicinal brandy (still undisturbed – I checked). However, he lay face down on the table in the common. He was attempting to masticate a bit of his ration when exhaustion knocked him out. Fearing he'd suffered a stroke or heart attack, I attempted to revive him.

"Are you keeping up with SETI?" he mumbled and returned, instantly, to dreamland.

SETI! The one scientific task assigned me, and I'd forgotten completely.

I rushed to the workstation – the extreme far end of the workstation. I paged through the project notes to discover the program was nearly two weeks off schedule. I scribbled some hasty notes for the next shlub who inherited this task and pecked at the computer to aim the search dish to the proper elevation and azimuth. There would be a gap in the search pattern. Someone, with far more interest and dedication than mine, would make amends. Of course, this would set the entire project back three weeks, but I doubt many people would give a big rat's ass.

Jens pushed himself as hard as Henri, but he maintained a high degree of common sense. He knew his spectrographs would suffer if he grew too exhausted. He retired for an uninterrupted five-hour sleep. When he woke, he took nourishment.

I was, once again, alone with my stars. My resentment was touched off by noise from the entry hatch. Moments later, Jens emerged. He secured the hatch and joined me in admiring the grandest view ever. I was jealous. I didn't want to share this scene with anyone.

"Can you see Saturn?" he asked, after several minutes of silence.

"If it's out there, I see it," I responded grumpily.

"What's the brightest star?" He teased.

Which brightest star? There were diamonds galore, but a few pearls stood out. Jens was disturbing my reverie. Selecting the brightest was a chore.

"There, I guess."

I pointed, vaguely, at a few hundred billion square miles.

"Well, let's look and see."

There was a toy telescope suspended from the ceiling. I'd been afraid to touch it and loathe to use it. The device would restrict my view. Jens fiddled with the mounting for a few seconds and pulled. It swung down and in. By earth standards, the eight-inch scope was bulky but merely tantalizing. The orbiting telescopes (one of nearly twenty inches) were far superior.

Jens spotted his target through a gunsight on the starboard side of the instrument, then shifted to the eye piece. He focused slowly and delicately with his right-hand fingers.

"You pass," he announced. "I declare you apprentice astronomer third class."

He pulled away and let me have a look.

Earth telescopes are such a tease. Smoke, clouds, air density and other factors make a hash of every image I'd ever seen – except, of course, the moon. I'd enjoyed views of the moon so detailed I could identify several of the craters by name. For any object further away, the atmosphere caused clutter, flutter, and twinkling. I cared for none of those.

This was different.

My eyes beheld a large, colored ball. The rings were nearly straight on to us and worthy of Tantalus. However, I saw – quite clearly – eight or nine moons. Titan, of course, was easily identified. As it lay between the planet and the sun, I could see Titan's shadow on that huge gas ball. As if standing inspection, smaller moons dotted the periphery. According to the most recent count, there are a hundred and fifty-two moons (more or less). There's a big brew-ha-ha over which are moons and which are of recent classifications of orbiting bodies. Being a non-scientist, I call them BDRs, "big damn rocks." I won't swear under oath, but I *think* I spotted a few of those as well.

If I couldn't take my eyes off the vast display of the moon's dark sky, it was equally impossible to tear myself away from this magnet sight of Saturn and her "pals."

"What do you think, Brice?" Jens prodded. "Is this worth the trip?"

"There ain't enough money in the solar system to pay for this view," I concluded.

He patted me on the shoulder and left me to get on with his work.

There would be no moon walks during the lunar night. Ergo, there would be no rock excursions and collections. It was important, psychologically, for us to remain together. Left alone in the dark brings out every childhood fear. Add to these, adult fears can push a previously healthy person into the deepest depths of insanity. Dark Side had an audio system. One could adjust the volume in certain areas, most notably, our sleeping "quarters." However, no one could turn it off. The shrinks learned that music hath more than charms; it has a calming effect. Moreover, it reassures the moon men and women that they may be isolated, but not alone.

The selections are classical in nature and are confined, largely, to nocturnes, barcaroles, and divertimentos (aptly named). Bach is, by far, the most often featured. I, at least, recognized his style if not the titles. The only vocal selection was Bach's *Coffee Cantata*. I never heard of it prior to take off, but it grew on me. Jens knew what it was. I vowed that, *if* I returned to *terra firma*, I shall add this little jewel to my eclectic collection of musical scores. It was, indeed, amusing and diverting.

The assembly who selected "moon music" are worthy of veneration. They may not have saved any lives, but they were experts at keeping people sane in the void of space.

Allow me this one moment in my confused memoir to mention that the greatest of the simple pleasures in my life remains my reading of Dorothy L. Sayers, in French, by the artificial light of my lunar sleeping "chamber" while listening to a collection of classical music. Relaxing by placid ocean waters on a sandy beach with a cool drink can't hold a candle to it.

Dr. dela Cour wrote a beautiful proposal that had the support of the top radio astronomers the world over. He thought he needed only a cycle Dark Side, and he would have enough data to keep a team of experts in work for years. Alas, he misjudged. He realized as much early on and begged to extend for another cycle. With only Dr. Schulte begging for a Dark Side billet, his extension was approved. Suddenly, Dr. dela Cour realized he mightn't finish. The more data he secured, the more "missing links" appeared. He could ask for another extension, but the idea of four more months in space was too daunting.

"He hasn't been on the exercise equipment for three days," Jens confided in me during one of his own infrequent breaks.

Exercising in reduced gravity is vital. If one becomes addicted to the moon's reduced gravity, a return to earth could be serious – even deadly. Nevertheless, Henri was the senior man on this side of the moon. We couldn't order him to get rest and exercise. Even if we could, how would we enforce our dictate. The nearest cop was a quarter of a million miles away.

Finally, the day of reckoning arrived.

Henri slumped down at his station. He remained inert for several minutes. Jens assumed he was asleep again. He attempted to revive him. There was no response. He felt for his pulse and was relieved to find it. Nevertheless, Henri wouldn't, or couldn't, respond.

"Brice! I need help!"

Ironically, I was working out. I was leg lifting three times my (earth) weight with ease. Mel's advice "It isn't the weight, it's the reps that are important" kept me going. Even on the moon, exercise equipment makes noise. I did not understand what Jens was shouting, but I realized he was shouting. One does not shout on the moon. That isn't an INSPAD rule, it's just common sense: yelling requires more air and produces more carbon dioxide.

I knew Jens well enough to know he would not shout because I was squeezing the toothpaste from the middle of the tube. This was serious. I stopped what I was doing and rushed in the direction of the voice.

"He's exhausted," Jens concluded. "Help me get him out of here."

"Want me to get the oxygen?"

We had four or five bottles of pure oxygen. These were medical emergencies only. If we used this stuff, we'd better have a super, super good reason. If we lacked one, Jens and I might share the same cell soon.

"Let's get him out of here first," he advised.

I helped him get the inert scientist out of the workstation. Now, our problem was compounded. The only place we could lay him out was on his bunk. There was hardly room for Henri. Neither Jens nor I could tend to him.

I have a feeling Jens had been pondering a situation such as the one we faced. Because he'd thought it over, he had a contingency plan.

I was ordered to take Henri by the feet. Jens got him under the shoulders. I backed through the common and toward the bunks. The "hallway," a narrow passage running parallel with the workstation axis allowed access to the four sleeping areas and the toilet on the opposite end from the air lock. Jens pulled the "doc" toward the airlock just enough so that I was free to get to most of the rest of the station.

"Get the oxygen," Jens ordered.

The bottles were stowed in the common under the communal table. I grabbed the first cylinder, roughly the size of large cucumber, and checked the pressure gage. It was full. I rushed back and handed it to Jens who used the receptacle to fit over Henri's nose and mouth. Slowly, gently, he turned the valve. He opened it only halfway and Henri began flopping like a fish out of water. Jens closed the valve and waited.

"What are you doing?" Henri asked in English.

"Saving your sorry ass," Jens replied in the same tongue.

"What am I doing here?"

He tried to sit up, but Jens forced his shoulders back down.

"Doctor, you just frightened me out of ten years," Jens scolded. "I asked you and begged you to get some rest and exercise. Now, I'm telling you: get some sleep and catch up on your exercise. I will lock you out of the workstation until you do."

"But," the man protested weakly. "My work. So much to do."

"And not a bit of it will get done if you do not get proper rest and exercise. You're too important to die out here from exhaustion. I like you, doctor. I like you too much to take you out of here in a body bag. I wonder how careless you've gotten and how many mistakes you've made because you're so exhausted. Get some rest, Henri. Catch up on your exercise. I repeat, I'm telling you, Henri. No sleepy; no workie."

Henri didn't like it. However, he was too tired and too weak to do anything about it.

"We're going to put you in your bunk," Jens concluded. "We will put you in, feet first. Brice, I want you to check him twice an hour. If he's having problems, give him another shot of that dope. If he's asleep, let him be."

I nodded. A visit with Saturn was in the offing, but I agreed that Dr. dela Cour was far more important.

We had to pick him up and turn him around so my end would go into the bunk first. I think he was asleep before we got him settled. We each checked to make certain he was breathing naturally. I put the oxygen cylinder on my bunk which was only three steps away from Henri if he needed another dose.

"I hate to put you on the spot," Jens said.

"I'll keep close," I promised. "When he wakes up, I'll see he eats and drinks something."

He nodded his thanks.

"Call me if you need me."

What a stupid thing to say. Did he think I'd insist on playing doctor alone? I may be a fake, know-nothing geologist, but there's no way I'm going to pretend to be a clinician. There mightn't be a thing that Jens and I could do as a team, but this was a responsibility I refused to shoulder alone.

PROCEED WITH CAUTION

Henri slept for seventeen hours. I know because I checked on him every thirty minutes, even during my sleep period. Jens made a point to check every thirty minutes as well, but fifteen minutes after my check. This interrupted both his own work and his own sleep period.

Following orders, I woke him when Henri began coming out of his coma.

"How long have I been out?" he asked, reasonably I thought.

I told him.

"Got to get to work," he croaked, trying to pull himself out of his niche.

We watched as he struggled. Since we intentionally put him into his bunk backwards, there was little chance he could extract himself without coming headfirst. When he realized his predicament, he ceased struggling and begged for help.

"You eat and exercise for thirty minutes before you go back to work," Jens announced.

"The sun will be coming up," he reminded.

"After food and exercise," Jens insisted.

"When the sun's up, I'll exercise," he promised.

"No, Henri. I'll not give you a second chance to give me a stroke. I'll let you have fifteen hours on station. I will place the same limits on myself. We're too smart to be so stupid."

"But, I'll never finish."

"You can come back later. Better yet, you can hand-pick and train someone to come in your place. Henri, you are too important to me and to your colleagues to do yourself serious harm. I warn you, Henri, I respect and admire you, but if I must, I will use force."

That made him think seriously about a good many things.

"Help me out."

"Food and exercise?"

He tried, but the words would not come. I thought he was about to cry. Finally, he nodded his head.

We helped him out. He staggered to the bathroom. Jens and I retired to the common. Henri could not access the workstation without going through us. We broke open a ration pack and started warming things up. I put the coffee on; it would be our last until we returned to earth.

"I need your help, Brice. I get carried away. I said fifteen hours, and I've been known to get so involved with what I'm doing, I don't bother to keep track. You must be our timekeeper."

I nodded.

"I can do that," I affirmed.

We three had a leisurely meal. I was left to clean up as Jens escorted Henri to the exercise station. There was room in the "gym" for only one person, so Jens acted as a coach. The moment he was "free," Henri stopped in the common long enough to take a ration of recycled water before staggering to the workstation. I noted the time and recorded it.

Jens remained to take his turn in the gym. He, too, helped himself to some recycled water. I showed him where I had recorded the "start time." He nodded.

"You going up to the telescope?"

"I think I'll sit here and read for a while," I announced. "If I go up there, I might lose track of time myself."

"I appreciate it, Brice. Make a note for debriefing: we need an alarm clock."

"I won't forget," I promised.

Beware of *woundy.*

That's from Johnson's dictionary. *Woundy* means "excessiveness." Johnson also adds that it is "a low, bad word." Perhaps, it is, but it is apt. Upon my return, I must have a chat with Mel about "all work and no play makes Henri a potential corpse." There must be a mission book that needs revision. *Woundy* certainly qualifies as a prime candidate for future inclusion.

I'd finished my Sayers' mystery just prior to Dr. dela Cour's breakdown. As interesting as Johnson's dictionary was, it didn't have much of a plot. Therefore, I pulled out my pocketbook mystery, turned to the title page, and began rereading.

Maybe, this time, I could spot the murderer before the final chapters.

THE NEW REGIME

Henri dela Cour was wise enough to realize he'd been a donkey's butt. His work had become so important, he neglected himself. What good was his data, he finally realized, if earth's gravity killed him? Though it was hardly necessary, Henri upped his twice-daily exercise period by thirty minutes. The extra fifteen-minute sessions threw both Dr. Schulte's and my exercise period back. This was but a minor annoyance. Having Henri back, and with his head on straight, was worth much more than our personal inconvenience.

Dr. Jens Schulte was our *de facto* station commander. There was no hand-over ceremony. Indeed, no one ever brought up the subject. Jens issued orders to Henri in that man's best interest, and the good French doctor carried out those orders.

The fifteen-hour work limit was, by lunar norms, draconian. Indeed, it inhibited Jens as much as it did Henri.

"If I'd only had another forty minutes today," Jens sighed beyond Dr. dela Cour's hearing.

I didn't respond. I wasn't certain I was expected to. We both knew – we all three knew – that Jens, by violating his own orders, would destroy the group dynamic. We were sitting on the edge of disaster. I had the most to lose. I was an interloper. If any serious repercussions were forthcoming out of a Dark Side "incident," Brice Duvall – as the only non-scientist – would be held accountable by INSPAD, the press, and myself.

Unexpectedly, the work restrictions allowed us more "down time." We fell into the habit of a post-meal retreat to the "observation deck." Our field of view was deteriorating rapidly because of the rising sun. However, while our immediate surroundings were largely unaffected, we enjoyed examining the salient features of the "spooky" moonscape. Henri and Jens found other objects to examine through the telescope, but Saturn remained my favorite. I noted the change of position of the moons, particularly Titan. The rings were gradually tipping enough for me to make them out. I hoped that during our next blackout, I'd get a proper view of them.

In the common, between our "promenade" on the "upper deck" and lights out, I would read fifteen minutes aloud from Dorothy L. Sayers. The doctors encouraged me until it became a ritual. I suspected, however, that they were very busy thinking of other things. One night, however, I mis-pronounced an esoteric word. Immediately, and in unison, the doctors blurted out the correct pronunciation.

I felt like an ignorant fool. Henri grew up with French; Jens grew up with German. Both, however, were more fluent (or seemingly so) in British English than I. Well, it just shows to go you that fluency in my mother tongue was a restriction rather than an asset.

There was another ritual which I did not share. Every lunar evening, before switching off the reading light, I'd open the cover of the Johnson selections. That is where I kept Elena's picture. I studied it daily. I compared the picture with my memory. The photo didn't hold up well. According to the photo, Elena was rather plain and forgettable. I, however, was fortunate enough to know this woman. Her physical features blossomed with her every mood. Her personality tweaked her limited attributes until she was captivating.

It was no wonder to me why Fedor Yelagin wanted to meet her – and to have her. In front of a TV camera, Elena, doubtless, bubbled irresistibly. She didn't need short skirts or low necklines to attract men; her smile, enunciation, and her flashing eyes could win over the most dedicated curmudgeon.

I'm satisfied, Fedor was no curmudgeon – neither am I. Nevertheless, Elena's photo was so disappointing. The very things which made her so overwhelmingly attractive could not be captured by a camera.

Fifteen-hour days led to an easing of tension. The atmosphere was further enhanced by Henri's acceptance of his "failed" mission. He called it that, but neither Jens nor I took that at face value. Clearly, he wouldn't return home with his entire project completed, but it was overly ambitious from the start. Henri figured if Dark Side were perpetually dark, he'd have finished in a cycle and a half. As it was, the dark side of the moon has much the same phases as the moon we view from earth. Henri was left with the realization that it is folly to curse the light.

Jens had seized power in a nonviolent coup. However, he deferred to Henri in most everything except strict working hours, a strict exercise regimen, and strict sleep periods. The moment Henri surrendered, our habitat experienced a good deal of serendipity.

One afternoon (morning, evening – the "moon clock" was our only determiner) Henri was taking bites of his "food" (whatever it was) between examinations of his printed data.

"Dr. Schulte," he said, slowly and deliberately.

My blood froze. When these guys addressed each other by their professional titles, it was frequently a precursor to an animated exchange. I knew from the expression Jens wore, he felt the same angst.

"Dr. dela Cour?" he said, softly and with trepidation.

"Do you think I might borrow you and your equipment for a couple hours before the sun comes up?"

Jens was slightly behind the schedule he'd set for himself. He suffered from the fifteen-hour rule as much as his French counterpart.

"Why?"

It was such a mundane and obvious question that Jens, wisely, dispensed with any preamble.

"I have encountered an anomaly."

I'm not a scientist. I don't pretend to be a scientist. I don't even play a scientist in the movies. However, I've been around two scientists for somewhile during this "mission." You will find the word *anomaly* in Johnson's dictionary, and it has every right to be there. Nevertheless, one of the first things I've learned is that the word *anomaly* is science's way of saying *oh, shit*. I made a note to ink in an addendum in the expurgated Johnson Dictionary I'd brought with me.

"I have a peculiar radio source which does not blend in with the rest of the system. It's a rather small system, five to eight light years across, but I'm beginning to wonder if it *is* in the system at all. Could it be nearer? Perhaps, it's beyond the system. I can't tell for certain. If I go off half-cocked, as our Ami friend here likes to say, I'd be tempted to suggest that it's been thrown out – ejected – from the system."

Jens was interested. Something must be very peculiar for a scientist to propose such off-the-wall speculation.

"Have you double checked?"

"Indeed, I have. It has a pronounced radio signal, but visible light is very faint."

"How can I help?"

"If you could get a reading from the system and another from the anomaly . . . There might be something at the invisible ends of the light spectrum that might explain – something."

Jens couldn't help himself.

"You need me to shed some light on it, then?"

Henri looked up quickly. I feared he was about to create a fuss. To my surprise, and the relief of the German, the radio astronomer smiled broadly.

"Precisely."

Henri and Jens did me the courtesy of speaking English. It was strictly for my benefit since they spoke each other's languages so fluently. It made me feel a part of the team rather than just an interloper.

Henri and Jens sat in the common for one of their fifteen hours working out their program "on the fly." It was mostly scientific, but there were many variables. For their joint effort to be of much use, they had to have both their instruments pointed at exactly the same place, at exactly the same moment, for exactly the same length of time. Only then could they announce that they had a radio plot and a spectrometry image which mirrored each other. Unfortunately, there were seven meters between Henri's radio dish and Jens's spectrographic – *thingy*. Seven freaking meters difference in a non-photographic photograph of a "something" hundreds of thousands, if not millions, of light years away.

Am I glad I'm just a rock collector.

Oh, this was just the beginning! For one of their fifteen hours a day for the next five days they stared at and compared their data in the common. Finally, after all their theories were hashed out, they ended exactly as they began.

They'd found an anomaly.

The pair carefully packed away their data, together with their photos, screenshots, whatever, in a large file and sealed it. Let the experts at home try and figure it out.

The sun was making itself known and the bulk of the scientific work was seriously curtailed. It was back to rock collecting. Both these learned scientists would defer to me – if you can believe it (I can't). It was my project, they insisted.

I don't know if they were having me on, or if they treated my geological lark as something serious. Either way, they took my orders and carried them out. Once a day, I and one of my companions would suit up and follow my lead. Using primitive survey equipment, I logged each find (we averaged six per foray) and noted their location by degrees from my arbitrary "south" and the distance from Dark Side. If there was ever a dispute, our footprints would allow anyone interested to correct any errors.

The doctors alternated with me. With little to do, remaining inside the station, alone, was both tedious and spooky. Still, they were judicious. Neither delayed when it was his turn to suit up, and no one expressed (aloud) derision about my project.

One day, I happened to step on something unusual. I stepped on it because it was mostly buried. I stepped back and saw sunlight glittering off an object. I picked it up and found the "discovery" of my lifetime.

It was a rock roughly four inches long and nearly as wide. For a moon rock in moon gravity, it was rather heavy. One third of the rock was run-of-the-mill igneous. Two thirds were translucent.

"Henri!" I could not disguise my excitement. "Tell me what you think of this."

He was several meters away and paid no attention. Of course, there was no air and no radio link.

My excitement had activated my reserves of stupid.

Quickly, I closed the distance between us and got his attention. I handed him the rock and let him study it. He was not being polite, I could tell by the way he handled it that he was excited. I felt his helmet tap mine.

"An impact could have done this," he deduced. "It must have been extremely hot to turn this into glass – or crystal. Look down here."

His gloved finger was very inexact, but I made out that place where the igneous turned into glass. Along the edge were tiny bits of a metallic substance that winked at us. It looked like gold. Well, all that glitters, etc. If it was gold, there wasn't enough to buy a Happy Burger.

Henri turned slowly around – the whole three-sixty. Upon completion, he signaled for me to touch helmets.

"There must have been a hell of a smash," he theorized. "This little puppy must have been thrown a considerable distance. There'd be more ejecta around if this thing came from nearby."

"I haven't seen any," I reported.

"The less ejecta, the longer this thing traveled," he replied. "Hang onto this, Brice. This is – as you say – a keeper."

We went nearly an hour beyond our scheduled time but failed to find anything even remotely resembling my *keeper.*

Jens was a little upset. He didn't like being alone more than necessary. Further, he was worried. He had no idea what had happened to us, and he didn't return to regular breathing until he could see us approaching from the "observation deck."

The crawler was no longer a major event. It was welcome, of course, but the thrill of its appearance was no longer a novelty. We were anxious for a time. It was nearly eighteen hours late. In addition to a minor breakdown, they paused to begin construction of the "wayside hut." When that became serviceable there would be a land line laid to our location so future delays would be announced.

Damned clever these engineers. They fixed the location of the way station at exactly (EXACTLY) the correct spot on the moon. A person (likely two) stationed there could communicate with Dark Side. Messages from earth and Base One could be sent to the way station by a special antenna. The radio transceiver would be placed just far enough earthside so the line-of-sight radio waves would not cause any interference with Dark Side monitoring equipment.

It was tricky. The radio would be in the hut, but the transmissions must first go to the antenna by landline to be automatically uploaded and sent to Base One or directly to earth. Any messages for Dark Side would be picked up and recorded at the hut. It would then be forwarded by landline.

That was two or three cycles into the future. For us, the only contact with Base One or the earth was hand carried by the crawler.

We had a visitor. Some swag from Base One was "inspecting" equipment and scientific progress at Dark Side. Since this was an INSPAD bigshot, he probably couldn't tell the difference between a telescope and a proctology exam, but he who had the gold makes the rules.

Consumables are so closely monitored and accounted for that crew numbers must remain static. Therefore, if someone at Base One wanted passage to Dark Side, one monkey must stay at Base One to make room for the passenger. Since three people were cycled to Dark Side, one person must stay on the crawler to make room for the visitor.

Guess who got kicked out.

I didn't mind. It was a break in the routine, and I welcomed that.

I took a few photos of the interior of the crawler as "souvenirs." In truth, I wanted to get a photo of that Rurik device. I didn't know if it was a gear box, a part of the suspension, an air compressor, or something other. All I knew was that it had a serial number and Elena's former husband was bound to be interested.

I had a meal with the crew, and we might have had a jolly old time. However, I was a victim of knowing too much. I was informed that I had a letter from Siss and a hastily produced, thirty-some page book on geology for elementary-school graduates. I became Tantalus. I so wanted to get my hands (and eyes) on my materials, but they were in the Dark Side air lock. I was trapped with people whose interests were much different than mine. I did enjoy two nice shots of illegal vodka which boosted my spirits considerably but left me queasy for most of an hour.

Finally, I met the hot shot "inspector" on the moon's surface. He was returning to the crawler; I was returning to Dark Side. I still suffered from the vodka which was made more volatile by the high-oxygen content of my pressure suit. Perhaps, they should post signs for future moon men (and women): Don't Drink and Walk!

I was extra, extra careful transitioning. If I screwed up and killed myself, Mel would be more than upset. If he learned that I'd been drinking, he'd be after the scalp of anyone who bootlegged the stuff. He would be particularly interested in the identity of the monkey who gave it to me. The lives of several people other than my own were dependent on me transitioning properly.

"Problems?" Jens asked when I finally entered Dark Side.

"I was just exercising caution," I reported.

He was close enough to smell my breath. Thankfully, he refused to interrogate me. He knew. I knew that he knew. He knew that I knew that he knew. That was enough. He'd either leave it for later or let it pass.

The geology "notebook" was on the table in the common, but it was the note from Siss that was my main concern.

She was so excited. She'd got to walk on the moon. She got to collect "pretty rocks" (her diction). She got to take a daytrip to Base Two and get high-quality photos of her home. She had a snap of her and her sisters' hut.

She thought one of her sisters was outside nearby. However, no matter how good the camera, the film, or the lens, taking photos through the earth's atmosphere is not recommended. Nevertheless, that print will remain her treasured possession. She couldn't wait to show her sisters.

I spent an hour composing a brief note of reply. There was no mention of my prize find. I didn't want to get my hopes up. If I got all excited, and I got other people all excited – well, I just knew some expert would take one look at it and announce that it was a coke bottle dropped by one of the astronauts a hundred years before and acted upon by the sun. That, or some equally mundane explanation would make me a laughingstock – not that I didn't deserve it, but I'd rather remain anonymous if given the choice.

If some scientist proclaimed mine the "find of the century," I would count on Henri to confirm that I was the one who found it.

The visit of the great high mucky muck was finished. Neither Henri nor Jens were very impressed by his imperial highness, but he left, they said, satisfied and impressed. We then spent much of our "evening" trying to figure out who this guy had pissed off to earn him a moon tour.

Back to business.

The monkeys filled the airlock with supplies and surprises. We brought them in and stowed them. When we filled the airlock with our recyclables, we left our correspondence in a conspicuous package placed in a conspicuous place.

In the morning, the monkeys collected our discards and performed maintenance checks and maintenance as required. They spent an inordinate amount of time on the oxygenator. That caused some concern. More so since this delay added to their tardiness. They were late arriving, and they took more time than normal in maintenance. People on earth and at Base One might be very concerned about them. Perhaps, this would expedite the construction and occupation of the way station.

Some swag realized that their fussing with the oxygenator would cause us concern. He scrawled a hasty message on a portable whiteboard.

Extra O 2
Boosts OXater
Performance

We all read it from the observation deck before the sun could reduce the message to indecipherable lines and streaks. He gave us a thumbs up. We returned it.

While we brought aboard our resupply and two more cylinders of ox-air, as we had come to call it, I hoped these cylinders would become SOP on future cycles. Letting INSPAD know of this smuggling might create turmoil. However, what INSPAD don't know, can't hurt us.

We set about to stow our imports. The monkeys set about to collect our garbage. Three hours later, we were buttoned up; the crawler was buttoned up. They would spend a sleep period in the crawler's parking space before returning to earth side. Doubtless, people would be camped next to the radio, eagerly awaiting word. If the crawler went "missing," that would force the remaining crawler to resupply all the bases and conduct a search. That would result in belt-tightening for everybody.

Yes, there was a dire need for an extra crawler – a *spare* if one dares employ the word. However, a crawler costs a tremendous amount of money. Assembly, disassembly and transport piece by piece would cost a tremendous amount more. Then, a crew would be required to reassemble it and make it operational, more money and no time for science. For a year (closer to eighteen months) all the human resources on the moon would be Space Monkeys. There'd be no room for scientists, new equipment, nor any time for projects and evaluation. The entire purpose of the moon bases was research. However, without crawlers, the moon bases were worthless. They'd be used as habitats for the off-duty monkeys.

INSPAD would cease to exist. Poor, poor Dieter Rolf would have to go back to organizing prostitution rings and overseeing the numbers racket. For want of a crawler, an entire gravy train may be lost!

Am I the only one who thought this through?

ROUTINE
DREARY, DREARY ROUTINE

It took a little over half a cycle, but we settled into a routine. The introduction of a fifteen-hour limit on research was one element in the introduction to monotony. The attempts to make me into a geologist by remote control contributed. I couldn't get my head around the study of rocks; it didn't help that the "experts" expected me to study the various types of sedentary samples and formations.

"There's no erosion on the moon, dolts!"

Those sections that did pertain to lunar geology were so esoteric, I gave up. Despite the best brains in lunar science, they could not communicate with a neophyte. They just assumed that I had taken all the required, lower division, undergraduate courses. Everything they dispatched to me went completely over my head. My pleading and explaining brought forth only more indecipherable manuscripts. I decided to stick with the science I knew – plain rocks and shiny rocks. Henri and Jens picked up on my frustration. We continued to log our search areas and the few samples we brought back, but there was no longer a sense of purpose.

Henri and Jens worked most days without exchanging a word. They were still working on their projects, but they lacked enthusiasm. Whenever we were in the common, the scientists were very careful not to talk about, or even mention, their work. We exchanged jokes (most of which would be funnier if lubricated with alcohol), humorous anecdotes, and autobiographical snippets of their non-scientific life and experiences. I was asked, on several occasions, to read two or three pages from the Dorothy L. Sayers mystery. They liked the author's style. It was precise and entertaining. It never failed to produce animated conversations.

Perhaps, I expect too much from learned scientists. I was disappointed to discover they weren't the least interested in knowing the identity of the murderer. If pressed, I doubt either could say who had been murdered.

I continued to read the book. It was the only thing available. The sinistrous (Johnson's word) geology texts lacked even the power to put one to sleep. I'd memorized several of the paragraphs in the mystery story, but there was nothing memorable (or pertinent) in the geology babble.

Our non-working hours were convivial, but the main theme was getting back to earth and "real life." We talked about the things we missed (big mistake). We told and retold jokes. We shared anecdotes of our pre-lunar lives. I spoke of Siss and my adventures at "the end of the earth." They were fascinated. I shared a summary of the communications we exchanged during our sojourn.

Siss had started her adventure with such enthusiasm. Her latest missive, however, was a syrupy harangue about how she missed her city, her home, her sisters, her favorite priest, her three part-time jobs, and – doing her "dreary" daily chores. It was obvious that her curiosity about the moon had been more than satisfied.

There were breaks in our evening conversations. There were three musical selections that we particularly favored. None of us knew the titles, or the composers of the "mystic trio." However, when one of them came up, we fell silent and felt the music as much as we heard it. These selections were soothing and beautiful. They made us miss earth even more.

Henri was the most contrite. When he returned to earth, it would be an absence of nearly eight months. Disappointed in his failure to complete his project (to his own expectations), he felt that being home and among family and colleagues was more important than anything else.

In an unguarded moment, I mentioned Elena Sidorov. Jens pounced. He knew her – well, he knew *of* her. He'd seen her reporting on sporting events.

"You understand Russian?" I asked (demanded) incredulously.

"No," he said with a touch of petulance. "But there's nothing wrong with my German."

"She did reports in German?"

It was my turn to be huffy.

"If she didn't, I doubt the networks would air her stuff in Berlin."

"I didn't know she spoke German."

Unexpectedly, and for no discernable reason, I was hurt.

"How well do you know her?"

"Apparently, not very well."

Persistent interrogation wore me down, and I related that she currently lived and worked in Atlanta. They assumed she was a sports journalist. There was no need (or harm) in allowing them to believe that.

I'd rather not think about Elena. I liked her, but I felt – somehow – betrayed. That's how far gone I was. Because she never mentioned her mastery of German, I felt slighted. My intellect insisted that this was not something vital for me to know, but my jealousy was aroused. I felt as if she were concealing the existence of a lover.

The second to last visit of the crawler brought a sealed message for me. By then, I knew the monkeys well enough to realize they read every piece of mail dispatched from Base One. They, probably, felt it was a minor transgression. Some messages were bound to be entertaining. Those messages which were science related were likely given short shrift. I wondered what they thought of Elena's message to me.

I wondered about Elena's message to me.

It was an eight by ten color glossy of her. She was in formal dress – as far as I could tell; it was either a gown or the most elaborate blouse ever designed. Her head and the deliciously provocative scoop neck were as much of her as the photo allowed. Her hair was professionally tended, and her makeup was equally attended. She was turned slightly to her left, so there was no way of telling if her three gnat's eggs were blotted out.

Elena's head was tilted forward, her eyes focused upward on the camera lens in unmistakable and high-octane flirt. The one visible earring dangled from delicate chain for an inch, perhaps. She smiled enigmatically with blood-red lips. Her left index finger touched the tip of her nose. The nail polish matched her lipstick.

This was no do-it-yourself creation. A professional photographer was clearly in evidence.

That was it. There was no note.

Why would a professional allow his subject to block her own face?

That was only one of a dozen questions which bloomed like dandelions in my muddled brain. Here was Elena dressed to the nines (as far as I could tell), professionally coiffured, and with a face made-up to please without being gaudy. Then she poses with a finger disrupting her lower face.

I knows

Yes, I was aware of that from my childhood game experiences. Beyond that . . .

I needed a scientific appraisal.

I caught Henri at a bad time. He was reading a precis of some radio-telescope experiment. He nodded his approval of the photo's subject but made no audible comment.

Jens was more interested.

"*That*," he announced, "is Elena Whatsername."

He wanted to study further. I handed it over but regretted doing so. He leered at the image in a way that made me jealous.

Neither of my learned colleagues made mention of the most obvious *anomaly*. If, I figured, they didn't notice the obvious, it would be pointless to mention it.

Elena is conniving and devious. She had some serious purpose behind sending this peculiar photograph *sans* written explanation. Perhaps, this was another expression of her peculiar sense of humor. Perhaps, my not getting the joke *was* the joke. Did she expect me to lie sleepless while pondering her non-message message? If so, she succeeded.

Was she still interested in me? If not, why communicate at all?

As if the final countdown to leaving my lunar cocoon was not agitating enough, she sticks a fork in me. How I wish I could speak to the monkeys who, likely, examined the photo and conjured a myriad of lured and obscene explanations as to its purpose. At least, they would be more constructive than anything my fellow prisoners supplied.

I retired to my zone. Before I hefted myself up onto my bunk, I took out the *"I nose"* photo and retrieved the image I kept in the pages of Dr. Johnson's dictionary. They both depicted a woman, but they were very different women. One was proud, even haughty, but with a subtle touch of – what? Vulnerability? No, decidedly not. "Human frailty" might be nearer the mark. The other photo, the one dispatched to the moon, was of a playful, mysterious and – dare I say – threatening person. She held all the cards. She wanted me to know that she was the master; I was some ignorant schmuck who had so very much to learn.

Which photo did I prefer? They were both honest representations of the same person. Both images were alluring. Without makeup, Elena was, maybe, a whisper above plain. With makeup, she was much more attractive, but – she remained a whisper above plain, only with frills. Regardless, she was special – to me, at least. There must be a thousand women more attractive, but few (if any) had Elena's appeal. *Appeal* leaked out of her shoes; it oozed out of her body; it radiated from her visage.

Damn

She was a quarter of a million miles away, but her essence surrounded me like cloak. I'd have given anything – everything – I owned or claimed just to hear her voice.

Well, I appreciated her sending me greetings from across the void, but I must put her aside. She was way, way, way out of my league.

I sighed.

I took out the Dorothy L. Sayers mystery. It was held together with rubber bands and portions reinforced with paper clips – the only items at Dark Side that were plentiful. I grabbed my pen and made an inscription.

If you enjoy the volume
thank the university people in Timbuktu, Mali
who made it available
for your pleasure

(donations will be appreciated)

I'd leave the book behind. I'd memorized parts of it. If ever I hankered to read it again "for old time's sake," I'd be forced to haunt second and third-hand bookshops. I'm certain I could find an English language edition.

Dr. Johnson, however, was returning to earth.

AND THE DAYS
DRAG ON

Just as with military enlisted personnel, we created a "short timers" calendar. Our evening ritual concluded with each of us crossing out the day just ending. If the crawler arrived on time, we knew exactly when we would leave the facility. What few personal items we brought with us were packed in our one allotted "carry on." In addition to Dr. Johnson and my photos of Elena, I packed away my ancient Coke bottle. This, of course, was *not* mine. However, until I was certain it would get into the proper hands, I'd keep it within arm's reach.

We were eleven days from "evacuation," but we were ready to go at a moment's notice. There would be no last-minute check to be certain we weren't leaving anything behind – it was all packed in our "hold baggage" or was with us in our "space purses."

We avoided, for as long as our noses would allow, cleaning our "flight suits." We were issued only two pair. When we first arrived, we changed suits every third day, but we lengthened that to once a week and, toward the end; we'd go as long as we could stand. The atmosphere inside the facility was pretty gamey. However, our "laundry" was managed by a machine that eschewed water, since we conserved as much of that valuable fluid as possible. Our flight suits and underneaths were heated slightly (no problem when the sun was out) and drycleaned (kind of). To be certain, the dirt, spills, spots, and oils were whisked away, but our "clean" clothes radiated a pungent, chemical odor. Initially, it didn't bother us much. Over time, however, we experienced bouts of nausea. Additionally, the chemical smell became so irksome that we preferred body odor over clean clothes.

Henri was not the first to notice, but he was the first to verbalize it.

"Those chemicals are what upset our stomachs."

What price cleanliness?

The lotions supplied to us were very good and, unlike most of our other supplies, plentiful. A good lotion bath (rubdown more like) every other day or (in my case) every day, delayed the arrival of "Bata Oscar" considerably.

Our pressure suits were the major bacteria factory. When on the moon's surface, our suits kept us at a comfortable sixty degrees – plus or minus a degree or two. However, they were cumbersome and required a lot of energy to lug them around, even considering the low gravity. The more we moved, the more we perspired. The more we perspired, the more stink we produced.

You won't find it in the facility SOP, but being as far removed from the airlock as possible was the standard procedure for the one person who remained behind during a rock sampling mission. It could get pretty pungent once the pressure suits were off.

Strangely, the lack of communication with the rest of humanity wasn't all that bad. We didn't have some INSPAD flunky issuing capricious orders or tasks, and we weren't bothered with periodic "news" bulletins. INSPAD was run by corrupt Neanderthals and the news was highly propagandized and, therefore, extremely inaccurate. There were times when being unable to speak one-on-one with a geologist who knew his onions were frustrating. However, when all things were considered, it was a joy to be "off the grid," as it were.

Life on Dark Side was shared by us three. Any problems arising were assessed and addressed democratically. We had no king, no commander, no dictator. We delt with life inside our living space democratically and without the need (or even the threat) of violence. True, Jens was a bit heavy handed when Henri suffered his breakdown, but no one thought he'd violated any reasonable boundary.

We were friends.

That's the part of my lunar experience I treasure. Who would think that some punk, card-stacker would get along with two dedicated scientists? We got along; we bonded. They never flaunted the flotilla of letters that sailed conspicuously after their names. They never once viewed me as an interloper. We got along as if we were friends on a camping trip. Would we ever keep in touch when we returned to earth? I like to think so, but that isn't vital. We learned to live together under the most appalling conditions. We had to. If we started hating each other, we could hardly leave and live somewhere else.

It had been an adventure, BUT we had ten more days before our relief appeared. There was still time for all manner of things to happen.

DEPARTING
IS SUCH SWEET . . .
ABOUT TIME

We saw the signal from the crawler after we made out its form. We'd been glued to an observation port for an hour. Before that, one or two of us kept a wistful watch for several hours. All the scientific equipment had been shut down, out personal gear strapped to our sides, and our "hold baggage" was stowed in the air lock.

"It's several minutes out," Henri said, needlessly.

Our trio dissolved severally for one last inspection. For two days, we looked in every nook and cranny for some personal item that we might have left behind. This final search proved as fruitless as all its predecessors. Henri's papers (mostly notes to self) and the data he had collected for nearly seven months was in a pouch in the air lock. The materials Jens collected were in a second pouch, clearly labeled.

The scientific data was run through the facility's primary computer and reduced to a single InfoRec, a compact memory device which, when connected to an earth computer, would recreate the fruits of his research. There was one InfoRec in the hold baggage. Henri had one in his personal purse, Jens had another in his, and I had yet another. This was only prudent. If one of these vital data sticks was lost or damaged, there were three "spares."

The data gathered by Jens would return in the same fashion.

My data wasn't worthy of computer storage. I had my Coke bottle and twenty-two pages of handwritten notes and a few photographs. If my "data" was lost, there were no additional copies available. Since botching lunar south, I figured my "scientific" contribution didn't rate salvage. If my materials were destroyed or went missing, so what? Any qualified goon could examine my samples, segregated by date and search area, and gather up any significant information for proper evaluation.

We watched and waited for the crawler to rest on its designated parking spot.

We watched as the monkeys accessed our hold baggage and got it aboard. Once they secured the outer door, we made our way to the exit. Henri went first, being the longest member of the facility. We heard him slam the outer door behind him, but Jens and I waited until we saw him enter the crawler's airlock.

Jen should have gone next. He was a scientist; I was a nobody. However, he insisted that I leave first.

I was hurt. Obviously, word had reached Henri and Jens (no matter how) that I was an INSPAD spy. It was only prudent that I leave next. This would deny me the opportunity to sabotage the facility, or place surreptitious listening devices or cameras, or deface the interior with childish graffiti. I was miffed by this palpable expression of mistrust, but I was more interested in getting the hell off the moon.

Mel should be proud of the way I transitioned. I was, in my estimation, perfect.

Ten minutes later, Jens appeared. Once the airlock was secure, we were given the signal to remove our hats. I'd forgotten that horrible air that greeted me on my first crawler visit and steeled myself against a repeat.

"You guys open a cylinder in here, too?" I inquired, in a voice very near my earth modulation.

"We got busted," a youngish monkey, possibly a trainee, responded.

"They didn't hear it from me!"

I was supposed to be a spy. Space Monkeys who earn INSPAD wrath are *not* understanding people. I'd been out of contact with earth for three months. Even a neophyte would know I couldn't contact INSPAD from Dark Side.

The kid wasn't impressed by my impassioned denial.

"They thought it was a good idea," the kid explained. "Now, the cylinders are included in the official manifest."

Leaving less room for illicit smuggling. I thought the sentiment but didn't vocalize it.

"Jenkins aboard?"

"He's been replaced."

I did some quick figuring.

"His cycle isn't over," I protested.

"He's waiting for evacuation. He got sick. We haven't heard anything."

"Where is he? He couldn't have left the moon."

"They're keeping him at Base Two. They have a doctor there and more room."

What a crappy way to start my flight to freedom. A pioneer of lunar construction was ill. It couldn't be anything communicable – viruses are scrupulously prohibited. Cancer!

I slouched down under the component marked RURIK and pondered. Between my escaping Dark Side and breathing passable air, I should have been euphoric. Instead, I felt defeated.

The garbage collection team was busy. They had to enter the facility to clear the empty food dispensers, finger-nail clippings, and discarded stationery items because they had to transfer the hold baggage. Handling garbage and hold baggage simultaneously was begging for terrible mistakes.

After stowing the trash in a designated area of the crawler – not accessible from inside – the pair of luggage handlers joined a second pair performing maintenance.

"You left a book in there," one of the workers said upon reentering. "I couldn't bring it out because I had to help with maintenance. There was no way I could carry it."

"Don't fret," I responded. "I've read it – three times."

I didn't bother to inform him that I left it on purpose. What was the point?

With four monkeys performing maintenance on Dark Side and one supervisor (not Jenkins) watching their every move and signaling by electric lantern every quarter hour, the three stooges had the run of the crawler. We took advantage of a fresh deck of cards and played three-handed spades for over an hour.

"Damn!"

It was the crawler commander. He was watching his crew and comparing their tasks with a checklist he studied at frequent intervals. One man in both of the two-man teams had an exact copy of the same checklist. When a team completed a task, they both gave a hand signal. The "crew chief" would respond with a single blink. When something did not "check," the team would affect repairs as needed.

"That kid ain't workin' out," the supervisor announced to everyone, and no one.

He flashed furiously for several seconds then paused to watch.

"Don't look at it, dummy," he muttered. "Check the connection!"

We three weren't interested. We were no longer assigned to Dark Side. The place could blow up, for all we cared.

That isn't accurate. We were as concerned as the Jenkins replacement. Lives were at stake. However, we were secure in the knowledge that we'd, likely, never see the interior of the facility again. What we really wanted was to be back on earth.

"I think I'll have a go at the treadmill," Henri said, throwing in his hand.

It wasn't a treadmill. It was a bicycle pedal system which could be set to any of several resistance settings. There were, also, weights for both leg and arm exercise. Jens opted to have a go at them. We were all anxious to prepare for our reintroduction to earth's gravity. People were known to keel over and remain inert for several minutes while struggling for breath. Not just a few people, either. Exercising in a low or zero gravity environment helped considerably, but it was no guarantee that you wouldn't take a header. Even the most judicious exercise fanatic experienced a few minutes of vertigo. Experience shows that, after three months on the moon, it takes, on average, five minutes to learn to walk normally again.

I would take a turn at both weights and resistance later, or I could go several rounds on the Space Master. Since both exercise stations were spoken for, my natural curiosity kicked in. I hefted myself up to the observation platform. Two could occupy the space comfortably or three uncomfortably. Only one could fit into the observation blister. That was the "team leader," and I'd rate not so much as a courtesy peek. The two teams working on the Dark Side facility would have to do without my expert direction.

"Get over there, you big, fat toad!"

This comment was not directed at me. It was a space prayer hurled at a person who had neither the means nor the inclination to hear it.

"Filling in for Jenkins?" I asked, just to get things started.

"I *am* Jenkins," he responded.

"You don't seem too pleased."

He never took his eyes off his crews. He had an optical device – all the better to see you with, my dears.

"I was in line for the job, but I was looking at one more year," he replied. "I think I'm several weeks behind where I need to be."

"Do they expect Jenkins to come back?"

"It ain't lookin' good."

I was sorry to hear that.

"This your first cycle?"

"My first full cycle. I finished six weeks of Jenks' last cycle. He was slated for retirement. Nice retirement package waiting for him. I doubt that he will ever take advantage of it."

"That bad?"

"The docs think there's nothing that can be done. They think the low gravity here is good for him, but . . . no one mentions anything about recovery."

I wanted to know as much about Jenkins as possible. I had thoughts of writing an article about the man, more than any other single person, who made living and working on the moon possible. Despite the corruption of the people who hired him to do an impossible job, despite the bureaucratic monster on his back every step of the way, Jenkins and a loyal band of volunteers accomplished the impossible.

Jenks

How remiss of me to not introduce this slice of moon slang earlier. Anyone who ever served in the armed forces knows about "field expediency." That term implies that one makes do with the materials on hand to accomplish a task or mission. It also implies a Rube-Goldburg device which will not last. On the moon, a *Jenks* is any on-the-spot correction or improvisation. Unlike its earthly counterpart, however, a "Jenks" is meant to be permanent. The paper pushers sent Jenkins and his team with a mountain of materials that worked well on earth (or on the drawing board). In the moon's reduced gravity and the restrictions created by cumbersome pressure suits, things sometimes did not meet design specifications.

Ryan Jenkins was no common contactor. The man had a degree in mechanical engineering. Rather than wait (forever) for parts or tools of need-to-order specifications to be created and launched, he devised ways to complete his work without compromising either safety or planned expectations. Many of his lunar improvisations were later manufactured on earth for use on the moon. They are there, in storage, and ready to serve. However, the Jenkins-modified equipment and parts remained in use and none, to my knowledge, have been replaced.

It was Jenkins who masterminded the spy-camera system. He would record every move the monkeys made during re-supply and repair. He would go over these recordings after each mission with those involved. He would make comments and suggestions. Each team leader carried a camera. If there were doubts about equipment, couplings, fittings, or hull integrity, the team leader would take several photos of the problem. Jenkins and the team leader would examine each one. If Jenkins wasn't satisfied, the offending materials were replaced as quickly as possible.

"You got a name?"

If this nervous crawler commander was taking the place of Jenkins, he should be recognized.

"Buonocore," he replied. "Andrew Buonocore."

"I wish you luck, Andrew Buonocore. You're filling a big pair of shoes."

"I had a great teacher," he acknowledged, never taking his eyes off the maintenance workers. "There are a lot of intangibles Jenks brought to this job. I'm not certain I have any of them."

"Do your best," I advised. "Lives depend on you."

"Don't I know it."

Later, when the common was filled with five people and precious little room for anybody or anything else, I took my turn at the exercise equipment. Andy was going over the maintenance check list, item by item, and his crews made comments for each one. There were a series of photos Andy examined very closely. He didn't like one of the leads to the oxygenator. He declared it must be replaced.

There was a collective moan. Routine maintenance work was a drag. Replacing parts required an extra "moon walk." It also required dexterity. The pressure suits were not designed for dexterity.

"Your choice," Andy said to the team leader. "Do it tonight or early in the morning. I want to make our departure time."

The frustrated team leader looked at his partner.

"Tonight," he declared. "I won't get much sleep if I fret about it all night."

"Okay," Andy nodded. "Grab some chow. After that, I want you two to lay flat for ninety minutes. You mightn't get any sleep, but you'll, at least, get some rest."

The meeting broke up. I could tell by Andy's expression, he didn't like sending those boys out again. Nevertheless, lives were at stake. If the oxygenator went on the fritz, there was no way to inform Base One. If the crew couldn't fix the problem, Andy would be moving corpses in the garbage compartment.

"Tough call," I said to display sympathy over his decision.

"Not tough at all," he replied without any sign of ire. "Jenks said to me once – just once – "'Imagine you're called before a court of enquiry, and they ask you about a failed system. How would you feel if you have to say, under oath, *I thought it would last through the cycle?*' I never, ever want to have to say that. Upset as the boys are, they feel the same."

Jenkins, thou art mighty yet!

THE LONG JOURNEY
TO
ANOTHER LONG JOURNEY

The repair was scheduled to take thirty minutes. On the moon, even time is rationed. However, thirty minutes in "moon time" isn't recognizable by we earthlings. First, you must secure the replacement part and stow it for transport. Next, the crew must suit up and check for suit integrity. Then, it's into the air lock – one at a time. Then, the team meets up, with their cargo, and make the short trek to the oxygenator. Then, one must use just the right tool in just the right way to remove the offending part. One cannot just turn off the oxygenator, so the team must use a bypass while an integral part of the system is absent. Replace the part and remove the bypass. Bring the original part back to the crawler. It must be returned to earth and examined by the "experts."

The thirty-minute repair took two hours. The replacement was easy, but the ceremony that went with it and the video from the crawler and the several camera shots taken by the crew of their handiwork, plus getting in and out of the crawler, plus getting in and out of the pressure suits ...

It was late.

I was trying to catch up with some sleep on the observation platform. I moved in the moment Andy vacated his video duties in the observation blister. He was required to meet with his team and examine the original part of the oxygenator. They presented their before and after photos.

I heard rather than watched Andy examine the offending implement. It took several minutes. There was some optical device in use, I was certain.

"Don't go away, boys," he announced at last. "I just remembered something."

The exhausted team did not care about the delay. They were exhausted by a very full day of dancing about in those ungainly pressure suits. They wanted a little time to recreate.

I peeked when Andy returned. In his hand, he had a pint of whiskey.

"I can't find a damned thing wrong with this POS," he reported. "Your mission was unnecessary, and I apologize. Meanwhile, I found this in your locker, Jake. Now, you know this is prohibited stuff. Get rid of it – tonight – now. If I see it in the morning, I'll have you up on charges – both of you."

"Sorry, skip," Jake said softly. "We'll get rid of it. That's a promise."

Jake and his co-worker slithered back down into the stern of the vehicle.

The junior member of the second team happened to be nearby.

"Boss," he announced. "I'm certain that we found a worn cable on the SETI dish. I – I guess, we didn't report it like we should, but I just now remembered."

"Next time, don't forget to remember."

The kid, the very same kid who reported my book was left behind, was crestfallen. I doubt he was too disappointed. Likely he or his team leader (perhaps both) knew where some hotch was hidden. They mightn't get to it that night, but it would be "examined" eventually.

Since I was nearest, Andy prodded me in the butt. I'd been sleeping in shallow fits and starts. My eyelids remained heavy, but I was "lunar rested" otherwise.

"I'd like you to take the first shift driving this thing," he said.

"Don't I get to volunteer?" I asked.

"You just did. I'll show you how to start the damned thing and get it in gear. After that, just stay on the highway."

"Any more whiskey you want disposed of?"

"You might get pulled over," he replied. "They won't let you return to earth if you have an outstanding traffic violation."

I sighed.

"You're right, Andy. You *are* Jenks."

I liked the way he apologized to his subordinates. The pint of booze hadn't been in Jake's locker, of that I was certain. With the monkeys it's quantity not quality. The whiskey Andy awarded his team was expensive stuff. Similarly, I liked how he handled the driving chores. Naturally, since we were eager to get off the "rock," Henri, Jens and I were expected to pull the dullest duty on the moon. We each drew lengthy stretches, but Andy took over for just as long. Additionally, each of his subordinates logged two-hour stretches.

We passed the way station. It looked ready for habitation but required the installation of an oxygenator. There were, at regular intervals, spools of commo wire. It wouldn't be fancy, but it would allow for a non-radio link between Base One and Dark Side.

"We will not waste people to man the station," Andy explained. "We will leave a couple cylinders or more in case of emergency, but once the link is established, there's no justification for wasting manpower on it."

Eventually, I'd have figured it out. Still, I appreciated Andy keeping me in the loop. There was virtually zero chance of me ever coming to the moon again. In fact, my interest would, hitherto, be confined to reading about research findings and results in those journals aimed specifically at the marginally literate. One never knows, however. I might be invited to give an unofficial lecture at a venue where adult beverages are the currency of the realm. It would be in my own best interests to keep abreast of moon news and events.

When we parked at Base One, there were no cheers or quiet celebrations. For the monkeys it was just one more stop which meant one more round of maintenance and resupply. For the three unwise men, it was merely the prelude to a half month of being cooped up in traveling telephone booths.

Does anyone, other than me who enjoys reading ancient texts, know what a telephone booth was? If you are one of the hundreds of millions who do not know, I encourage you to try and find out. If the facts get beyond your incredulity, you may find my metaphor quaint and, just maybe, amusing.

At that time and in that place, we were not amused.

The slide-rule people (look up that while you're at it) tried to keep wait time to a minimum while allowing for unexpected delays. Our ship had to depart during a very tight window to reap the advantage of "optimal" fuel expenditure. We had to catch the space station at exactly the right moment just as the Space Master had. In space, gravity is both an asset and an inhibitor. Our flight plans existed only for the assets. If we missed a launch window, we had to wait until another appeared – weeks or months depending upon several variables. This is why a moon cycle is never exactly ninety days. It is also why the crawl speed of the crawlers is maddening.

We were another day in the crowded crawler before we suited up for transfer to the launch vehicle. There were six suited monkeys tending to our escape Arc. We were "invited" to stand in the "parking area" until issued further orders.

Since we were no longer on the dark side, our suit radios were enabled. We could speak to one another on a frequency reserved for chatter. The important communications were on other frequencies segregated according to function.

I noticed how the moon dust had been trampled upon repeatedly until it had become as firm as any tarmac. I left no noticeable footprint.

Finally, the monkeys around the launch vehicle were reduced to two. The other four were tasked with loading. A hand-pulled trolly was brought out to us. We had to identify our hold baggage before the monkeys would load it. Any unclaimed bags were taken away and either destroyed or left to vaporize under the relentless sun.

"Mr. Duvall? Are you here?"

It was Siss. I recognized her voice.

"I'm somewhere on the moon. Where are you?"

I had turned to face Base One. That, apparently, gave away my position. I saw a figure holding up a hand.

"Is that your hand?"

"And my arm too."

I didn't know if I was allowed to leave the parking area. Let Siss come to me.

It was impossible to see her face behind the protective sun visor. The voice, however, was welcome and reassuring.

"I'm told we will share the same compartment," she reported.

She was told a hell of a lot more than I was. I didn't care. My desire to return home was such that they could have tied a rope around my leg and dragged me to the station.

"Do you know Jenkins?"

"Yes," she replied. "He was on our station for three days before they took him to Base Two."

"I wish I could have said goodbye to him. What is the problem."

"Leukemia, we were told."

One does not develop that overnight. Why, I wondered, didn't the doctors catch it before?

I had a thousand more questions, but I didn't intend to share them, or the answers, with everyone who happened to be on our frequency.

"Talk to you inside," I promised.

"I can't wait," she replied.

We watched as people were lowered out of the rocket. Dark Side was first. It was a trio. They were herded toward the crawler. Before they were allowed into the airlock, they identified their hold baggage. Two monkeys proceeded to load these packages and cases into an external storage hold. One at a time, the men disappeared upon entering the airlock. Their names and research areas would remain anonymous until we boarded the launch vehicle.

Next out were two people bound for Base Two. I hoped one, or both, were doctors and could help Jenkins. They followed the same routine as the Dark Siders and disappeared, one at a time, into the second and smaller crawler.

The final contingent consisted of three people destined to work from Base One.

These transfers took slightly more than half an hour.

Eight of us were guided to the airlock of the "launch vehicle." Dark Siders, having come furthest and having waited the longest, were admitted into the airlock. This one was larger and could have accommodated two people at a time, but procedure is procedure. Henri went first. A few minutes later, Jens took his turn. Finally, I was the last to transfer into the tin box that would get me off this rock.

There were two monkeys aboard. They would leave prior to launch. For the moment, however, they had the important task of "disinfecting" the very sweaty and gamey pressure suits. They had other, more important duties, but this one was most appreciated – by me at least.

Our pilot and his apprentice, a.k.a. "spare" never set foot on the moon. Their sole entertainment consisted of greeting passengers and bidding them good-bye. Until they were cycled out, their only other home was a tiny compartment on the space station. Save for launch and landing, their job was nearly as tooth-achingly dull as driving a crawler along a lunar "highway."

Siss and I found our compartment without aid. Perhaps, some psychologist will one day work out how space and moon workers take such solace in knowing where they will be sleeping. Finding an extra bunk on the crawler was nearly traumatic. My latching onto the observation platform was, for me, the space substitute of clinging to a teddy bear. No one objected and no one announced any prior claim. Sleeping in the fetal position was preferable to not having an assigned spot.

Siss was happy to be headed home and happy to recount her experiences. Since she could speak three languages and was stationed earthside, she was featured in two or three broadcasts a week. She enjoyed talking to and fielding questions from school children. She was thrilled to spend ninety minutes with children from Mopti, Mali. Additionally, she was subjected to a Q and A with university students in Brazil and a convent in France. She loved responding to questions and, even, occasional pot shots. She had become a media super-star amongst the under-thirty demographic.

There were serious matters as well. As a supernumerary, she was tasked with escorting Jenkins to Base Two and remained until the doctor could no longer be proactive. When it became a matter of waiting for special equipment and meds from a resupply ship, she bade the terminally ill patient goodbye. He was disappointed that she was unable to stay, but Base Two was not equipped to handle the INSPAD PR work she was assigned.

Siss dominated the conversation. This was not a hardship. I could report only my campaign to separate moon rocks from deformed moon rocks. The episode with Henri's "break down" I kept under wraps. If Henri wanted to talk about it, fine. Until he did, I would keep my oar out. I did, of course, speak of the view during "nighttime." That was splendid, but it defied my limited powers of description. Similarly, I could get very excited about spying on Saturn, but I could do little more than describe the sensations I felt and the thoughts that flooded my mind when taking in that beautiful view. A picture is worth a thousand words, we are told. After two or three of my words, a picture was vital.

We were doomed to remain on the ship for five days because there was nowhere else to put us. Our launch time was predicated on the optimal time to rendezvous with the space station.

I had a chance to memorize my mail. I had three lengthy missives from Elena and a nice picture, in crayon, from Arina depicting (I guess) me standing on a very tiny moon.

Elena's letters were chatty. She recounted Mel stopping by twice just long enough for coffee. She reported her mother had an "episode" and was in the ER for four hours, but she was sent home with the proverbial "clean bill." She announced her most recent promotion; she manned the cash register only when Happy Burger was caught shorthanded. Otherwise, she was in charge of timecards, signing for and inspecting orders, and supervising her underlings. It wasn't enough to order the floor mopped or the rest rooms cleaned, she had to inspect to make certain those tasks were up to company standards. She could hire and fire as required. She was paid for six hours and could divide them up however she wished, but she was normally away from home for nine or ten hours. When she wasn't tending to her duties, she would "hang around." She chatted with customers and patiently listened to and wrote a synopsis of their complaints and concerns.

She ate her lunch at Happy Burger.

"It's good PR," she wrote. "People who know me are relieved to see me eating the food. It makes them think that it must be pretty good. Either that or its safe."

The problem with being confined to the launch vehicle is that its "deep space" configuration is on one axis and its attitude on the lunar surface is on a different axis. The first essential modification was putting in a gravity-assist toilet for use on the moon. The first "evacuees" were forced to put on a pressure suit and toddle of to the Base One facilities.

With only the zero-gravity "powder rooms," bladders swelled, and tempers flared. In our case, eight people were cycling out, and we must wait six earth days for our optimum launch condition. With the pilot and the spare, there were ten bladders and bowels. The two, tiny facilities saw much use.

Our couches were on one axis for best results during launch and landing on the moon, but the moon's gravity placed us on another axis. We could sit and sleep in our assigned couches, but to stand, we were confined to the lower bulkhead behind which were the engines and their propellant. There isn't enough room for all ten of us to pretend we're at a cocktail party. There isn't enough room for us to circulate. Therefore, we were allowed out of our couches to mingle with two or three others according to a prearranged schedule.

There was a ladder for moon use. It ran through the long axis so the pilot, and the spare, can access the control room. Similarly, we used this device to reach our couches or descend to the "promenade deck." Once in weightlessness, we could float around at will and, when we wished to sleep, we'd fly to our bunks and strap ourselves in so we wouldn't wander about the cabin while in slumber.

It may sound spacious. However, as in all things, the first consideration is weight. This facilitates the orange-concentrate type of design. Most of the water is forced out. In space parlance, the interior of a space vessel is squeezed until the ends overlap. Ten people are left with precious little room. If I sneezed, the person three couches ahead would feel it.

Privacy is reserved for those who remained on earth.

After six days, we knew each other very well. We were all extremely cooperative. We obeyed all the rules and regulations since troublemakers were marked for "special training" upon our return. No one knew what such training would involve, but we were assured it would be memorable.

Among our group, there was a considerable lack of curiosity about special training.

We were curious about Jenkins. To placate everyone on the moon, in the station, and on earth, Jenks medical updates were broadcast every two hours. The specialist and his equipment were hustled over to Base Two. The bland "updates" were poorly thought out. This new doctor was a doctor, not an INSPAD plant. He played the game close to the vest, but his generic updates tipped his hand. Had there been a glimmer of hope, he'd have thrown us a bone.

Together with news about Jenkins, we began getting unauthorized information. It isn't difficult to send a signal to the moon. Not a high school student with a basic knowledge of radio can fail to make. The trick, of course, is knowing which frequency to tune. Somebody, decidedly not a high school student, was broadcasting from various mobile stations on four continents.

These "pirates" were clever and persistent. They were obviously coordinated. Just as INSPAD was run by a powerful cartel, so was Radio Free Earth. It existed for years prior to my leaving earth, but the Jenkins story set it on fire. The propaganda ministries of half the world were in a tizzy. The greatest weapon in the propaganda world is withholding information. Radio Free Earth was not inhibited. Among other tidbits, it not only announced the budget expenditures of INSPAD, it compared them with documented purchase orders.

Someone inside INSPAD was not playing by the rules. Indications were that several somebodies were off the reservation. I hoped that Mel was one of them, but I prayed he wasn't. The last news I wished to hear was the discovery of his body washing up on some beach.

The wheels were coming off the wagon.

The propaganda ministries worked tirelessly to put out the brush fires. However, with every success, three more popped up. People were coming forward – people who are not anonymous; reputable people: scientist, engineers, government ministers, bank executives –

The common theme among all these "leaks" was that the people on the station and on the moon were not getting the support they needed. A case in point: if INSPAD medical personnel were performing proper if routine physicals, Ryan Jenkins' malady would have been detected long before he was cycled back to the moon. His children were creating quite a stir. The sharks promised a series of lawsuits. There were rumors that criminal charges might be forthcoming.

This was unofficial, of course. News was not news unless the propaganda ministries gave us the "official" (and highly expurgated) version. It was a standard maxim among those no longer of tender mentality, that official reports were next to worthless. The imperative part of any news story is what the "officials" were careful to leave out.

The pirates were forcing the (so-called) news organizations to, at least, acknowledge that INSPAD was subject to intense criticism. Of course, they insisted, these criticisms were baseless, but their (imagined) credibility would go down the drain if the "news" media refused to mention what millions of people were hearing.

Our "pilot" was not a fan of the news media. He listened to the pirates. After all, his job might be threatened if INSPAD were investigated (by whom?) A few of our fellow internees were similarly interested in "non-official" news reports. They would take turns climbing up the ladder to be near the pilot's earphones during a pirate broadcast.

I was getting nervous. INSPAD, out of pure spite, might cease all operations and use Jenkins, Siss, me and all the people on the moon and on the station as hostages. If the pirates did not shut down their "*slandercasts*," we would be stranded. Without supplies, we would die.

The pilot was besieged by passengers asking if we would "blast off" on schedule. This poor man was helpless. He was there to monitor the automated systems. He could override those systems. However, unless he had a tremendous amount of data available to him, he couldn't fly worth a damn. You would be amazed at how easy it is for a spaceship to "miss" the earth by tens of thousands of miles – never mind finding the space station, an invisible pin prick in our galaxy. One must consider gravitational forces, fuel expenditure, burn time, and a myriad of other factors that no one person could know or figure out on one's own.

"If I ever get back to my sisters, I'm not leaving again – ever."

There are many lessons we can learn from a lunar sojourn if we have the facility to be introspective.

"We've been family seven years. We are Mali's answer to the three Musketeers. Camaraderie is the glue that keeps us together. We think differently, act differently, speak differently, but our friendship comes first and foremost."

I offered up a platitude because I could think of nothing germane. Siss should have been angry with my shallowness, but she is an exceptional woman.

"I was doing – fine," she continued.

The word *fine* was loaded. It was full of emotional subtext.

One of her "sisters" was the survivor of an abusive marriage. The other was fleeing from an arranged marriage to a man whose virtues were, at best, well hidden. He, apparently, preferred to dawdle with men. This did not bode well in a Muslim community. The marriage was cancelled when the groom, or parts of the groom, were found being picked over by wild carnivores.

Three women from three points on the compass found each other in Timbuktu, their chosen place of refuge.

"My sisters are Muslim, you know. They knew I was Catholic. Despite our differences, we became very close. We appreciate our differences as much as we enjoy our commonalities."

"I envy you," I confessed.

Siss was never what I would describe as perky. To say truth, she was frequently and uncomfortably somber. When delivering a lecture or relating an anecdote, she was prim and exact. I'd never seen her step out of character – until that moment on the launch vehicle.

"You envy me?"

She was incredulous.

"You have Elena and her children. There's a lot of pain and frustration to test you mightily. That will make your friendship and devotion ever stronger – every day, stronger. There'll be much happiness too."

"She frightens me," I confessed.

"You're afraid of letting her get too close. That's your demon, my friend. Conquer it or carry it with you. I, and my sisters, have conquered our demons. It was difficult at first. It was hard work, but we're stronger for it. *Envy?* Do me a favor and save your envy for someone else."

This was too cryptic for me. The one thing I took away from one of our last lunar exchanges was that she wanted me to go after Elena. Maybe. Was she referencing Elena or her children? They hadn't known each other very long, but they got to be very tight.

Some women positively frighten me. Those that don't frighten me are – well, not very interesting. Reclining in the couch while waiting my turn to stand up, I could play patient while Siss, the shrink, could do the "shrink" bit. She didn't have a pad and pencil which killed the illusion. However, she got me thinking about many things. Isn't that the point of therapy?

I do not want to give the impression that my forced captivity was spent with Siss and her psychoanalysis. We spent a great deal of time talking about everything – and nothing. She found my memories of childhood fascinating. She related a pair of childhood memories. Recall, her childhood was crammed with terror, abuse and anguish. However, out of the slime, she salvaged two "precious" anecdotes that – according to her – presaged better times ahead.

Henri, Jens and I remained cordial, but we didn't engage in conversation. Practically anything we had worth saying to each other was hashed out at Dark Side. In fact, Henri found two other scientists with whom he enjoyed lengthy discussion. I don't think either shared his expertise in radio astronomy, but they had something in common and exploited that. Jens was a "free floater;" he enjoyed exchanging science chit-chat with just about anyone.

Finally, we were thrilled by the digital display ticking down the seconds leading up to our launch. We'd no word from earth that the scheduled launch was scrubbed. All the internal systems were given the green light by the pilot and his shadow. All exterior checks were performed by a team of eight monkeys working in shifts. They signaled both a visual and audible thumbs up. We were ready to go.

With two hours to go, I slid over to the couch nearest the bulkhead and strapped in. Siss was taking her scheduled stand-up time. When she returned, she could ease into my couch rather than climb over me.

The last thirty minutes, we watched the digital clock flash off the seconds. We tolerated no distractions. No one said a word. Nothing stirred – not even a mouse.

Zero!

For one horrible micro-moment, I thought the thrust rockets had failed to fire. No sooner did that thought streak across my brain than I felt a heavy weight pressing against my chest.

VOYAGE HOME

The plan called for a sling shot. Two orbits around the moon, each timed to the second, followed by a three-minute burn on the far side of the moon which, with gravity assist from luna, would hurl us toward the space station.

As we passed over Dark Side, I could make out the facility. It may have been more imagination than observation, but there was no mistaking the crawler "highway." From its terminus, the station would be only a few yards to the "east."

There were three people in our replacement party. We were informed within minutes of getting settled in the launch vehicle. It was an all-female crew. One was a geologist from Chile who, in all likelihood, would ignore my segregated sample piles and gather her own specimens. A second woman was from Canada and would study the moon's interior with seismic instruments and small explosive charges placed at various points around Dark Side. It is rumored that she intended to grow earth plants in lunar soil. Unless she was loaded down with necessary nutrients, she'd be disappointed. There was a chance, however, and carbon dioxide would be plentiful. The third scientist, from the United States, was a shrink of sorts who doubled as a radio astronomer.

I hoped the geologist would know dark-side south. It's a fair bet, coming from the Andes, she was knowledgeable about igneous rock and wouldn't waste her time searching for sedentary exhibits.

I wondered who would get stuck with SETI. Perhaps, they would take turns.

For the better part of two days, we drifted towards the Space Master's apogee. The computerized launcher/lander fired an exact retro less than two-hundred yards from its target. For the only time during any normal mission, the pilot switched to manual control and eased us to within the transfer parameters. It took forever as only a whisper of fuel was expended to urge our lunar taxi forward. After thirty-eight minutes, a whisper of fuel was expended to "lock" us into "neutral buoyancy." The computer calculations are exact, but there is always a tiny glitch in the machinery that could not bring us into a perfect rendezvous. After watching our radar returns, the pilot announced that the two ships were drifting towards each other at a rate of six or seven inches an hour.

Allow me to insert information that, in my excitement outbound, I neglected to include in the narrative.

First, INSPAD measured in imperial rather than metric. According to "informed sources" (drunks in a bar?) the original INSPAD pioneers ordered stationary from an American supplier. They ordered "standard size." The American vender complied. Since the office paper was measured in inches, it was decided that all INSPAD measurements would conform to with "the king's thumb to his royal schnoz" measure. Likely, there was another, more believable, explanation, but I have yet to hear it.

Second, the "leap of terror" was the transfer from the Space Master to the Lunar Lander/Ascender. Neither INSPAD nor anyone else wanted two space craft to "bump." The distances must be adhered to religiously. The Space Station and any other vehicle must remain a quarter of a mile distant. People transferring to and from the station were highly trained in using a Buck-Rogers rocket (two cylinders of compressed gas) which is released by the spaceman/woman in delicate increments. They aimed themselves at the station or the Space Master and pressed a hand-held valve. They could apply mid-course corrections as needed with the understanding that any further release of propellent would increase velocity – *not* a good idea.

There were, at least, four suited personnel deployed around the target vehicle to "catch" the "fish." The quartet were tethered to the target vehicle and were trained to apply just the right amount of counter thrust. It was an extremely delicate operation. If a "free floater" and a "catcher" crash, they were in danger of taking the tether to full length at which point the vehicle would be pulled out of position creating a dangerous situation.

To date, there had never been a catastrophic "freak out" by station personnel. It remains, however, a disaster just waiting to happen.

For us peons, there was no rocket-man transfer. The lead person would "jump" out of the airlock with a two-hundred-foot cable attached to his or her suit. Four spotters would wait to catch the transferee and hook them up to a three-hundred-foot cable affixed to the target vehicle.

A specialist would then, very gently, reel in the "fish" until he or she could access the airlock.

Of course, there were forces acting upon both vehicles and they, invariably, were pulled out of station-keeping position. If these vehicles came within seventy meters (don't ask how meters got in there), operations were halted until the vehicles were repositioned.

INSPAD (supposedly) was working on a safer and less traumatic means of transfer, but – well, R and D were always in need of more cash. Until they devise something "cost-effective," the Leap of Terror was the best (only) means of transfer.

Mel had us simulate the Leap, but it required a full day and a huge swimming pool, so "familiarization" was the objective. Proper training required ten or twelve additional days (of funding).

There were several freak-outs during transfers. It was time consuming and dangerous. The freakee must be reeled back in and shot up with a tranquilizer. Someone had to aim them as accurately as is humanly possible (very inaccurate and exceedingly risky) and pray that the spotters can retrieve an inert lump before it pulls the mothership into an erratic slip.

Henri would be first out. Due to his medical "episode" on the moon, he was given a shot prior to suiting up. He later related that he was awake and aware of every moment of his transfer, but he was unable to move. He was handled like a suitcase and eased into the airlock by a spotter. It took another thirty minutes before he was mobile again. Meanwhile, he was put out of the way and left to himself while the transfers continued.

Siss was a trooper. She let a monkey aim her and she went at a nice, gentle speed down the cable which was kept taught by one of the spotters. If she was frightened, it was impossible to tell, packaged in the pressure suit. Later she confessed she sang "weeee" for much of her journey. Floating away from the lander was absolute fun. Being reeled in for the second half of her journey wasn't nearly as enjoyable.

I didn't freak out because I saw nothing of it. I shut my eyes and trusted in the pitcher and the catcher to do their jobs. They did. I did not open my eyes again until I felt the hatch of the airlock. Vision restored, I transferred like a pro and closed the hatch behind me.

Transferring the whole lot of us was time consuming, but we were a long way from perigee. However, since Space Master had disgorged its cargo for the station and the supplies destined for the moon were loaded prior to transfer, we were bringing back only hold baggage. That meant there was considerable, wonderful, beautiful, fantastic room for all the passengers. We could relax on our assigned couches, sleep in our assigned bunks, or just float around and not create a major disturbance while doing so.

There's more!

The Space Master greeted returning earthlings with non-regulation "goodies." There was no liquor, but there were taste treats, a.k.a. "junk food," that constituted a joyous "welcome home." Well, we weren't home yet, but we could (literally) taste it.

There was, also, news – pirate news. The flight crew were particularly interested as their careers and payrolls were at the mercy of unknown factors. They and a few of the passengers were huddled near a radio receiver. The volume was kept down. Most of us suffering from "space fatigue" were more interested in the soft, recorded, instrumental music that was piped through the passenger cabin. Over the years, INSPAD tried several genres of compositions, but jazz, classical and "moldy-oldie rock" were the most preferred. The persnickety voyagers were encouraged to bring their own music and listening devices with the proviso that they not "share." Several arguments and a few fights climaxed unsanctioned "concerts."

The idea struck me. With a little research and a series of interviews, I might draft an article about music in space. How did INSPAD hit upon the formula most influential in promoting felicity or, at least, tolerance among such eclectic congregations one finds on the Space Master? Music hath charms that soothes the savage beast but only within certain limits.

What were those limits?

Understand, I was returning to earth unemployed. It was important to have some plan to obtain funds. If I begged hard enough, Elena might get me a job with Happy Burger, but I doubted I'd be any good. It's my fault, of course. I spurned the idea of an exclusive deal with the fiction artists. Meanwhile, I was without a job and was left with damned few options.

When Jens floated past, I asked about the news.

"Nothing new," he said. "Authorities in three countries are looking for fraud. They're not committing themselves."

"INSPAD is a pretty big outfit," I mused. "Before anybody takes anything into court, they're going to have to have all their ducks in a row. I wonder if these investigators are working with authorities in other countries."

Jens shrugged.

"It would be the smart thing to do," Jens concluded. "Notice the air in here?"

In fact, I had. It wasn't moon stuffy. Neither was it moon stuffy with a gas cylinder boost. It seemed like the refiltered air one experienced in commercial aircraft. It wasn't anywhere near real, earth air. Nevertheless, when compared with the stuff we'd been breathing for months, it was most refreshing.

"I could go for some exercise in this air," Jens continued. "I have a feeling that earth's gravity is going to hurt."

"You're in pretty good shape," I reminded.

The exercise regimen Jens established after Henri went la-la was bound to reap benefits. However, we hadn't enjoyed a proper exercise period since we climbed aboard the launch vehicle. A lot of muscles can get flabby very quickly.

I retired to my couch. Siss was fastened into hers, leafing through a magazine Space Master brought up from civilization. It was only a month and a half old. It was a society peep, but she found it interesting – particularly the pictures of people at fancy do-dahs in their finest togs.

Siss lived in Timbuktu, not on Pluto. She knew what the cultured set wore, but she enjoyed studying the photos.

"When you go on your tour, you'll be liveried in fancy duds like those."

"I can't wear that stuff," she sniffed. "I'd feel like a freak. I will insist that I wear something that people in Mali would recognize."

"The people who own your story might have something to say about that," I reminded.

"They can say what they want," she reported with amazing reserve. "I read the contract. There is nothing in it which allows them to dictate what I wear, eat, or drink."

I was pleased.

"I admire you," I stated honestly.

"What do I do when people ask me about these pirate reports? I know they will ask."

It was my turn to display a little of my public relations sophistry.

"You remind them that these reports come from unnamed sources and have yet to be verified. Remind them, also, that the *mainstream* media has not verified any reports."

She never took her eyes off the magazine.

"Ah! Is it considered ethical to lie?"

"In news, one lies by deliberately excluding information from the text. That is ethical and accepted in their world."

"It isn't my world."

"I know it isn't. I admire you for that. However, you should play the game. As of now, we have no concrete evidence. It's all unconfirmed. Don't fall into the trap of passing judgement based only on your own feelings."

She folded the periodical and looked me in the eye.

"You sound as if you've read the Bible," she concluded.

"Not enough to hurt me," I dodged.

"Save that line for those who will appreciate it."

I nodded.

The Gospel According to Duvall?

I'd have to think very hard about that, but I doubt I had the audacity to write such a work.

CRAVINGS INTERRUPTED

The Space Master shared the Space Station's elliptical orbit. We remained a quarter of a mile behind it (give or take a few inches) as it zipped around earth. It loomed large, as popular authors are prone to write, and appeared just beyond arm's length. We watched it as it rotated and envied those people who had some semblance of gravity. The RePlat was visible only if the sun's rays reflected off it just so.

The Space Master is a marvel, but so is it's quick turn-around time. We would break from orbit and enter the earth's atmosphere at a shallow angle while maintaining an "insanely" low velocity. This feature eliminated the need for bulky heat shields. It did, or so we were informed, get uncomfortably warm for a time, but it maintained a leisurely, ever decreasing orbit until it was low enough – 50,000 feet – to resume flying like a regular transport plane. After several orbits of our planet, the Space Master would make a very long final approach and settle onto the runway.

The returning Space Master became the "backup vehicle" for the second Space Master. After two days of maintenance, it was, theoretically, fit to return to the Space Station. The second Space Master would be loaded with cargo preparatory to catching up with the space station. If the second Master didn't pass inspections or final checks, the just-returned Space Master would be loaded with cargo and sent out again. This had yet to be attempted; the need had yet to arise. There were many who felt that proper maintenance and repairs would take the better part of a month and returning to space after such a short time was exceedingly dangerous. However, the Space Station couldn't loiter. It would continue in orbit and if the Space Master didn't take off by a certain time, there was no way it could catch up.

Well, once Siss, Henri, Jens and I were back home, the Space Master was no longer on our to-do list. INSPAD and the computer gurus would have to figure it out without any help from us.

We were, metaphorically, sliding down hill. When the earth computers and those on the Space Master agreed that it was time to initiate re-entry procedures, we'd be warned to strap in. They promised to give us thirty-minutes warning, so people had plenty of time to visit the necessary, stow any floating gear, and return to our couches. After the Space Master's retros fired for eight minutes (plus or minus a few seconds), we would be in descent mode and free to float around for another day and several hours. When we made contact with our atmosphere, we would be advised to strap in once more. The engineers promised that we would remain perfectly safe without returning to our couches, but we would experience turbulence eventually. Better safe than sorry.

The seconds ticked by – very slowly. We were, all of us, ready to be earthlings again. The wait became more and more intolerable.

"I want to be home," One man groaned. "NOW!"

"What do you want first?" I asked Siss.

"I want to know my sisters are well," she replied.

We'd be held in the facility for four days. This would not be a quarantine. People had been known to sneak out before we were paid and officially released. If, however, these bolters were caught, they forfeited their pay and were prohibited from participating in any future projects. Most of us, save for the monkeys who were very well paid, never intended to go into space again. Still, putting in all that time and suffering and all the hardships and not get paid – well, it was a tough choice sometimes.

"What do you want to do first?" she asked me.

"I want to eat real food and take a real poop."

These are two items at the top of every itinerary, so Siss got little satisfaction from my response.

"There must be someone you care about," she pressed.

"Mel," I replied.

"Harden? Our drill and systems instructor?"

"We started at INSPAD together. We're as close as any two people can be."

"He will be at the facility when we land, won't he?"

"He makes a point of it. He is a part of our out processing. He will interrogate us very carefully. It helps him and his underlings modify training procedures."

Siss nodded.

"You're not married," she reminded. "Still, there must be someone."

I snickered. She presented her – shall we say? – *ultimatum,* and it put me on the spot. I hadn't given it much thought.

"I want to see Arina."

"That's better," she concluded.

"Perhaps," I teased. "Arina is a beautiful blond who thinks I am the lobster's dress shirt."

She smiled over my diction. The woman's English is as acute as that of any educated native speaker. As with most non-native speakers, she collected linguistic oddities. My "lobster's dress shirt" was filed away for future recall.

"Do I hear wedding bells?"

See! She picked that up from somewhere. It's a safe bet she didn't get that expression from any textbook.

"Not for me," I assured. "Ariana is a beautiful blond, to be sure, but she's five-years old. I'm anxious to know if she still thinks well of me. It's possible that she's forgotten me. It's, also, possible that I have been replaced in her young, innocent heart."

Siss required elucidation. She didn't ask for it, but her attitude and facial expression made her expectation clear. I told her about our kiddie-park outing; the one I nearly missed. It amazed me how much I remembered. The details, both visual and sensory, That I recalled amazed me. The sights, sounds, sensations, even the smells entered into my narration with ease. I hadn't expected to enjoy the outing, but it was a treasured memory. I shall always think fondly of Siss for shaking it loose.

How many days we drifted in our parabolic orbit is a fact I can't answer, even under oath. Days are earth measure. In space, there's the sun and there are the stars. The Space Master rotated slowly on its horizontal axis (earth terms, again) to keep the hull from overheating. One of the pilots attempted to explain it to me when I expressed concern over the possibility of our expansive wings from melting or, at least, suffering structural damage. I don't speak calculus, and there were no translators available. I had to be satisfied that a ship with several earth landings in its history was, likely, good for one more.

Finally, after several card games (computer generated cards), a hundred get-to-know you confabs, and hours of anticipation and introspection, we were ordered to strap into our couches. There is no noise in space, but there is atmosphere in the passenger cabin. We were treated to both noise and vibration. The noise was not deafening, but it was unpleasant. We'd spent months in mostly muted quarters. Save for our launch from the moon, we enjoyed silence politely interrupted by the background music INSPAD provided us.

Similarly, we were gently pressed into our couches. It was not excessive. Indeed, it was pleasant. We were experiencing a sensation very similar to earth's gravity. After eight minutes, we were weightless again. The Space Master returned to its heat-dissipating rotation. We were informed that we were "falling" toward earth and would meet our atmosphere in twenty-seven hours. We would be given an hour's notice so we'd have plenty of time to "take care of business" before buckling in.

I felt as if I were in a slow-motion video. I was anxious to get back on *terra firma*. Unfortunately, the Space Master was built for a "gradual re-entry." It was a cost-effective means of transferring people and cargo. The design of this craft eliminated ten to twelve launch and recoveries by the old "blast-off" method. It required spot-on computers and computer programs. The pilots and co-pilots (there were relief crews for every mission) had to be able to take manual control and fly us down should we experience a system failure. There were back-up computers that, with the aid of communication with the ground, generated data that the pilots turned into hands-on control. Barring an emergency, the pilots only had to turn certain knobs as required by the automated flight control.

I wasn't paying attention when told how many orbits we'd make before landing. I was too anxious to bother to ask someone. All I knew – and all I needed to know – was that each orbit brought us nearer and nearer to a regular airliner type flight.

"Feel that?" Siss asked.

Shaken from my daydreams, I turned to bring her into view. I studied her wide-eyed expression. She reflected perplexity. Siss thought she'd felt or experienced something but wasn't certain. Gingerly, she pulled a pen out of the sleeve pocket of her flight suit. She held it up over her chest and let go.

The pen hovered for a moment in the recycled air current before slowly sinking onto the perceptible swell made by her breasts. Without pause, the implement slid off the mound and settled into the hollow of her neck from whence she retrieved it.

"Gravity," she whispered as if sharing a state secret.

She had to be correct. It was nothing near earth's gravity – or even lunar gravity, but the pen had, decidedly, floated *down*. Soon, others in the passenger cabin discovered what Siss had. An electric current of gaiety and relief flowed through the cabin. If the Space Master blew up, our remains would be scattered on Mother Earth and not wander, for eternity, in the void of space.

Jens started a "gravity watch." Every hour, on the hour, he and his fellow conspirators would check the rate at which an object fell. The five people involved in this "club" (for want of a better term) watched the clock with disturbing intensity.

The Space Master clock, mounted on the bulkhead separating passengers from the pilots, was a reproduction of Big Ben. However, since the Space Master went through time zones like a pack of pigeons through a peck of popcorn, the clock was equipped with the minute hand only. Siss and I weren't interested in the hourly report. We were satisfied to half float and half walk around the cabin. When the ability to float was denied, we mourned very little.

Finally, Siss announced that she could no longer detect the curvature of the earth. The Space Master was, from that point on, the slowest airliner since the old propeller days. Because the huge aircraft maintained a large support crew on the ground, commercial air traffic was rerouted away from the Space Master flight path. A midair collision would prove catastrophic, no doubt, but the size and bulk of our monster craft would probably do considerably more damage than it would absorb. Picture a modern tank plowing through and over an ancient jeep; if the tank crew wasn't paying close attention, they might never suspect they'd run over something. Nevertheless, despite our size, no one cared to test our resilience.

There were two reasons why we would be held in the INSPAD departure/arrival lounge for a calendar week. First, we must adjust to real food. Our bodies would experience a shock if it were forced to cope with a proper meal after a long period of breaking down moon rations. Second, even the most experienced Space Monkey needed a few hours to learn how to walk again. Some muscles we use every minute of every day were rendered dormant in moon gravity. Granted, it only took an hour or so to regain pre-launch mobility, but most moon men and women complained of cramps and soreness.

More than one macho scientist or monkey experienced the utter humiliation of falling flat on their faces during egress or immediately after disembarking from the Space Master. I didn't want to be humiliated. While most people railed against a week-long jail sentence, I welcomed it. As much as I wanted to loop a lip over a Happy Burger, I'd be mortified to be rushed to the hospital because my stomach couldn't deal with it. Similarly, I'd never want to be using a crosswalk when my weakened legs and knees decided to go on strike.

Then, there was the press. Siss would be subjected to the bulk of the attention, but the "scrub team" of the reporters would be on me like red on an apple. I'd fraudulently worked my way to the moon just to poke the INSPAD cyclops in the eye. Unfortunately, that made me cannon fodder.

The great, unanswered mystery: why do reporters have to hound (mostly) innocent people when they're going to make up their reports anyway? I don't see the point. My story, likely, was composed before we ever left the ground. Much of Aissata's story was already in the hopper. True, photos and interviews would boost sales, but Siss had signed an exclusive contract which would keep most of the ghouls at bay. That left me.

"What's your favorite color?"

"What kind of flower would you like to be?"

Mercy!

I hope my moon experience sapped the bulk of my strength so I couldn't strangle anyone. Still, is killing a reporter a crime? It might be a good idea to consult a lawyer.

I had an entire week. Maybe, I'd remain a prisoner for that time, but I'd have unlimited access once the warden returned my PoCo.

We were, at last, on an airliner. We were free to walk around and fetch our own drinks and snacks. We could eat; we no longer had to suck our meals out of a tube.

Henri, Jens and I had made a tacit treaty that we would not disclose Henri's "breakdown." There was nothing to be served. No one made a point of reminding ourselves. We didn't even exchange knowing glances. We'd made an agreement. Nothing more need be said or done.

While still in airline mode, we got word (through the propaganda ministry and, therefore, highly suspect) that Sir Albert Whitley, the officer in charge of INSPAD procurement, died of heart failure. This left a gaping hole in the quadrium of INSPAD. In the scope of INSPAD power, he was second only to Dieter Rolf.

I take no joy in any person's death, but I couldn't help wondering if he had anything to do with the theft of the Rurik component in the lunar crawler. This was uncharitable. However, I did not share my thoughts with anyone, so I couldn't feel too guilty.

The crew of the Space Master were curious. As with much of the rest of the world, we took "official" news with several grains of salt. A crewman played around a bit with the radio equipment and picked up a pirate news broadcast. According to the "unofficial" news organizations, Sir Albert's heart failure was aggravated by two .32 caliber bullets.

The great side-effect of news organizations that put "agendas" and "correct thinking" into their news bulletins is that more and more people dismiss them as inaccurate or outright false. Pirate news proved so much more reliable. I wasn't prepared to believe either version of the story. That didn't stop me from thinking about it.

Thirty-two caliber I knew from ancient detective fiction. It was the weapon of choice by those who were paid handsomely to eliminate "problems." The professionals who used these "pop guns" did so because they wanted something light and easily concealable. Such professionals did not, as a rule, require two shots. Also, the thirty-two was considered by many as a woman's weapon. Conclusion: the shooter (if there was one) was not a professional killer.

Tell me why I should not consider Dieter Rolf as the trigger man. It was the release of purchase orders that created the tempest for INSPAD. Who had access to such information other than the top procurement officer?

There was a flurry of speculation that people like Dieter and Sir Albert were to testify before an investigating committee. How and who would put together such a panel? INSPAD was an international leviathan. The layers of international law and law enforcement organizations was imponderable. It might take decades to establish legal authority to investigate INSPAD. That would leave Dieter and his crowd plenty of time to find some nice, cosey, neutral nation where international law might not mean more than a pint of warm piss. With the ill-gotten gains they have acquired over the last several years, they could buy an entire country.

I recalled how Dieter threatened me. He threatened Elena as well. If the assassin had taken Rolf out, rather than Sir Albert Whoseits, I would breathe easier.

That brought me back. Damn scruples! I didn't wish anyone dead – not even Dieter Rolf. I was afraid of him and what he might do, but I draw the line at murder. I will defend myself. I will defend Elena, if I can, but I'll not participate – even vicariously – in a mob war.

I sought out Siss. She was concerned but puzzled. Lucky for her, she knew very little about INSPAD prior to my recruiting her. Since she entered the United States, she knew little more than Mel and his uncompromising approach toward training neophytes. He was nasty and abrasive, but he taught his trainees well. Siss knew that much. The politics of the international community and INSPAD – that was way too confusing. The politics of Mali was confused and, at times, brutal. Understanding enough to survive or, at best, earn an honest living was tricky and required a copious amount of savvy. Multiplying her Mali political experiences by a hundred times was simply too much for her to grasp. She felt bad for the late Sir Albert, a person she neither knew nor knew of, but that's as far as she could go.

I envied her. In a few months, she would be back with her sisters where life was a challenge, but one is ever cognizant of the obstacles one must face. With INSPAD, it's all to play for, and the deck is always stacked in favor of the house. If the INSPAD Empire was crumbling, no one would know what to expect or when.

Siss and Henri were leaning against a vacant couch comparing French. The language had evolved considerably under the desert sun. Native French, or the regional variation (Henri was born in Provance) and the Mali "frontier" dialects made for hilarity as well as erudition. Several times, Siss was convinced her leg was being pulled. I assured her that Henri was not one to mislead anyone just for sport. Contrarywise, he never suspected that she might be having him on. They were both amazed by how the French vocabulary has evolved since the colonial times.

The discussion was too esoteric for me. Realizing their exchange offered me minimal profit, I walked (we could walk normally) back to the galley and helped myself to some coffee. It was the real stuff. However, when made in large quantities, it lacked quality. Still, bad coffee was exponentially superior to no coffee.

One of the flight crew was topping off his with cream and sugar. It made me sick to smell it. How anyone could adulterate coffee was an inexcusable abomination – in my estimation, at least. Why not throw in a lump of cow poop?

"We are now, officially, on final approach."

The coffee heathen's announcement lacked any meaning. It was pitch black outside. We were bathed in minimal interior lighting. The bulk of our passengers were sleeping; a few of the snoozers were seated upright on their respective couches, eschewing the comfort of their overhead cots.

"Aren't we still over the Pacific?" I asked.

"Everything is big on the Space Master," he informed me.

Did he really want to make conversation, or was he postponing having to sip his yuk coffee?

"We're lined up on the runway," he continued. "It's a matter of making our altitude match that of the runway. That will take a while."

"What are the chances we won't meet exactly?" I prodded.

"Slim or less than slim. Only changes in air pressure and gusting winds can affect us now. The computer compensates faster and more accurately than we can."

"Does the computer land us?"

"Hands-off landings are several years away – at least in the Space Master."

I nodded.

"Good to know."

Was it? The idea of any human handling this massive machine was sobering. However, it was fantastic to think that a giant machine could land itself unassisted. If I were a pilot, I suspect I'd like to keep my fate in my own hands.

After coffee and a nice chin wag with one of the flight crew, I returned to find Siss jotting down notes in a composition book she'd brought with her from Timbuktu. She kept a careful record of her Moon "adventures." It was an interesting amalgamation of sketches, crude maps, printed observations, personal recollections and random thoughts. Her precise handwriting made it a work of art. Perhaps, one day, it will find a place among those ancient celestial observations that pre-dated Newton by several centuries.

Siss worked with stream of consciousness. Her writings were in English, French, and one or two other languages unfamiliar to me. When I caught up with her, she was making note of the anomalies she'd picked up from Henri.

As with many of her experiences, Siss focused on oddities or, at least, novelties. Her conversation with Henri sparkled with linguistic treasures she did not want to vanish from her memory. Homer spoke of the *winged words*; if they aren't recorded or memorized, they fly away.

Siss did not chance any didactic sensation to "fly away." They were scrupulously recorded in her composition book.

"I thought I was fluent in French," she confessed. "How wrong I was."

"How often will you be speaking Henri's dialect?" I dared.

"Maybe, never, but it is nice to know certain things. One thing I've learned from French visitors to my city is that they are linguistic zealots. If they don't like your diction or pronunciation, they let you know."

"Let them get their pants in a bunch," I advised. "If their French means so much to them, they got no business leaving the country."

It might be a long, long while before Siss was forced to take up being a tour guid again. Her exclusive contract – well, I hadn't seen that many zeros since the last no-hitter. Siss, however, is a serious student. She's always learning.

She didn't slight me or shrug me off, but she made clear her intent to record her findings while her experiences remained fresh. Considering we had several hours remaining before we landed, I decided to sample the coffee again.

HOME AGAIN
(Kinda)

We were notified two hours out to make ready. Most of us were glued to the view ports. We were seeing the world again from close up. We saw grass and houses and deciduous trees and irrigation canals and puddles of water and cars and carts and farms and farm animals and a myriad of everything we could not see from space. We weren't on the ground yet, but we were home.

Home!

One forgets about INSPAD and taxes and cheap, tiny apartments. One, also, forgets that one does not have a job – that "one" person being me. Well, I'd get a nice package in space pay, but that wouldn't last more than a few months. However, first things first.

I wanted to see Arina again. That little imp had tunneled right into my heart and took up lodging there. Of course, Elena and her enigmatic gnat's eggs would constitute a visual blessing. To see and speak to and tease Mel Harden again would be worth a hundred times my accumulated space pay. Next to the electric sensation of these thoughts, my hankering for a Happy Burger or a scotch and soda shrank to insignificance.

Behind all my anticipation, my thoughts were burdened by Dieter Rolf. Was I still a target? Could he continue to hold life and death over me and all those dear to me, or had the same bullets that induced heart failure in the chief of INSPAD procurement stayed his hand?

I was safe on the moon. Back on earth, I was a walking target. I hoped that I would have a few days left to enjoy all those inconsequential things and sensations that one ignores until deprived of them.

First, I experienced the sensation of breathing again. During the last twelve hours of our return, we were treated to earth air – or a reasonable fac simile. The manufacturer of the Space Master provided air vents. When activated by sensors, these vents scooped up earth air, ran it through a filter, and introduced it into the recycled mixture we breathed since our transfer at the Space Station.

My lungs burned a bit at first. Within an hour, however, I was breathing earth's atmosphere. What a sensation! It was almost worth spending months away – yes, *almost*. I suspect that Henri's appreciation far outstripped mine. He was positively giddy.

With that huge wingspan and the whisper of the fan jets, the landing of the Space Master was noticeable only because we watched through the view ports. Not until the monster swerved off the runway was I assured we were, once again, earth bound.

Mission rules required assistance during egress. There were twenty-seven rather substantial steps on the portable stairway. It was wide enough for three people. Each of us was "assisted" by a half-dozen hulking brutes. Two would take the nearest arm of the returnee and gingerly see them to the tarmac. The next pair would scurry up to the Space Master and secure the arms of the next person. The last pair would – and etc. until we were all safely on level ground.

As with the airlock transfers, we must exit individually.

Another wait.

Siss was one of the first to deplane. I was fifth from the last.

Normally, I would resent being treated like an invalid. Looking down an endless row of steps, however, I was appreciative of my escorts. Earth gravity, despite all the exercise mandated by Jens, proved very tricky. One false step, and I might require a protracted stay in hospital. Even with a weightlifter on each arm, I tired quickly. They were there to catch me if I stumbled; otherwise, they offered no practical assistance. I was forced to greet the ground under my own power.

I was more tired when I mounted the bus. There were handrails, but it was a struggle to pull myself up the three steps to the seating level. Of course, the seats nearest the entrance were all occupied, and I had to shuffle to the back of the bus.

The drive to the facility required five minutes in first gear. Then, the tedious march to the front of the bus and a very slow and careful negotiation of the steps. I slid over to allow the next person to exit while I leaned up against the vehicle to catch my breath. My legs were quivering.

There were three "attendants" eyeing me suspiciously. One of them would respond if I motioned to them, but I refrained. When I felt up to the task, I slowly shuffled toward the entrance of the facility.

"Duvall," I announced to the smug, desk-bound manikin. He drew a line through my name on the manifest with one hand and offered the cardkey for my assigned quarters with the other.

"Hold baggage will be delivered within the hour," he muttered.

It was a phrase he'd memorized long before this troop of space travelers ever signed up.

I shuffled into the facility and settled down at the first vacant table. I was not alone. Several of my fellow refugees opted to take a time out prior to searching for quarters. Earth's gravity, though much appreciated, required serious re-adjustment on our part.

These quarters were the same ones we had occupied prior to our departure. I expected to have the same quarters I had then, but it was not to be. There were no grounds for objection as my "arrival suite" was nearer the great hall – where we would take our meals. Meantime, I lay on my bunk and breathed deeply until I felt both refreshed and comfortable.

I hadn't bothered to close my door. Privacy was not a necessity at the time. I was content to be an exhibit for anyone who happened by. My first visitor was Jens. He looked as if he'd spent the past four months in a resort hotel. He showed no sign of fatigue.

"You wear earth's gravity well," I muttered.

"They're putting out fruit plates for us."

I took this as an invitation. I threw my legs out and put my feet on the floor – not without effort – and stood. Just the thought of real fruit had my glands working full speed.

It was not fancy. The plates were paper but had a cheery, colorful if abstract design. Each was placed in front of a name plate; role was being taken. Anyone who skipped the snack would be tracked down. We all knew the food and drink had been treated with something. After so long a period on space food, we needed a little help readjusting to real victuals.

My serving was identical to all the others. I had a slice of peach, a slice of apple, two sections of orange, five grapes, and two strawberries. The clear, plastic cylinder contained lemon water with a small slice of lemon floating atop. We were encouraged to chew and eat slowly. This was a chore. Left to our own devices, the fruit would have vanished in a matter of seconds.

Our "evening meal" appears modest on the printed page, but I felt uncomfortably full. I didn't want the lemon water but was prohibited from leaving the table until the vessel was empty. Brice Duvall was but one of five who were "kept after class."

Our food and drink were designed to ease the transition from packaged rations to earth food. Not only did it ease the shock on our stomachs, the fruit helped awaken our intestines. The sooner our bodies adjusted, the more efficiently nutrition would be utilized, and the sooner I would enjoy a good "poop."

During our "dinner," unseen staff used unseen hands to deliver a schedule of the following day's events. After examining mine, I was tempted to seek out Siss and compare notes. I knew her day would be busier than mine. I prayed she was up to it. My itinerary was hardly taxing, but it constituted an intrusion.

Brice Duvall
Dark Side

05:30 Wake up call
06:00 Breakfast
06:45 Morning exercise
07:45 Debriefing
08:15 Personal time
09:30 with Aissata Sissoko – meet with print and broadcast reps for Q&A
10:30 Exercise
10:45 Team sport (TBA)
12:00 Lunch
12:45 Main Hall: Visitor Mel Harden
13:15 Main Hall: Visitor Elena Yelagin
13:45 Exercise
14:00 Free Time
18:00 Evening Meal
18:45 Forms and Pay Card (Assistance will be available)
21:00 Lights Out

Lights out, by the way, meant exactly that. The power was shut off in the dormitory area.

We were free to have battery-powered devices, to include video comms, but we'd be forced to utilize them in the dark. There were no windows in the dorms. People had been known to sneak around after curfew, but those apprehended by the INSPAD "Storm Troopers" enjoyed a huge bite out of their finances.

Some people aren't too smart. Others are genuine dumbasses. What would induce a person to leave their assigned quarters? I might understand if it were possible to leave the facility and go out drinking and carousing, but it's easier to leave a high-security prison than to get out this facility undetected. Perhaps, one might be tempted to do the Romeo and Juliet bit, but there were no balconies – only security cameras and heat sensors enough to make a Stassi master envious.

I "declared" my ancient soda bottle before my hold baggage was delivered to my hovel. Two uniformed men were with me when it came. One was a security guard; the other was from the Lunar Geology Institute. The latter shared my excitement over my "discovery." He agreed that the sample had been subjected to tremendous heat and promised to inform me what conclusions the institute reached after careful, and thorough, study.

He made out a receipt for my find. A copy of this paper would be left with the facility administrators. In the past, INSPAD had claimed full credit for important scientific materials until many who were stiffed made a loud and legal fusses. In the interests of muting unfavorable publicity (*and* avoiding huge financial payouts), INSPAD instituted stringent regulations. Additionally, Henri and Jens signed an affidavit that I had, indeed, found the sample and noted the discovery location according to *my* system (bogus South and all).

Truthfully, I didn't give a rat's ass if I got credit for the find. If the scientists thought it useful, they were welcome to it. I did not go to the moon to collect souvenirs, nor did I take (as many have) small items along to sell to unsuspecting dupes at inflated prices. Were I such a gyp artist, I'd pawn any number of small objects claiming they had been on the moon with me.

This, by the way, has become a thriving industry. People (many – if not most – of whom have never been on the moon) sell keychains, nail clippers, paperclips and all manner of things to the ignorant and the gullible.

Yes, there's a sucker born every minute.

SERENDIPITY

My narrative has gone on long enough. I have excluded masses of material simply because I didn't care to be bothered recounting them. What I have omitted, in many cases, is much more interesting than anything included herein. Just as an example, Siss became an international celebrity. She was articulate and smart. It took her over a year before she could rejoin her sisters and resume their pedestrian, if contented, life. Even then, hundreds of people trekked to Timbuktu to seek her out. Fortunately, Siss has many friends who jealously protect her privacy.

I fended off much of the publicity and limelight to which Siss was subjected. Within days of my "release," I was working for a furniture manufacturer. Yes, I, a person who couldn't rub two sticks together, landed a nine-to-five office job creating, sorting, and filing a myriad of "necessary paperwork" – not that anyone used paper. However, even in the computer world, it takes a no-talent schmuck to know which files go where – particularly around tax time.

INSPAD is being shunted aside by government agencies eager to keep the monster in its cage. It is more decentralized, but the loss of efficiency is more than balanced out by a procurement system devoid of the "free-for-all" which existed before. INSPAD executives are limited to specified stipends and bonuses are predicated on demonstrable results.

When Mel and I met, I was adamant in my scorn for INSPAD in general and Dieter Rolf in particular. That bastard had threatened me! Perhaps, I was as much at fault as Rolf, but I was scamming. He was threatening. Mel, however, never caught fire. He took a less passionate view of INSPAD and its "reorganization."

"I hope they hang him!" I announced, foolishly and without thinking.

Mel reached across the table and gripped my wrist. He didn't use force. Had he, my wrist and hand may have been out of action for some while.

"Let me remind you of something," he said in his low, yet well-modulated baritone.

He had my complete attention.

"The evidence against INSPAD began coming out *after* Agamemnon."

That was the dope slap of all dope slaps. Had I bothered to put two-and-two together, I would have realized this item for myself. If Rolf seized power to curb INSPAD abuses – !

"Don't be Russan into anything . . ."

Suddenly, that didn't strike me as a threat. It is entirely possible that Rolf was turning the tables on me for my Adam Kane routine. I could not be positive, but I began viewing Dieter Rolf and INSPAD through a different lens.

During my time away, I realized I was in love with Arina. She was so cute and excited that day we shared at the kiddie park. Her smile was infectious, her laughter hypnotic, and her affection for me superlative. I was very anxious to see her again. I feared that she had grown up in my absence and was much more selective in her choice of companions. That – well, it hurt me to even think of it.

I wanted to see her, talk to her, hold her, hug her!

When you are relatively alone on the moon, yearning becomes the focus of one's existence. I hardly gave her a thought while on earth, but on the moon I could think of little else. It was my one great hope that I would find an anonymous rock or a crater or topographical feature so I could christen it with that little girl's name.

That day Elena came to the facility –

Please, bring Arina!

If Arina was with mommy, mommy was likely with Elena – and Eduard. That would not constitute a hardship. If I could just see Arina, talk to her, hug her, then my irrational longing might, at last, be satisfied and, finally, set aside.

Remember how Fedor had no time for home and family?

I did. I took it to heart.

Once again, Fedor was away from home and on business. The business was in Atlanta. His family was in Atlanta. It is well that I didn't know. Of course, I learned all about it – later.

If ever I wanted to see Elena, I could find her at Happy Burger. If I pursued my newest craving, Arina, I could go to the apartment and have Elena's mother fussing over me. Suddenly, I was forced to modify my simple-mindedness.

Visitors were allowed into the facility during re-transition. However, visits were confined to several "interview rooms." These were modeled after prison visitation areas except there were no wire screens and you were allowed to touch as well as talk. There were no guards, but, of course, there were the ubiquitous cameras. Presumably, a few "transients" were prone to reacquaint themselves in ways not conducive to a publicly owned facility. Some people had scores to settle. Others had – um – long-denied exercise.

I opened the door to discover a round table surrounded by four cheap, plastic lawn chairs.

Across the table was Elena. She wore a bluish dress – sack, more like. Her head, hands, and ankles peeked out from the voluminous, button down the front (to, practically, the floor) sartorial nightmare. Her shoes had thick soles and heels to give the illusion that she was five and a half feet tall.

Her face was lacquered. I couldn't tell if the gnat's eggs were able to peek through because, by chance or design, I was unable to see all the left side of her face. Her lips were the proverbial ruby red. When they parted in a smile and her overbite manifested itself, I couldn't have hoped for a better, more beautiful portrait.

The scene was spoiled by a large figure standing next to her. He was broad shouldered and handsome. There were whispers of white around his temples and sideburns. He was hardly the ancient mariner, but he was getting on. Elena, in the shoes she wore, came up to his broad shoulder. I think he wore a suit. I resented his being there sufficiently to blunt both my powers of observation and my memory.

Elena took this man's arm and grinned at me as if I were a person who mattered.

"Brice," she began with pride in her voice. "This is Fedor, husband and father of two."

My heart sank. This was not the homecoming I'd imagined. However, I recalled that I had a photo and a serial number of a crawler component, two items he would find interesting. If he was here to spirit Elena away, he could whistle for them.

Elena, with the practiced ease of a ballerina, dropped Fedor's arm and slid around to my side. She took my arm, exactly as she had her husband's and faced him.

"Fedor, this is Brice, a good friend and father of one."

Whose eyes were wider? I couldn't imagine mine were. Fedor's amazed expression included two amazed orbs straining to be let free. We stood as statues for several seconds. No one moved. I'm not certain anyone breathed.

This was too rich! Under the circumstances, Fedor had every right to take a powerful swing at me. I was too stunned to react. Part of my paralysis was the result of earth's gravity. Most of it, however, was pure bewilderment. Would Elena be so petty as to lure me into an ambush? If so, I had been expertly deceived about her character.

After time enough had passed for a glacier to melt, the tall, muscular man extended his hand. I was too dumbfounded to not grasp it.

"Congratulations," he said, without a hint of rancor. "I swear, I had no idea."

Elena tittered.

I knows!

I should have been angry. Fedor should have been angry. No one seemed to be angry.

"I wasn't sure," Elena spoke softly into the silence. "I didn't want to get too excited too early because – well, I'm a little beyond my 'sell by' date, but the doctor is satisfied there's little risk."

"I hope I'm up to this," I muttered.

"I'm still in love with Elena," Fedor spoke with an obvious lump in his throat. "Please, give her what I could not."

"What," I croaked.

"My time," he announced. "Make certain you give her as much of your time as you can."

I didn't know what to say. There was no script boy standing by to give me my next line. The best I could do was to swallow – hard – and nod my head.

9 781961 254619